Wayfarers

Other books by Knut Hamsun
published by
Farrar, Straus and Giroux

PAN
translated by James McFarlane

HUNGER
translated by Robert Bly,
with introductions by Mr. Bly
and Isaac Bashevis Singer

VICTORIA
translated by Oliver Stallybrass

MYSTERIES
translated by Gerry Bothmer

THE WANDERER
translated by Oliver and Gunnvor Stallybrass

THE WOMEN AT THE PUMP
translated by Oliver and Gunnvor Stallybrass

Wayfarers

KNUT HAMSUN

*Translated from the Norwegian
by James McFarlane*

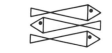

FARRAR STRAUS GIROUX
NEW YORK

Library of Congress Cataloging in Publication Data
Hamsun, Knut, 1859-1952.   Wayfarers.
Translation of Landstrykere.   I.   Title.
PZ3.H1903Way   1980   [PT8950.H3]   839.8'236   79-27034

Part One

1

TWO MEN CAME TRUDGING NORTHWARD FROM THE neighboring village. They were dark-skinned and had lank grizzled beards. One of them carried a barrel organ on his back.

Nobody in the locality had expected that particular day to bring anything special: then up turned these two strangers. They made for a conspicuous position among the houses, set the barrel organ up on a pole, and began to play. Everybody in the place came flocking round, women and children, the adolescent and the lame; a ring of people formed around the music. There was so little to get excited about, now that it was winter; all the men were away in the Lofotens; nobody danced and nobody sang; the whole village was poor and miserable. These strange minstrels were therefore a great event, something fabulous. An event which it is doubtful if anybody in later life forgot.

One of them turned the handle. There was something wrong with one of his eyes; he seemed blind in it. The other carried a pack, but otherwise did nothing. He was merely the partner. He stood looking down at his shabby boots. Suddenly he snatched off his hat and held it out. How could he possibly expect money in this godforsaken place where everybody was simply hanging on till the spring, when the men got back from the fishing! He got nothing and put his hat on again. He stood for a moment; then he began talking to his companion in a foreign tongue, gradually louder and more insistent. Seemingly he wanted to stop the music and get his companion to come away. But the musician went on playing; he switched to a new piece and he ground out a soft sad melody which moved the audience. One young woman who was a little better off than the rest turned quickly, meaning perhaps to go in and fetch a coin. This the partner must have misunderstood

3

and thought she was leaving altogether. He shouted after her and made a face.

"Ssh!" said the musician to him. "Ssh!" The partner was not the kind of man to be hushed like that. He became furious. He leaped at his companion and struck him. That might not have been so bad, but the half-blind musician could not defend himself. He had to cope with the barrel organ, which stood swaying on its pole. His hands were occupied; he merely ducked his head. A gasp went through the crowd at this unexpected assault. The circle at once spread out; children became frightened and screamed.

It was then that Edevart ran forward, a young lad of thirteen, blond and freckled, wild-eyed with excitement. He was quite reckless, and prepared indeed to face death. He tried to get a trip hold on the assailant. The first time he failed; a second time he was lucky and threw the man to the ground. The lad gasped like a bellows. His mother screamed at him to come away, but Edevart stood there. He seemed beside himself; he grimaced, baring his teeth.

"You come home this minute!" cried his mother, in despair. She was thin and sickly, a poor mite, who all her days had been quiet and religious. She had no authority.

The stranger picked himself up from the ground. He scowled at the boy but did not attempt to do anything to him. On the contrary, he looked embarrassed and brushed the snow off himself with exaggerated care. Then he spoke again to his companion, shook both fists threateningly at him, then slunk away and disappeared.

The musician remained behind. He sniveled a little, and wept. A red streak ran across one of his cheeks—a color strangely bluish to be blood, but that was doubtless because he was from a foreign land and was so dark-skinned.

"He should have had a stick across his back!" muttered the young woman, turning to look at the assailant. Then she went in to fetch a coin.

4

When the other women saw this, they, too, felt they wanted to do the same; and one after the other they went in to get money. God knows, the musician probably had more by way of worldly goods than those who gave. They were all so very poor, but their hearts were overflowing and they contributed their offering. They came with their small coins—though some were larger copper pieces, which in those days meant real money—and with these they comforted the weeping man.

But now it was the musician's turn to be forthcoming. Suddenly he pressed down a catch on the barrel organ and a theater, a paradise, was revealed. Ah! breathed the audience. Never before had the likes of this been seen in the village: small figures, colored and gilded, stood on a platform. As the musician turned the handle, they moved. They turned and took a step forward, turned about, halted a moment, and turned around again.

"Napoleon!" said the musician and pointed to the central figure.

All of them had heard the name Napoleon; and they gazed at him, rapt.

He had two generals with him; they were also painted wearing their decorations, and the musician named them by name; but it was Napoleon they all looked at. He wore a gray cape and held a little short telescope in his hand; now and again he raised the telescope to his eye and let it fall again. In front of all these great men stood a strange figure of a lad, ragged and bareheaded, laughing. He held out a little empty bowl for money; when a coin was put in the bowl, the lad would give a jerk and empty the coin into a box. What a marvel! The lad was alive. He seemed to laugh more than ever when he held his bowl out again.

And the musician played on. Marches, waltzes, and other melodies went floating off over the people, over the houses. A black dog sat in the snow some distance away and howled at the sky. It was an unforgettable day.

When no more money was forthcoming and the lad had stopped his jerking, one little girl had the idea of putting a bright button into the bowl. It might well have been her one and only bright button, but it wasn't money. And now came the greatest marvel of all. The lad suddenly gave a jerk in the opposite direction and sent the button far out into the snow. For a moment everybody was silent. What in the world . . . ! Was the lad human? The young woman was the first to laugh. She put a dress hook into the bowl and saw it, too, land far away. Then everybody laughed. But the little girl went down on her knees in the snow to search for her bright button, which had been so disdained.

Then things got out of hand. One after another, the onlookers placed worthless things in the bowl: nails, pebbles, wood shavings. Finally the beggar lad grew weary of this; he shook the bowl unceasingly so that nothing could remain in it. Was he then the only one of them all with any sense?

The musician stopped playing, shut the lid, and unscrewed the barrel organ. He sighed heavily.

"Why are you with *him*?" asked Edevart darkly.

The musician explained as well as he could: they owned the barrel organ between them, but his partner was bad. Look, once he'd stabbed him in the eye with his knife. The musician never dared show Napoleon and the other figures when his partner was around. The man was so hot-tempered he would smash the entire theater.

"Where are you from?" asked Edevart.

He was from Armenia.

"Where is that?"

Far away. Past all other lands. *Gewiss.* Across many mountains and a great sea. A year's journey . . .

"Come in and have something to eat," said the young woman.

They followed him in, as many as the room would hold; the rest stood outside and looked in through the windows. There wasn't a great deal to the man; he merely sat inviting sympathy, hanging his head. They watched him say grace and eat herring and potatoes, after which he had some barley gruel. Then he said grace again and started to get up and say his thanks.

The young woman said: "If I'd had any coffee, you'd have had a cup."

"I'm not entirely out of it," said another woman helpfully.

"Well, then, you can loan me a spoonful."

All was well as long as the man sat there. The women combined to find ways of holding him there and of keeping him away from his inhuman partner.

"Which way did he go?" they asked.

Nobody knew. The man didn't know, so he said.

"Perhaps he's gone for good?"

"Oh, no!" The man shook his head and sighed. He began moving his feet and knocking his frozen boots together.

They asked him if his feet were cold. They were. Then they asked him about his stockings. Yes, he had holes in his stockings, many holes, big ones.

They looked at each other and nodded; and again the better-off young woman went and brought out a pair of new stockings, knee-length, and gave them to him. And they had a blue border around the tops. Lovely stockings.

"Oh, Ane Maria, there you go again!" the other women murmured admiringly.

"Put them on!" said Ane Maria.

The man didn't want to. No, he behaved as though he hadn't the heart to spoil the stockings. He held them to his cheek, then tucked them inside his shirtfront. Everybody was touched.

One person stood in the farthest corner, turning things over in his mind. It was Edevart. When the musician had said his thanks for what he had received, he lifted the organ case onto his back and trudged off. "The Lord be with you!" they called after him. Sorrowful eyes followed him for as long as he remained in sight. But Edevart surreptitiously followed a little way behind.

When the man reached the forest, he slowly turned around with his burden and discovered Edevart.

7

"Where are you going?" he asked.

"Nowhere," answered Edevart.

"Nowhere? Eh?"

Edevart said: "I'll help you with that partner of yours."

"Help? No."

"I'll knock him senseless!"

At this the man smiled: his partner terrifically strong, a Hungarian, great warriors. Uses a knife.

Edevart paid no heed. He strode past the man and began to walk on ahead.

"Fool . . . fool!" the man shouted, suddenly angry. "Go home! What do you want here?"

Then all of a sudden another man, the partner, stepped out from behind a juniper bush, as large as life. First he took in the situation, then put a question, which the musician answered. Then they both laughed.

Edevart stood there glaring. The Hungarian moved forward belligerently. This in itself would not have deterred the crazy boy, but then the musician set down the barrel organ and also began to make threatening remarks. What was the meaning of all this? Edevart's head was not used to coping with complicated matters; he was deplorable at reading and arithmetic. But he had two good fists; and when he was worked up showed a ready courage. But now he retreated.

The strangers were quite unconcerned about him and let him stand there. The musician took a handful of snow and rubbed the red bloodstain from his cheeks. His partner told him when it was all gone. Thereupon they opened the compartment in the barrel organ and counted the coins. The stockings were also inspected and they ended up in the Hungarian's bag.

Then the musician slung his burden across his back again. The two of them nodded to Edevart and continued on northward to the next settlement.

Edevart was still no wiser than before about the strangers' behavior. He had calmed down. When it finally dawned on him that he'd perhaps been made a fool of, he snatched up some snow and packed it into a ball; but when he had made it good and hard, he dropped it and let it lie.

He came home a changed lad, rather shamefaced, sorry for himself, dispirited. He went over to the little girl in the snow and asked: "Haven't you found the button?"

"No," she said.

"You mustn't worry about it."

The girl didn't answer, but went on searching.

Edevart was bad at books and hopeless at school, but his instincts were sound, seemingly. He went over to where the barrel organ had stood and measured with his eye the distance the button could have been thrown; then he, too, began to search. The girl stuck close to him with renewed hope. "There was a crown on it," she said of the button.

While they were searching, there was a call to the girl from one of the cottages: "Where have you got to, Ragna?" Ragna did not answer. They searched patiently. They each took a stick and dug with it; finally they found the button. The girl herself found it. Her joy was great and she hurried in.

The whole thing marked an event and a turning point in Edevart's life. He probably did not draw any immediate conclusions from his experience in the forest, but it laid a foundation in him upon which later experiences could build. The next winter he was taken on as a half hand fishing in the Lofotens, although he was still not confirmed. This was no small thing; older lads than he remained at home. It was good for him to have got out. He gradually lost his reticence; he began to speak out in discussion.

But in the spring he was failed by the priest. This was in everybody's eyes a great shame, and particularly of course for his father and mother, both of whom were able to read and were also religious. He had to stay at school another year, and this blunted his spirit again. Finally, at fifteen, he was confirmed and accepted more or less as an adult. He read badly and was frightened of books, but he was no stupider than many another and he had grown big and strong, a capable lad at work, and kind and good-natured. He gave all support possible to his parents and to his brother and sisters.

A MUCH-TRAVELED young man returned home to the village. He was called August, and was an orphan. Actually, he was from another district but had grown up here. Among many other things, he had been to sea for a number of years and visited many lands. The things he could tell of his life were something miraculous. He was not rich, nor did he pretend to be; but he had beautiful blue clothes, a silver watch, and a daler or two in his pocket. As he had no close kinsfolk, he stayed with the woman who had brought him up. But he ranged far and wide in the locality and was well regarded by everyone. The young girls had him much in their thoughts, and the small boys listened to his stories openmouthed. A close friendship had arisen between him and Edevart.

It began this way:

An accident at sea had caused some damage to August's mouth, knocking out some teeth. He had made up for this as much as possible by growing a mighty mustache and wearing a set of gold teeth, a so-called bridge. Edevart had never seen such glorious teeth, and he planned to buy some similar teeth for himself as soon as he could afford it. August told him quite readily where he had acquired this set of teeth and what it had cost. It wasn't pennies; he'd saved for months and years to meet the expense, he said. The girls for their part found no fault with August's teeth, but the young men began to laugh at them and mock him. They were jealous of August, and angry that he should come here and collect all the girls around him.

As time passed, things got worse. The young men joined forces to scoff at the sailor lad and even seemed about to turn the girls against him. One day the young woman Ane Maria even said to him in everybody's hearing that he shouldn't open his mouth so when he laughed.

"Why not?" asked August.

"Well, you shouldn't show off those teeth."

Many laughed at this; and August—good-natured and even-tempered as sailors are—said nothing.

But it was more than Edevart could stand. He turned to her and said: "You shouldn't have given the organ-grinder those stockings."

"Why not?" asked Ane Maria uneasily.

"What stockings?" asked her husband. His name was Karolus.

"New stockings," said Edevart.

Ane Maria went and busied herself over by the window, and asked from there: "Why shouldn't I have given them to him?"

"Because he didn't need them. He sold them for eighteen skilling at the village north of here."

"How do you know?"

"I know, all right. He didn't want to be burdened with them. I saw those stockings again up there."

Ane Maria said: "I don't understand what this has to do with you."

But then her husband spoke up again. "What stockings are these, I'm asking?"

When it was explained to him, he sat there, his face dark; and Ane Maria began to cry. Her husband said: "So! That was the year I came home and you had no change of stockings for me. And you thought you were grand enough to give stockings away!"

"I'm sorry I did it," said Ane Maria, sniffing.

A young relative of hers called Teodor broke in: "In any case, it's none of your business, Edevart."

"No. But what business is it of yours if August has gold teeth?"

"Listen to the little brat!" Teodor burst out. "He's forgotten that the priest failed him."

Edevart, pale and wild-eyed: "You know what *you* arc forgetting? You are forgetting that you've got a rupture and wear a truss."

Teodor gets up snorting.

The man of the house, Karolus, drags him down onto the bench again. Edevart was in no mood to draw back; he was roused and was afraid of nothing.

The young man Teodor ended up saying that he had his own good teeth and didn't need any blacksmith working on them. To which Edevart replied that it was just as well, because he'd never be the sort of man who could afford teeth like those August had.

After that, Teodor couldn't let things rest there but started up again and continued his abuse for quite some time. He might have taken less time if Edevart hadn't constantly answered back —but he did.

From that day on, August and Edevart became partners in inshore fishing. They caught much codling and haddock for their domestic use, and weren't above giving away a meal of fish to others when they had enough for the day for themselves. More than one housewife blessed them during the long autumn.

When the time came for them to get ready for the Lofotens, Edevart asked one day: "Are you fixed up?"

"No," said August. "Nobody's mentioned anything."

"Aren't you going to have a word with somebody?"

"No. Not when all the men are against me."

"So what will you do this winter?"

"I'll take myself off to sea again," August answered.

Edevart said: "If only I could come along, too!"

Neither of them got away that winter; and Edevart didn't even go to the Lofotens, though he could have signed on as a full hand. This was a disappointment for his parents. His father was not a fisherman himself, but earned a little looking after the telegraph wires over a wide area. Edevart, on the other hand, disappointingly had no job to fall back on. The lad ought to have thought more about his own interests, but now there was nothing to be done about that. August began buying up furs and hides in the district, and took Edevart along to help carry them.

It transpired that August wasn't all that short of dalers in his pocket, and he arranged to pay Edevart the same wages an ordinary hand would get for a winter in the Lofotens. This was thus a very fair arrangement, and Edevart did not lose anything by it. Moreover, he learned much from August, and looked up to him as a great sea dog and one hell of a fine fellow.

So they bought skins: mostly calfskins, occasionally a sheepskin or two, now and then a cowhide. Suddenly all the dogs came down with sickness; a stray dog brought in distemper and infected the whole district. August and Edevart, as the only grown men left at home, were often called upon to destroy an animal for humane reasons, whereupon they flayed it and got the skin free. But fur trading: did August know the business? He was not without some knowledge of it, he claimed. Among his many occupations in foreign lands, he had worked for a time on a sheep farm in Australia.

With the approach of Lent, August expanded his business. He began buying more valuable pelts—otter, fox, and ermine. He got hold of a gun and a couple of traps of different kinds and had a go at hunting. It worked. No shot had been heard for a long time in those parts. Foxes and otters were by no means rare; and one fine day August came home with both a silver fox and an otter. It was his ambition to catch an ermine; he explained to Edevart how ermine was used for trimming the robes of royalty. But these shy animals were rare and difficult to get.

Time passed. Daily they worked on the skins. They spread them out on walls or hung them stretched on stakes to dry in the wind; and when they dried out, they were sorted and bundled. By the time the crews had returned from the Lofotens in the spring, the two partners had a mass of skins stowed away in barns and lofts which had become emptied of hay. They had no ermine; but one day when the ice had melted and they were rowing out to shoot seabirds, they were lucky enough to shoot a seal—a rare visitor to the bay. That was a good skin.

People shook their heads over August's fur business. "Don't you want to buy any mouseskins as well?" young Teodor asked scornfully. At all events, August's speculation was new and un-tried in these parts; and when he tried to hire an eight-oar boat to transport his skins, Karolus (who owned the boat) replied that he ought to give up the idea since the trip wouldn't even pay for the hire! But August knew what he was doing. He had bought each skin for next to nothing; moreover, he had been in touch with the great leather firm of Klem, Hansen & Co. in Trondheim —the one known all over Nordland by the round stamp on their blue-tinged, oak-tanned shoe leather. From them August had got precise instructions. Klem, Hansen & Co. were to come north this summer and operate a stand at the Stokmarknes Fair. It was there that August was to deliver his goods. But he had no boat.

August was made to feel the general hostility. Now there were other young men who had returned from the Lofotens with money in their pockets and goods of various kinds. As for Au-gust, he only had skins in barns and lofts around the place and had presumably spent all his money on these.

The day the eight-oar Lofoten boat was due to be laid up in the boathouse till next winter, August again expressed a wish to hire it. But the owner refused. He used the excuse that it was a new and expensive boat; he hadn't even paid for it all yet, and still owed for the equipment, the sails, the rigging, the anchor. August walked away a few steps, returned, and said: "Will you sell the boat?"

"Sell it? Are you perhaps thinking of buying it?"

"Yes," said August.

Karolus gaped. "Ha! Buy it?"

Edevart was standing near. He too gaped.

But when the man heard that August was still well enough off to be able to buy an eight-oar boat and all its gear, it gave him something to think about, something that took him around to all the cottages. The whole village talked it over; and once again August wiped the floor with the other young men of the district. Damn it, was this returned sailor lad made of money? The boat owner became amenable. He went himself to August and said: "I can't part with my eight-oar. It's all I have to live on. But I'll rent it to you if you like."

"No, I'd rather buy it," August answered, bridling.

Karolus said mildly: "Can't be done."

They discussed it up and down. What would August do with an eight-oar boat once the trip was over?

He would dispose of it at the fair.

"It's a long time to winter and the Lofotens fishing," said Karolus. "You'll not sell a big boat like that in summer."

No, August admitted it might be difficult. But he had his reasons.

"What reasons?"

August intimated that much was going on behind the scenes for him at the moment. He'd spent all his ready cash on skins, and he couldn't really pay the modest rent.

The man was bewildered. "But you have money to buy the boat?"

"Indeed I have," answered August. "I don't want you to pass it on, but it's rather a large banknote I have. Several large notes, if it comes to that. I can't pay the rent for the boat before I've changed them."

Karolus, rather crestfallen: "Well then, you can pay for the hire when you've changed your notes at the fair."

This they agreed. And the two partners, August and Edevart, loaded their skins, took on provisions, and sailed for Stokmarknes. Actually, they were too small a crew for such a large boat, but it was fine weather and a summer's day, so they didn't worry.

All went well until they were nearly across Vestfjord. There was a fair wind and the sun shone night and day at that time of year; they took turns at the helm while the other leaned back on the bales of skins and dozed. While August was on watch, he sang and talked English to himself. When Edevart woke and looked up, August swore with pleasure and boasted that the trip was going splendidly, and that, in fact, if they wanted, they could nicely carry on right across the Atlantic!

August had rather watery blue eyes; and, all in all, he didn't have all that much about him, God knows. He gave the impression of being competent in certain things—of the head or of the hands. Indeed; but he didn't seem particularly inventive. But now he felt happy. It was sheer delight to sail easily along like this. And he'd be making money, too!

They had set course too far north. They saw Hindø in the distance. Here the wind freshened as night fell, but there was no sea running as yet. August was at the helm. What was this—the wind rising? He was not used to these square-rigged vessels and he became seasick. Strangely it also began to hail. A blizzard arose, the sun was extinguished; he looked back at the darkening sky. They reached a stretch of open sea; the weather turned rough, a hailstorm. August woke Edevart, screaming at him. Edevart leaped up.

"What are you doing with the steering?" he shouted.

"I want to turn around," August answered, sick and afraid.

Edevart said: "Are you crazy? You can't turn in this wind."

"I didn't know," said August, cowed.

"Slacken sail!" commanded Edevart. He managed to lower the sail and took in a couple of reefs at once.

No, a square rig was no real ship. August could not stand upright in such a boat, only sit. He had to keep down. If need be, he could kneel. But here the sailor lad was scared to death.

"God Almighty, how will all this end?" he whimpered.

"Hard over again!" Edevart ordered.

This was done. The boat shipped some water, but righted herself. What mattered now was reaching Raftsundet.

August hadn't much to say now. He looked despairingly at Edevart and shouted: "The Lord wants to punish me!"

"What do you mean?" Edevart's face seemed to ask.

"Well, Edevart, you see I hadn't enough to rent the boat and I lied when I said I wanted to buy it."

"Ah!" said Edevart. "So you didn't have the money?"

"No!" answered August. "And now God help us!"

Edevart decided there had been something wrong with the steering. They were taking in a lot of water; the sea had risen. "Go up forward!" he ordered his comrade; and the sixteen-year-old lad took the tiller himself. He pulled it in and pushed it out twice for every wave, splashing a drop or two of water over August's back, but nothing into the boat.

"You were steering like a clot and getting your skins soaking wet," he said with an experienced air. He allowed himself the comment.

"I don't care about the skins, just as long as we stay alive," answered August.

Edevart shouted: "Take in the third reef!"

August did so, perfectly content to take orders. This he was used to. Sure, August had been to sea, as he had never tired of telling people; he had lived a precarious yet carefree life aboard ship, had been patient and submissive, and had enjoyed celebrating ashore. But he had also changed his job and his livelihood many times. He excused himself by saying that he had no particular mission in life, and could therefore turn his hand to anything on earth—indeed, for that matter, *under* the earth, mining. This is what he said, at all events; and it all sounded very modest. But deep down he could well have been boasting. Here he had followed the plow, there he had had a town job, often in a tavern, very occasionally in church. Everywhere he'd been one among many, it seemed; a common man, a subordinate. At times he had known happy days. He had been ashore on coasts where scarcely any clothes were needed and where your food could be shaken off the trees; at other times he might have wandered about a cold town where a proper meal was too dear for him, and where liver was the cheapest meat. Should one then expect all that much of him? Like other lads similarly placed, he was reduced now and then to living on his wits, he would confess with a laugh. But August never killed anybody! No, no, never killed anybody! It all sounded honest and innocuous, and perhaps he was right. He suffered for his sins later every time he found himself in danger, for then he was afraid.

They took in one reef after another, finally running before the wind so that the boat scarcely answered the rudder. August sat on the forward deck, pale and wet. There were more and more things outstanding with God. There were these gold teeth. He confessed that he hadn't paid for them, only a little on account, and then he'd fled the country. "I'd be happy to see them at the bottom of the sea!" he said, and tried to wrench the teeth out of his mouth.

"You'd do better to bail the boat!" said Edevart, being very adult. He probably felt a little superior at his companion's humiliation. He sat at the tiller like one in command.

"What should I bail for?" said August in despair. "It's getting worse, not better. I can't see us being saved."

"Don't be such a fool!" shouted Edevart. "Can't you see I'm making for emergency shelter!"

August did as ordered and bailed out the boat as best he could, but his thoughts were far away. He had doubtless heard tell of a life after death and he wanted to use his last moments to confess his sins and pray to God. "That's all I can think of at the moment!" was how he concluded his confessions.

They kept going like this for an hour. It was approaching midnight. The sea rose; the sun was nowhere to be seen. The hail showers were over, but the sky was still blue-black. There was more to come. In this half light, navigation was tricky. Neither of the two men was familiar with these waters. Edevart steered as best he could, edging toward the land on his right. They still had a glimpse of Hindø. It was a matter of finding an inlet, a refuge. The land far away to the left, the Lofoten mountains, would have been more in the lee, but the wind was wrong.

"We aren't all that far from land now," said August. Perhaps he had taken hope; he had confessed his sins and was feeling a bit lighter in his mind.

Suddenly it thundered. Edevart cast a quick glance backward. Hail again rattled down on the bales of skins. A sudden squall whined around the mast. Edevart failed to ease the sail in time and the boat keeled far over. Shortly after, the hail came pelting down.

August had lost his courage again and cried with upturned face: "Save us, oh, Lord! If there's any chance after this, I've still got thousands of sins to . . ."

"Bail out the boat!" ordered Edevart.

August didn't hear. "There was that time we had shore leave," he shouted, humbled, "the time we were in Negro country and we met her and four of us went after her."

"Bail out the boat!" shrieked Edevart.

August fumbled with the bailing scoop but did not succeed in using it. He was absorbed in his ugly memories and shook his head like one annihilated. "We're sinking," he said.

They were close to land. Edevart saw, to his terror, that he had not reckoned with the strong current. "Let out another reef!" he shouted in mortal fear. He wanted to give the boat a bit more sail so that he could steer it away from the breakers.

August must have grasped what was at stake. He did as ordered and the boat answered the helm. A quarter of an hour went by; the boat was half full of water and August gradually began of his own accord to bail. If Edevart had been able to leave the tiller, he would certainly have thrown some of the bales of skins overboard; but it would have taken time to cut the lashings, and he dared not mention it to August, who had lost all initiative. Instead, to encourage his companion, he said: "That's right, just keep bailing!"

A short while later, a rift appeared in the island, and that was a change. Farther along there was a new rift, which widened into a gap, a black hole. Edevart resolutely altered course; he pulled the tiller toward him as far as he could and sent the boat into the hole. It was a gamble; they might have been smashed there. Neither of them knew the coastline; luck would decide. But

Edevart's nervous energy was pretty well exhausted; he was no longer capable of facing the open sea; his face was gray. When August saw land on both sides, it galvanized him into life again. He finished bailing, seized the boat hook, and sat tensed to save himself if they ran aground. "When I shout, heave out the anchor!" Edevart commanded, still thinking ahead.

There was no need to throw out the anchor. They had fools' luck and did not run aground. The black hole which bored into the island swung around and ended in a bay. A boat lay there ahead, four-oared, in calm water, moored with a simple anchor. Here there was no wind; in the end they had to take the oars and row ashore to the beach.

They were saved.

Edevart might have crowed now, but he made no great fuss. His mouth was bloodless; it looked frozen stiff and he said nothing. August did what had to be done: took the rope ashore and tied up the boat, bailed it dry and spread out the sail. When all was done, Edevart braced himself and, in order to seem calm, said: "Negroes, you said. What Negroes were they?"

"Well, it was in one of those hot countries," said August shyly and shook his head. "But that doesn't concern us now!"

Edevart might well have liked to press him on this and not let him off so easily, but his esteem for his comrade dissuaded him. Apart from that, he couldn't face it just now. He was no longer so grown-up and self-assured as he had been on the voyage. When he came ashore, he began to feel terribly ill; the tension was lifted; he began to retch. August stood by him and helped him over the first painful moments.

"Do you feel rotten?" he asked.

"No," answered Edevart, and was sick.

It seemed to be a long way to people and houses; there was a little boathouse, but it was secured with a wooden lock. August wanted to break down the door, but Edevart objected. They ended up by sitting in the shelter of the boathouse, ate some of their provisions, and waited for morning. Edevart revived a little;

he wanted to know more about his comrade's various confessions, but August answered evasively. Edevart wasn't a sixteen-year-old for nothing. He couldn't forget the Negro girl.

"What did you do to her?" he asked.

"What did we do to her? Nothing!"

"But there were four of you to one of her?"

"Did I say four? You mustn't ask. She was only a youngster, so we didn't do anything to her, you understand. It was somebody we met on the road."

"Did she scream?" asked Edevart.

August did not answer this; instead, he said: "She was no bigger than Ragna back home. But the thing is that in hot countries they are adult while they are still children. They get married at Ragna's age. They're strange—people in hot countries. Ah, there comes the sun again!"

August went down to the boat and carried the wettest of the skins ashore to dry. He had confessed his sins and was once more a free man. Now he could get down to his work again.

They left the island that night in fine weather. There was no wind; they had to row. When they got out of Raftsundet, there was again a favorable wind.

2 AT THE FAIR THERE WAS MUCH NOISY COMING AND going. Many vessels and boats, large and small, lay there; and more arrived by night and by day. Crowds of people swarmed in the streets. A couple of men from Namdal had had too much to drink and were looking for a fight. Every man was his own policeman.

Edevart found it both amusing and instructive to be here; and while August was delivering his consignment of skins, Edevart wandered about looking at everything. There were stalls with wares of all kinds, for everyday use and for special occasions; masses of goods with a much greater selection than in Lofoten. And there were tightrope walkers, organ grinders, wild animals, bowling alleys, street hawkers, merry-go-rounds, gypsy fortune-tellers, coffee and lemonade stalls, the world's fattest lady, and a calf with two heads. And here, making his usual appearance, was Papst, the venerable old Jewish watch dealer with all those mysterious pockets in his greatcoat. A remarkable man.

Edevart remained a while in the vicinity of the old Jew, not because he thought he might buy anything from him, but because the glittering pocket watches made a marvelous sight. How rich he must be to have so many watches! thought Edevart.

Old Papst had simply settled down in Norway, although it might have been more profitable for him in other places. He had traveled Nordland a whole generation, moving on from town to town, calling in at the fishing stations, turning up at the fairgrounds. He spoke excellent Norwegian, knew all the words, though his pronunciation sounded a bit foreign. All in all, Papst was well regarded everywhere; people knew the fat little man with all those watch chains across his big belly. He hailed young and old, and had gold watches for the rich and cheap silver watches for the poor. He used many different approaches when selling, depending on who the customer was.

To the young people who hung around him looking wide-eyed at his display, Papst might say: "I've got a good watch for you, too. Look here! Hold it in your hand." When the youth learned the price and had rejected any idea of doing business, Papst would ask: "How much have you got?" The youth might mention a sum half or even a third of the price. At which Papst did not abandon the lad, not at all. He became friendly and sympathetic. It was as if, in this particular instance, he might even be willing to go to the length of lending the lad a little money himself to enable him to buy the watch. Indeed, it sometimes happened that Papst gave credit till the following year. "You come of good folks and you are an honest man," he would say. "You will pay a poor old Jew!" In the face of such an enormous, such a fabulous display of confidence, the lad for his part could not hold back. And showing the kind of honesty he had little use for in daily life, he would pay the following year. Seldom, if ever, was Papst swindled.

Such was the way the old Jewish watch seller did business, conducting his itinerant affairs year in and year out with the same quiet dignity. He cheated when he could; but when caught out, he would cheerfully rectify the fraud, though sometimes, to be sure, by committing a new one.

He had a keen eye for those little upstarts who critically inspect a watch and pretend to be great experts. These Papst would cheerfully defraud. Self-important and familiar, they come up to him, calling him Moses: "Well, Moses, have you got a good watch for me today?" Papst takes a watch out of his pocket and makes a great show of displaying it to the prospective customer. "Look at that!" he says. The man looks at it, opens it, and asks if it is a good one. "Good?" answers Papst. "I carry the same sort in my own pocket. Look for yourself!" And he pulls one of his own watches out of his pocket for comparison. Then comes the price. Papst asks a stiff price of everybody; but with upstarts who pretend to be experts it is generally double. If he is then offered half, his face grows sad as though greatly blighted by the thought of so much wickedness in the world. He takes the watch back. No business that day.

But the customer knows about Papst from hearsay. He shows up again later, and Papst recognizes the man again. "Make me another offer!" he says. The man might add on a few coppers. "No, no, no!" says Papst and brings out the watch again and shows it off, opens and shuts it, and puts it back in his pocket. But when the man's face shows he is about to leave, Papst gives a deep sigh at all the wickedness in the world and concludes the sale. He is selling at a loss, indeed he is. It will bring ruination and the grave, but there is no help for it! When the man has counted out the money, Papst takes out the watch and hands it over, resplendent and shining, with fine engraving on the case. The watch ticks magnificently . . . but it is not the same watch! Papst has been into one of his mysterious pockets and found another one. It looks the same, but it is a cheaper watch.

It can of course happen that the upstart really is quite smart and has also had his suspicions aroused. He might catch Papst out in his cheating and start making a fuss. Then Papst will shake his head sadly at himself and say: "There, you see! I know nobody smarter than you. I didn't notice it myself, but *you* saw it!" And in order to appease the customer, he gives him his own pocket watch—which the man assumes is a kind of guarantee. But, in fact, he walks away with a third and very ordinary watch.

Here at the fair Edevart saw the Armenian again, the organ grinder from back home; and the Hungarian was still with him. He ran across them one afternoon down by the quayside. They had taken up a stand on a crowded stretch and they were hard at it with their music and the peep show.

The two men had not changed wholly beyond recognition in the three years since their appearance in the village back home: merely that the Armenian now had two black eyes and was thus totally blind. Poor man, to be an organ grinder in a strange land! Such is fate! Some felt pity for him and put coins into the boy's begging bowl; children and young people flocked around the marvelous barrel organ with Napoleon and his generals in their gold and bright colors.

"I know them," whispered Edevart to the man beside him. "I have seen them before!" And he turned directly to the organ grinder and asked: "Have you become blind?"

"Yes, blind!" answered the man sorrowfully, and shook his head.

"I don't believe it," said Edevart. For he had noticed that the good Armenian looked intently at him when he heard the question.

Now the Hungarian joined in, shouting and attacking his companion as of old, with blows and hard punches. A thrill of horror ran through the spectators. They fell back and shouted to the older people to come along. Fine! Everybody here was his own policeman. The two men from Namdal were nearby; they set about the Hungarian with their fists, picked him up, and hoisted him above their heads, shouting coarsely that he was just a big baby not yet breeched and they ought to chuck him in the sea. Well, the two men were too much for the Hungarian. He fought back for a while and tried to wriggle free, but then gave up and began to plead with them. The Namdalers were merciful; as they had so totally defeated him, they gave him a kick on the backside and let him slink away. They stood and watched him go, laughing. And then there was no end to their boasting. They should have made mincemeat of him and fed him to the chickens! The Namdalers now turned to the victim of the assault, expecting his thanks. He did not thank them. He stood sniveling and wiping his cheek.

"Have you ever seen such funny blood?" said the Namdalers to each other. "Just as though it had something blue in it."

"It's not blood," said Edevart. "It's something he smears on himself. I have seen these two before."

"Isn't it blood?"

"No. And he's not blind, either," said Edevart.

A voice in the crowd supported him. "No, he's not blind. I have seen these two rogues up in Finmark. They played the same tricks then to get money out of us."

The Namdalers walked over to the man and looked at him. "Aren't you blind?" they asked.

The man sniffed and replied: "Yes, blind. *Gewiss.*"

One of the men took out a knife and thrust it near his face; the blind man flinched and drew back in terror. No, he didn't survive the test. In great haste he began dismantling the barrel organ, intending to make his getaway. The Namdalers didn't touch him; but they felt rather silly not doing anything about him, after getting mixed up in such a ridiculous affair, which in fact hadn't been worth fighting about. They stood there embarrassed, thrusting their hands into their pockets and taking them out again. They had actually thought of throwing the wrong man into the sea!

"Away with you!" they commanded. "You are no more blind than we are."

"Yes, I am," mumbled the Armenian. "Almost blind, very blind."

"Away with you, do you hear!"

And thus it was that their act was ruined. The Armenian and his companion vanished from the fair. They presumably made their way across the island of Hadsel to Melbo, playing at the various farms, putting on their performance and fiddling their way onward, a little step at a time. What else were they to do? They were human beings, stumbling on, carrying on as circumstances permitted; and they lived until they died . . .

Then there were more events and experiences for August. Edevart lost sight of him one morning as they came off the boat, where they had slept the night, and didn't see him again until the afternoon of the following day. Then he was drunk and in high spirits. Ah, August! The sailor lad had awarded himself shore leave again!

He came wandering down the street to where Edevart stood staring at old Papst and his watches. August was rather merry and pink-faced, and he talked English to himself. He was wearing a shining gold ring which he had bought for himself, and had some silken finery around his neck that was doubtless meant for ladies. Anyway, it was fringed.

When he caught sight of Edevart, he waved and asked: "Have you eaten? Come, we'll go to a place I know!"

They went to a place that sold sandwiches and hot meals and sat down. A woman and a girl were running the business. August was known here. He patted the girl on the arm and called her his darling. "Bring me my bottle, Mattea!" he said. Then he turned to Edevart and invited him to order any food he happened to fancy. "There's no food in the world too good," he said, "that my darling Mattea here won't rustle up."

"*You bet,*" he added in English.

And Mattea brought food and a bottle of spirits.

While they ate, August explained what had kept him away. He'd delivered his skins to Klem, Hansen & Co. of Trondheim, and then got the idea of going out and celebrating. He'd met a number of very nice people.

Edevart asked: "What did you get for the skins? How did it go?"

"Marvelously!" replied August. He'd never imagined he'd get so much! And then he went on to explain that, because he'd become engaged, he might not have time to sail back again with the boat.

Edevart was alarmed. "I can't sail it back home alone."

"What do you mean, alone? That's not my idea. I'd rather buy the boat."

But surely it wasn't for sale?

August snorted: "Don't you worry about that!"

They ate and drank and chatted. Now and then August would hum. Edevart had never been so richly entertained before. If only those poor people back home could have seen all this splendor!

"But what do you want the boat for?" asked Edevart.

August hadn't really considered this. No doubt he only wanted to buy it to get out of the business of sailing it back home, and thereby taking himself away from his sweetheart. Perhaps the terrors of the voyage coming north were still in his mind. In any case, he didn't want to discuss serious matters now. All his thoughts were on fun and games. "Look at Mattea!" he said. "Beautiful girl! She's well worth that heavy gold ring I gave her. Isn't it heavy?"

The generally taciturn August grew garrulous. He talked more freely than at other times. The drinks were having their effect. His thoughts grew swifter; he laughed, showing all his gold teeth; and was in a good mood.

Two young lads came in, and August began showing off to

them. He began to tell about other places round the world, about hot countries. In India, for instance, they had rings on their ankles made of pure gold and without any kind of clasp, forged straight onto the limb, along with a few diamonds and trinkets to jingle. But once a girl had broken her ankle and they had to file the ring off to be able to set the bone!

"Come over here and have a dram with your coffee!" he shouted to the two youths. He felt a need to share with others; he didn't want to celebrate alone, and Edevart hadn't much capacity. "Skol, lads! I'll have you know that I'm a much traveled man. I've been all around the world, and I can well believe that Calcutta and Sydney and such places are unfamiliar cities to you. Be that as it may, here I sit on this stool just as you see me. What d'you think brought me to this place? Furs! Yes, I'm a businessman. And this much I can tell you about the skin trade: there's no trade like it for putting fur on your back! Ask my friend sitting here what kind of cargo we came with! Which reminds me, Edevart," he said suddenly, "I must pay you your wages!"

Edevart was embarrassed. "It can't be much. I got such a lot last time."

August took out a fat wallet and counted out the money, and was not too persnickety. "Here," he said. "If you are happy with that, take it!"

Edevart thanked him even more shyly and said it was marvelous. He'd been given much more than he should have been.

"Yes," said August. "I'm like that. I don't begrudge you it." He called for Mattea and asked if there wasn't another bottle.

"No," she answered.

"Bring another bottle!" he said, friendly but firm, and gripped her arm. When she complained, he gripped her tighter and said: "The louder you scream, the worse it'll be."

"Let me be!" she cried, red in the face.

But he didn't let her go until she had promised to bring another bottle. All in all, he treated her harshly, with no real sign of affection, as though she were some insignificant creature in comparison with himself. Like one of his ribs. A strange relationship for an engaged couple. "And now bring some cigars," he said. "Extra good cigars for everybody!"

One of the young lads seemed to know the girl rather well. They made eyes at each other; and young Mattea rested one of her hands in an unnecessarily affectionate way on his shoulder when she reached out for something on the table. August noticed nothing. He rose to greater and greater heights; he turned fanciful and foolish, playing the rich man and the fool. He began to tell about a fight on board some schooner. Perhaps it was sheer invention. The Malay had taken his knife and pretty well carved up the mate, but then August had thrust a marlin spike into the Malay's belly . . .

August fell silent.

"Well, I'll be darned!" one of the young men broke out. "What happened then?"

August prepared to draw the moral significance of his story. He said: "Wait a moment till I remember it properly! What happened then? He rolled around the deck seven or eight times and then got to his feet again with the marlin spike still in his belly . . ."

"Ah!" said the listeners.

"Yes," said August, himself overcome. He shook his head. Perhaps he had exceeded his own expectations.

"But did you kill him?" the lads asked in horror.

August drew back. Mattea was standing there listening. He didn't want to seem a monster and a murderer. "I didn't kill him," he said. "A Malay and a Mohammedan like him—he doesn't die from a piece of iron in his belly. No, he continued on with the marlin spike in him till we reached harbor and a doctor."

"Why didn't he pull it out?"

"Don't you realize he would have bled to death . . ."

Many more stories and a great deal of crazy talk followed throughout the afternoon. Time passed. Edevart began thinking about practical matters and asked: "Have you written home about the boat?"

"No," replied August. "I shan't write. I'll just send a telegram, express and reply paid and all that sort of thing. Ah, yes!" he added. "Those of us who know the ways of the world use the telegraph. Mattea, let's have some coffee!"

But before the coffee arrived, August began to feel unwell. His face turned deathly pale and he had to go out. Our good August was by no means a practiced drinker. Not at all. He couldn't take spirits. What happened was that when a suitable occasion offered he would go out on the loose. Given a chance, the carefree lad's head would be swimming. He had plowed and harrowed the seas and reaped its harvests; and with every shore leave he had sown his seed anew. That's the way it was. He said it himself often enough, made no attempt to conceal it.

He managed to mumble: "I'll be back soon!" And went.

Edevart followed him out and said: "You should come aboard and lie down for a while."

He answered: "Lie down? What do you mean? No!"

"If you lie down, it will soon pass."

August, innocently and stubbornly: "What is there to pass? I'm not drunk. It was that cigar . . ."

Edevart: "But if only you were to sleep for a little while. I wish you would!"

August, stubbornly: "Sleep! In the middle of the day? Not likely!"

No, August was not receptive to new ideas of this kind. And, like drunk people everywhere, he was definitely not drunk. He was completely sober, utterly sober. It was just that wretched cigar . . .

Anyway, he recovered quickly outside, got some color back into his cheeks, and stood firm again on his feet. They both went in again.

What a sight met them! That damned young man and Mattea standing in the corner openly embracing each other!

The immediate result of this vision was that a stool suddenly hit the ceiling and fell back again on the table, smashing cups and glasses. After which August grabbed a bread knife from the table and vaulted over in the direction of the couple in the corner. The effect was instantaneous: the young lad, roaring with fright, re-leased the lady and rushed to the door, his companion following on his heels. The place then seemed rather empty; there was nobody left for August to set about. He stood there looking at his lady love: a swordsman disarmed, a fool, speechless and stupid.

"It didn't mean a thing," said Mattea, trying to smile.

The proprietress came in from the kitchen, rather fright-ened, and demanded quiet in the house. She didn't immediately seek to throw out a man like August—such a good customer for her moonshine liquor—but now she felt she had to ask him to be so good as to pay up and leave. He could always come again later. "Let me have the knife!" she said.

August still had the look of one who was bent on extermina-tion, but little by little he gave way. It wasn't as if he were on a bear hunt now. He handed over his triumphant saber to the woman.

Mattea spoke again: "It didn't mean anything, you know. I just happen to know him. He is from Ofoten—son of a skipper. He's called Nils."

"Yes, but . . ." stammered August.

"We weren't doing anything. We were only talking," Mattea insisted. "We weren't doing anything, hardly."

"Wasn't he kissing you? I saw him."

"No, no! Are you crazy!" cried Mattea. "We were just play-ing around." In the end Mattea was talking as though really she'd scarcely been there in the corner with Nils at all that day—which left August greatly bewildered and stupefied. All right, perhaps he hadn't all that many eyes in his head, two at most, but he could, after all, see with them both! Meanwhile, Mattea fussed about him, spoke disarmingly to him, and persuaded him to sit down while he paid the bill. When he ordered a new bottle from her to take away, he was not refused it. And when he put his arm around her and asked for a little tender favor, he was given that, too. In short, Mattea could not have been sweeter. That also seemed to bring solace to August.

But when he got up to go, his suspicions returned. He de-

31

manded that she should repudiate Nils and everybody else in the world.

"Yes!" she made haste to reply. "Yes, I do, believe me."

"Because if you don't, you can just hand over the ring," he said.

She made as if to pull off the ring and began sobbing a little. This compliance on her part had a remarkably good effect on August. He wasn't far from tears himself now, and said: "You can keep the ring for the time being."

He turned to ask Edevart: "She promised to be faithful to me forever, isn't that so?"

Edevart felt honored to be playing a part in all this, and he answered: "Yes, to that I am a solemn witness."

"Yes, on that you may stake your life," replied Mattea, weeping with emotion. "I won't give him so much as a single glance ever again."

"Then you can keep the ring!" he announced magnanimously.

But Edevart clearly considered the betrothal to be somewhat uncertain. When they were standing in the telegraph office, he quietly asked whether it might perhaps not be better to delay sending the telegram until tomorrow. "What do you think yourself?" he added, afraid of giving offense to a man who had been all around the world.

"No, I'm going to buy that boat now," replied August firmly. "You heard what she promised!"

"But how am I going to get back home again?"

"By the steamer," replied August. Meanwhile, he had been scrawling on a number of blank forms; finally he got the telegram straight and handed it in, reply paid. He had sobered up somewhat.

What about August going aboard the boat now for a little sleep and rest? No, certainly not! He was a free man, he had plenty of time, and he had money in his pocket. Not that he was intending to throw his wealth away by buying useless things. But,

32

for example, he did very much want to treat himself to a dark coat which he might wear at his wedding. Moreover, for a long time he'd needed a revolver . . .

"What's that?" asked Edevart.

"Don't you know? It's a thing to shoot with. A pistol."

"Wouldn't you be better off with a gun? I don't know."

"No, I can't put it in my pocket. Really, I should have had a revolver just then instead of that knife. Then you'd have seen something!"

August went on to explain that there were various things he needed: here he was wearing a watch chain whose gilt had worn off. Abroad, not even the lowliest sea captain or mate would be seen with a thing like that on him. Away with it! Get a new one instead! He'd show Mattea what sort of man he was! He'd also discovered an accordion on one of the stalls, with two banks of keys and broad silken straps. Ah, a superb instrument! It appealed to him.

"But can you play?" asked Edevart.

August answered with some embarrassment: "What do you think?"

Edevart didn't know. He had his doubts. But what a hell of a fellow August would be if he really could play!

Edevart wasn't thinking of buying any splendid things of the sort August had in mind, but he, too, had plans: a shirt of many colors and laced up the front; a cap with a shiny peak. It depended on what he could afford. A length of dress material for each of his sisters he would certainly have to take home—to those little ones who, speechless and bashful, could only thank you by pressing your hand.

That night, after Edevart had turned in, August came aboard; and he, too, crept in under the sail. Sure enough, he had bought both the accordion and the gold chain; and he offered Edevart a cigar from a full box.

"Did you buy the coat?" Edevart asked.

August slapped his knee and shouted: "That I forgot! Well,

33

it's not too late tomorrow." Anyway, he said, it was a miserable fair compared with what he was used to. There wasn't a revolver to be found.

In the morning he went ashore declaring he was going to buy the coat and then he'd be coming back again, for this was the last day of the fair. Good. Edevart waited, but August didn't come. He waited till afternoon, then he, too, went ashore and began wandering up and down. He stopped as usual near the watch seller Jew.

"Where are you from?" asked Papst.

Edevart told him.

"Whose son are you?"

Edevart told him his parents' names, but Papst didn't know them. He asked the lad what he was doing here, how old he was, what he was called, and if he was going to the Lofotens next winter. And Edevart gave an account of himself. When that was finished, Papst turned to others.

August was nowhere to be seen. Edevart went to Mattea's shop. August had been there twice that day, but had gone away again. He'd been all smartly dressed, with a dark coat and a gold chain, she told him. Edevart waited for him there quite a while, but finally left.

The stall holders were now busy packing up their unsold goods and preparing to return home. They wanted to sell endless things to Edevart at ridiculous prices: a neckerchief, a pair of suspenders, a long-stem pipe. "Come and see before I pack everything away. There you are: a first-rate razor. I can see you need one already. Take it for what you feel like giving, have it for next to nothing!" Edevart had begun to grow a fair amount of down on his cheeks, and he bought the razor. But he was red with embarrassment.

August came aboard that evening. And very smart he looked in his new coat. But his spirits had slumped. Whatever else might have been the cause of this, it was doubtless in part the hangover effects of his drinking. Edevart at once asked him if he had had any reply to his telegram. No. Had he made any inquiries? No, he hadn't done that, either.

Edevart looked at him. The blue of his eyes had somehow become pale and blurred, and his face was wan. Edevart remarked that he ought to get some sleep.

"I ended up playing cards with some fellows," said August.

"And you lost?"

"Yes, they were like fiends. Yet in fact I didn't lose all that much. What I was going to ask was: were you out looking for me today?"

"Yes. And I looked in to ask Mattea, too."

"Well, what did she say?"

"She said you looked smart. One of the smartest people she'd ever seen."

"Yes," responded August. "When I buy anything it's always the best!"

They talked about the price of the gold chain. It had been a stiff price, and Edevart wanted to have another look. He couldn't. "No," said August, "and I wish I'd never bought it, because now it's gone."

"Gone? You lost it gambling?"

"But I've still got my watch," said August, and turned away, his mouth trembling.

"You ought to go to bed," said Edevart.

Again August wouldn't listen. He had decided that there was no longer any pleasure in sleeping. He had a hangover and was deeply dejected.

But when Edevart woke in the morning, fatigue had nonetheless overcome his companion. He sat outside asleep on one of the thwarts of the boat, fully dressed and as gray as a corpse.

The vessels and boats had already left the harbor in the gray light of dawn; a small steamer lay alongside the quay taking on passengers and packing cases. Edevart felt inclined to go aboard himself, but decided that he would first dash ashore and inquire about the telegram. It had arrived. He took delivery of it and ran back on board with it. August was sitting on the selfsame thwart; he was awake now. He was busy counting his money.

"Here's the telegram," said Edevart.

August answered: "Can't be bothered with it."

"Don't you want to see what it says?"

"No. Chuck it in the sea."

"You are being stupid," said Edevart respectfully. He looked across at the little steamer and said: "Isn't that the steamer I'm supposed to be going home on?"

August merely sighed and sat there, pensive.

"For there's nothing more to keep me here," continued Edevart and began collecting his bits and pieces.

"There's no hurry," said August.

"No hurry?"

August suddenly ripped open the telegram and read it, or pretended to. "Just as I thought! Karolus thinks he can ask me some outrageous price for the boat. Look here!"

Edevart slowly spelled out what the telegram said; but as far as he could understand, it seemed a reasonable price. It was a new boat with all its equipment. August said: "No. It's better we both sail the boat home and return it!"

That was different; and Edevart had absolutely no objection to that. August had come down to earth again and was acting sensibly.

He came even farther down to earth later that day; was indeed laid quite low. Mattea had disappeared! When the two of them went in search of a bite of hot food, they found the place deserted. In the kitchen there was only a cold stove surrounded by bare walls. The woman was gone. Mattea was gone.

August burst out idiotically: "What! . . . Have you ever seen anything like it?"

"They must have left," said Edevart.

August: "Left? No. Let's go out and find them."

They went out to search, with August still carrying his accordion, for he had meant to play for Mattea. They couldn't

36

inquire of the neighbors, for there were no longer any neighbors there. Nearly all the stalls were deserted. They searched the entire fairground but found hardly any people there. They went to the quayside, but now even the little steamer had left.

The jilted August had obviously taken things to heart and was in need of consolation. Now and then he simply stopped and stood still. Edevart said: "Well, perhaps it's all for the best. You never know, but if she *was* the kind who . . ."

August did not answer.

Edevart suddenly cried: "But she's gone off with the ring!"

"Where was she from, do you know?" August asked darkly.

"How should I know! Don't you know yourself?"

"Goodbye and good luck to the ring. But that's not the worst," said August. "She got my watch yesterday."

Edevart, thunderstruck: "You're joking!"

August was not joking. There was certainly nothing funny in it for him. He was well and truly stunned. It was Edevart who had to see to the necessary provisions for the return journey and in general to take command. The other man was incapable of anything.

And August's misery was naturally exacerbated by the strenuous work they were then faced with. They had a reasonably fair wind over Hadselfjord; but then it dropped and they had to row with their heavy oars the entire length of Raftsund. For August this was a tough ordeal. He rowed till he was dripping with sweat; he peeled off one garment after another; and when the time came for their evening meal, he simply slumped back in the boat, incapable.

"Isn't there a dram for you to have?" said Edevart. "I've heard that sometimes helps."

But August was no drinker. He wasn't the kind who can cure a hangover by taking a few more drinks. On the contrary, the very thought of it brought a feeling of nausea.

Suddenly August asks: "What am I going home for?"

After a moment or two, Edevart answers: "What are we

going home for? The main thing is that we have to return the boat."

"That you might well say. But I can't."

"How's that?"

August rests on his elbow and answers in desperation: "I'll tell you why not. I can't pay for the hire of it."

Edevart is silent a long time. But August goes on talking—foolish, excited talk: "What are you looking at me like that for? I tell you—I can't meet the cost of the hire."

Edevart ventures to say: "Yet you wanted to buy the boat!"

"Yes," replied August. "But that was then. Don't you understand? At that time I could have bought the boat for straight cash."

"That I don't believe," Edevart might have said, but he kept silent. What was he to think of his companion? He had a suspicion that the good August had overstepped the mark. After all, what in fact could he have made out of that consignment of skins? Not all that very much. Not a fortune. Just enough one-daler notes to plump out a wallet. Not enough to keep him in gold chains and rings for the rest of his life.

"Have *you* any money left?" asked August.

"Who, me? What would I have!"

"You must help me. You can have my new coat."

"I don't have enough for that," said Edevart.

They counted his money and August said: "There's enough here. You can take the coat!"

Edevart: "You can't give your coat away like that!"

August, careless and magnanimous again: "You need it more than I do."

He would now be returning from his voyage in rather modest style. And if ever he'd thought of trying to lord it over the lads back home, that was all over now. Nevertheless, August's spirits gradually began to revive. For the time being, he had been saved from the worst of his difficulties—he was able to pay for the hire of the boat. And he still had his gold ring and his accordion in hand. That wasn't *too* bad with which to confront the poverty-stricken little village. August suddenly found his appetite and said he wanted to sample the provisions they had brought from the fair. August began to pull himself together. When they came to Vestfjord later that morning, they had a following wind the whole way and so were relieved of rowing.

"What are you thinking of doing this summer?" asked Edevart.

"Oh, something will turn up," said August cheerfully. "Why do you ask?"

"I don't know what to do myself," answered Edevart.

August fell to thinking. He was acting as tack man and had nothing particular to attend to in the boat. He seemed to be dozing. Then he said: "What will I do this summer? Are you concerned about me, Edevart? You mustn't worry!"

Edevart was far from convinced that the whole world lay open to his companion that summer. He kept silent.

Suddenly August began to wash his hands in the sea and then dried them very carefully on his trousers. Then he seized hold of the accordion, placed his fingers inside the silken straps, and played a lively march. Edevart could not restrain a cry: "Marvelous! So you *can* play!"

August spat into the sea and replied: "You needn't spread it about at home!"

Edevart was deeply impressed by his companion. He had never once mentioned that he could play. How much more remarkable he was than other men: a fool and a madman, maybe, but a real live wire! Could anyone really make him out? Hadn't he behaved incredibly badly on the voyage out, weeping in terror at a mere hailstorm! And hadn't he confessed to many sins and misdemeanors during his roving life! But now this same man sat here playing marvelous music—dance music and wedding music, and finishing up by singing an English song. He had great gifts.

"I've played for the highest and lowest of company in my time," said August.

"Where did you learn?"

August ignored the question and continued: "Once I played for a king."

"You don't say!"

"The King of Burma. He was black and had great fangs. He was surrounded by thousands of headhunters. But he and I got on very well. 'Play a dance for me, August!' he said."

"What was he called?"

"Caphavaripeilinglog."

"What on earth! That's a bit of a mouthful!"

"Yes, that was his name," said August proudly. "Caphavaripeilinglog. And you should have seen the rings in his ears. They hung right down to his shoulders and they were made from the teeth of all his enemies. I presented him with my accordion."

"You *gave* your accordion away?"

August smiled cunningly: "Let me tell you, Edevart, that I didn't do it for nothing. I got many chests, all full."

Edevart's face went blank with incomprehension. "Many chests full of what?"

"You mustn't ask that, because I'm not one who likes to brag," answered August. "Nor do I want you spreading it all around the village. But those chests are still in the capital of Further India waiting for me to come and collect them."

Edevart: "Not a word of this is true, is it?"

"What do you mean: not true? Have I ever lied to you before? Will you believe me when you see these keys?" August asked, and he brought a huge bunch of keys out of his pocket. There were eight keys and a corkscrew.

Edevart was speechless. August had also kept this concealed —that he had eight chests waiting for him in India. Moreover, this was the first time Edevart had ever seen the keys. He capitulated.

3 IN THAT POOR LITTLE VILLAGE EVERYTHING SEEMED TO be in a torpor. Nobody showed any enterprise, any initiative; people lived from hand to mouth. Their little patches of land grew hay, potatoes, and barley. The animals went out in the summer to graze, and remained in their stalls in winter. It was all so eternal, so unchanging. Children learned what their parents knew, no more and no less. And the days went by, and life went by. When the men had done their Lofoten fishing in the winter, and had gathered in their modest crops in the autumn, they had done what was expected of them. The remaining time was without significance. What were they to turn their hands to? What was there to do? Oh, they were so lazy! Loafers, all of them! They drifted around from cottage to cottage, gossiping. Idle, sleepy, hungry. They went to church to get the latest news.

In the neighboring villages they had a small but regular income every spring when the sloops and other boats arrived from the Lofotens carrying fish to be dried on the rocks along the shore. It made a welcome penny or two for flour and coffee when young and old turned out to handle the fish, with everybody earning a little. Whereas in *this* village nothing had been done to clear the drying grounds of heather and turf to make them suitable for use. It was scandalous, thoroughly despicable. And our sailor lad August had a word or two to say about it one day: What about their going out and clearing the thin layer of turf from the rocks? All the men from the village could get together and do the work in a few days. August himself would also lend a hand.

He got no response. They all turned their backs on him, and muttered among themselves, and shuffled on. Did August think he could teach them anything! Karolus, the boat owner married to Ane Maria, didn't think it altogether impossible. What else had they done in the neighboring villages a few years ago but get a number of men to go out and clear up the rocky grounds? In this way they had assured themselves of drying places forever after. "In any case, it's too late this year," they told him. Another serious objection was that nobody in the village knew anything about drying fish; there was nobody who could take charge of the work. So what would they do with a drying place? August declared that he knew about drying fish.

"You?" they said.

"I've been in Newfoundland," he said.

"Where haven't you been?" they said.

August got nowhere.

Then one afternoon, one fine Sunday afternoon at the beginning of July when the men hung around waiting for St. Olaf's Day in order to begin their mowing, something happened. There was the sound of music from Karolus's barn. What—music? Had the two organ grinders come back again from foreign parts? Children rushed to the scene from all directions. They saw August and Edevart sitting there, and August had his accordion, all silk straps and gilt and bright colors. Sublime music came pouring forth from a double keyboard, with bass and treble. August's fingers never stopped. Then the adults came running. They had just got back from church and had thought of having a sleep. But there was no thought of that now. Karolus arrived. Soon it was a full house.

Everybody stared! August, what was he not capable of! When he played and sang a song about a girl in Barcelona, everybody was touched.

August paused and mopped his brow. "He can do more than we can!" said Karolus.

"Where did you learn that?" they asked him.

He did not answer. After a while he packed the instrument away in his box; and it was no use their asking him to play any more.

A number of the men had heard accordion music before both in the Lofotens and in the towns of Finmark; but nobody had expected anything so remarkable from August. He had now been one of them for years and had never said a word about it.

There was thus more to him than was apparent. God knows, maybe it was all true—all these stories he told about his life? All these improbable things they had previously simply taken as lies? From now on everybody looked at him through different eyes. He was not without mystery for them. They hadn't yet seen his bunch of keys from India, not yet. But they had seen the double keyboard on his instrument, and it was incredible the way his fingers coped with them both. Where had he learned this skill? Perhaps in some extraordinary way! Perhaps from the Prince of Darkness himself!

Edevart felt a quiet pride for his companion, and did not stand in his light. He went to Karolus and said: "You all saw him sitting there playing. But I have seen and heard even greater things of him. Now he wants us to clear the rocks."

"Yes," said Karolus.

"Then you'll support us?"

"Yes."

"Then I suggest we make it tomorrow."

Quite a number of men turned up, including the awkward Teodor. If Karolus, who after all owned the boat, was willing, the others couldn't hold out any longer. And when a week later the work was complete, everyone felt well satisfied. They now had a drying ground capable of taking several thousand fish, the sort of cargo they could reasonably expect at any one time in Polden.

August said to Edevart: "Now you and I will do quite well for ourselves this summer, don't you fret!"

In the winter, Edevart joined Karolus's crew for the Lofoten fishing, and August went along as a passenger. August was meant to promote the new drying grounds, and take on the role of manager. With his gold teeth and his gold ring, he was clearly no ordinary fisherman. Moreover, he had borrowed the black coat back from Edevart, and looked very prosperous. Ah, August was no mean ambassador! He was also in luck. After he had rowed around the various fishing vessels for a week talking to the skippers, he made contact with one who could only be described as a find: a peasant skipper from Hardanger, owner of both boat and cargo, a splendid man with a black beard and a golden locket which hung on his chest by a hair chain. Moreover, he showed himself in time to be very companionable and fond of a glass. With this man August started negotiations. August was carefully questioned and had to give a full account both of himself and of the drying ground; but it ended in a signed contract. The man from Hardanger had brought along a good store of salt biscuits, a whole barrel of liquor, and a bulkhead full of nuts. All these things were meant for those who would dry the fish. The skipper's name was Skaaro and his vessel was called *The Seagull*.

August spent the winter aboard the Hardanger vessel and gave the skipper a hand buying in his fish, and doing other odd jobs as they occurred, like relieving the fish splitter when necessary. August could do that, too. He probably didn't get much of a wage, but he got his board and lodging, and August's appearance didn't seem to suggest that he needed payment for every job he did. He was more like a guest on a visit. In the light summer evenings he sat playing cards with Skipper Skaaro, winning and losing nuts. He might also take a dram to be sociable, but further than that he refused to go. A thoroughly decent and reliable fish drier; there seemed nothing whatever wrong with him. When he spoke of his experiences in foreign parts, he toned down the coarser stories; and the skipper, who hadn't been beyond Hardanger, Bergen, and the Lofotens, listened with interest.

The second half of April saw the end of the Lofoten fishing, and *The Seagull* took on its final load. Edevart came on board to pilot the vessel across Vestfjord. For this he was to receive little or nothing; on the other hand, he was well fed. One glorious spring evening, with the sun shining and a gentle breeze blowing, *The Seagull* glided into Polden and put a line ashore. People stood on the high ground all around looking at the proud sight.

The business of cleaning the fish began with a drink and salt biscuits for one and all. August went round with the bottle and Edevart with the biscuits. Cleaning was highly paid work because it was both heavy and dirty—paid by the "fisherman's hundred," i.e., 120 fish. Some of the men hauled the fish up out of the hold; these were then loaded into boats and taken ashore. Here stood men and a number of women knee deep in the sea, cleaning the fish. It was a matter of removing all the dried blood and gutting them and leaving the white flesh. When the fish were clean, they were carried away on two-man stretchers and spread out over the rocks. August with Edevart at his side supervised everything from the deck of *The Seagull*. They had a full view of everything; now and then they shouted something down into the hold; they pointed and directed the boats. Karolus with his eight-oar was earning good money; he could manage an entire "fisherman's hundred" at a time in his big boat. Skipper Skaaro often came ashore to see how things were going there and to joke with the fisher lasses. His joviality was well received.

Some days later the entire catch had been gutted and cleaned and *The Seagull* was swilled clean. The fish lay now in small heaps on the rocks, waiting only for the last patches of snow to melt. Then the drying would begin.

Every morning began with a dram for the men; the women and children got a salt biscuit or a handful of nuts, but no dram. It was a mild *brennevin*; nothing very strong. The morning drink was but a token of goodwill, and had become customary at all the drying grounds. Edevart got on good terms with many a youngster by secretly slipping them an extra biscuit or a few more nuts. They then set about their day's work with a will and with never a complaint. By the time the fish had been spread out, it was dinnertime, and time for an hour's rest; then the fish were turned and lay the other side up for several hours. In the evening they were once more collected. The drying grounds were crowded with people.

Everything now ran smoothly; the only interruptions were for Sundays and the occasional rainy day when the fish remained in piles and were not moved. Already while in the Lofotens, Skipper Skaaro had sent home as superfluous the men he had brought with him from the south—the fish splitter and the other man—since they would be without work for the entire summer. Skaaro himself began going off visiting other skippers in the surrounding drying grounds; and August and Edevart were left alone on board. On the whole they did a good job and didn't waste their time. While August cooked and supervised the drying, Edevart painted the vessel and scraped and oiled the mast and the bowsprit. If there was a problem of bringing in the fish before the rain, they both went ashore and lent a hand. When the skipper came back on a quick visit, he found nobody idle, and he became more and more satisfied with his two Nordlanders. This was helped by the fact that August had presented him with his gold ring. In the eyes of the man from Hardanger this was a magnificent present; but August, who was a good-tempered and generous-minded sailor lad, didn't think it amounted to all that much. Skipper Skaaro praised him in all the neighboring villages and made him a man of some renown.

One afternoon the skipper came home from one of his visits to the other drying grounds cheerful and happy and pleased with life. He had a plan to throw a party for a few of his friends. There was to be food on board and dancing ashore. August was asked to find a musician. August nodded with a little smile. He was also to find the largest barn and some dancing partners. August nodded again. But what about food? Fresh meat? Now that it was close season for seabirds and all game? August pointed to a flock of sheep on the edge of the wood and said: "There should be plenty of choice there!"

They did not have regular shepherds on these northern farms, and the flocks often came grazing along the edge of the drying grounds. The sheep were in good shape about now, and Skipper Skaaro spoke to the young housewife Ane Maria about buying a ram for fresh meat, as he was thinking of giving a party. Certainly, she would talk to Karolus about it. The next day she came back with Karolus's approval, and the skipper asked her to come with him up into the fields and show him the animal. They went, and Ane Maria wasn't away more than a short while before she returned alone, agitated and breathing hard, and began work on the fish again. The other women and girls pulled faces at each other and seemed to be amused. "Didn't you find the sheep?" they asked her. "What have you done with the skipper? Surely he wasn't after you?" Ane Maria did not answer. Skipper Skaaro returned from the fields a little later and went straight on board; he then set about bathing one of his eyes with cold water.

It was August who had to buy the ram and act as middleman again. Not that he had any difficulty. Both Karolus and Ane Maria behaved as though nothing had happened, and sold him the animal at the first asking. Karolus also lent his barn for the dance.

It proved to be a pleasant occasion, with everyone enjoying themselves, and drinks and salt biscuits all around—and for those who preferred it, there was wine from the store. As visiting guests there were two young skippers; young wives and girls from the village made up the party, and the musician was August himself playing his accordion. It was a great and rare event to get August to sit down and play his marvelous music on that double keyboard and the twin bass keys. It was like music for a wedding. Even the three skippers had never heard anything like it.

So was all splendid? Well, Edevart wasn't doing too well. Because of course Ragna was there, little Ragna, who had grown into a tall and in every way a beautiful girl. Yes, she was there, with all the skippers competing to dance with her. Nor was a man like Karolus particularly pleased to have to sit there and watch Ane Maria dancing endlessly with Skipper Skaaro, and never once sitting out. What could you do! She was young and healthy, liked to be in the swim and to be pursued as she had been before she was married. Perhaps she also discovered that this man from Hardanger was a powerful dancer, strong as a bear when he swung her. Perhaps it was also not without significance that this same man also bowed and thanked her after every dance—some-

47

thing she was not accustomed to and hadn't once experienced since she was a bride!

"Shouldn't we go outside and cool off a little?" asked Skipper Skaaro.

"No," she answered. "I don't think so."

"I have a little flask of wine in my pocket," he said.

"I don't care for that," she said.

So the skipper went out alone and stood by the wall. Then along came Olga, the one with the beaded belt. She really belonged to the neighboring parish, but she was in service at the storekeeper's. She was small and brown-eyed and like a willow when she danced, but not strictly pretty. How was that? Her nose turned up too much, but what of that! Skipper Skaaro stood there talking to her a while, gave her some wine from his hip flask, looked at her beaded belt, fondled it, and had never seen anything quite so pretty.

And there sat Ane Maria inside, watching everything through the open door. Finally she began dancing with her husband; but it wasn't the same. He stamped; he didn't bow and thank her. There were many things she found fault with. How cold his hands were, even though it was a warm summer night; how clammy they were to hold. That was doubtless because of all the drinks he had taken. His breath was pure brandy; nor did he attempt to do anything about it by chewing roast coffee beans as the Hardanger skipper had done.

Skipper Skaaro came in with his lady, the bead-belted Olga. They now danced unceasingly, never leaving the floor. Brazenly they stood in the middle of the floor waiting for the next dance. Skaaro was wild with excitement. As he went whirling round he shouted out in delight to the musician for more.

"Make it last!" he shouted. "Stretch it out—twice as long!"

Oh, what marvelous fun!

But now the musician needed a breather. His right thumb had become white and numb in the tight silk strap. The two visiting skippers each took out a daler note to reward him for his playing. They said they were afraid it wasn't very much and that they had never heard such playing. They also wanted to know where he had learned it, but once again he did not answer. In the interval the skippers lit their pipes and talked to the ladies. Edevart went round with refreshments.

Whatever it was that caused it—there began to be a smell of smoke. In the half dark of the barn, where the only light came in through the open door, there was no fire to be seen. But the smell of the smoke got worse. Everybody sniffed and looked around; the skippers put their hands over their pipes and let them go out. Suddenly a flame shot up from the hayloft on the left. "Water!" came the shout. "Water!" The women screamed. Karolus and his neighbors went running to the houses for buckets. There was great confusion. Edevart went streaking down the road to the beach to get some pails from aboard *The Seagull*. Skipper Skaaro had just been thinking of taking a walk outside with Olga when he discovered the fire. He turned back, quickly tore off his coat, threw it over the flames, and trampled on it. It was all done so quickly and cleverly. He smothered the flames. His coat was scorched, but what did he care about that! What a hell of a fine fellow he was! A hero! The sleeves of his violet-checked calico shirt gleamed resplendent in the hayloft; a knife in a bright silver sheath hung at his side. Ane Maria could not take her eyes off him, and said as if to herself: "He's ruined that splendid coat of his!"

When they arrived with buckets of water, it was only a matter of damping down and thoroughly wetting some of the still-smoking hay. But Karolus remained frightened and uneasy for a long time after. He now had the best part of the year's hay harvest in that building and it would completely ruin him if he lost it. "I'll pay for any hay you've lost," said Skipper Skaaro, in the presence of witnesses. What a decent man he was! And Karolus took him by the hand and thanked him for what he had done; and similarly Ane Maria took his hand, very moved, and brushed ashes and hay from his coat. Skaaro said: "No, don't thank me.

We were the ones who lit our pipes and started the fire—whichever one of us it was!" He looked around for his two guests, but they were gone. They had slipped away in the uproar and confusion. It turned out that a couple of the girls had also gone. But Olga was still there.

Edevart came running up from the beach with a bucket of sea water in each hand. When he saw that he was too late, he gave a quick glance round at everybody, put his buckets down, and went off again. He picked his way carefully along the edge of a barley field to a little wood. He seemed suspicious about something. He heard the whisper of voices from a little way off; a big clump of bracken shook agitatedly. He ran up on tiptoe. Aha! One of the visiting skippers was busy kissing her. Perhaps he had already kissed her many times! A cold shiver ran through Edevart and he began to beat his breast as though in despair. Ragna discovered him first and gave a little cry. The skipper let go of her and allowed her to get up.

Things might quickly have turned serious then; but the skipper recognized Edevart as one of the men from *The Seagull* and did not pick a quarrel. Naturally, he was both embarrassed and angry at being disturbed in his bit of sport; but he forced a smile, took a half-full flask from his pocket, and said to Edevart: "Come and have a swig as well, my friend!" Edevart scowled, on his guard against such friendliness. The skipper passed the flask to Ragna and she sipped daintily and thanked him.

"Is he your sweetheart, this lad?" the skipper asked.

"Not that I know of," she answered.

"So what does he want here?"

"I don't know."

Edevart heard this. He wasn't one to step back. He stepped forward. Ragna came between them and asked: "What do you think you're doing?"

Now the skipper made the mistake of acting all superior, and said disdainfully: "Let him stand there and beat his breast!" With this he started to take Ragna by the arm and lead her away.

The first blow to land on him sent him sprawling backward into the bracken. Edevart must have helped things along with his legs, using the wrestling throw he'd learned at school. Ragna gave a scream but stopped abruptly. She was struck by the skipper's appearance; it was strangely altered. All evening he had danced with his hat on. Now he had lost it in falling, and he revealed himself as being completely bald, all shiny and bare. Ragna was on the point of dissolving into laughter—the little scamp didn't know any better. The skipper got up, put his hat firmly on, and got ready. The next thing that happened was that Edevart was hurled on his back into the bushes, with the skipper in a rage, calling him a dirty little brat. Things didn't end there. Edevart was on his feet again in a flash, a look of fury on his face. He clenched his fists and leaped at the other. The skipper snarled: "You dirty little brat! You dirty little brat!" And the fight was on again. Ragna screamed in earnest now and ran away.

"What on earth . . . what's going on?" people shouted as they ran up. The combatants were now rolling about on the ground, now one on top, now the other. Both were looking tired, and both were bleeding. People separated them, taking it all in good part and laughing: surely they were only fooling about! It was a wrestling match, a contest. "Look at Edevart! He won't give in!"

Indeed, no! Edevart wasn't going to give in. He was only a bit of a lad, but he had courage.

It was now well on to morning and the dancing was over. Even the most ardent dancers had left by now, among them the skippers, including Skaaro, as well as the bead-belted Olga, Josefine from Kleiva, and Beret. They came slinking back separately from woods and paths, curiously separated couples who had gone out with their arms tightly around each other but who avoided each other's company on the way back. August had packed up his instrument in its box, but took it out again to play a grand march as the skippers took their leave and made their way down to the sea. August and Edevart were to sleep ashore that night to make room aboard for the visiting skippers. They settled down in Karolus's barn, but woke an hour or two later, when the work was to begin again on the drying grounds. They were a little lacking in sleep, but otherwise all right.

There were others who lacked rather more, lacked peace of mind and any sense of satisfaction. Ane Maria was in a bad mood. She suffered unbelievably from jealousy, and had great difficulty in putting the bead-belted Olga out of her mind. What was that bitch doing at this dance? Who had sent to that distant village for her? And whatever could Skipper Skaaro see in that stupid little upstart! She'd been working now at the store for two years and still wasn't married! Ane Maria was filled with bitterness toward her.

Karolus, on the other hand, was in every way content. He'd had his hay harvest saved, and had another daler's rent for his barn from Skipper Skaaro. Moreover, he'd got his wife back, so to say; he'd danced with her and had fun as though they were newlyweds.

"I found this pipe in the hay," he said, showing her the pipe.

"In the hay? How come?" asked Ane Maria.

"When we damped down the fire."

"It's Skaaro's pipe," she said.

"You're probably right," he answered. "I forgot to give it to him."

Yes, indeed, Karolus was very satisfied with everything. He'd even found this pipe and had immediately sliced some tobacco in it and begun to smoke. "It's a meerschaum, that I do know!" he said expertly, wanting Ane Maria to understand that he knew about these things.

Everything then returned to normal. The visitors left Polden; August and Edevart moved back aboard *The Seagull* again; and the fish drying continued. The fish were now well on the way to being dry; already birch bark had been put on the roof of the stacks in case there should be rain in the final days. Money, too, had arrived for Skipper Skaaro; two thousand dalers for the rent of the drying grounds and for the workers' wages. The skipper walked about with pockets bulging with money. Yet nobody understood why he needed so much money. It must be sheer arrogance.

August said to Edevart: "It isn't everywhere in the world that you can walk about with two thousand dalers in your pocket and not get killed!"

Edevart: "Huh! What it must be like out there!"

August: "I don't know what to say about it. You could often pick up quite a bit. Once I was given twenty-five dollars just to keep my mouth shut!"

"You don't say!"

"It was during a fight. And you never saw a fight without a corpse being left behind. When they'd killed him, they took his watch and his money."

"And then you got twenty-five dollars?"

"Yes, but not for nothing. I'd stood there watching. They were very decent. They said to me: 'Either we kill you as well or else you keep your mouth shut!' 'I'll keep my mouth shut,' I answered. Then they offered me his watch, the corpse's watch, a huge gold affair. I didn't dare take it, for then I might have been caught. 'Give me fifty dollars instead,' I said. They gave me twenty-five, and promised me the rest later. But I never got any more. All the same, if I ever meet them, they'll pay me. They were decent fellows."

Edevart shook his head pensively and said: "It's rotten to kill people!"

"That's what you and I think," answered August. "But it depends very much on the circumstances. Take me, for instance: the thought would never occur to me, but then I don't feel the need. I can simply go back to India and have more than enough of anything you care to mention."

Then came the day when the fish was ready for loading. A great day with sun and screaming gulls and much bustle. Boats large and small ferried the fish back aboard the sloop. Karolus was there with his eight-oar, earning good money again. Skipper

53

Skaaro had had a lucky summer; he was at least two weeks ahead of the skippers at the other drying grounds, and would be able to take fine valuable cargo to Bergen.

The stackers were already standing on deck on *The Seagull* waiting for the first fish. The stackers were always women. They climbed down into the hold and placed the fish neatly in layers. At all the drying grounds these women were generally chosen from among the prettiest and the cleverest and were particularly well paid. It was in a way an honor to be picked for this work of stacking; but the word went around from the neighboring villages that it was not altogether without its hazards, for it meant food and drink in the cabins, and occasionally something a little wilder.

Ane Maria was not one of the stackers, but Beret was there, and Josefine from Kleiva was there, and later Ragna and another girl who were to lend a hand as trimmers. But Ane Maria was not there, and had not even been asked. The women on the drying ground asked her if she wasn't going to be aboard, if she wasn't one of the stackers.

"Do you think I would go aboard and stack?" she answered. "I wouldn't lower myself."

Ah, but she resented it greatly, and she continued to give vent to her spite. It was all right for Josefine from Kleiva; she was a young widow and could do what she wanted with herself. But Beret had her husband in one of the boats and a two-year-old child at home. What was she doing there stacking?

"You get well paid for it," answered the woman.

"Well, I hope she gets all she deserves!" said Ane Maria spitefully.

The loading took several days. On the very first day, after the meal break, Skipper Skaaro came down into the hold and said to Josefine: "What's wrong? You look a bit unhappy!"

"It's the smell down here," she answered.

"You must go and lie down a bit till you are feeling better," said the skipper.

She objected a little, but the skipper led her away to the

cabin and made her lie down. She recovered later but declined to go back to the stacking because she was sure Beret and Ragna would give her dirty looks. She was taken ashore, and she told everybody at the drying ground artlessly that she couldn't stand the smell on board.

"Who is going to take your place?" asked Ane Maria.

"I suppose he thinks he can manage with Beret and Ragna," answered Josefine. This answer left Ane Maria thoughtful.

That night this same Ane Maria must have developed a strong sense of honesty and justice. She found Skaaro's pipe, which Karolus had put away in the sideboard, and took it with her the next morning to the drying ground. She borrowed August's dinghy and rowed herself aboard.

Skipper Skaaro immediately recognized his pipe and thanked Ane Maria and poured her a drink.

"I suppose it's made of pure meerschaum?" she said of the pipe.

"No, it's made from a foreign wood called vine root."

They talked some more. Ane Maria glanced into the hold and asked: "Are there enough down there?"

"No," he answered. "But what's to be done? I suppose you wouldn't want to go?"

"I haven't been asked," she said.

"Well, we didn't think it was any good. But what do you say now? Is it any good?"

"No!" was Ane Maria's answer.

Skipper Skaaro tried asking her more insistently to go down and replace Josefine. He was shorthanded, he said; and now Ragna was already beginning to hint about taking a rest.

Ane Maria seemed to waver. "If it meant helping you out," she said. But she doubtless expected him to beg her some more, so she again said no.

Then Skaaro became angry and turned on his heels and said: "You and all your nonsense!"

He wasn't going to ask any more! Not a bit of it! Off he went, down to his cabin.

Ane Maria climbed into the dinghy and rowed back to the shore.

She was now on the verge of tears and bitterly resentful. She'd get her own back on that Skipper Skaaro! What if she told Karolus that he'd been after her that time in the woods. Then Karolus would do something, don't you fret! That same time in the woods the skipper had asked her to pick a bowl of the splendid cloudberries growing there and bring them aboard. And out of the goodness of her heart she promised him she would. She said: "Wait till they are a bit riper!" Catch her picking any cloudberries for him now!

She told the women on the shore that she regretted having given him his pipe back. "So much the worse for him."

"What's he done to you this time?" they asked.

"Done? Didn't he ask me to go down in the hold? Begged me? But I've no desire to stack for him! I'm not that kind!"

Meanwhile, young Ragna, too, came up from the hold one afternoon announcing that she couldn't stand the smell down there any longer. Look at that young hopeful, Beret doubtless thought. She already fancies she's old enough to tempt the skipper. Thus it was that this man from Hardanger, with incomparable scrupulousness, allowed one stacker after the other to feel tired and poorly, and had them in the cabin till they felt better again. One of the girls who was giving a hand with the trimming visited him yesterday, and now Ragna wasn't going to be passed over any longer! He! he! he! Beret smiled in a superior fashion.

When the skipper came by and saw Ragna on deck, he was immediately very sympathetic. "Yes, if you're tired, go and lie down for a bit!"

But this time Edevart was on hand. Edevart was in charge of the tally and of arrangements generally, acting as a kind of mate. At that moment he was up in the rigging. When he heard what the talk was about, he took one leap and landed on the deck. That was enough of a hint for Ragna. There was no mistaking Edevart! To save herself, she replied: "I'm not going to lie down! Just let me sit here a little while!"

And it was in fact for a very little while. Perhaps Beret was not really superior but in fact madly jealous. God alone knows! In any case, she screamed up through the opening: "Am I to be left entirely on my own to stack the cargo?" Ragna called back to pacify her: "You needn't think I'm going to the cabin. I'm just sitting here a wee bit!"

Edevart had as yet only scant knowledge of the ways of the world; but he had begun to grow somewhat enamored of little Ragna, and Skipper Skaaro was perhaps not very trustworthy. He might take it into his head to kiss her, bend her head back and kiss her. He must not be allowed to claim that! Apart from that, here was Ragna herself sitting and saying no to him; and when the skipper had gone, she tossed her head and sneered after him: "Fancy him thinking he could get me to do that!" Edevart felt much better when he heard these words. He said: "If you don't feel well down there, you mustn't stay there. I'd rather have somebody else come aboard." She replied that she was better now, and with this she went down below again.

Sunday came and there was a respite from loading. Some of the villagers went to church, but Ane Maria wanted to see to the flock that day. Somebody had to do it and she wasn't going to shirk it. Karolus offered to go in her place, but she very flatly said no. Karolus and his wife hadn't quite seen eye to eye for several days; this was on account of the pipe which Ane Maria had given back.

"Why did you do it?" asked Karolus.

"Why did I do it? Were you thinking of stealing the pipe?"

"I could just as well have bought it, and paid for it when he settled up."

"Very well," she said. "It's still not too late."

That was no stupid reply; and in consequence Karolus became angrier still. He said: "Are you sure he'll part with the pipe now that he's got it back?"

"No, I'm not!" she replied.

"You're not, eh? But what I do know is that you could have left that pipe alone."

Ane Maria gave in and said: "I'm sorry!"

With that it ended. But Karolus was dissatisfied and his wife was in a bad mood for several days. She eased the tension by relieving her husband of the job of looking after the flock. "*You* do it?" she said. "No, I won't hear of it. It's not right for you to have to see to the animals."

Possibly Ane Maria had her own reasons for wanting to do it. She was a moth fluttering around the flame. She drove the flock all the way down to the drying ground and to *The Seagull*, making sure that those on board could see her. She had put on her best finery and was looking quite dressy, but maybe this was only because it was Sunday and for no other reason. When she had placed herself in clear view of Skipper Skaaro, who was walking about on deck, she quietly drove the flock over toward the woods and the fenland.

Sure enough, the skipper followed.

"Good morning! What about those berries I was to have?" he said.

"Isn't it a bit late?" she asked him sharply.

"Yes, time is passing. We're taking the last of the cargo on tomorrow. And if there's a wind I shall be sailing."

"I wanted to let the berries ripen first," she said.

He took this good-humoredly and hinted that she probably wouldn't give him the berries now. She begrudged him them. "It's probably best I pick them myself," he said. "But then you'd put the constable onto me, I suppose?"

She wanted to show that she didn't much care to talk to him, so she drove the sheep away from the bog and followed them. That was damned difficult for Skaaro; he couldn't just leave it at that and go; so he shouted at her, angry and embarrassed: "So can I pick myself a few berries?"

"Yes," she replied. "As many as you like!" She pointed across the bog and said: "The ripest are over there!"

He followed her direction, and sank deeper and deeper into

the quagmire with every step. Ah, such diabolical evil—to point where she did, and not warn him that the bog there was bottomless. She knew that if he went out far enough, if he did not turn around and come back, he'd never be able to lift his legs clear, but simply sink—sink. She knew precisely the position of the fatal area. Everybody knew it. A little green tuft always lay resting on the slime; and if anybody trod on that tuft to save himself, it would roll over and make him lose his footing. Ane Maria had once seen an ox which had not been reared in the place disappear completely. She had also heard the story—not knowing whether fact or fiction—of the girl who had met her death here, a young girl who had taken her life following a broken heart. She had lit upon this manner of dying in order to be able to pray to God the whole time during her slow death. When she had sunk to her neck and her arms had also already gone under, she must have been seized with terror, for a cry was heard from the bog, cry after cry; but by then it was night, and when people eventually reached her it was too late. God have mercy on her soul!

They dug down into the slime and took a good grip on her hair. They pulled the hair out by the roots. They dug some more and tied ropes around her neck and pulled. Many men helped to pull. It was dark night and they couldn't see. They pulled her head off. Then they gave up and said the Lord's Prayer. It was either fiction or fact.

Skipper Skaaro jumped over onto the tuft. It spun around like a ball. He sank in beside it and stayed there. At first he didn't make much fuss. He wasn't going to have her think that he was concerned about his shoes, even though he had given them a high polish for Sunday. He looked up and laughed a little. It didn't occur to him to worry. "Nice street this one is!" he said. "Fine old pavement! He-he-he!"

Ane Maria did not answer.

The skipper began struggling to lift his legs. He became impatient and stamped his feet. That wasn't much use. He sank farther in and burst out: "What the devil is going on?"

Ane Maria answered calmly: "You should have gone around."

The skipper was no longer laughing. He was now struggling hard and was already up to his knees in the slime. Anger seized him. He leaned over one way and tried to raise himself, then leaned over the other way and tried, but it only made things worse. He sank in deeper, and realized that while struggling thus he had lost one of his shoes. This was funny! Very very funny! He ground his teeth, waved his arms about in desperation, and snarled like a dog. Suddenly he stopped and said as if to himself: "Am I to stay here!" Perhaps it was beginning to dawn on him that the woman over there on firm ground was going to let him be swallowed up. "Why are you standing there not helping me!" he screamed at her.

"You haven't asked me," she replied stolidly.

He thought about it. So, he was to ask her! Let us see. If he were to let out a cry for help, he couldn't expect to be heard on board. The sloop lay over in Polden, and the wind was blowing from there. On the other hand, a good shout ought to be heard over by the houses. He was now up to his waist. The bog was sucking him down. He let out his first shout.

It wasn't at the top of his voice; it was intended more to scare Ane Maria. "What do you think people will say about you when they come?" he asked.

"There's nobody at home. They've gone to church," she answered.

He turned on her furiously and shook his fist at her. "If you are going to stand there and watch me go under in cold blood, you're worse than any monster!"

Ane Maria answered: "You must pray to God!"

"Help!" screamed Skaaro at the top of his voice; and he heard with satisfaction the powerful call as it echoed among the hills. He yelled at the woman: "I'll settle with you, you devil, when I get out of this!"

"Rather you should pray to God," she repeated.

"I'll tie you to the mast and flog you."

"Will you now?"

"And after that I'll report you to the authorities."

She sat down in the heather, smoothed her skirt, and looked indifferent.

"You are waiting for me to die," he shouted. "But you won't have that satisfaction. I still have my arms free. He-elp!"

The echo again answered; but nobody was there to hear.

The skipper had been unable to keep himself still and had thus hastened his sinking. It was nearly up to his chest. He tried to lie flat to prevent the weight of his body operating straight up and down; but he had sunk down to beyond his waist and could no longer bend forward. "He-elp!"

Ane Maria got up, brushed the heather and the twigs from her skirt, and looked about her. Everything was still.

"What have I done to you, you animal?" he snorted. "What I wanted from you that time here in the fields this summer surely isn't something you want to kill me for. It was enough that you gave me a black eye. And since then I've never suggested anything. I danced with you at the barn and you wouldn't even step outside with me to cool off. Did I ever use force on you? No! What is there you want to kill me for? You go your way and let me go mine. I'm not all that desperately in love with you. Anyway, you yourself brought me my pipe. That's something I don't understand. What in the devil's name did you do it for?" He stopped and looked wildly at her and waited. "No, you don't answer! You are too stupid! I'll tell you what you are! You are a shit of a woman who hasn't the sense or the brains to know what it is she's doing! You are just wooden—wood from the neck upward. That's it exactly. Perhaps now you'll open your mouth!"

Ane Maria began to wander slowly along behind her sheep.

"So you are going! I shall remember you on Judgment Day!" he said menacingly.

"I'm going to seek help," she said, and walked away.

"You are lying!" he shouted after her. "You are walking away from where people are! You want to destroy me! That's what you want!"

61

When he was alone, he became quieter. He raked down into the mire and got hold of his watch, wiped it clean, and moved it to a higher pocket. After that he thought of trying to save his wallet—those two thousand dalers as well as those important papers. It was a fat wallet. He would hold it aloft with the hand which went under last, perhaps finally throwing it onto dry ground. Presumably somebody would find it. He owed for the cost of the drying grounds and he owed wages to all the workers.

Strange how things go! He'd turned out of his bunk that morning lighthearted and singing. Now he was a condemned man, only a few steps away from safe ground. Of course he might have spoken nicely to Ane Maria instead of letting fly; he might have offered her a nice fat sum of money to throw him a branch or two, which might have supported him. Indeed, he might. But that thought presumably never occurred to him, not for a moment. And doubtless he didn't regret it. He was so beside himself with anger toward this creature, so bloated with ill will, that he himself blocked this particular escape route.

Hours passed. He shouted his calls for help, but nobody answered. Everything was quiet. The sheep bells had long ago died away, so far away the flock had wandered. Even the wind dropped more and more as the sun sank lower as the afternoon advanced. First it was two o'clock, then three. He looked at his watch, wound it, and thereafter held it in his hand. The slime had now risen chest-high. He no longer had much courage left; he wept a little at the realization that he was going to die. His arms were free, but he could no longer move his legs. They were as though encased in lead from top to bottom. If, as Ane Maria had said, people had gone to church, they must surely be back home again now. It was quite a long way to church and they always allowed themselves plenty of time for exchanging their news; but it was now late, terribly late. Was there to be no rescue? He screamed and yelled for help, kept silent for a moment and listened, screamed and yelled again, wept, beat the slime with his hands. But even his cries now became gradually fainter. He had lost courage.

All this emerged from Ane Maria's account a long time afterward. She had not gone on with her sheep. She had seen it all and even heard what he said when he talked aloud to himself. One or two things about his conduct Ane Maria had not understood: he suddenly began to write something on a piece of paper taken from his wallet. She thought: Now he is writing down that I am the one who has killed him! Then a change came over him. He fell silent; but he wept so that his whole body shook. After this he took the piece of paper and tore it into small pieces and pushed them down into the bog by his side. He seemed humbled and crushed. The bog gradually sucked his arms down; there was not very much more of him above ground. Ane Maria felt a pressure about her heart. She rose stealthily to her feet and fled, ran screaming in the direction of the houses . . .

The last thing Skaaro had done was to throw his watch and his wallet onto firm ground. He had written nothing. Since he had no family and no kinsfolk, he had left no word of farewell.

4

NORWAY IS NOT LITTLE. NORWAY IS VERY LONG.

When Skipper Skaaro of *The Seagull* was lost in a bog up north, it had no greater consequences in the south than a brief mention in the newspapers and perhaps a little shudder down the spine of one reader or another.

The village, on the other hand, is little. The village is close. When a man is lost in a bog *there*, the village long remembers it and talks about it and avoids the bog and fills the minds of young and old with terror.

To be sure, Ane Maria had raised the alarm at the church. There was no fault to find with that. She had run the quickest way to the houses, shouting as she ran. But it was too late. When they got there, there was nothing to see on the surface of the bottomless bog but a green tuft turned on its side. People couldn't believe it. Couldn't believe that Skipper Skaaro had been silly enough to walk right into it; but in the end it couldn't be denied. It emerged later that one or two people had heard sounds but hadn't taken them seriously. Yes, the skipper had lost his life in the bog. His wallet and his watch were found.

August and Edevart were summoned on board *The Seagull*. August took charge of the wallet, counted the notes in the presence of witnesses, and was clearly the right man to deal with the situation. Ane Maria was frank and consistent in her initial accounts, not only to the neighbors, but also to the sheriff: it grieved her that she hadn't been able to warn people in time; apart from that she couldn't understand, simply couldn't fathom, what the man had been thinking of. He must have delayed shouting for help until the slime was up to his neck; and in the hour or two she needed to raise the alarm and get people to the place, the skipper had gone right under.

A dark and terrible misfortune.

August at once set out for the neighboring parish to consult Skaaro's two friends there about what to do about the vessel and the fish. Meanwhile, Edevart continued to supervise the loading. He had no difficulty getting stackers now; in the shadow of the fate which had befallen the skipper, everybody wanted to be nice and helpful. Even Ane Maria let it be known that she would help to stack if necessary.

The women on the drying ground talked in low tones to each other and shuddered.

"Ugh! I hardly dare look across at the bog any more! What he must have gone through—it doesn't bear thinking about!"

"Don't speak about it! Don't even mention it! I didn't sleep last night. I thought I heard shouts again!"

"You heard shouts? I suppose that means that he hasn't found peace."

Ane Maria asked: "Why shouldn't he have found peace? What do you mean by that?"

"What do we mean? He is dead and buried in the bog.

Nobody helped him. Not even by so much as the Lord's Prayer. Not a word of blessing. That's probably what he is crying out for."

Ane Maria said: "That's nonsense. He isn't shouting. You're all scared, that's all."

"Well, aren't you scared?"

"No! I could quite readily go and sleep out by the edge of the bog tonight."

The women doubted this and said offendedly: "Ah, yes, you are always ready to go one better than us!"

When the fish was loaded aboard, Edevart went round the drying ground for the last time with drinks and salt biscuits. It was something of an occasion, but without joy, without gaiety. People said little and spoke in low tones. It was disquieting to remember the man who had lost his life in the bog—a decent fellow, an excellent man in every way. But it only shows how precarious life can be!

August returned from his deliberations. Once again he was the right man for the occasion: quick-witted, decisive in thought and speech, a wholly different August from the earlier one. He who had always been the subordinate, who had taken orders, now took command. He fixed the following morning as the time to settle up with the workers. "We'll start at the usual time," he ordered, "in case there is a favorable wind for sailing."

"Who'll sail her?" somebody asked.

"Who do you think?" was his curt rejoinder.

His accounts were impeccable, and nobody had any occasion to object. None of those workers who had kept their own records of their working days, making chalk marks on the roof-beams at home, could catch him out. He saw them two at a time in his cabin, so that one could witness the payment of the other. It was a trick he had doubtless learned from his time at sea. It struck Karolus—and it also made Edevart wonder a little—that for every transaction August entered up the details of the amount in a special kind of daybook. It was as if he was keeping a private record of labor costs or whatever else it might be. This daybook he put safely back in his pocket after each item.

When the payout was over, August announced that he would take over as skipper and sail *The Seagull* to Bergen himself. There was nobody else who could navigate by compass, chart, and clock, and the skippers at the other drying grounds were not able to leave their own vessels.

It cannot be denied that people met the news with open mouth, even though it was not entirely unexpected. August had astonished them before; they believed he was capable of many things; but this really was setting his sights high. Skipper and captain of a big and heavily laden sloop, navigating by compass, chart, and clock the entire length of Norway—that man must have learned a fair amount somewhere!

He had Edevart, but he was still one man short for the voyage. He mentioned Teodor.

"Teodor has a rupture and wears a truss," objected Edevart.

"He's the one I have in mind," said August firmly.

Edevart reminded him that Teodor had been in the forefront of those who had poked fun at August and hurt him. He was a nasty piece of work.

"Then he can expect to be paid back," said August.

They didn't get their wind. They had to tow *The Seagull* out of Polden. This was heavy work, and they hired Karolus and a second man to help him out. Out in the fjord they found a light breeze and set sail.

This time, too, people stood around on the high ground and watched them. They bade farewell to the sloop, and they felt deprived. The bay lay empty; and there was no sign of life on the drying ground.

Before they had even left Vestfjord behind, August settled up with Edevart. He gave him a generous sum for the summer's work.

"You have been a good man and I want to do the proper thing by you," he said.

Edevart thanked him, but couldn't really comprehend why he had so much coming to him, given the time he had put in.

August took his private daybook out of his pocket, studied it, and said: "It's confirmed by the book."

Edevart: "What book is that?"

August: "I'll tell you. It's an account of what you and I have earned."

He began to explain. "You remember what I said in the spring about you and me earning good money this summer?"

Edevart: "I remember."

August: "I went to Lofoten. I got Skaaro and *The Seagull* to come to Polden. I dried the fish. You have never heard of anybody to equal me, of any other man who could have done what I have done."

Edevart pondered and said: "Napoleon perhaps."

"Yes," admitted August. "I'm not bothered about Napoleon. But if, for instance, you were to ask me about lots of things in this world, I'd be able to tell you. I kept the whole calendar in my head this summer and never a day lost."

In this August might well have been right. He had calculated the days exactly. What Edevart was meant to gather from his companion's lengthy explanation was this: not all the workers had put in the same number of days. Karolus, for instance, had skipped ten days in all; Teodor three days. In addition, over a number of rainy days the entire drying process had come to a stop all down the line. So there! But August had very shrewdly booked a fair number of these miscellaneous days to his own credit, thus supplementing his own wages. These were the entries his own little daybook contained. Every worker received his proper due; but for the absentee days August took the payment for himself. He could do this entirely without danger, because he had organized the drying with extraordinary efficiency and had been ready to sail a couple of weeks before the other vessels. This amounted to a nice fat sum of extra earnings for August; and he generously gave a substantial share of this money to Edevart, so that they should both stand together in the arrangement.

Edevart's mind was confused, though he was greatly impressed. He permitted himself to ask: "But supposing Skaaro had lived and had been there at the payout, how would you have managed to put aside so much money?"

August answered: "I'd simply have put two or three more names on the payroll and made receipts out on their behalf for the money to be passed on later. That would have been the simplest of my tricks."

Very smart, very audacious, our August! A devil of a man in many ways.

Edevart accepted the money, but brooded for several days. The affair was unusual and left him feeling undecided. It was impossible to regard it as unsinful; the question was how much good might it bring. And there was the problem of whether or not Skipper Skaaro might come and appear to him. One day he said: "The skipper is in that bog and knows what we have done!"

"It is, however, a fact," August answered, "that I gave him my gold ring as a present."

Edevart, wonderingly: "Well?"

"Gave it to him for nothing. And why should I do that?"

Edevart: "I didn't give him any present."

August was not at a loss for an answer. "So what? Didn't I wear out your coat, a brand-new dress coat? Were you supposed to let me do that just for fun?"

On the whole, August achieved a good mix: right and wrong, truth and fiction. He never felt shame. He still talked about following an honest course, and about the need for straight dealing. August smiled with his gold teeth and told how Karolus had asked him for Skaaro's pipe.

"He no longer has any need of it," Karolus had said.

"No," August answered. "But our dear departed Skaaro did plenty for you by saving your hay!" Then Karolus had asked for a coat or some other article of clothing, a hat, some little thing to remember the skipper by. Never heard the likes of it! August replied: "I won't defile myself by having anything to do with such low-down greed, and you can put that in your pipe and smoke it!"

"And don't you think that was the right sort of answer to give him?" he asked Edevart.

Edevart, even more confused and stupefied by all this oblique talk, finally gave up. August must know, surely. He knew so much. There was more to him than met the eye.

They had taken on provisions at Bodø, and lacked for nothing. The nights were still light. They sailed down the coast of Helgeland, the three of them taking shifts at the wheel. Skipper August studied the charts intently even when they sailed close to land, making sure that Teodor saw him doing this. Sometimes August would hasten over to the compass, stop, take Skaaro's watch out of his pocket, calculate the minutes and seconds, nod, and go away again.

Teodor didn't count for anything on board. Skipper August didn't deign to answer if such a miserable nonentity tried to offer an opinion. Off Folla they ran into a storm and high seas, and then Teodor was really given the runaround. He had no experience of sailing, didn't know his way about the vessel, didn't even know the names of the various ropes and lines. At the start he did so many things wrong that the skipper threatened to set him ashore and get "a grown man" in his place. Here off Folla they had to take in both topsail and mainsail, and run only with the foresail. Skipper August stood at the wheel shouting orders and having to give instructions to both his men. August was no faint heart this time; his watery blue eyes were keen; he stumped the deck. It was one thing to lie prostrate in the bottom of an eight-oar, and quite another to stand upright on a real deck. The two things did not bear comparison.

They passed Folla, went in again behind the skerries, and found better weather. The whole situation improved, and August brought out his accordion and played for the first time that voyage. He was in a good mood. Up to this point they had made good progress, had passed the Rødø lighthouse, were traversing Frohavet and approaching the Trondheim Straits.

"You realize now I can sail?" he asked Edevart. "What about our sailing *The Seagull* straight on to foreign parts?"

"What do you mean?"

August looked around and spoke in a low voice. For a moment he looked uncertain, indeed almost shamefaced. "I'm wearing Skaaro's watch, and I won't be very happy to part with it. I'm also carrying more than a thousand dalers, which belong to Skaaro. It's no small thing to hand over all that in one go. What do *you* think? I just don't know."

Edevart, not particularly interested: "What would be the point of that?"

August continued: "And then there's the ship and the cargo. Worth a lot, a whole fortune. We are the ones who have grappled with everything, and it isn't going to do Skaaro any good. By rights we are the ones who should inherit from him."

"Oh, a lot of things go on in that head of yours!" Edevart laughed.

"I just thought I'd mention it," said August.

Nothing more was said about it just then, but later in the day August returned to the subject. "I didn't mean that Teodor was to be with us on that voyage. I'm not all that stupid."

"What voyage?"

"To Spain. We'd get rid of Teodor. And you and I would have to see eye to eye. Anything you didn't understand, you would have to let me understand for the two of us. I've already done this once before."

"I don't understand a single thing you're talking about," said Edevart.

It had indeed gone over Edevart's head. He wasn't all that sure of himself any longer. His companion had been all around the world and learned too much. There seemed to be something about his life that was mysterious and obscure . . .

At Fosenland they put into a green bay to take on water. They had heard the roar of a waterfall somewhere up in the forest. An isolated farmhouse stood at the head of the bay. From it two children came down to the river and stood looking at the strangers from the sloop. Shortly afterward a young woman came running down to them. She was barefoot and very scantily clad, wearing only a slip and a skirt. They mustn't be offended, but she'd come to ask them if they'd kindly lend her a hand. A sheep had got lodged on the rocks behind the house. It had been there now for two whole days and she couldn't rescue it, being as she was on her own. The woman had tears in her eyes. It was such a nice sheep, such a pretty sheep.

August: "Aren't there any men around here?"

"Yes," said the woman. "But they're working over on the island just now."

"The island is marked on the chart," said August, very much the master mariner. "What kind of work have they got there?"

"On the estate at Fosen, of one sort or another."

August had clearly asked these unnecessary questions to demonstrate his importance. He looked up at the house and murmured something; but as he was still in a good mood, he promised to come.

They rowed back to the ship with the water barrel, took block and tackle, and returned to the dinghy. August also brought his shotgun with him and sat with it on his knees, but this he did mainly to impress the young woman.

They walked up to the farm and had the place pointed out to them. The sheep had ventured out onto a ledge where there was green grass, but the ledge was so narrow that the animal couldn't turn around and get back. Below it was a deep drop and death.

August asked the woman: "Will you sell the sheep?"

"No! Oh, no! Sell it?"

"Because I'd buy it and shoot it from here, and it would roll down."

"Shoot it? Oh, no! It's such a nice sheep, a lovely big breeding ewe."

August went with his men up to the cliff edge, lowered Edevart down to the ledge, and let him decide what was necessary. The sheep stood quite still; evidently it was used to the presence of humans and showed no signs of fear. Hanging on the rope, Edevart took a firm grip on the animal and turned it back to front. It happened so quickly. He seized it by its fleece, lifted its forequarters, held it momentarily standing on two legs, then let it drop its front legs again. The sheep itself seemed confused by this and didn't quite know what had happened. Had its head somehow shifted to its rear end? Edevart patted it and tried coaxing it, but in the end had to shove it and prod it before it would go back the same way it had come.

Edevart pulled himself up a few feet on his rope and swung himself in and onto the ledge. He stood there a moment and pondered. Then he unloosed the rope and let the rope end fall. "Haul away!" he shouted up to the others. He heard the creaking of the pulley at the top of the cliff face, and he saw the rope slide upward. Then cautiously he made his way along the ledge, and followed the sheep.

Down below at the house, the woman and her two children stood and looked up. The woman wept, sick with fear for both the sheep and the man. Now and then the children gave a shout. "Not so loud!" the mother warned them. "They might fall!" She herself gave a shriek of joy when it was all successfully over; and when the men came down, she seized them by the hand and thanked them. She told the children to do the same and they held out their small hands—the right or the left, whichever happened to be easier. The woman looked at Edevart with wondering eyes and thanked him specially, and her cheeks reddened—to be sure, the young woman saw that he was the handsomest. And Edevart, for his part, was no better; he, too, turned red. Ah, youth! Blessed youth and innocence!

They were invited in and were given milk to drink; and the woman once again singled out Edevart and gave him the milk first. At this, August's mood seemed to turn sour. He took Skaaro's watch out of his pocket and said: "Well, lads, let's get back to the ship. I want to press on with that cargo!"

The woman was so filled with gratitude she wanted to make them coffee. August answered: "No, we have coffee on board. We have provisions for the whole trip. Thanks all the same! Is that your sweetheart there on the wall?" he asked jokingly.

"That's my husband," she replied.

"Is he also working on the island?"

"No. He's gone away."

"A handsome man," August said then. "Was he lost at sea?"

"He's gone to America."

"So he's in America. I know it well. How long has your husband been away?"

"Four years."

"And he's coming back soon?"

"God knows," the woman answered.

"You must know that, too. He writes, presumably?"

"No, he doesn't write. He's never written."

August slapped his knee. "He's never written? Then you don't even know if he got as far as America?"

"Yes. He landed in New York."

"And then went off?"

The woman did not answer.

Edevart's heart bled with compassion. He was facing something he didn't understand: a destiny, a cross of a strange kind. This woman might be about twenty-five or twenty-six years old; there was something affectionate—or if not affectionate, then tender—in the way she hung her head, in the meekness of her eyes. Where was her husband living? Was he indeed anywhere? What did the woman live off? There was a loom standing in the room; wool in various colors hung about the walls and on chair backs. Nothing in the room was painted. Edevart sat, every now

73

and then moistening his lips. He was in no way cold or indifferent. He trembled, perhaps from humility, perhaps from love. Something sweet.

There was now nothing left for August to inquire about. He rose and went over to the door. Edevart was the last to leave the room. The woman followed at his heels and said outside in the passage: "Thank you and a blessing on you for everything you have done! What's your name?"

Edevart, taken aback: "Me? Oh, Edevart's my name. And you?"

"Lovise Magrete Doppen."

"Well, my name is Edevart Andreassen," he said. "I wish you farewell."

Ah, youth! They did not shake hands. They both stared at the floor and whispered like thieves . . .

"Did you kiss her?" August asked later.

Edevart was speechless for a moment. He would have to make himself out to be more a man of the world than he was, and laugh off this cruel question. "No, she wouldn't!" he replied.

"She wouldn't? Now, if it had been me . . . !" said August.

But Edevart felt as though a painting, a rainbow, were being torn apart within him.

He immediately had other things to think about. The sloop had drifted close into the shore and had to be towed out of the bay again. Together with Teodor he toiled away, rowing with his face turned toward the houses. The whole time he could see the young woman sitting by the wall of the cottage. Not once did she raise her hand to wave—perhaps because there were two of them in the boat.

Then they set sail.

"That sheep took a hell of a time!" said Skipper August. "Now we can't put into Trondheim."

"What would we want there, anyhow?"

"Various things. But we'll stop at Kristiansund. It's right on our course."

Edevart asked: "Where do you think her husband is?"

"Her husband? Either he's run away or he's been killed. That's all."

"Can you understand why things are going so wrong for her?"

"How do you mean? How can anybody ever tell? She was a pretty woman, and I'm quite happy to have taken my crew and rescued her sheep. Not that I haven't seen prettier women in my day, both on land and on sea."

Edevart, hurt: "Anyway, she was a lot prettier than Mattea."

"What? Oh, her!" August laughed and shook his head. "Yes, she was a real horror! I wonder where she is. If I had my hands on her now, she'd know about it! But goodbye and good luck to her. I wouldn't have wanted her, anyway."

THEY STOPPED at Kristiansund. August went up into the town and bought himself some fine clothes and a gold ring. He took with him Skaaro's bulging wallet and took pleasure in opening it good and wide when he paid for anything. Edevart wrote home that now he'd seen lots of new things, the open sea and great stretches of coast, as well as many people, towns, and ships. Many greetings to all!

Here again in the streets of Kristiansund they once again ran across Papst, the old Jewish watch seller. He was the same strange person as before, fat and friendly, with his venerable beard and many watch chains on his chest. The watchmakers in town doubtless looked on him with displeasure, but nobody else did. He was a well-known figure and had sold watches to high and low. Everybody stopped for a gossip with him, youngsters, merchants, consuls.

"A watch today?" asked Papst.

"I've got a watch," said Skipper August.

Papst was allowed to look at Skaaro's watch. He opened it and said: "A good watch!"

"It's got twenty-two jewels," August announced. "Perhaps it was you who sold it in the first place."

Papst: "I can't remember. Perhaps." He turned to Edevart, asked him his name and where he came from, and recognized him again. "It was at Stokmarknes Fair last year. I often saw you. But you've changed a lot. You've grown. You haven't yet bought a watch?"

"I thought of waiting till I got to Bergen."

"You shouldn't. They'll cheat you," said Papst.

Skipper August asked: "What are you asking for a first-class watch for my first mate?"

Papst reached down into one pocket, then into another pocket, and came up with two watches. "A first-class watch, did you say, Skipper? Here is a first-class watch and here is a first-class watch. Here you are, look at them. Anchor escapement."

August opened each of them in turn, knowing all about watches as he did, and said: "In my view, this is the best."

Papst nodded.

"I saw that at once," said August. "What will you sell this watch for? Your lowest price?"

"Eight daler."

"Eight daler—you must be joking! Eight daler may be all right for a skipper, but where is a mate to get eight daler from?"

"You could well be right," admitted Papst.

Edevart, somewhat crestfallen, asked: "And the other? Is that also a good watch?"

"Yes, very good."

"What does it cost?"

"I can sell that for double—sixteen daler."

Both men gaped. August said, perplexed: "Twice as much for the more ordinary watch? How come?"

Papst handed him the watch and said: "Look at this watch again, Skipper, and tell me what you think."

August took the watch, opened it, and looked at it; but now he had become wary. "There's no doubt this is a good watch.

76

Even a child can see that. But that it should cost twice as much as the other . . ."

Whereupon Papst came out with a strange pronouncement: "It's because of the engraving on the case," he said. "A very expensive engraving. It'll never wear out."

"Engraving?"

"Yes. Moreover, there are three more wheels in this watch than in the other. Perhaps you would care to count them, Skipper."

August stood firm. Declining to count them, he said, offended: "However that may be, Edevart, I'll get you a first-class watch in Bergen at a much lower price. Don't you worry!"

Papst asked: "When are you sailing?"

"Later. With the night wind."

They parted and went their ways. August inquired for the finest hotel in town and went there. "I might have taken you along," he said to Edevart, "but you haven't bought yourself any clothes yet."

"I'll go back to the ship," answered Edevart, "and relieve Teodor."

Edevart wasn't like his old self. He had money in his pocket but had lost his zest for life. For several days now he had been suffering the torment of love; he had lost his appetite, was pale and despondent, and was feeling really low. He might have written to her, but hadn't got her address. Apart from that, he was no great letter writer. She was almost certainly much cleverer at it than he and would laugh at him. Oh, those events in Fosenland! Little Ragna back home dropped out of his life. He could easily have seen her as somebody else's sweetheart without feeling greatly upset. He was overwhelmed by something else, something more powerful. It felt like an attack of something. As though he were under some spell. What was to be done! To hope was out of the question. The future was closed. Never again would he put into that green bay for water. Lovise Magrete Doppen would live and die in her cottage and he would live and die far away from her. All they could do was remember each other. He could well have slipped a little money into her hand . . .

Just then old Papst came shuffling down to the quayside, as though by chance, and stepped aboard *The Seagull*. He was so pleasant and quiet. Edevart was glad to see him.

"Well, so I meet my old friend, I do declare!" said Papst, surprised. "Is this where you live?"

Of course, Papst wanted to sell him a watch; it couldn't possibly be anything else. And Edevart livened up and prepared to begin to bargain. Papst proposed that he should first be told how much money Edevart had all in all; whereupon he then suggested that four daler ought to go to the purchase of a good watch.

"Look. You can have the one I showed you just now!"

"The one that cost eight daler?"

"Yes. I want to sell you a good watch. You have always spoken nicely to old Papst, and you can have it for four. Oh, I'll not make anything on it. In fact, I'm losing a little. But I'll do it for friendship's sake. The watch is honestly worth six daler, I assure you. Now you must wind it up carefully every night and not force it. It has a fine movement. I don't want you to do a bad deal with me, for we're bound to run into each other again."

Edevart bought the watch. His innocent pleasure must have touched the old watch seller. Papst knew what a bit of finery meant for a young lad, and he presented Edevart additionally with a handsome chain for the watch, whereupon Edevart gripped his hand in gratitude and Papst yelled at the pain in his fingers.

They took leave of each other. "But don't press so hard," said Papst. "You are too strong." This he said doubtless to flatter the young man. But God knows whether possibly something miraculous hadn't happened: this wandering Jew, who surely must have swindled thousands in his day, might possibly on this one occasion have been more than honest and sold at a loss.

August came aboard, throwing down a roll of navigational

charts he had bought. He strutted about, smoking a cigar; but he was quite sober, merely a little proud of the fact that he had eaten at that fine hotel and had had a cut of veal and imported macaroni. "I met another captain in the hotel," he said, "and we had a long chat at table. What? Have you bought a watch? Let me see!"

When August heard the details of the deal he was immediately suspicious. "Watch out that the old scoundrel hasn't fooled you. You should have offered him two daler—that's what I'd have done. You are none too bright when it comes to business matters. Do you suppose it's ever been adjusted?"

Edevart: "I don't know. He didn't mention that."

August: "Ha! no! Of course he didn't. Well, you'll soon see. I won't say any more!"

They sailed that evening.

Their next stop was Aalesund. August also wanted to show himself in this town, with his fine clothes and his gold ring. They remained there a few brief hours and sailed again; but here, too, August had bought a few charts, this time charts of the French coast.

Now the fine weather seemed to be over. They ran into rain and a head wind; they had to tack. There was no great sea running; but then the wind stiffened, and off Stadt they had a difficult passage outside the skerries. August swore like a trooper as he dished out orders, driving himself and his men with sheer arrogance. Both Edevart and Teodor asked if it wouldn't be wisest to turn back. "Turn back?" snorted August. "What is this compared with what I'm used to!" All three were on constant watch and they got no sleep. Only when they again reached the fjords and the narrow sounds with land on both sides of them could Edevart and Teodor each take a spell in their bunks. August was inexhaustible and remained on watch the whole time.

At length they reached Florø and hove to. It was tantalizing to have this stubborn head wind just when they were so near their destination.

A lively little place, Florø, inviting and attractive; but August was discontented. What he feared most was that the other fishing vessels from the north might catch up with him. "We wasted too much time on that sheep," he said. On the third day August went ashore and came back aboard in the evening drunk. He then took a brighter view of things generally, having calculated that the other vessels were at least two weeks behind *The Seagull*.

In the morning he again went ashore. A short time later he sent word aboard to Edevart, asking him to come at once and bring the accordion.

Indeed, August had ended up in just the right place: a lodging house with a hostess and a barmaid and girls and drinks. Here he was having a high old time. The sailor lad had awarded himself shore leave again. The events of the fair last year repeated themselves; he took a fancy to the barmaid and bought her a ring. She was from Bergen, an attractive and lively lady with a well-rounded figure and bright eyes. August! August! He had had ample opportunity to drink brandy from the barrel that summer but hadn't touched it. He wasn't a drinker in that sense. There had to be high spirits and girls and fun, there had to be shore leave and a party mood. Good!

The ladies were doing everything possible to charm August; the hostess called him captain and offered him a room ashore for as long as he was in port; and the girls were given tips for merely coming in and briefly showing themselves. Edevart arrived to find a great party; when August began to play, the barmaid took Edevart by storm and waltzed him round, whereupon August laughed good-naturedly and encouraged them: "That's right! Let me see you swing that mate of mine!" Edevart, for his part, was in no mood for any such thing; he was nursing a sad, sweet memory, and the fact that he now had a watch and chain to show off didn't actually help very much.

Things went on in this way till quite late in the day; but in the end August became less willing to play the accordion. He wasn't getting enough of the barmaid's admiration. On the contrary, she became more and more eager to chat with his mate and to dance with him. Once she even danced the lad out into a dark corridor and threw her arms around him and said "Oh!" At that, August wrinkled his brow as though in suspicion and packed his instrument away and wouldn't play any more. "Let's have something else! Bring some coffee!" he shouted, in order to give the barmaid something to do.

Later that evening Edevart went on board, but August wouldn't hear of sleep. He demanded a new bottle and he made all the women of the house sit up and listen to his stories. Finally, toward morning, one after the other slipped away and August landed up in bed, still fully dressed. He muttered angrily, plotting revenge because his barmaid sweetheart was nowhere to be found. He'd show her!

A day and a night went by. August was now tired; and he slept. When he woke and counted up how much money he had squandered, he took a grip on himself and didn't touch another drop. He was in a pitiful state. Edevart came up from the sloop and asked him to step outside with him; he had read the weather report and thought there would be a sailing wind. They both looked at the sky and talked it over and agreed. August went into the house to settle up for his room. He was away a long time; when he came out again, he said: "I can't understand what she's done with herself."

Edevart: "I saw her on the quayside late last night."

"On the quayside? So she was one of those!"

"Perhaps she was looking for you?" Edevart suggested.

"No, she knew where I was. Did she shout to you on board?"

Edevart might have answered, Yes, she did. But he spared his companion and said she was probably only taking a walk to get some air.

"Well, it's good luck and goodbye to her!" August broke out.

Edevart: "Then you won't get your ring back!"

"Get my ring back? What do you reckon!" August grimaced. "And let me tell you this, Edevart: there's no trusting these womenfolk."

They went aboard and sailed at once.

August had a hangover and was in a filthy mood, but there was nothing else he could do but grit his teeth and buckle to. They had settled weather and a decent wind, but it didn't help much with August. He complained that he had never felt so low. It seemed it was all the fault of the sherry, on top of which came that poisonous coffee, and finally there were those bottles of Crambambuli Cream he'd had to drink with the ladies in the course of the night. A fine thing to do!

Edevart had heard that a glass of neat brandy taken in tiny sips might help. At this August spat far over the side of the ship and said the very thought turned his stomach.

The stupid fool! It wasn't as if his binge had been in any way the consequence of surplus *joie de vivre*. He had nothing to draw on, no reserves. Nothing but time could cure him.

One morning, when Edevart came on deck, August was at the helm. And surely a devil must have entered into him, for he beckoned to his companion to come close and said: "We're not putting into Bergen. Look at me like that if you like, but we're not going into Bergen now. Believe me, we've already passed Bergen."

Edevart, skeptical: "What's that you say?"

"Do you think that's so crazy? Now we'll make some money and get somewhere!" August's pale-blue eyes grew hard and cold. He announced that he wanted to go to Spain with *The Seagull* and sell cargo and vessel and become a rich man. Edevart was to go along with him; they were to stick together.

"Don't think I don't know the way," he said. "Haven't I bought the charts! We go down to southern Norway and head straight across the North Sea, then through the Channel and all the way down the coast of France to Santander, and then we are in Spain. I know Barcelona well, but unfortunately we can't go there because it lies on the other side and we'd have to go into the Mediterranean and that's twice as far . . ."

All these names and places left no impression on Edevart. He merely asked: "Shall I take the helm?"

August paid no attention. "I know what you're thinking," he said. "You are afraid the vessel will be posted as missing and recognized. But I've got a scheme. I've been through this kind of thing before. We'll put in at some remote point on the Scottish coast and repaint her and give her another name. Not a soul will recognize her, no matter how much they cable."

"This is sinful talk—and worse," said Edevart.

"Are we doing anybody any wrong, do you think?" August asked. "Skaaro is dead. Anyway, Skaaro wasn't exactly an angel himself. No saint he, that I can tell you! What do you think he wanted Ragna down in the cabin for? He spared neither mother nor daughter, the swine!"

"Why don't we let Skaaro rest in peace!"

August: "I'm just telling you. Skaaro is dead. And when a man is dead, he isn't hurt by anything we do. Now, if he'd been married! But no. The skippers up north told me he had no family of any kind. Some second cousins from Hardanger were supposed to be coming to take over the ship, they said. Do you think that's right? That I should tamely hand over the ship to these cousins?"

Edevart: "How can you stand there and say such things!"

But August *could* stand there and say these things; nor did he seem to be joking. The sheer impossibility of his scheme he scornfully rejected. He wanted Skaaro's watch, money, ship, and cargo for himself. What was remarkable about that!

"I know what you're thinking," he continued. "But it's of no significance. We don't want Teodor with us in this. Ha! That ruptured dolt! No, thank you! He would just go and blab everything like some old woman!"

Edevart sighed, wearied by the whole thing; simply to say something, he asked: "You mean the two of us should sail the ship to Spain?"

"No, no! We'd sign on some new man in a Scottish port."

"Well, and how would we get rid of Teodor?"

"In the North Sea. We'd heave him overboard."

"Ha! ha! ha!" Edevart laughed heartily.

August was displeased by this laughter. After all, he was the skipper. He wanted to assert his authority. Presumably he meant to be reasonable, but all his control went to the winds. With cheerful naïveté he said: "Of course, we'll shoot him first."

Edevart looked intently at his skipper and said slowly: "You're crazy!"

"Stand where you are!" screamed August at once. "Don't you set yourself up against the commander of a ship! That's mutiny! Stand where you are! It's too late to draw back, let me tell you. We are already past Bergen."

"Then we'll turn back," said Edevart.

"We'll not turn back!" August replied.

Edevart's face blanched. He went forward and called sharply: "On deck, Teodor! We're going to turn about!"

August fell silent. He stood for a moment before giving way. Even then there was no collapse. He said, with forced gaiety: "Ha! ha! You believed it! It's as I said, Edevart, you aren't particularly bright. But let's turn about."

Teodor came on deck; they turned about and made for Bergen.

For a time August pretended that his great plan had been nothing but a joke. At the same time he asked Edevart how he thought he would have fared aboard a proper ship if he had disobeyed the captain. He'd have been shot.

As they lay in Bergen harbor he settled up with his two crewmen and paid them their due. All in order. He reverted to their old friendly relationship, but bolstered himself after his defeat by offering Edevart some good advice: "Now, do as I tell you and take care of yourself here in Bergen. Don't you go falling into the clutches of some rogue or other. How is that watch of yours? Is it still going?"

"I've never known it otherwise."

"It'll stop soon enough. I haven't time to come with you, because I must hand over the ship. But you must go up into the town yourself and call in first at one big watchmaker and then at a second and find out what that watch of yours is worth and whether it's been properly wound and adjusted by the chronometer. Afterward we'll meet back here on board and pack up our things."

Not a word was said to Teodor.

Edevart went up into the town. He bought some necessary clothes, bought gifts both large and small to take to those back home, and also remembered to call in at a watchmaker's shop. Hundreds of clocks ticked on the walls around him, all telling different times. Two young lads sat at a table busy with gold-colored wheels and other clock parts. One of them got up and looked at Edevart's watch and spoke to him about it: where he had bought it and how much he had paid. While this was going on, a man came out of an inner room; he took over the inspection, put a glass to his eye, and scrutinized the watch. "A very fine watch," he said. "Excellent movement! Where did you buy it? From Papst?" asked the watchmaker in astonishment. And when he heard the price he was more astonished still. He adjusted it by a clock in a mahogany case on the counter and handed it back.

"That's an unusual clock," said Edevart of the one in the mahogany case.

"It's a chronometer," said the watchmaker.

Edevart went to another large watchmaker's shop, all glass. A young lady stood behind the counter. She summoned an old gray-haired man who put a glass to his eye and peered in Edevart's watch. He asked the same questions and was astonished at the answers. This time there were questions about where he came from and what had brought him to Bergen. The watchmaker eyed him suspiciously, as though he might have stolen the watch. Finally he said: "If what you say is true, then you've bought a bargain!" He took two gleaming watches out of a glass case and said: "I'd give you both these watches for yours."

"I don't want to exchange," said Edevart . . .

It was lucky that August had had his fling in Florø and had only just regained his equilibrium. Here in Bergen he felt no temptation to award himself shore leave again. When he had handed over *The Seagull* and settled up with the cousins from Hardanger, he was eager for them to set off for the north again immediately. There was nothing to keep them; the two men from Hardanger were not the kind of people you wanted to make friends of; they had looked closely at the documents and asked about a number of details, though anybody could see that the records were accurate and correct. Why, for example, had they wanted to give lengthy scrutiny to that largish item at Florø: repairs to sail. They even seemed as though they wanted to unfurl the sail to see what had been done to it. But that is the way with people who inherit things—they never seem to get enough!

August looked somewhat reduced when he boarded the northbound steamer. He no longer had any watch chain across his waistcoat; no longer any wallet bulging with another man's money. His baggage was a sailor's duffel bag. Yet even so, there was more to August than met the eye. He had acquired those navigational charts by padding out the accounts for provisions; moreover, he had in his bag a pair of sea boots—which Skaaro had no more use for. All in all, it seemed the two Hardanger men had not been particularly close-fisted. They were astonished and impressed that there was so much brandy left in the keg after it had been drawn on for a whole summer; and they nodded assent to more than one obscure item in the accounts, because August was obviously a man with an orderly mind.

On their journey north, the two men found one day very much like another; they were bored and longed to be home. August was once again wearing his watch chain; and he unrolled his charts to point out the various lighthouses and reefs and seamarks to the other passengers.

"So you got Skaaro's watch?" Edevart asked.

"Yes, but don't think I didn't have to buy it," August answered in an offended tone.

A certain suspicion passed through Edevart's mind and he

asked: "Why haven't you been wearing it until now? Why were you so eager to get away from Bergen?"

August flared up. "What do you mean? Wouldn't it simply have meant more expense for both of us if we'd waited for the next steamer? You've got me to thank for that."

But whatever the truth was, the suspicion remained with Edevart; and August was aware of this. A certain tension sprang up between the two men. Edevart couldn't resist poking fun at their great piratical scheme of running away to Spain; and August was provoked into defending it. "If I had stood there with a revolver, Edevart my lad, you wouldn't have dared disobey the commander of a ship," he said. "But for that bloody sheep and the time it took, I'd have been into Trondheim and found myself a revolver. I went looking for a revolver in Kristiansund and Aalesund, but there weren't any to be found."

Edevart: "Then, as far as I can see, you are a murderer."

August snorted scornfully: "I treat that remark with the contempt it deserves. You are an imbecile, just like Teodor. Still wet behind the ears. Do you know what we could have done? I do! In Spain we could have bought a clipper and sailed her away to the Pacific and had the whole wide world before us . . ."

August did not seem able to convince his companion; and it obviously preyed upon his mind that their relationship was not as good as it had been before. While the steamer was lying in Trondheim, August went ashore alone. He was pensive and depressed. When he came aboard again, it was to collect his bag. He had joined the crew of a bark bound for Riga.

When it became apparent to Edevart that this was in earnest, he felt bad and regretted that he had driven his companion to such despair. "You mustn't do it," he said. "You must come home with me. We have been through so much together. Surely you don't want us to split up?"

"Just to Riga. A short trip. It's nothing. The ship's name is *Soleglad*, if you want me for anything. Address: care of the Norwegian Consulate."

They were both feeling down, but there was nothing to be

done. August was signed on. He gave Edevart his gold ring as a present and wouldn't take no for an answer. Then he himself raised the matter of the trip to Spain and he asked Edevart to say nothing about it back home.

"I'll never say a word," said Edevart.

"I'm sure you won't," said August. "But let's shake hands on it?"

Edevart, surprised: "Yes, I can always do that . . ."

"Then it's like your Bible oath. You can't ever escape it. That much I have learned. You would be a banished soul . . ."

Parting from August was a matter of no small importance for Edevart. He thought things over. In one way his hands were freer, but this was no unmixed blessing for him. There was an empty place at his side. Living these two years alongside August had taught him many things. His horizons were wider. His native village was no longer his whole world. He had seen many many people, and many ships and cities and landscapes. August was a good lad, a remarkable fellow. Goodbye and good luck!

Edevart walked about the steamer somewhat confused; he was sad and lonely. Teodor wasn't the kind of man to confide in.

When the steamer made a stop off Fosenø, Edevart boarded the launch and went ashore.

5

THE HOUSES LAY IN THAT GREEN BAY, WITH THE ROAR of the falls around them. And Lovise Magrete Doppen and the children were just as they had been before. They stood outside the cottage, scantily dressed, silent and lovely, and watched him approach. The young woman smiled uncertainly as she looked at him in his new clothes. Her eyelids quivered. She said something like: "What's this I see . . . !"

He set his pack down and held out his hand, embarrassed. "Good day! I just happened to be passing." He was helped by the fact that his clothes were new and he was obviously doing well for himself. Without that he perhaps wouldn't have uttered a word.

"Fancy seeing you again! You who were so clever and helpful!" she said, simply and artlessly, though her face had gone red. "You got somebody to row you here? Where is the sloop?"

"We handed over the sloop in Bergen. No, you see, I began thinking about that sheep of yours. We didn't block off that path, and I thought it might have got stuck again. I just wanted to look in and inquire."

She clapped her hands. "Did you really think that!"

To emphasize the casualness and inconsequence of his visit, he explained that his companion, the skipper, had left him in Trondheim and was off to sea again. So he was now on his own, he said with a faint smile, and he might just as well make this little detour.

"Good heavens!" she whispered, overwhelmed.

There was no doubt that new clothes, money in his pocket, a watch, and a gold ring helped to make a man of Edevart. He nodded to the children and said: "I've brought one or two little things for you!"

Lovise Magrete: "Please come in. You must take us as we are."

The young woman had not been idle these last weeks. She had set up her loom and had woven the greater part of a rug, a real work of art in many colors and a fine pattern. "That's how I make my living," she said. "I spin the yarn and dye it myself. Wool from my own sheep."

"Marvelous!" said Edevart, without understanding. "Make your living—how?"

"I send them to Trondheim, and from there they go farther. I had them on exhibition and won a diploma."

He shook his head in wonderment when he heard this; and

this was enough to fill her with childlike pride. "Don't you think this is a nice piece of weaving? You do! But then I've woven many finer hangings than this. This one is more for everyday use."

"Where did you learn this?" he asked.

"Learn? I don't know. It came gradually. That's the way things happen. My mother taught me to spin and weave when I was little."

He opened his pack and the children got their presents— they were the things he had bought in Bergen to take home to his younger brother and sisters. Now he gave them away here: silk kerchiefs for the girls, a splendid pocketknife for the boy, and a pair of much too large shoes for each of them. Only when their mother prompted them did they remember to say their thanks, so excited were they at their treasures.

"You are much too kind!" the mother said.

When she had given her guest food and drink, she took him out and showed him the little barn, which housed one cow and ten sheep, showed him the hay barn, the path for bringing water from the river, the woodshed, and all else that was hers. Everything was tidy and well kept. A door with a key in the lock led to an outhouse under the eaves. With a certain pride she opened up and showed him in. Several finished rugs hung over the beams; in addition, there was flour and other food, one or two skirts and a single Sunday dress, a little wool, a little butter, some sheepskins. She clearly didn't feel she was too badly off, seeing how she showed it all off to a stranger. She displayed it like the family silver. He looked at it all and honestly thought the same as her: that this was a great deal, more than enough. "Marvelous!" he said.

Happy creatures! To be almost nothing is also something.

He went over to his pack and began taking out his work clothes, getting ready for the mountains. She suggested—of course he must do as he wished—but couldn't he stay the night? It could wait till tomorrow, this business of blocking the path to that dangerous cliff edge. He ought to take it easy today; and as it happened, tomorrow was Sunday. He must do as he wished, but there was always Monday . . .

She rattled off all this at once, doubtless to cover up her blushing embarrassment.

Thank you, yes. He could stay over if she liked. He could sleep in the hay.

Yes. And he could have some nice rugs over him and under him, lots of rugs . . .

So the photograph on the wall was her husband. August had said he was a handsome man. Perhaps by showy foreign standards he might be thought handsome: curly hair, hooked nose, wild eyes, large mouth. Edevart asked how old he was, and then he too said: "A handsome man!"

"Yes," said Lovise Magrete. "A handsome man. He danced much better than all the others and he was great at playing the accordion."

"August was, too. He played the accordion," Edevart interrupted. "That skipper of mine you saw. Masterful! Up north where I live they say he learned it at the School of Wittenberg."

"Is that so?" she said. "My husband was so spry he could walk enormous distances on his hands. And you see that clothes pole out there? He could clear it with a standing jump."

"No!" said Edevart incredulously.

"I'm telling you he could. Well, nearly, at least."

"That's tremendous."

"He also sang nicely. But he was too headstrong, and he's probably landed up in trouble—in America, I mean. He was fond of his liquor, too. Because he was lively and got invited everywhere and acquired a taste for it."

"I can't understand why he doesn't write."

"No, he doesn't write. But it could well happen someday that a letter will come, or even he himself. What do you think?"

Edevart shook his head and did not answer.

"He sang so nicely," she continued dreamily. She took stock

of all his good qualities, all the things which had impressed her. All in all, she remembered him with affection.

"But the fact that he never writes . . . !"

"No," she said. "He was funny that way. When he left, he said himself that he wouldn't write until he had something worthwhile to write about—made a lot of money or made something of himself. Perhaps in five years' time, he said."

"And you and the children were to manage with nothing coming in from him?"

"I don't know. He knew we wouldn't starve here at Doppen, because I could weave. I had begun weaving some time before he left, for he wasn't earning anything."

They sit and talk together, these young people, and anybody could have listened to them, for there was nothing wrong in what they said. In the evening she had to make up a bed for him in the hayloft, and naturally he lent a hand and carried the heavy rugs for her. Together they busied themselves in the hay; she played the little mother, claiming to know more about making up beds than he did. Occasionally, they would laugh. There was in truth nothing hangdog about her.

When she left, he followed her, finding it hard to part from her. His love for her was great. He intimated as much to her in simple, humble words and shyly stroked her arm. This was bold, but she did not take it amiss. She shook her head and smiled gently at him. He was young and good-looking, strong and sturdy from a lifetime of work. She accepted his tenderness.

Outside, she peeped in through the window to see if the children were sleeping peacefully and had not kicked off their blankets. She said to Edevart that they could go into the cottage again and sit, if he felt like it. It was Sunday tomorrow and they didn't have to get up early.

But it became clear that they couldn't talk inside. The children became restless in their bed; they weren't used to voices in the cottage at night. At length the girl opened her eyes and asked: "What is it, Mama?"

"Nothing. Go to sleep!"

They could not sit here disturbing the children, so they went back to the hayloft. Nothing took place between them, nothing. Only that they shyly held hands while he told her all his thoughts had been of her during his trip to Bergen. Oh, it was all so youthful, so foolish, so wise. Now and then he would wet his dry lips with his tongue, all the time looking down, his heart thumping. "Hm!" he would say from time to time very forcefully to bolster his courage. Perhaps this wasn't necessary. She sat and smiled and listened and probably returned his love. It seemed so; for when she left, she let him kiss her. Oh, dear God, he kissed her! It just happened. He didn't ask her, but their lips met.

He dived down under the rugs fully dressed and lay flat on his face, as though wanting to shut himself in with some great secret.

From now on in the evenings they sat in the hayloft, for they could not sit inside the cottage and disturb the children. There was always something to talk about, and they never wearied of finding things. He told her how difficult it had been for him to find his way back to her. When he left the steamer and came ashore, nobody seemed to know where Doppen was. "A place called Doppen?" they said. "No." But one young man said: "But I used to know a man called Haakon Doppen." "Yes," said another, "I also used to know him . . ."

"Yes, that was my husband!" Lovise Magrete exclaimed. "You see, everybody knew him! A great lad!"

Edevart, surprised: "Your husband? No! They said he was in prison."

"Oh, then it wasn't him," she murmured.

"In Trondheim, they said."

She shook her head vehemently. "No, no! It must have been somebody else."

Edevart continued: "It must have been. I got the two young lads to row me over here. None of us knew the way. There are so many green bays between the landing stage and here, and all

93

three of us rowed for quite some time. But then I remembered where we sailed in with the sloop that time we wanted water and we heard the roar of the falls—then I knew where I was. There isn't a green bay anywhere as pretty as this one."

"You think so?" said Lovise Magrete. "I think so, too."

Edevart: "All I wish is I could stay here all the time."

"Yes," she said reflectively. "I wish that too, but . . ."

Thus they would sit and talk of an evening. During the day they were each at their own work: she at the loom and he outside. He had been here now for over a week and had long ago blocked the approach to the ledge. He found other things it was necessary to see to: he mended fences and cleared things off the land. Now finally he had decided to break a few stones lying irritatingly on the hayfield which got in the way of the scything.

But he couldn't do that on his own, she objected.

He wasn't sure. Perhaps he could manage it alone. But at all events he would need a crowbar.

Yes, they had enough to talk about. Where would he get a crowbar from? Where could he borrow or buy one? At the trading station, but it was a long way, across the mountains. It was a trip which Lovise Magrete made only every few months. There were two small pioneer settlements nearer, but they would hardly have a crowbar. They talked and talked.

In the morning Edevart decided to do the best he could as it was. He trimmed two poles of stout rowan and began clearing. Yes, he shifted one stone after another, filling the holes with soil and turf. When occasionally he needed a greater weight on the pole, the two children—and, at a pinch, Lovise Magrete herself —would hang on and lend their weight. All four of them then thought that clearing stones was great fun. A family clearing its land.

After the midday meal Edevart prepared to return to work. He had had porridge and milk. It was good food, but Lovise Magrete would have wished it better for him. She was sorry she had no fish. He found it flattering that she brought him into these domestic affairs, making them like man and wife. She asked him to go into the storeroom and cut a shank from one of the sheep carcasses, crush it and bring her the marrow. She wanted to start spinning and had first to grease her spinning wheel.

Edevart went. He sneaked in with him a large cardboard box which had lain in his pack the whole time. In the box was the present he had bought in Bergen for his mother: a fine all-wool skirt and a shawl, a kind of cape without arms which was now the fashion and which in his home village was called a "rampe." He hung the garments hastily on the wall, cut the sheep shank, and went out of the storeroom.

When he came in with the marrow, he said he had to go at once to the trading station. He had been thinking about it for a long time.

She looked at him: "What is this? You want to leave?"

"No, no! I want to look around. I want a crowbar. These wooden poles aren't any good. They bend."

Seemingly relieved, she said: "I thought you wanted to leave for good."

He laughed and answered: "I'll be here till you chase me."

She shook her head sadly and sat silent for a while. "I'll come and set you on the right track," she said, and got up from her loom. "A path leads to the first two farmsteads, and from then on the road is better. But it will take you the rest of today to get to the trading station. There'll be no time to get back."

They stood and looked at each other when they reached the top of the hill. As usual she was barefoot and wore nothing but a skirt and a blouse; flushed now from the walk, her nostrils dilated, she was beautiful. There was nothing unseemly about her dress, simply that she was sparing in her ways and her needs were modest.

"Ask at the post office as soon as you get there if there are any letters for me," she said.

He was away twenty-four hours. She had washed and mended his clothes and been like a mother to him; but now a day and a night had gone and he must surely come soon. He had hung some fine garments up in the storeroom, and she did not fail to understand. It could only mean one thing and she was touched by his shyness. Was she longing for his return or was she indifferent? It wasn't exactly that she was walking in a daze, but she did begin to climb the path to the mountain, perhaps to meet him, perhaps to help him carry. When she reached the hilltop she happened to look back and saw some distance out in the bay a man rowing a boat. It was Edevart. Yes, of course, he was rowing. He could not carry that heavy crowbar such a long way across country. She ran down the path and met him on the beach. Yes, he had bought the crowbar; he had also bought this boat and some fishing tackle. He was going to fish in the bay.

"Heavens, whatever next!" she said.

What? It was nothing to brag about, nothing at all. Fishing for him was as simple as ABC. Nor was the boat new . . .

"But, good heavens, all these things you've done and planned for me!" she said, overwhelmed. "And those fine clothes you've hung up in the storeroom! I don't know what to say . . ."

They walked up from the boat. She helped him carry various packages and things: food, one or two more things to wear, tools. Sweets for the children, a white collar for Lovise Magrete —if she didn't disdain it! Besides this, he placed on the table two new spoons.

That was good. They needed spoons. He thought of everything.

Gladness filled the house. Edevart himself was perhaps the happiest of them all. Lovise Magrete happened momentarily to lean against him. She probably only meant to get past his chair; she scarcely more than brushed his shoulder. But a sweet warmth surged through him and he breathed heavily.

Food was served but he could hardly eat. They drank coffee and ate the cakes he had brought home. They lacked nothing. While Lovise Magrete opened the parcels and stacked the items of food in the cupboard, he secretly emptied her coffee cup and placed his lips where hers had been.

Evening approached; but they were not to retire to rest before something sad and strange had happened. Oh, so sad and strange!

Lovise Magrete remembered something. She said, "Did you ask about letters?"

Yes, he did have a letter for her. He'd nearly forgotten.

As soon as she saw the handwriting, her face grew tense. She opened the letter and suddenly cried: "It's from Haakon!"

Edevart and the children watched her as she read. She turned pale, then red. As she was reading, she exclaimed: ". . . Great act of clemency . . . Yes! . . . No, no, no! . . . Oh!"

"Is it from your husband?" Edevart asked.

"Yes," she rejoiced and stood up. "Now he is coming, children! Papa is coming! Do you understand, Papa is coming!"

Edevart moistened his dry lips. "But didn't I see that the letter is from Trondheim?"

"From Trondheim? No! Yes, it is! He's come to Trondheim . . . from America. Look, it's postmarked Trondheim. But imagine that he's coming now. It's a year earlier—earlier than he said, I mean. It was divine fate that took you to the trading station. He's giving himself a little time to recover—after the journey, I mean—and then he'll be coming!" And involuntarily the young woman began tidying up the room and putting things in order.

Edevart went out. He wandered down to the river and sat there a while listening to its rippling sound, thinking, thinking. What was there for him to do now? What use a crowbar, and what use a boat?

About the time he judged Lovise Magrete must have put the children to bed, he walked back to the house again. She came out at once. She said she'd read the letter again and that she could expect her husband any time.

"Well?" said Edevart.

She showed no inclination to come with him to the hayloft as on earlier evenings; and in general she seemed changed. Very absentminded, very preoccupied. As he left she made no move to follow him. He looked back once, then continued on his way. He would not ask her. Stubbornly, deeply unhappy, he undressed and lay down in the hay so as not to be tempted to go back to her.

A little later she came and sat down hesitantly by him. She was doubtless sorry for him and wanted to be nice to him.

"You mustn't take it so hard," she began, and went on to say what had to be said: that there was nothing to be done about it, that he would get over it in time—good, commonplace truths which might even have comforted her once. Perhaps, who knows, when her husband had left her.

Edevart remained darkly silent.

"It can't be otherwise," she continued. "But thank you and God bless you for all the kindness you have shown me."

"I don't know what I am going to do," he said.

"You? Oh, you'll soon find yourself a girl," she replied. "As for me, I'm married and can never be anything to you." At this, she seemed to be about to get up and go.

How unreasonable, how resentful he became! *She* wasn't in despair, didn't even take it seriously! What was she made of? He threw his arms about her and drew her down to him. She didn't care what happened to him. He was superfluous now. He'd been shamefully deceived. He wanted to hold fast to her. That's what he wanted.

"You have no feeling for me," he said.

"I have! I have!" she replied. "Oh, how can you say I've no feeling for you! I have thought more about you than . . . I have thought a great deal about you. You are good-looking and you have dark-blue eyes. What do you want me to say? Tell me and I'll say it! But as things are now—my dear, you must find another girl, because I'm married. You must know that. I don't know what we are going to do . . ."

"Can't I stay? No, I suppose I can't."

"Here?" she asked, terrified. "No."

"But nearby? At the trading station?"

"No, no, you mustn't think of it. My husband would find out."

"So you love him?"

"Yes," she said. "But I can never thank you enough for all you've been to me."

They lay there silently for a time. Then he took her and kissed her and she let him. But when he shyly and inexpertly wished to go further, she said: "No. I dare not."

Miserable and embarrassed he hid his face against her breast, and thus they lay a while. He heard her heart hammering under the thin blouse. Suddenly she raised his face and kissed him. She whispered against his mouth: "I don't suppose I dare, do I?"

"Yes, you do!" he whispered back.

And yes, she did. She did dare. Whether from motherliness, from compassion, from love, God alone knows. She initiated him, and then their night hours were filled with a wild passion beyond compare, a tumult of the senses, wholly natural, guileless. He was insatiable, and not once did she cry out for mercy.

It was the gray light of dawn when she left him.

Ah, but this only made things worse. After he had slept some hours, she stood over him again, scantily clad as usual, and woke him: "I am so afraid he will come," she said.

"Let him come!" Edevart answered defiantly.

"No, no! You mustn't be here!"

He stretched out his hand and wanted to have her again, but she drew back. He moaned that it was their last time. Was he not leaving, weren't they about to part . . . ?

She had to smile, and she kissed him in a moment of tenderness. But that made things worse for both of them. "God, how wild you are!" she whispered, and gave herself . . .

It was still early morning and the children were not up yet. Edevart was given a hurried meal; he packed his bag, lifted it, and said: "It weighs heavier on me today than it did the day I came."

"You mustn't carry it. You must row."

"Row? Don't you want the boat?"

"I dare not," she said. "A boat—no! I might have bought

those other things, so it's all right for him to see them when he comes."

Edevart: "But if nothing else, the children are going to tell him I've been here."

"Yes. I will say only what happened: that a man came to work for me and was kind enough to clear away some stones. You must take the crowbar with you."

"No," Edevart answered. "Set him on clearing stones. Now that he'll have a crowbar!"

She thought it over. "Yes, a workman might have left his crowbar behind, but a boat is too much."

Then he stood ready to leave. Her mouth began to tremble, and she said: "I suppose I'll never see you again as long as I live?"

"I don't know," he replied dejectedly. "Would you have wanted me to stay?"

She, whispering: "Yes, I think I would . . ."

He was still sobbing as he ran down to the sea with his pack, but it was for joy at her answer. He had known a great happiness. And as he rowed out across the bay, she stood outside the cottage. Finally she waved.

THE TRADER was called Knoff. He had a big place, with a white-painted main building and two huge dockside warehouses, each four floors high. In the harbor, a ketch and a sloop lay moored, and on land there were many buildings and workshops. Knoff himself was an enterprising gentleman, a go-getter, proud of his place and his business, not altogether without vanity or always conspicuously honest; but nevertheless, he was looked up to in the district as an excellent fellow. But so vain: in conversation he would refer to Mrs. Knoff as "My lady wife," and he had baptized his two children Romeo and Juliet. He had many lines of business: his general store, boat building, bakery, coopering. His greatest regret was that the Nordland coastal steamers, purely by tradition, called in a good way farther south and by-passed his place. It was not only a matter of pride for him. It cost him a lot of money to bring all his goods by boat from the landing stage. He had long sought a change in the situation.

When Edevart asked him about work, he began by saying no, and was sly and reluctant. The question was, what could he do? Edevart said he thought he could turn his hand to most things. Could he saw and chop wood, look after the horses, row a boat, keep the books in the office, help out in the bakery? Edevart answered smilingly that he could certainly take on some of these things. "Yes," said Knoff, "but I already have people for these things."

But Edevart had learned a thing or two from August. He said: "I see two boats in the harbor, big vessels both of them. Have you full crews for them?"

Knoff thought. "Well, they are moored there because they have already been to Trondheim with fish. They'll sail to the Lofotens this winter, but it isn't even autumn yet. So you can't wait for them."

Edevart kept silent at this. Of course it was autumn. It was the end of September, and there was frost in the fields in the mornings. Autumn was well advanced.

"Have you been to sea?" Knoff asked. "Have you worked on a boat before?"

Yes, he had. And he knew the Lofotens.

"You're not thinking you'll be given charge of one of the vessels?"

"No," Edevart replied. "But I'll take any job you care to put me to."

Knoff looked at him and assumed the posture of one who is too important to think about petty details just now. He said: "Anyway, I have my old skipper for the ketch. Have you ever been on a trip to buy fish?"

"Yes," Edevart replied.

"Where have you come from? That landing stage farther south?"

"No, I've come from Bergen. I helped to sail a fishing sloop there."

He was a good-looking lad, well dressed, with a gold ring and a watch. He appealed to the conceit of this important man; he was not given a flat rejection.

"Come and talk to me in an hour," he said, and looked at his watch. "I haven't time now."

Edevart wandered down the road to the warehouses, and feeling somewhat low, he threw himself down on the ground. He was tired and preoccupied after recent events. Until today he had had enough to do getting away from Doppen and presenting himself at the trading station. He had had no time to think things over. Even his conversation with Knoff had been pretty well unprepared.

When he went over the wonders of the night, he could scarcely keep silent. He lay there whispering to himself. He had undergone a revelation. He trembled inwardly in wonder and gratitude. Strange! He placed his hand over his face and sensed again her tenderness. He saw her brown eyebrows, straight and delicate as brushstrokes, and with an expression that made them seem strangers above her otherwise quite ordinary gray eyes. Lovise Magrete, dear sweet Lovise Magrete! He did not mean to row back and make things hard for her. He would simply seek work here. He desired only to be somewhere near her . . .

As though obeying an order, he kept an eye on the time; and when he stood in front of Knoff again, he knew that he was punctual to the minute. Knoff took out his watch again, looked at it, and nodded: "On the dot! You can stay on here," he said then, "and for the present you can help at the warehouse. Some flour has arrived. What's your name?"

"Edevart Andreassen."

Ah, but Knoff always had to be grand and distinguished. "Knoff" was distinguished, "Romeo" was distinguished. He wrote a note in which he referred to Edwart Andrésen, and said: "Deliver this to the warehouse foreman."

Done . . .

As the days passed, he helped in turn the warehouseman, the baker, and the boat builder. He was called upon when he was needed, and when called he went. He slept in the baker's pantry and ate in the kitchen. It wasn't at all bad. And autumn had indeed arrived; it began as early as October. Time passed; he did not die; he endured his love.

The place swarmed with workmen, boat hands, store assistants, and domestic staff. Knoff did not like turning anybody away, especially anybody who had failed to find work at the steamer landing stage farther south. How that landing stage preyed on Knoff's mind. It was only an old country store on a headland, but it had a liquor license, was an egg and down-feather center, and had accumulated capital. But above all, it had the Vadsø-Hamburg boats, something which in Knoff's indignant eyes was the great jewel. If a man had been turned away from there, he was pretty sure of getting a job with Knoff. "What's this! Don't they do anything down there?" he might say. "Don't they want anybody at all? I can't take on all the people they dump on me from there. Look, take this note to the man at the farm and ask him if he can't use you in the forest!" Something like this he might say.

Edevart settled in well. He was young and quick to learn. The girls in the kitchen took notice of the young man because of his good looks; and even the housekeeper, Miss Ellingsen, asked him where he came from and what his name was. He couldn't complain that nobody paid any attention to him. The children clutched his hands and asked his help with various things, especially the boy Romeo. And one day out on the estate Madam Knoff called him over and asked him to go down to the store and get some peas for the doves. Every Sunday he was well-dressed and generally kept company with those men more or less on his level: the cooper and the baker. The foreman boat builder was also friendly and helpful. He had already taken back the boat from Edevart and refunded his money. This he had the power to do; he had worked for Knoff so long, he was allowed to act on his own authority. From the boat builder and others Edevart also heard a lot about Haakon Doppen—more than enough, indeed, about Haakon Doppen.

Edevart took a look on board both the ketch and the sloop: nice vessels both of them, and well maintained. He did not understand much about the arrangement of rigging and sails on the ketch; but the sloop was straightforward and it appealed to him.

It occurred to him that he might write to August, on the bark *Soleglad* in Riga, and tell him where he was and what work he had. Eager to have his companion back with him again, he wrote in glowing terms about the place, about Knoff and all the other people, and urged August to come. There was a place for him here. He would surely get command of the sloop to take it to the Lofotens if he came. "Think about it. Reply requested! Postscript: If I know you, you won't be too worried about deserting the bark in Riga!"

Three weeks later he had a reply from Dünamünde. August declined. It was not his custom to desert from Norwegian vessels. He was in the habit of acting honorably. The bark was now taking on a cargo of rye for the return journey and he would be back in Trondheim again at the beginning of December. Edevart could come to Trondheim some time about then and talk to him. Bark *Soleglad*. "Warm greetings from your friend and God be with you."

Huh! There was August putting on airs. August summoning him to Trondheim! But it might perhaps just be possible that August had turned religious . . .

The weeks passed. The snow had come. It was sleighing weather and Romeo and Juliet had brought out their skis. Knoff had taken to his bed with a cold, perhaps for fear of becoming ill. He was chicken-livered. From his lair he kept a close eye on everything that was going on and sent one instruction after another to his workpeople. Edevart became uneasy when, one Sunday after dinner, Miss Ellingsen said that Knoff wanted to talk to him. Was he going to be dismissed? She opened the door and led him through the sitting room to the main entrance hall, then up a staircase to the first floor.

On his way through the room, Edevart's sharp eyes had been wide open. He had a vision of splendors quite unknown: a mirror from floor to ceiling, a gilt-painted sofa, a piano and a daughter playing it, Madam Knoff with gold jewelry on her breast, the house tutor, office employees, pictures on the wall in gilt frames. He was allowed to peep over the fence into another world—perhaps not a particularly high fence, but high enough for Edevart. The things he saw he had never seen before.

Why had he been conducted through the sitting room? God alone knows if it hadn't been an order, if the lad hadn't been made to traverse this paradise in order to make him feel small, make him feel like an ant. Edevart had heard things that hinted at his boss's calculating methods in these matters.

He stepped into the bedroom and halted by the door.

It wasn't a big thing Knoff wanted to see him about, he said; and it wasn't to talk about his dismissal. Like the big businessman he was, with little time to spare, Knoff came straight to the point: "I hear from the office that you got some things on account yesterday evening?"

"Yes. Some oilskins," Edevart replied in astonishment.

"Why did you put them on account?"

"I thought they might be thought of as an advance."

"An advance? We've never said anything about wages," said Knoff. And as Edevart was speechless, Knoff continued: "I can't pay any wages to speak of during the period you are waiting to sign on."

"Oh?"

"You must understand that."

"I'll pay for the oilskins," said Edevart.

Knoff: "So you have money?"

Edevart: "I'm not exactly broke."

"That's good," said Knoff. "As for wages and that kind of thing—you have board and lodging and that ought to be enough during this waiting period. You know of course I really haven't any use for you. You realize it's not exactly poverty that leads me to do this. It's just my method."

Edevart became angry, and said: "I'm not working here for my keep."

Knoff seemed surprised. "What else do you expect? It's wintertime and at least you have a place to stay."

Edevart: "I shall leave."

"Where will you go?"

"In the first place to Trondheim."

Knoff was silent for a moment. He wanted to step up the tension still further. "Very well, off you go to Trondheim. But I don't suppose you have anything to do there?"

Edevart, short and to the point: "Yes, I have." Then he left.

He immediately began to pack his bag. While he was doing this, it occurred to him to take back the oilskins, which were new and unused; but then Knoff would probably believe that he had no money to pay for them. By rights he ought to take the oilskins and dodge paying for them. That's what August would have done. He wouldn't have waited until Monday to go to the office and pay some piddling little bill. Edevart had already learned to take a less exacting legal and moral view of his conduct. He abandoned the idea of running away, for the sole reason that it might have consequences. Inquiries might be made of what he had been doing; and he was still in the neighborhood of Lovise Magrete.

Lovise Magrete! Strange that nobody from Doppen had been here at the trading station all this time. Edevart had kept a lookout every day and even made inquiries, but nobody had seen anything of them. The boat builder was of the opinion that

Haakon Doppen was too ashamed to show himself; it was also conceivable that he had saved up some money during the four years he had been in prison and had bought a lot of things before leaving Trondheim. But, at all events, both Haakon and his wife would come to do their Christmas shopping . . .

On Monday morning, when Edevart had settled his debts and was ready to depart, the chief assistant in the store, a man called Lorensen, came with a message from Knoff that Edevart could be taken on as a regular member of the crew of the sloop from today. Edevart was still angry and said "No, thanks," said that the sloop clearly wasn't ready to sail yet and he wasn't going to take Knoff's money for doing nothing. "Tell him that from me."

All the same, Edevart left his pack behind so that he could make a trip back to collect it. He took with him only some clothes in a bundle.

6 ALTHOUGH IT WAS STILL ONLY THE MIDDLE OF NOVEM-ber, the bark *Soleglad* had in fact already returned home and had begun discharging. It had made a quick voyage. Since several of the crew belonged in Trondheim and were living ashore, August was given permission to house Edevart on board. They were both greatly pleased to meet again, and they had much to tell each other.

August was wearing several rings on his fingers and a gold watch chain on his waistcoat. He scoffed at Edevart's idea of coming up to Froland and taking a sloop to the Lofotens. Not likely! He had other plans! August was very secretive about what he was planning to do, but he wouldn't conceal from Edevart that he was on the way to winning an international reputation. It would, for example, be time for the Levanger Fair in a few days time—

"What are you going to do there?"

"There? You'll see!"

Not another word for the time being, but August indicated with a sweeping gesture that he had valuables concealed all over the *Soleglad*.

In the evening, August produced eight full boxes of cigars from one of the bulkheads, wrapped them in a cloth, and gave them to Edevart to carry. "We're going up into the town," he said. "We'll look in at a place and do a little deal. But you're not to say a word."

They went into a tobacconist's. August seemed to have been there before. He nodded in familiar fashion; and to Edevart's amazement was almost unable to speak Norwegian, interspersed a number of strange words, and made himself understood by signs. He opened every box of cigars, showed their contents, smelled them, hammered the boxes shut again with a gleaming pocketknife, and handed them over. Then he was given money. August thrust this carelessly into his pocket, nodded, and said: *"Hoberpomere!"* "Yes," was the answer. The two men went.

"Did you sell the cigars?" asked Edevart.

"That was nothing. A few boxes," said August. "I wanted to help him out."

The next evening he sold a dozen boxes to a grocery store. Edevart carried them to the place. The deal was done in a back room where August opened up the boxes, showed off the cigars, invited the grocer to smell them, then held out his hand for the money. *"Hoberpomere!"*

"What's that you say when you leave?" Edevart asked.

"Haaper paa mere Handel! Hope for more business!" replied August. "I'm a Russian. Hurry up, and we'll do one more trip this evening. It's nice and dark."

Edevart carried another dozen boxes of cigars to a little tobacconist's shop where a lady was standing at the counter. She also had bottles of wine on her shelves. The lady smiled as they entered and immediately showed them into a side room with a sofa, chairs, and a table. She might have been in her thirties; she was tall and well built, with a pretty face and a lively manner. She poured them wine; they drank, and August spoke strange words to her. Edevart remained silent. It appeared that the lady couldn't pay for the cigars that evening; and August, with his devastating golden smile, indicated that this didn't matter, *nichevo*. It could "stay to an evening after." Before they left, he took her behind the door and kissed her and seemed to make some arrangement with her by pointing at his pocket watch and talking his crazy language.

"Why are you a Russian?" asked Edevart.

August answered: "They're more ready to believe me that they're getting a good deal. And they do, too. I sell cheaper than the other wholesalers, and I also have better cigars. Extremely fine cigars. Not that they cost me a great deal. I got them from the makers who roll the cigars in the factories in Riga. They'd stolen them, of course, and sold them for what they could get. Nor have I paid any duty on them. Not likely!"

"Why do you have me carry them?"

"Of course, you don't understand. But I simply must have a servant. When you come to Russia, you'll see that nobody carries even as much as a parcel himself. He has a servant for that. And if he has several parcels, he has two servants."

"How many boxes of cigars have you altogether?"

August looks superior, tosses his head, and says: "There can't be all that many hundreds of boxes left by now. I sold a thousand or so boxes before you came."

"Who did you have for your servant then?"

August stared: "What . . . servant? Oh, I let the customers come aboard and collect the boxes themselves. Why do you ask?"

Edevart, thoughtfully: "Oh, I just wanted to know. But is this what's going to make you so famous?"

"I don't deign to answer that," said August, offended. "I'm not telling you today all the things I've got on board. But let me ask you one thing, anyway: have you got all that much more than me? If so, let me see it!"

"No, I have nothing."

"Well, then there's no point in your sitting here and our being bad friends."

"Bad friends?" cried Edevart, repentantly. "Let me tell you this, August, there isn't a person on this entire coast I think more highly of than you. I only wish you had a whole cargo load to grow famous on, believe me."

They went on talking things over in their curious Nordland dialect. It had many peculiar words, unexpected words, and was a masterpiece of absurdity, but it expressed their meaning. August regained his good mood and began boasting as before. He said it was incredible what he'd achieved on the trip. "I got to Russia and went ashore and did things nobody else managed to do. Ask any member of the crew!"

Edevart: "I don't need to ask. I can see well enough. Apart from anything else, those gold rings on your fingers are unlike anything anybody's ever seen."

Again August tosses his head. "I have more like these."

Edevart was allowed to try on a few of the rings, heavy and exotic rings, some like snakes, some with stones. He weighed them in his hand and asked the price. Ah, August! It wasn't like the time he was in the fur trade and had to part with his best coat to pay for the hire of the boat. One might almost think he'd gone and opened his chests in India.

"Try this one!" said August, and took a snake ring out of his waistcoat pocket. "Does it fit? Well . . . you can have it!"

Edevart didn't believe his ears. "Not to keep?"

August drew himself up and appeared to be angry. "You are not to shout like that every time I give you a gold ring as a present. It's as if you don't really take me at my word. I say you are to have the ring. You can show it off to that man Knoff you wrote to me about. Ask if he's got anything like it."

Edevart, overwhelmed: "I'm speechless!"

They talked about Knoff. Edevart had bragged about him in his letter to Riga, so he couldn't condemn him too harshly now. But he no longer concealed Knoff's weaknesses, the tricks he got up to, his conceit. That little landing stage farther south was Knoff's mania.

"What's all this about a landing stage?"

Edevart explained what was known to God Almighty and to everybody in Fosenland: that for years and years the Vadsø–Hamburg boats had used this particular landing stage and by-passed Knoff, even though he ran an important business. This was a completely ridiculous situation, but Knoff had been unable to get it changed.

August took in the whole situation at once. He was a man of wide experience, and he wasn't slow in proposing solutions. What were the approaches like to Knoff's place? How deep was the bay? Was the surrounding area well populated?

Much more so than the old landing stage, which stood merely on a headland, Edevart thought.

"Then Knoff must be a fool!"

"How so?"

August immediately became excited. He was already hatching a scheme. Quickly he asked: "You say they have to unload things into boats at the old landing stage?"

"Yes."

"And didn't you say just now that Knoff's harbor is ice-free?"

"Yes. The bay is ice-free. Like Svolvaer, you know."

August, emphatically: "Then he must simply build a quay."

"Build a quay . . . yes. Should he, now?" said Edevart uncomprehendingly.

August couldn't help being astounded by this man Knoff. Couldn't help laughing. Why hadn't he built a quay long ago? Then he would have had the boats. Nobody could tell August that they were going to sail past a quay where they could tie up and be nice and secure, as in the bigger towns. What kind of boats were going to prefer being serviced out in the open sea in all kinds of weather when they could be lying alongside the quay?

After a while Edevart began to see daylight. "Ah, August!

What a stupendous man you are to think of a thing like that!" he exclaimed.

August swelled. "If only I could get my hands on that man Knoff!"

"You must come!" said Edevart.

"It would serve him right if I went and bought a strip of land from him and built the quay myself and got the boats to come to me. Then Knoff would kindly be allowed to rent the quay from me, and how he'd pay through the nose! But when I'd soaked him long enough, I'd let him buy the quay off me. I would do the decent thing."

"Yes, you must come!"

August, scornfully: "I'm not coming! Far from it! And if you want to know my opinion about taking the sloop to the Lofotens, I think you ought to take it over."

"Me?"

"Who else but you! Think about it! And at the same time, remember that if this man Knoff is disposed as he is toward you and won't pay you properly, as you say, then you needn't spare him even unto the third and the fourth generation, you know. You can arrange that when buying the fish."

"I can't sail a sloop," said Edevart, rejecting the idea.

"That's strange! Didn't I train you on *The Seagull* and teach you all about charts and compasses and reefs and lighthouses and how to set the sails. You know, I'm ashamed of you, Edevart!"

"Anyway, I wouldn't get command of the sloop, either."

"Well, there's something in that," August admitted. "You never were very bright when it came to pushing yourself forward and using your head. Never. But however things are, I don't want the sloop. You can tell Knoff that from me. I have other irons in the fire . . ."

They disposed of a few more boxes of cigars in town. They were together the whole time, and August kept away from temptation. He said: "No shore leave this time. Nothing doing. I am a businessman. I'll be greatly surprised if I don't make quite a fortune!"

A few days later he announced that he was going to the Levanger Fair, and generously invited Edevart along. They left early one morning in murky weather, with freezing fog. That suited them very well, said August, for then neither the customs officials nor the police would see very far! He was acting very mysteriously, carrying a little box under his arm and intimating that it contained things of great value.

When they arrived in Levanger, August locked the door to their room in the little hotel and positioned himself in the middle of the floor. "Now the hour is come when I shall reveal something to your mortal eyes!" he said, behaving like some prophet. When he opened the box, it very obviously did contain valuables: gold, silver, and precious stones. How had he got hold of them? There were rings, jewel boxes, necklaces, chains, earrings, brooches. Edevart sat dumb, staring at these splendors. Ah! August, August! There were probably no outstandingly valuable pieces and they were all old things; but they caught the eye with their brilliance and their strange barbaric splendor. August, pale with solemnity, mentioned now and then some large sum in respect of a ring of unusual thickness or a medallion in blue and gold set with tiny pearls. They were doubtless cheap trinkets, and the diamonds probably nothing but paste; but the effect was splendid. One wonders whether they weren't things out of pawn-shops or antique shops, perhaps even in fact stolen goods from private homes. God knows! All of them were old and second-hand. There was a little silver box, engraved and inlaid in black, quite evidently from deepest Russia, a fine piece of niello work. August lifted the end and took out a small gold watch with a blue stone set into the case. "Like to exchange your watch?" he said, making an outrageous, improbable joke about this so precious thing. "It was the czarina's own pocket watch. It has fifty rubies and every wheel in it is gold!" Finally August took out of the box a length of silken material with interwoven gold threads, lovely as a dream, in pale fading colors of red and blue, and long fringes at the ends.

Edevart sat, understanding nothing. He was seeing a mystery. Agreed, August must have made himself a pretty penny when he was skipper of Skaaro's sloop; and he might well have saved every bit of his wages during those months aboard the *Soleglad* as well. Edevart didn't know exactly what the prices were for ornaments and jewelry, but the whole of this lot might well be worth a million. And where had August got hold of that? Edevart sat uneasily.

August doubtless realized that his friend was sitting there trying to make him out; but for the moment he was too full of himself to offer any explanation.

Finally, Edevart asked: "Are you selling them for somebody?"

August had to answer, had to admit: "What do you mean? I'm selling them for myself. What are you thinking?"

Edevart: "Well, it's nothing to do with me."

August, immediately incensed: "Nothing to do with you? Do you think they're not mine? They are, so help me, so indisputably mine that . . . Look, I'll show you how I would defend them!" At this August pulled a revolver out of his pocket and held it up.

"All right," said Edevart and gave in.

"Hah! Nothing to do with you! It has nothing to do with anybody!" August continued. "Look, Russia isn't like here. There was this fire in Riga, and where should it be but in a building full of valuables for sale—actually, three other buildings on either side also caught fire. I and some others helped to put it out and this we did for nothing. But a lot of people simply helped themselves—villains and scoundrels and criminals who deserve to be flogged, I can tell you, for they weren't like Christian people. And afterward they came and sold off the stuff. Wouldn't take no for an answer. I had to buy to save my life. That's what happened. But some of them were very decent. They didn't ask much. Practically nothing. I gave them my address in order to get away from them, for I thought that once I was back in Dünamünde they'd never follow me there. But not a bit! They tracked me down, and one evening they brought some rings and another evening various silver boxes full of things. They said that if I didn't buy, somebody else would. And they wept and begged me to save them. Where was I to turn? But when they made the sign of the cross and fell on their knees, I had to do them this service. I hadn't the heart to drive them away. Would you have done so?"

"No!" replied Edevart, won over by his friend's account. "I'd have done the same as you."

Afterward Edevart doubtless thought about this answer: that it was weak and did not express his feelings entirely. Only a year ago he would have shaken his head at himself about it—now he had learned a few things from August and others, from Knoff and from daily life. He had begun to take a less rigorous view of right and wrong. Sure thing, he'd now got a bit of backbone. He could look after himself. The miracle of Lovise Magrete was still held just as purely in his heart, but not even that was as immediate and overwhelming as before. It was a long time since that miracle had happened.

LEVANGER FAIR wasn't much. Edevart had soon seen everything. On the second day he ran into Papst again, the Jewish watch seller. It was a happy encounter for both of them. They immediately recognized each other and met as good friends. Edevart produced his watch out of his pocket and held it out to show that he still had it, that he had taken good care of it. He also recounted what the two watchmakers in Bergen had said about the watch.

Oh, what great friends they became—like stablemates, buddies even. Not an hour had passed before the good Papst had got Edevart dressed in a topcoat, because he was freezing in his light suit. The coat was excessively large, but that didn't matter. It was nice and warm and had lots of pockets, and in the pockets were bright new silver watches which Edevart was to sell. But he wasn't to say that he was from Papst—that was not necessary.

How could Edevart start dealing in watches? He was given

his training by the master, many useful hints. Tests were held, and the lad was not without ability. Later, he learned from doing the job itself. Oh, it was a school, an occupation which matured him quickly and effortlessly. Things were falling into place. The lad's fortunes were beginning to rise. Now that he had valuables passing through his hands, he was approaching the level of August. He felt greatly honored by Papst's confidence in him and determined to apply himself diligently.

He sold a watch or two to young working lads of his own age. He would begin by asking some unbelievable price and then come down. It paid well and was fun. Very entertaining. He learned the art of talking about his wares, of drawing the customers' attention to their merits. But the most exciting thing was when he swapped the watches about in his innumerable pockets, made them disappear, brought them out again, and finished up by, in fact, selling the first of the three or four watches he had shown off—the main trick of the master himself. Ho! It was simply that the quickness of the hand deceived the eye. He couldn't help laughing to himself.

When he came home in the evening and presented his accounts, Papst nodded and put the money away into a huge wallet. He'd done well, said the master. Couldn't really expect any more. Five watches the first day wasn't bad. Out again tomorrow!

The next day he sold at least twice as many. Yes, indeed, he had learned his trade, but it had to be admitted that he soon began to lose his taste for selling watches. Not being particularly resolute, Edevart let a watch go at a rock-bottom price to a young lad who stood there, bare-necked and freezing, counting his pennies only to discover he was one daler short. The young watch seller gulped when the lad seized his hand to thank him. Dear God, innocence comes in truth from heaven and all else is of the earth! Then again, it greatly confused Edevart to discover that even this sale, which was meant as an act of charity, also turned out to be profitable. He made money on it. The lad was so delighted with his buy that he couldn't keep silent about it. He talked about it to everybody, which attracted new buyers. And although Edevart had to keep his prices up, he was sold out by midday. The word had gone round that he was selling amazingly cheap. Where had he got his goods from? God alone knew if they might not be stolen! No matter—indeed, so much the better. The customers saw their chance, a chance that had to be taken.

In the afternoon, Edevart went out again with more watches in his pocket. He moved around a little from place to place, selling one watch here and another there. He passed August, who was also doing business. Here, too, August was a Russian, uttering peculiar words and offering jewelry for sale in a rather more wary fashion. In his crowd there were both men and women, but mostly women. He seemed to be doing good business. He was pretty inventive despite his helplessness with the language. Edevart heard him say about one ring that it had magic powers, that this pair of earrings had been found in an earthquake, while this brooch with blue stones had once been part of a martyr's crown. Imagination he certainly had; and if some laughed and shook their heads, others excused him because he couldn't speak better Norwegian. He held up the lovely length of silk with its interwoven gold threads, showed it to a lady with a hat, and gave her to understand that in his own country, Russia, it was a royal bridal veil. The lady smilingly replied that she wouldn't use it over her face, but she bought the silk.

Toward evening the young lad came back to Edevart. He stood there, bare-necked and greatly distressed, with fearful eyes. His watch had stopped. It wouldn't go. This came as something of a blow to Edevart. True, he had had misgivings already about these cheap watches. Perhaps they weren't really dependable. He asked the lad: "Has it just stopped?" No, it had stopped a long time ago, and he'd also been to a watchmaker with it. "What did the watchmaker say?" Shyly, the boy hesitated, reluctant to answer, and Edevart did not want to press him. He shook the watch. No! He tried to wind it up a little more. No! Edevart's mind worked quickly. He could give the lad another watch. Papst wouldn't notice that among the unsold watches which he got back one was stopped. The apprentice was planning to cheat his master. Why not?

"You can have another watch," he said to the lad.

"Thank you! And it'll go all right?"

Edevart was touched. He was not particularly resolute. "You can either have a new watch or your money back," he said.

The lad beamed. "Can I? Oh, thank you!" The lad was in doubt as to which to choose.

Edevart offered him advice. "I can't really vouch for these watches. If I were in your place, I think I'd rather have my money back. I'm only saying what I think."

The lad took the money, thanked Edevart, and went away relieved.

But two other lads were watching out for Edevart on his way home, and they promptly threatened to beat him up for selling them those watches. They had been to a watchmaker and discovered that their watches weren't even worth one daler and they had paid three! Edevart couldn't start a fight with all those watches in his coat pockets. He asked: "Have your watches stopped?"

"Not stopped, exactly. But they weren't worth the money!"

At that, Edevart left them. True enough, they followed him all the way home, hurling abuse; but they didn't do anything to him.

There had to be something or other wrong with those watches. When Edevart turned in his accounts for the day, he announced that tomorrow—the last day of the fair—he would be busy doing something else.

"But why?" asked Papst. Things were going well, and the last day would be best of all.

Edevart pretended he had to help his friend with something.

"I have seen your friend. Watch him! He is selling stolen goods," said Papst. "Listen to me now. You're not going to leave me sitting here with all these watches on my hands?"

Yes, Edevart was firm.

Papst looked desolated. So great a misfortune was almost impossible to bear. He recalled that he had virtually given away that expensive watch which Edevart had in his pocket; and now he was meekly asking a favor in return.

But Edevart was now made of sterner stuff. He said: "I have now sold twenty-five or thirty or I don't know how many watches for you. That's not what I want to talk about. But tell me this: what sort of watches have I been selling?"

"Well, cheap watches—at cheap prices, too."

"Are the cases made of silver?"

"It looks like silver," Papst answered. "I don't know."

Edevart: "I don't know, either. But a man came today who had scraped his watch and he said it was brass underneath."

Papst threw out both hands. "Well, they're cheap watches and cheap prices."

"Why don't you sell these watches yourself? Why always the others?"

"I thought you might do me that modest service."

"Yes," said Edevart. "But here am I simply making a lot of enemies. They follow me about and threaten to beat me up."

"Ho! Ho! You're a strong lad!" Papst laughed. "Besides, you'll never be returning to Levanger. But I will. Old Papst must keep roaming around from place to place and returning regularly. Yes, indeed!"

Yes, of course Edevart should have shown more gratitude toward the friendly old Jew and worked one more day for him. But he couldn't bring himself to. For all that, they didn't part as enemies. On the contrary, Papst patted him on the shoulder and said: "We'll surely meet again!" Edevart was not offered any payment for his work, but neither did he expect any. He left behind the large topcoat and walked back to his lodgings feeling relieved.

August had returned dissatisfied. He expressed himself bitterly. "You can't get any kind of price here. Ask what you like to begin with, but you have to cut things right to the bone. What kind of people do you get coming here? Verdalers, the lot of them! And the ridiculous offers they had the nerve to make! Levanger!" he sneered. "Did you ever set foot in a more villainous hole? I'll try again tomorrow and sell for what I can get and then I'm leaving."

"Have you sold the czarina's watch?" asked Edevart.

"Have I sold the czarina's watch! What do you think I'd get for it in this one-horse place."

"Does the watch go?"

"Of course it goes. Why are you asking?"

"You can sell it in Trondheim," said Edevart.

"Yes, and get arrested on the bloody spot!"

Everything looked black to August. He was displeased and impossible. Here he was in the market town of Levanger with its five hundred inhabitants, having come in the expectation of conducting extensive business in ornaments and jewelry, and having found only frustration. Not that he was the least bit worried: he'd made some money on his gold trinkets. But he was angry and sore at his setback, for any thought of achieving great fame had now gone by the board.

In the morning he counted up his valuables, estimating them roughly at Levanger prices, and mumbled some embarrassingly small figures. Edevart bought for cash a little gold medallion which could be worn on a chain. It wasn't anything very much and August didn't really want anything for it, but was talked into accepting what he had valued it at.

Edevart remained behind in his room, alone and bored. He had a feeling he had better not show himself outside too much, in case he was recognized and pursued again. On the other hand, he had nothing to occupy himself with in his room. There was little point in just sitting there thinking; and he detested reading just as much as he ever had. After August had been home for dinner and had gone out again, Edevart lumbered out after him. He decided to risk it; the days were short now and it was already beginning to grow dark.

August was nowhere to be seen. On the other hand, old Papst was there, walking along some distance away. He had a friendly word for all, and now and then he would take a watch out of his pocket to let a customer see. Edevart recognized every movement of the hands and could almost guess what the words were.

Suddenly August came out of a building. Was he drunk? Not likely. But he was in high spirits, triumphant. "I've started going from house to house," he said. "I should have done that before. I've even been to the goldsmith's and sold him one or two little things. But he couldn't afford anything very much. I've just been now to the chemist's. I sold the gold watch."

"What!"

August nodded. "And got a high price. The chemist's wife was none other than the lady who bought the silk. She wouldn't believe that the watch had belonged to the Czarina of Russia. But I made the sign of the cross over my eyes, and then she called the chemist in. 'Well,' said the chemist. 'If you want it, have it!' Oh, Edevart, things are beginning to pick up. Now I am going to call at another place. There are lots of officers in the town. A rich captain is said to be resident here. What do those lads want with you?"

A couple of lads had started talking to Edevart, furious customers of the previous day complaining that they had been swindled. Their watches were worthless, they'd made inquiries, and they wanted the deal canceled. Money back, please!

But now Edevart no longer had his pockets full of watches he had to take care of. He waved the more persistent of the lads away and asked to be left in peace. What in fact did Papst's rotten watches have to do with him, anyway? He had acted as an agent. He had sold goods, and those goods were possibly worthless, but what then? A deal was a deal. None of the others was thin-skinned, so why should Edevart be!

They made their way down the street, quarreling the whole time. The lads shouted to everybody they met that this was the man who was passing brass watches off as silver, and now he was going to get it, indeed he was! They caught up with Papst and the lads also explained to him how they'd been swindled by this man here who'd been around selling watches these last few days. They pointed at Edevart, stabbed their fingers at his chest, saying there he was.

Papst shook his head sadly that such was the way of the world he lived in and began to act as honest broker: let the young man take himself off, let him not waste any time, let him be on his way! "All you have to do is let the watchmaker repair your watches," he said to the lads. "It won't cost more than a few coppers and then you'll have your watches."

"But they are brand-new watches," they shouted. "Are we supposed to have brand-new watches repaired? I've never heard anything so stupid! They stopped as we were buying them. They only went because he shook them . . ."

Yes, Papst was overwhelmed; but he persisted in his attempts to mediate. The last thing Edevart heard was the old man saying: "You mustn't go buying watches from just anybody. You should buy from Papst. He doesn't swindle!"

Edevart made his way back to his lodging and did not go out again. He had had enough. Again he had had a glimpse over a fence. No great mirror to see this time, no gilded objects. It was a world where everybody pulled the wool over everybody else's eyes . . .

August came home at the end of his day's work. He was not entirely sold out, but he had abandoned the chest somewhere or other and now carried the whole of his shop in his pockets. "I had to chuck the chest away," he said. "I ran into trouble. There isn't a rat hole anywhere which is worse than this town. God, if only I were well away from it! Let's leave, Edevart, this very night if possible!"

"We can't leave tonight."

August told his story. "I sold a few expensive things to the captain. He lives outside the town, a long way out, and I tramped and tramped to get back. I passed a big building and couldn't see what it was, but I went in all the same. It was the school. What was I doing in a school! Then the headmaster came and asked me what I wanted. I was a Russian and wanted to sell some things— something *nichevo* or whatever it was I called it. He barely glanced into my chest, for no schoolteacher like that ever has a penny. "So you are a Russian," he said. "What fun! Do sit down. I learned some Russian when I was teaching in Hammerfest!" And then he started speaking Russian to me. That damn well did it! I nodded and smiled and made the sign of the cross, but he was probably asking something he wanted an answer to; so I said *hoberpomere* a few times and threw in a few other broken words. These he didn't understand and he shook his head. Of course I had my revolver, but to shoot a man just because he knew Russian was something I didn't have the heart for. So I became raving mad, slammed the lid of my box, and stormed out of the building. But when he remained standing there trying to puzzle me out, so to speak, I was afraid he might do a dirty trick and report me. I don't even feel safe sitting here."

"What have you done with the chest?" Edevart asked.

August: "I emptied the chest as I was running through the streets and stuffed the things in my pockets. I threw the chest away so as not to be recognized by it. Oh, I know what I'm doing, believe me! The mistake was in not being either a Malayan or a Siamese, for I can be anything. Don't you think we can get away from here tonight?"

"No," said Edevart. "But, anyway, you haven't done anything wrong, have you? Or have you?"

August: "Done anything wrong? What might that be? I didn't even have my revolver out!" But August didn't feel safe. He hadn't eaten and would have liked some supper. But he didn't dare risk it. He went to bed hungry.

THEY GOT BACK to Trondheim safe and sound, and August was a bit easier in his mind. And this was with good reason, for his wallet was good and fat. It hadn't been such a bad trip to market. So what was wrong? "It didn't turn out as well as I expected," he said.

Ah, well, it hadn't resulted in anything very special. No fortune, nothing to boast about. The more easily satisfied Edevart thought things were all right as they were, but August snorted at this. He was different, had bigger ideas: he felt he must make one more coup and sell much, much more. What did it amount to, all in all? A little for clothes, a little for the winter's board and lodging, nothing. And what about that woman Edevart had taken the dozen boxes of cigars to? She couldn't pay for them now, either. Twelve boxes—a considerable loss to his business. Yes, all right, the woman had done what she could, but—

"No," said August emphatically. "I must make one big haul!"

"Yes, you must come north with me," said Edevart.

August, pausing a moment open-mouthed: "How can you think such a thing! Me! Who has been all around the world! Anyway, I haven't been discharged from the bark and she's all ready to make another trip to Riga."

"So you'll go with her again?"

"I'm going again. I've thought it all out. Oh, I'll buy a lot more and come back with a cargo load of stuff. I'll charter my own vessel! How about that? Great!" And August boasted expansively and beamed with pride.

Edevart: "But how will you dispose of all that? You had enough trouble selling what you had this time."

"Dispose of it? Don't you worry about that! I'll try a different market."

After a moment, Edevart said: "All right, so long as you don't come to regret it!"

His quiet words merely irritated August. What did this big baby know about things, anyway! August turned away indignantly, suggesting it was somehow scandalous to try to restrain him or to sow doubt in his mind at that moment.

The friends stayed together a few more days while the bark

took on its cargo of dried fish and various piece goods. They went into town and sold the remaining trinkets. Neither of them went out on the loose. They even visited churches and museums. They looked the whole town over and kept their eyes open. When they went walking down by the harbor, August was able to point out certain constructional features of the various quaysides. Knoff should have been there from Fosenland to hear him talk about the different types of wharf.

No, August was not going to cut loose now. When he had a full wallet, he steered clear of any stupid "shore leave" business. It was at those times when he had little or nothing in his pocket that he blew his wages on some binge and then endured his hangover. Wages were something for the day, not something to hoard. Let them go! A wallet was something different.

7

THE TWO FRIENDS PARTED AND EDEVART RETURNED TO Fosenland. He was drawn there. He had his pack there. But, oh, dear God! He forgot something in Trondheim! Had he not given away to strangers those presents he had bought in Bergen for the people back home: the lovely shawl for his mother, the little shoes, and all the other things for his brother and sisters. All these things he had handed out at Doppen. All this time he hadn't once written home, or sent any money to his father. He might have put things right in Trondheim and sent a big parcel or perhaps even a crate. But he had forgotten; he had occasionally thought about it, but each time had put it off and finally forgot it altogether. He groaned when he thought about it now. It was a sin and a shame. There they would be at home, inquiring about letters, his father silent, puzzled, greatly subdued, his mother devout and patient, kindly in her thoughts. "Perhaps there'll be a letter today!" His brother, Joakim, would be confirmed by now, would have shot up and grown out of all his clothes. How delighted he would have been with a new suit . . .

They asked him at the trading station whether he had come back to stay. No, not that he knew of. But he was to collect his pack. He stayed over Sunday and Monday. Knoff came and said: "So, are you back again?" "Yes," Edevart answered. That was all that was said. Knoff walked away, a big and important man.

The cooper told Edevart that Haakon Doppen had been at the trading station and had bought various things. He didn't seem greatly changed. They had asked him to play his accordion, but he refused, saying that he'd given it up. But when they'd given him a few drinks and some laced coffee, he played for a dance in the servants' hall. One felt sorry for him. They egged him on, saying: "You haven't forgotten how to play yet!" He stayed the night. Edevart asked if his wife had been with him—Lovise Magrete. No, she hadn't, but they'd presumably both be coming for their Christmas shopping.

Tuesday passed. Edevart finally got a letter written home and sent some money. This eased his mind and cheered him up; and in this happy frame of mind he promised to come home himself with things for them all.

Knoff came to him again and said: "Are you just hanging around? Don't you want to work?"

"There's no great hurry," Edevart replied.

Knoff, taken aback: "You want to lord it?"

"No, not exactly, but . . ."

"Well," said Knoff curtly, "he who doesn't work doesn't eat."

Edevart wrinkled his brow. "I don't eat your food."

"Oh? Whose then?"

"I'm staying with the cooper and paying my way."

Knoff remained silent for some time; then, wanting to smooth things over, he said: "I didn't mean it that way! Where have you been all this time? Ah, in Trondheim and at the Levanger Fair. No, I didn't mean it that way at all. You can stay on here as before. And if you want to join the crew of the sloop on its Lofoten trip, I have room for you at ordinary seaman's rates. I meant to ask if you came ashore at the landing stage? Is there no sign of a spark of life in the people down there yet?"

"I saw no change."

"If you'd asked for work there, you wouldn't have found any."

"I had no wish for that. I was on my way here for my pack."

Knoff muttered something to himself, perpetually obsessed as he was by the one ridiculous idea: why doesn't that rotten old place fall into the sea!

Now the moment had arrived that Edevart had been waiting for. Experience had taught him how to exploit a situation. He said: "Why isn't the landing stage here at your place?"

Knoff shakes his head and answers almost piteously: "I can't get it here."

"That's strange. Then it's your own fault."

"What's that you say? You don't know what you're talking about!"

"I know what you ought to do."

Knoff smiles coldly at the young man. "As if I hadn't already done everything."

"You should build a quay," said Edevart.

A minute passed in complete silence. Knoff had had his hand halfway to his pocket for something or other, but stopped with his hand in the air. He seemed thunderstruck. "Should I?" he said.

"Then you would get the boats."

"A quay?" said Knoff. "You think so? A quay, a docking area, eh?"

Edevart now had the upper hand and did not try to conceal it. "I must say I'm astonished you never thought of it."

"Thought . . . thought . . . Anyway, what assurance have I that . . . what I mean is . . ."

Edevart held forth: No detour necessary to speak of, a bay deep enough for all ships, ice-free harbor. Here you had a place with thriving businesses, in excellent surroundings. The old landing stage lay far out on a headland a long way from habitation. Build a quay here, Edevart said, and he'd like to see any boat which wouldn't prefer to tie up nice and secure to being serviced out in the open sea in all kinds of weather!

"Come on down with me," said Knoff. "I want to show you something . . ."

They went down to the waterfront and looked around. The quay would have to be built to connect with the furthermost warehouse. It was deep enough there; freighters had regularly delivered flour and salt to that warehouse.

Now Knoff began to recover his wits again. He pointed and said: "I've always thought the quay ought to be here when I got around to building it."

Edevart let this pass and was clever enough not to try to answer. As they walked back to the house, he noted with satisfaction that Knoff was very friendly and looked at him with very different eyes. Wanting to make the most of the situation, Edevart led the conversation on to matters of construction and materials. He drew attention to certain common and certain peculiar features in the different kinds of quays, insisting that there were quays and quays, that you could build in stone or build in timber . . .

"Stone!" said Knoff. "Stone is the most substantial."

"But it's also the most expensive."

Knoff gesticulated. "I said stone is the most substantial! Listen to me now! If you really are thinking of joining the crew, you can have the usual seaman's wage as from today. And you must move out of the cooper's house. My own people must live at my place. It'll soon be Christmas, and after Christmas and New Year's it's no time before you sail. Is that agreed?"

"Yes," said Edevart.

Yes, he had succeeded in his intentions. He had been taken

on here permanently. What did he want here? Nothing. To be here, to breathe here. Memory once again stirred powerfully.

He was put to work on such jobs as happened to come along. Nor did it matter greatly if he did nothing. When the Christmas trade started, he was promoted to help in the main store. He wasn't much of a hand when it came to writing, but he was a demon at mental arithmetic—just what was needed. Moreover, he had a way with people, was well-dressed, and wore both a plain gold ring and a three-coil snake ring. So he stood his ground. He now took his meals along with the other store people in the dining room, together with the boss himself and his family.

This was a terrific rise in life for him, and it affected him greatly.

Then one day Lovise Magrete came. She had her husband with her. They were on foot and had walked that long and difficult road under bad conditions. Lovise Magrete had snow on her legs and dress. It was unusual to see her in so many clothes, and she looked strange, lacking her childlike charm. Edevart stared at her and bowed as he did to the other customers before he recognized her. He also looked at the husband. He, too, looked strange. He didn't greatly resemble the picture in the cottage at Doppen; but he looked handsome enough, nothing wrong there, and he had curly hair.

"Fancy seeing you again here!" said Lovise Magrete. She spoke simply and directly to Edevart, and it was her voice. But she had a scarf about her head and woolen mittens on her hands and all those other clothes on, a mass of clothes, and on top of everything else the cape which he himself had given her.

"Who's this?" the husband asked. And when Lovise Magrete had explained, he turned darkly to Edevart and addressed the following words to him: "So, you were the one who did that work back at my place. What did you get for it?"

"Get?"

"I asked what you got for it!"

"My keep," Edevart answered.

Lovise Magrete: "Yes, he got his keep."

Haakon asked: "His keep—only his keep?"

Edevart bestirred himself. "I wasn't looking for more," he said. "I was a wayfaring man at that time and glad to work for my keep."

Haakon had to stop. Finally he turned to his wife and said, seemingly as a joke but maliciously: "Did this man get anything done? He looks a bit of a ninny to me."

"Do behave yourself," the wife answered softly.

They made their purchases and put the things in their bags. During this, all three exchanged brief remarks. Edevart asked after the children, and was given a reply. Haakon began to recognize acquaintances among the other customers and started chatting to them. Edevart and Lovise Magrete wandered back and forth along the counter in search of the various articles she wanted. At length they reached the far end of the store and were alone together, but they spoke only about the goods. No whispering secret words. Oh, where was the glory now? Had they both forgotten what they had been to each other? Finally Edevart says: "Is everything all right with you?"

She cast a quick look behind, then answered: "He's not there. He's gone out. Yes, thank you, everything's all right."

"How is he taking it now that I'm around the place?"

She: "I suppose I must see where he's gone . . ."

"No!" said Edevart. "Listen, Lovise Magrete, I've been waiting so long for you."

She shook her head gently and said nothing.

"I've a little thing here in my pocket I want to give you."

"I suppose you've heard a lot about him?" she asked.

"Yes," Edevart answered.

"Yes, but he was pardoned," she said eagerly. "His conduct was so good that they reduced his sentence by a whole year. Wasn't that something?"

"Yes, indeed," Edevart mumbled absentmindedly.

"Just as long as he doesn't now get hold of any drink," she said uneasily.

Edevart: "Wasn't he standing talking to a girl? The one with the red hair. She won't give him anything."

"I know her," said Lovise Magrete. "She isn't altogether the best person for him to be with."

"Let them be." Edevart fumbled in his pocket and began: "I have a little thing here . . ."

"No, you mustn't give me anything," she replied. "I wouldn't dare. Wait a moment, I must see where they are. I'll be back immediately."

Edevart followed her with his eyes all the way across the floor and out of the door. He did not call out. Did not swear. But where was the glory now? This harsh treatment was unexpected; it was a cruel, an insane experience; it reduced him from a somebody to a nobody. He pulled out a drawer from under the counter, sank down on the edge of it, and remained sitting.

When she came in again, she said with relief: "No, he was only with a few of his friends . . . I'd like to see a string of beads—or perhaps just a silk ribbon. I promised my little girl."

Edevart rose and brought out the articles one by one. His mind was far away; he was scarcely aware of what he was doing. Nor did he say anything to her except to mention the prices. When it was time to pay she had to go out and find her husband. She came back in again with him as if nothing was the matter, though he must already have had a fair amount to drink.

To begin with, Haakon was jocular and good-humored toward his wife. He said: "So you're finished. But I still have my shopping to do. I want to see some pipes."

Edevart brought out pipes, many pipes to choose from.

Haakon said: "Fair's fair, my friend! Of course you haven't done anything wrong? Or have you?"

Edevart remained silent.

"Come now, pick yourself a pipe!" said Lovise Magrete.

"These pipes are a load of junk," Haakon replied. "You find me one!"

"This one!" she said, pointing.

"Very well, if you say so!" And to Edevart: "If you give me

a reasonable discount on this pipe, I'll take it. And eight ounces of tobacco, Virginian. Then you'll be rid of me. That'll please you, eh?"

Edevart remained silent.

"At least you can tell me how much I owe you for all this?"

Edevart said the amount.

"Ah! That you do know! But it doesn't sound as if you know very much. You don't say anything! Didn't he say anything back home either, Lovise Magrete?"

"Please!" she begged gently.

"Please? Why does he stand there not answering me? Hasn't he been a workman of mine back home . . . ?"

"Please pay now!" she begged urgently. "Then we can make our way home!"

He was slow to pay. It was a large bill, with many small items. Edevart had it all in his head, but he had to add it up several times for this half-drunken man. And in the middle of the calculation, Haakon found it appropriate to say: "But of course you didn't do anything wrong, eh?"

Edevart turned away from him and began to serve another customer . . .

When the store was shut for the night and he was passing the servants' quarters, he heard accordion music and the sound of dancing. He saw Lovise Magrete standing in the doorway. So the people from Doppen had not gone home yet. Edevart wanted to walk on past. He felt so empty, so drained. He had nothing more to say to Lovise Magrete.

She came after him and said: "We're staying till tomorrow. He's promised to play the whole evening. Well, our neighbor is staying with the children, so that's all right. What were you saying—that you had something for me? But I dare not. It's very kind of you, but I dare not. What was it you were going to give me? Perhaps you don't want to tell me, but I thought it might be your picture . . ."

"And you wouldn't want that?"

"Yes, I would, but you know . . ."

"It wasn't my picture," said Edevart. "I haven't got one."

"So that's that, then. Heavens, how kind you've been to me!"

"I was so in love with you," he heard himself say.

She shook her head sadly and made no reply.

He: "Have you completely forgotten the things we did together—that you gave yourself to me and everything? Have you forgotten that?"

"I shouldn't really stand here any longer," whispered Lovise Magrete, and looked about her fearfully.

"And don't you remember what you said the morning after?"

"What was that?"

"You said you'd have liked me to stay with you longer."

She sighed. "Yes, but he was coming home, you know. We couldn't have gone on. Now I must go."

"Ah, yes," said Edevart, hurt. "Go back to that husband of yours."

She started. "He's not as wild as you think, Edevart. You should have answered him and talked to him. You didn't treat him in the right way."

Edevart grew deathly pale. Furiously he said: "What the hell do I care about treating that man in the right way, as you put it! Just let him try anything!"

"No, no, no, Edevart! You must watch out for him! Listen to me! I'm so afraid!"

"Ha! I know well enough he uses a knife . . ."

"But then he was drunk," she said to excuse him. "And you have to remember it was for my sake, if you've heard about it. He didn't mean to take life. Even the man who died said that. He said he'd provoked Haakon and he called on God as his witness."

Edevart, still furious: "I'm not standing around here just to talk about him. He means no more to me than this pair of old boots. And you can tell him that from me."

"Edevart, please be nice to me now!" Lovise Magrete entreated, placing her hand on his arm. "You'll soon find some other girl, and you'll not care about me any more . . . There he is!" she whispered in terror and at once ran toward the door of the servants' hall.

Haakon came to meet her and asked her who she'd been standing talking to. Edevart did not hear her reply; but in the lamplight from the passage he saw Haakon tear himself away from her and make toward him.

It was a very short scuffle. They wasted no words but flew at each other like madmen. Edevart's towering rage proved decisive. Not a blow was needed; just that old trick with the foot, that wrestler's throw, and a thump under the ear from that heavy young fist. These were sufficient, and Haakon lay crumpled in the snow.

Lovise Magrete had raised the alarm in the hall. The dancers came running out and surrounded the two men; but it was too late and they were cheated of their entertainment. They did not look too kindly on Edevart. This stranger from Nordland had risen too rapidly, from casual laborer to store assistant. And now he had laid out their musician and spoiled the dancing. They muttered threateningly and began siding with Haakon. In spite of everything, he was no interloper but one of them. They began closing in on Edevart. That made no difference. He just stood there, not budging an inch. One young man from the village came a bit too close and was given a word of warning. They had of course all been drinking. Haakon Doppen had been drinking and was a bit shaky on his legs; otherwise, he would have made a better showing. He laughed, bewildered and embarrassed, as he got up. Lovise Magrete brushed the snow off him.

"We're not finished yet," he said, turning to Edevart. Those few moments in the snow had sobered him and hardened him. He began to leap about. Lovise Magrete screamed and some of his friends tried to restrain him. There was confusion and uproar. Edevart stood there, silent.

"What's all this?" a voice suddenly demanded. It was Knoff. He looked from one to the other.

"It's nothing," somebody answered. Others thought it more prudent to tell the boss the truth, seeing that he had promoted the stranger and might be expected to stand by him. "It's only Haakon Doppen shooting off his mouth, nothing serious."

Knoff glanced at Haakon and said: "If you want to stay till tomorrow, take yourself off to bed!"

"I can just as well go home tonight," said Haakon bad-temperedly.

"As you will!" said Knoff, and left.

The respect for the master was such that his word prevailed. Haakon was taken off to bed and the place grew quiet.

Edevart wandered about for a long time in the moonlight. After all that had happened to him, he should have been sensible and gone to bed himself. But there were still lights here and there in the houses, and there was a light still on in the little building they kept especially for putting up casual visitors. So what about these lights? Nothing, only that it still wasn't very late and he was probably hoping that Lovise Magrete might appear and talk to him some more. Oh, the craving he felt! The sense of being captive! Naturally, Lovise Magrete would be staying in that little building with her husband and she wouldn't want to come out. And what if she did come out? Did he expect her to look at him with ecstatic eyes because he had beaten up her husband? She wouldn't even appreciate his courage—all that manliness thrown away!

No, he meant nothing to her any more. August would have said: "Good luck and goodbye!" and been unmoved. Edevart grew soft and sentimental. He felt sorry for himself and grieved. In this languid mood following the great excitement, he began to wonder whether Lovise Magrete had any fire in her stove in there. There was no smoke visible from her chimney, yet she had had snow over her legs and her dress during the day and she might well want to dry her clothes.

Good night! he thought, and left.

He considered taking a turn down by the waterfront to pass the time. What was he doing here anyway in these strange parts? He might have been at home in Polden, winter fishing in the Lofotens, and summer fishing for coal fish in Vesteraal; he might have gone seine fishing for herring; he might have gone fishing in Finmark. Many, many were the things he might have thought of doing, and lived his life in peace. Then he might have married little Ragna and taken over the homestead after his parents, kept a few animals, and grown enough potatoes and grain for his domestic needs—aye, and never been forced to wander the winter night through, tormented by grief and love.

He walked on, feeling so forlorn that he grew homesick. He wanted to go back home. The village might be poor, but it was bright and friendly in summer, and full of fairy folk and fanciful legend in winter. Never was there a place like it! Even in little things: like how prettily Ragna opened her mouth when she laughed, both as a child and the whole time she was growing up. But then all the children back home laughed prettily. And if he were to turn his attention to bigger things, too: where in the whole wide world were the mountains as beautiful as they were at home? Nowhere! Already in March came the starling, and shortly afterward the wild goose. Ah, God! that marvelous wedge-shaped flight of beating wings and bird cries across the sky at which he took off his cap and stood in silence as his father and mother had taught him! Ah, yes, he wanted to go home. He *would* go home, would sail north on Knoff's sloop and then make for home from Lofoten. He could be there in a few months. By then the hare and the ptarmigan in the forest would already be starting to turn brown, and the water in the beck would throb beneath the ice, and the willow would be in bud . . . And what were those little birds that used to swarm around the houses and which he couldn't remember having seen here down south? Ridiculously small they were, mere yellow-and-gray nothings! He felt the deepest sympathy for these poor creatures—it was unbelievable what they suffered from hunger in the winter. Edevart felt his eyes fill with tears as he walked, and he said angrily and harshly to himself: "Just a few paltry birds! Makes no difference whether there are any left at home or not! They were only brown sparrows and gray sparrows, lousy little birds, do you hear!"

Noisily he cleared his throat and only saved the situation by breaking into a snatch of song.

"Is that you out singing at this late hour?" a voice asked.

He had arrived back at the estate buildings and had run into Miss Ellingsen, the housekeeper, at the corner of the servants' quarters. A shudder ran through him. She was wearing a fur coat and seemed to have been out for some time. Was she there keeping an eye out for somebody? Did she know why he was wandering about?

"Yes, it's me out singing," he answered. "I couldn't remember if both the warehouse doors had been shut, so I went down to see. You are out quite late yourself."

"To get some air. I'm in the house all day."

He made to walk on past her.

"That was quite a flare-up a little while ago," she said. "You ran foul of that Haakon Doppen?"

"It was nothing."

"I think it was quite something, so help me! You're a brave lad to do a thing like that!"

"He was drunk and stupid," said Edevart deprecatingly, though inwardly he swelled with pride at the housekeeper's praise. Here was somebody who admired him. Indeed, Miss Ellingsen wasn't all bad. She was young and capable, saw to the daily running of that large house herself, and had several girls under her. Nice-looking? Nice figure, good carriage, brown eyes, firm breasts. And now there was this new and splendid fragrance she had taken on and which Edevart breathed in deeply.

"You must watch out for him," she said. "You know what he's done, I suppose?"

"Yes," he said offhandedly. "But he's not dangerous," he added, feeling very superior.

Miss Ellingsen: "You know his wife?"

137

"Not really . . . I worked at her place a while last autumn. She needed help badly."

"Did you like her?"

There was no doubt that Miss Ellingsen smelled a rat. She had probably been watching what he had done, listened to his conversation with Lovise Magrete, perhaps observed the fight from some window.

"Did I like her?" he replied. "I'm sorry for the woman. Yet she doesn't complain. She never says a bad word about her husband."

"You mustn't stand there freezing," said the girl. "Look now, let me . . ." She tried to put her fur wrap around him, but he smiled and pushed it away. She wanted him to go into the house and was very solicitous about him. "Off you go to bed now," she said. "I'll see you to your door!" And at the door she said . . . Miss Ellingsen, this naughty, skittish little imp of a girl, said: "Good night! Aren't you going to ask me in?"

He gaped at her. "What . . . ?"

"Ha! ha! ha!" she laughed and was gone.

Toward morning Edevart was wakened by snow being thrown at his window. Both he and his roommate, the baker, leaped up and looked out, but nobody was to be seen outside. The moon had dropped behind the mountain, and it was still not daylight yet. Edevart threw on some clothes and rushed out. The craving he felt! The sense of being captive! A desperate hope flared up in him again. Indeed, she stood waiting at the corner of the house, her heart in her mouth, waiting.

"You must stay awake," she said.

"I am awake," he answered in astonishment.

"Because now he's mad! He drank too much!"

"Was this what you wanted me for?" he asked, immediately grateful. "You wanted to save me?"

"No. Well, yes, that too! Just as long as you stay awake. I'm so afraid!" She stood for a moment, then ran back to the guest lodging.

Naturally, it was her husband she wanted to save, save from getting mixed up in something else! She didn't want him going to jail again! Edevart went back to his bed and lay there the rest of the night telling himself that all he wanted was to leave this miserable place and get back home to Polden as soon as he could manage it. He'd now had a letter from his father thanking him for the money: it was a fine present and a great help. It would go toward food for the winter and a new turf roof for the storehouse, which had been leaking, and, besides that, on some nice dresses for the little girls—Josefine, the girl from Kleiva who was so capable, had made them up. The letter had been written by Joakim, who was an adept at reading and writing, much better than Edevart, a freckled and formidably smart lad who was also good at wrestling holds and throws. About himself Joakim wrote that he'd joined Karolus's crew for the Lofoten fishing, and after that he wanted to go seine fishing if there was any chance of herring. He was fourteen on the fourth of August, but was accepted for confirmation ahead of time, and was to have full seaman's rates on the Lofoten trip.

Yes, indeed, Joakim was all right. Edevart had no doubts as far as he was concerned. You wouldn't find him daydreaming or getting involved in stupid schemes and going adrift.

In the morning Edevart took up his place in the store and began serving. Not many people were there. He saw Lovise Magrete and her husband in that long passage out where the stoves and the spades and other ironmongery were kept. She clung to his arm and seemed to want him to leave. Instead, he came into the store and stood by the counter. He put his bag down.

"We'll be going at once," said Lovise Magrete. "It's just that we forgot something yesterday."

Haakon must have slept off the worst. He looked shamefaced, and his eyes were red-rimmed. He wasn't exactly friendly, but he asked for the things he needed and paid without fuss. The red-haired girl he had talked to yesterday came in and began buying from one of the other assistants. Lovise Magrete paled when she saw her and interposed herself between her and Haakon. But this was doubtless nothing more than dislike and foolish jealousy on the part of Lovise Magrete.

Edevart couldn't help feeling sorry for Haakon for a moment. He, too, had been thinking things over that night: it wasn't altogether unreasonable for Haakon Doppen to suspect him and to feel hostility toward him. Edevart himself would have been furious in similar circumstances. He had, after all, lived for several weeks in the same house as Lovise Magrete, and had only been sent away a few days before her husband returned home. Haakon was within his rights.

"That was a sudden stop to your dancing last night!" It was Haakon talking to the redheaded girl.

"Yes," she answered, smiling. "How did that happen?"

"Ask him over there, the one with the gold rings!"

Lovise Magrete: "Please now, try to be nice!"

Haakon did as he was told; mildly he turned to Edevart and said: "We weren't very good friends yesterday, were we, comrade?"

Edevart, still feeling sorry for him, simply murmured: "It was nothing."

This answer must have irritated Haakon. He wasn't easy to talk to today, and now this red-haired girl was standing there listening. That a fight with him should be considered nothing was an affront to his manhood. This man, Edevart, and the girl visitor must not get the impression that it would always be as easy to beat him as it had been the previous evening. He said: "I wouldn't say it was nothing exactly, eh?"

Edevart did not reply.

"And more can come of it!" said Haakon, laughing in the direction of the girl.

Lovise Magrete: "We're ready to go now!"

Haakon looked at her: "Oh, yes, Lovise Magrete! I suppose I'm not all I should be. I'm not one of your dandies with four gold rings on his fingers like some I could mention . . ."

"Dear God! Haakon . . . !" she moaned.

Haakon quickly threw his bag over his shoulder and went out through the door with her. Edevart heard him say as they crossed the room: "All I want to know is whether he needed all those gold rings when he was working up at my place."

Thus passed the Christmas shopping, then January and a little of February. Edevart was now given the task of supervising various things aboard the sloop in readiness for her departure. "Who is to be skipper?" he asked.

"A man is coming," Knoff answered.

In any case, Knoff had no time for getting mixed up in such petty details now. A man was apparently coming. Perhaps he would come; perhaps he wouldn't. Knoff was occupied. You could see how busy he was with his own horses, as well as with other hired horses from the village, hauling stones from a scree way up the mountainside. Stone upon stone, huge blocks of rock, transported out to the farthermost warehouse and meant for the construction of a quayside. Knoff blessed the fact that snow and frost and settled weather made for good transporting conditions. It would greatly serve the future quayside to have all those stones piled one on top of the other in a straight line. The long outer wall beyond the seabed shelf would already be thirty feet below water. They would have to bring divers from Trondheim for this part of the work—as well as masons and laborers and huge cranes and barges and rolling stock. The cost? Colossal! Knoff already had a foretaste of the cost when, on Saturdays, he now had to pay the wages of ten men and their horses for hauling stone, as well as another ten men who did the blasting and who split the blocks and loaded them for transport.

When the vessels were ready to sail, Edevart was given the task of signing on a crew for the sloop; and when he objected that this was the skipper's job, Knoff hemmed and hawed. The skipper seemingly wasn't coming. No, the man he'd had his eye on had dropped out. There was nothing else for it but that Edevart should take over.

"I can't," said Edevart.

Knoff looked at his watch, for time was short. But he explained: "All you have to do is follow the schooner. It has my regular skipper aboard. Anyway, didn't you tell me you'd been in the Lofotens before, buying fish. Fine! Buy fish! You'll get money from the schooner. Settle up with the skipper there!"

As Edevart continued to object, Knoff replied: "You don't want the sloop to stay tied up here, do you?"

"No, but . . ."

"I haven't time to stand around here. Take the sloop."

The position he had been given was a great honor, and Edevart resisted no longer. Of course, August had taught him how to sail a sloop. No problem there. And he was sufficiently familiar with the charts to be able to manage a Nordland voyage. He decided to risk it.

He caught up with Knoff and said: "You've an old seine net hanging up in the warehouse. What do you want for it?"

"That herring net? What do you want to do with it?"

"I just want it."

Knoff thought a moment and said: "All right. Take it. We can agree on a price later."

Yet more evidence of the great confidence the boss had in him. Not everybody would have had a herring net handed over merely for the asking. But then not everybody had brilliant ideas about building a quay, as Edevart had.

The final days had arrived. Everything had to be seen to; and provisions and the brandy cask and the biscuits and a great mass of salt had to be taken aboard. Edevart also had to take leave properly of Miss Ellingsen. This couldn't be evaded. He had enjoyed her company several times recently and was damned if he could understand her, but she had attached an exaggerated importance to their friendship as though it were meant to last forever. He didn't care all that much for Miss Ellingsen, and was certainly not in love with her, merely very proud that a woman who was a housekeeper should want anything to do with him. She hadn't so much as glanced at any of the other lads in the store, only at him. This increased his self-confidence.

He immediately found himself on good terms with Skipper Norem on the schooner. He was a grizzled elderly man, prosperous, who had a small farm at the top end of the village. Edevart was invited to his house and spent a whole day and night there with an abundance of food and drink. It dawned on Edevart later what all this friendliness signified. The skipper had only sons; it wasn't therefore that he was seeking to marry off a daughter, but he wanted to be sure of Edevart's goodwill in another matter.

Then they sailed, the schooner leading and the sloop *Hermine*, skipper Edevart Andreassen, following. There was no problem: nothing but fair weather, starry nights, and lazy days. Edevart stopped off at Bodø and bought new presents for the people back home: a skirt and a cape for his mother, shoes and various little things for the others. It gladdened his heart to weigh these things in his hands and imagine to himself how they would be received—his sisters would come and hold out their little hands to thank him.

A good three weeks the voyage lasted, because the weather had been too fine and calm. Eventually they reached Skroven, that ancient wealthy place. Edevart was on familiar ground. The fishing had only just begun; there were few people about, not many buyers. Following Knoff's orders, they were at all times to keep themselves informed about the catches in West Lofoten, and if need be sail west.

When Karolus arrived with his eight-oared boat and its crew, Edevart tingled with excitement. These were neighbors and people he knew from Polden. His brother, Joakim, had grown into a real man, with the family's huge fists but with his own round, freckled face. What a reunion and what a surprise it was! The people from Polden couldn't believe that it was Edevart who was in command of this sloop and who was to buy their fish. It was terrific! And how had it happened? He must have inherited from some Englishman! He must have been in the land of Canaan! The whole crew came aboard and had drinks and refreshments. Teodor came along, too, the one with the rupture. Since he had taken part in the voyage to Bergen and was thus the most experienced of them, he was well placed to talk about Edevart. He said: "What I've seen of him, he can turn his hand to anything!" Teodor asked after August.

"Ah! August!" said Edevart. "He's a miracle! Put him on an island in the sea and he'll grow wings and fly ashore! One minute he's in Riga, then he's in Levanger. And he grows richer and richer every time."

The fishermen stared wide-eyed at Edevart's finery and he had to show off his snake ring to prove that it had three coils. Karolus said: "This is how it is when somebody makes his way in the world!" One of the crew, old Martinus Halskar, responded thus: "Ah, yes, Karolus, but then you've become the village spokesman and all sorts of things, and the rest of us think you've done well. But what are we? Dust and ashes!"

They asked Edevart if he would be coming to Polden to dry his fish, and he said he was. They asked what he would be paying a day, and he said he'd be paying the same as at the other drying grounds. Thereupon they thanked him and left.

Joakim remained behind on board. He brought news from home and couldn't thank his brother enough for the money he'd sent. The storehouse now had its new roof, and the little girls had fine dresses to go to church in. Mother had been in poor health this winter, and she was in bed when Joakim left; but she said herself that it was nothing serious. Father was well, and had inspected the telegraph line once during the winter. Apart from that, there had been no great changes in the village. Well, Karolus was now the district's chairman, for the local businessman who had been chairman before him wanted them to build a road but Karolus didn't think they could afford it, so he was elected. "But the thing about Karolus now," said Joakim, "is that his wife has changed so much."

"How?" Edevart asked with interest.

"She goes about mumbling to herself. She's become so simpleminded that people think she's been bewitched."

"Ane Maria?"

"Yes, can you believe it?" Joakim exclaimed. "She was so spirited and independent before. When the men were away during the winter she was quite capable of slaughtering a calf. Nobody understands it. Now she keeps hearing cries from the bog, and says it's Skaaro, whose soul can't find peace. When Karolus came home and got himself made chairman, she said he must set the whole district to work digging out the bog and recovering Skaaro's body. She takes it all so terribly hard, this business about Skaaro. After all, she did all she could to rescue him at the time. So it's really rather difficult for Karolus. He hardly dare leave home these days . . ."

Edevart showed off all the gifts he was meaning to bring home with him in the spring. He gave Joakim a shining new sheath knife and took him down into the hold and showed him the seine net. "See that seine?" he said. "You can have it!"

Joakim didn't understand. "Have it?" he asked, and began feeling the net. It lay there all heavy and brown, a great mountainous heap. Some seine net, indeed! "What's this? Surely that seine net is not for me?" he asked.

"You're to have it!" said Edevart, and swelled with pride.

Joakim was overwhelmed. "Well, I'll be . . . !"

They both laughed with tears in their eyes, so moved were they. It was almost too much for them. A fantastic vision rose up before Joakim's eyes: he was a seine owner, could stand in a circle of men and set each man in his place, could put out the seine across an open channel and catch a fortune within it, for half the catch belonged to the seine owner . . . The brothers talked about the net, how long it was, where it came from, what it had cost. Joakim would really have liked to take it with him there and then. But a seine net is no pocket handkerchief; it's a whole boatload. They came to an agreement that Karolus would have to collect the seine with his eight-oar. They hired a place ashore to store it.

The days passed. The fishing was still poor and the weather changeable. Edevart had everything ready for splitting the fish and for storing the cod liver oil. The salt was at hand. Every day the man who was to split the fish fussed over his great heavy knives. But the fishing continued poor. Edevart bought everything he could get his hands on, but this hardly covered the bottom of the boat.

Skipper Norem came over and said he'd had reports that the fishing was no better westward of them; but then there were no buyers there either, so he thought it would be best if one of them were to sail west, and it might as well be the schooner. He handed some money over to Edevart, and spoke to him in a friendly and fatherly fashion. He had something in particular he wanted to say to Edevart . . . to say to his young friend . . . something they might agree on. Nothing all that important, but . . . He'd been with Knoff a long time, had been buying fish for the last twelve years, and things had always gone all right. Well then, there was no reason for them to be any more stupid than the other skippers and not make something out of it for themselves. One vessel might pay a few pennies more, the other a few less, and the firm wouldn't be able to check the prices from day to day—that was impossible, and Knoff had other things on his mind . . .

When it came to the point, Skipper Norem was wanting to inquire ever so gently of Edevart whether they couldn't agree to cheat Knoff, cheat him on a very small and modest scale, over the buying. What did his young friend think about that?

To begin with, Edevart didn't answer.

The thing was that if they got the fish a couple of skilling cheaper, that money could be theirs, couldn't it?

"Of course," said Edevart. "But when is fish ever a couple of skilling cheaper? It never is. There's a standard daily price."

"Ah, yes!" said Norem in response to this vast inexperience. "But we are the ones who decide the day's price, and we can put it up a couple of skilling so that there can be something in it for us as well."

"Oh, so that's how it's done!" said Edevart. He remembered

what his friend August had hinted: that it was an accepted thing
to look after your own interests when doing the fish buying. The
methods seemed to be well known. August knew about them—
August knew all these sorts of things.

"Yes, that's how it's done," Norem continued. "Knoff will
never ask the other vessels how much they paid on such and such
a date last winter, and even if he did, he'd probably get the same
answer from them all, for the other skippers are doing the same
as us. I learned it from them."

"Well, if that's the way things go . . . !" Edevart said finally,
and did not resist.

Everything would be just fine, said Norem, this much re-
spected, prosperous man of property. All they had to do was
agree that one of them didn't enter one thing in the books and the
other something else. It would, in fact, help things now if the two
vessels parted company and the schooner sailed west; but they
had to take care that the differences in the fish prices didn't
become too great in the two places.

When Skipper Norem left, he held out his hand to his young
and very dear friend, and Edevart accepted it as a kind of oath of
agreement. What else was there to do? If he reported matters to
the firm, he'd never be believed, for Norem had been a long time
with Knoff. And why should Edevart want to be any better than
the others? Why should he stand in his own way? But of course
Norem was a cunning scoundrel who, by extending friendship
and the generous day-long hospitality of his home, had induced
others to be the same.

That's how people were.

Then the fishing began in earnest and lasted a fair time.
Edevart bought and bought, and those dear little extra skilling
lived happily in a secret drawer in his desk, their numbers in-
creasing all the time, until a severe storm unleashed itself about
the middle of March and put a stop to everything. Storm signals
were hoisted and remained there three days.

People long remembered that storm, an equinoctial fury that

shook the earth and struck terror to the heart. It began with an unusual calm: all around everything was dead, even the seabirds were silent, and the world seemed swathed and muffled. This heavy immobility was almost the worst: it alone seemed to exist, a state of things beyond man's comprehension. For twelve hours the world seemed stuck fast, out of order, an aberration enough to send the senses drunkenly reeling. Then a poor little blade of grass on a fisherman's turf roof begins to tremble; then comes a puff of wind; the stillness has sprung a leak; the sea lives again. Somewhere far distant something is coming, coming as though being trailed along, a torrent of approaching sound, coming, coming. Bringing in first one flute, then the shrill whine of other pipes, bringing in bassoons, organs, roaring and raging. Within a couple of hours the sea was in a mad white fury.

Things did not go so badly for the people, however, for they had had twelve hours in which to secure their equipment. The roofs of some of the houses and cottages they made fast with hawsers. By the third day the worst was over; all that remained was the ceaseless booming of the sea and a half moon running aslant among the clouds and looking like a squinting eye. The storm signals were hauled down.

It took a week before the fishing got properly started again, and this was in fact the fault of the fishermen themselves. They sought fish in the area where they had been before, but it wasn't there. They went looking farther out, but no. So they turned and came back in and found the shoals as they were making their way out again. It seems they had made toward land to shelter from the storm. For a few weeks then the fishing was good and Edevart bought and bought. The extra skilling became banknotes, and the banknotes the beginnings of a fat wallet.

At Easter Karolus and his crew paid a visit home. Karolus wanted to see if his wife was any better. Joakim seized this opportunity of having his seine net transported back home across Vestfjord in the eight-oar boat. Edevart sent a few daler of his "extras" back with him to his father—that father who practically never said a word but merely shook his head, overcome, at every little help he received!

But Easter came and went and Karolus and his crew did not return. The fishing had already started again after the holidays and Edevart was again buying, but it was a week after Easter and still there was no sign of Karolus at Skroven. What could be wrong? Edevart telegraphed, but did not get any answer until the tenth day after Easter. The reply was from Joakim. He had already made a catch with the seine; it was in Hommelvik outside Polden. Really fine herring, a pretty big catch, already a couple of buyers, salt and barrels also arrived. The crew would not be returning to Skroven that winter. Best wishes . . .

A good deal was said and written about that herring catch. It was the will of providence, a sign from heaven, a fairy tale.

Joakim, the young devil, certainly had eyes in his head. Moreover, he could think of nothing else but the seine net. As they were passing Hommelvik on the way home, he saw some birds and the spouts of a couple of whales making toward the coast. Joakim had been out herring fishing the year before and he recognized the signs. He called to Karolus to stop and haul. Karolus was at first reluctant. He was in a hurry to get back to Ane Maria. But whales and birds are things every Nordlander is interested in. He gave in. They conferred for a minute; they had to act quickly. How they were ever able to lay hands on a four-oar boat in Outer Polden, how they ever succeeded in making one end of the seine rope fast to a rock ashore and got ready to receive the shoal at just the right moment was something they marveled at afterward. The whales and the birds came driving in—they mustn't turn away now! Joakim, very much the seine owner, very much in charge, waited for the decisive second. He wanted to cut through the shoal in a great arc and run the net from shore to shore. The birds were already overhead; they were surrounded on all sides by herring.

"Row!" Joakim ordered, and every man lay on his oar. They were literally rowing in herring; the boat tilted as though running aground. Karolus thought they were making too small an arc and wouldn't take in enough of the shoal. But Joakim, still very much in command, shouted and pointed: "Make in again! Right! Now straight ahead! I don't want the whales as part of the catch!"

It was a miracle the way things went. The shoal divided up just the way the seine had split it, and the whales followed the arm which again swung out to sea. When they reached the shore on the other side of the bay, there were still a few fathoms of net to spare.

The catch had been made, but they worked until evening making things secure. They had no water glass, but they knew from before that the bottom was clean and white in Hommelvik. They attended to one or two places in the net where they feared it might be torn; and they reinforced the ropes going ashore because of the enormous weight of the herring. So long as the seine now held!

The catch had been made. The crew had had an enormous stroke of luck. As far as Karolus and the other men of experience could tell, it must have been that selfsame blessed storm at work here, too, driving whales and herring in toward the coast. In Polden, people had many somber and uncanny things to tell of those days of storm: how they had heard the heavens roar as never before, how they had lived through a storm so violent they had never known the like of it. A woman had been hauling wood from the forest, and both she and the horse had been blown right over; a roof here and a house there had gone flying into the sea—no wonder, then, that people wept and clung fast to each other and prayed to God. And no wonder, either, that Ane Maria, who was already somewhat deranged, very nearly broke down altogether and went to bed with a gag over her mouth as though to keep herself from screaming something out loud.

Oh, but scarcely was the hurricane past when people got up again, rather embarrassed at having prayed to God. But that wasn't all. When Karolus and his crew came home with fish scales on their clothes, after having made a great catch right off Polden and with the prospect of making a lot of money, everybody's spirits rose in that poverty-ridden village. Even Ane Maria got up from her bed, removed the gag from her mouth, and for a time was as cheerful as all the rest.

8   THE DANGER THREATENING THE CATCH WAS THAT WINTER was already almost over, and the thing was to act quickly before the herring were attacked by parasites. In any case, they wouldn't live long with nothing to feed on in Hommelvik.

That night Joakim hurried to the local storekeeper to get him to telegraph and spread the news and organize salt and barrels. Gabrielsen, the storekeeper, had taken umbrage at having been defeated in the recent election for the district chairmanship and said: "Why don't you go and ask the new chairman?" Actually, they both laughed a little at the idea, and it finished up with Gabrielsen taking charge of the whole business. It was late at night, but telegrams were sent out in all directions. By Easter Monday a little cargo steamer had already arrived at Hommelvik and was loading herring; and the next day two sailing vessels arrived.

The folks of Polden had no Easter to speak of that year; none of the usual snoozing, no lazing around, no churchgoing. They gutted and salted and laid down herring from dawn till dusk. In time several vessels arrived. There was such life and bustle that it even drew in people from the neighboring districts. Money? Money rained down! It came with the boats, and it came by post and telegraph. Hommelvik became a place of note; the cottages and the haylofts served as accommodation for herring workers. It was pennies from heaven. The housewife charged two skilling a night for each guest, and the daughter of the house went prancing around engaged to two of the workers at once, even though she was only sixteen.

And of course Gabrielsen, the storekeeper, would not let this incomparable opportunity pass without exploiting it. He had stocked up with goods from one ship after another, but that didn't suffice. It was gone before the next ship arrived. Finally he sent his wife off to Trondheim and got her to buy up masses of fabric and glassware and sweetmeats, rugs and long-stemmed pipes and silk scarves, even fiddles and barrel organs. These she bought and brought home with her. But then Gabrielsen's little store proved to be too small; it wasn't big enough to take all these goods. He had to build on. From the south came planks and boards and carpenters; they worked for several weeks, and they erected a building the likes of which Gabrielsen himself had never dreamed of owning. In this way, one advance followed another. People found they could afford to buy expensive things, and dressed themselves in the imported fabrics which Gabrielsen sold. His servant girl Olga, who earlier had owned a beaded belt, now had a crinoline and factory-made stockings, no less. Fashion decreed waistcoats in imitation astrakhan and string mittens for Sunday wear. Fruit wine from the cask was no longer acceptable; wine arrived in crates from the south, the bottles all gold and colored labels. Previously weddings were the only great festive occasions; now feasts were introduced for baptisms, confirmations, and funerals. Gabrielsen stood there in his new premises endlessly selling Roquefort cheese from France and Danish eggs for these parties, and thus raising the standard of living for miles around . . .

The weeks slipped by as though on wheels; and Joakim, always very much the seine owner, very much in command, slept no more than was absolutely necessary. His whole time was spent working on the herrings. He had plunged into this fabulous undertaking and could think of nothing else. No wonder it took him till the tenth day after Easter to report to Edevart. He was so young, so taken up by it all; moreover, his new sense of importance had quite gone to his head. He already had all the young girls eyeing him, even though he was only fifteen and freckled. And he had men old enough to be his father taking orders from him. He had got himself a man-size coat, which was too big for his youth's trousers, which were themselves too short—but what did details like that matter! He sold his herring and kept a close eye on things. Eventually, he had to lower his prices a little. But he was a demon when it came to writing and doing sums, and nobody could put anything over on him. How remarkable that this was young Joakim, who only a few years ago had been running around with a runny nose and was always cutting new teeth! With God's help he had become the miracle man of the village. Every household had somebody in his employ, and his own little sisters stood and cleaned and salted herring and earned money, even though they could scarcely reach the bottom of the barrel. Young Joakim had with God's help created a time of greatness for all, a golden age—the only thing was that his mother lay there in pain and was unable to die.

The last remaining herring went bad. That was only to be expected, with spring sunshine and the snow already melting in late April. Joakim now sold herring for lamp oil. He let the people of Polden have herring for animal feedstuff, which was a blessing at this difficult time of the year. The beasts stood up to their ears in herring; the milk tasted of herring, the pork tasted of herring. Gabrielsen kept chickens, and their eggs tasted of herring. Finally the bottom of the seine was scraped, and this time the herring went as fertilizer.

All in all, great days, golden days. True, Hommelvik once again lay deserted, but what did that matter? For then along came Edevart with the sloop and anchored at Polden.

Edevart came too late to delight his mother with the fine cape and dress he had brought. Two days earlier and she would have glanced distantly at his presents and smiled—an infinitely tender smile to her son for the last time. Edevart stood there with his gifts, yet also somehow empty-handed. He deeply regretted his long neglect of her. With a few warm clothes he might perhaps have saved his mother; but he had thrown away those Bergen presents in that love affair at Fosenland. If only he'd made it good again in Trondheim by sending a big parcel, or better still a packing case! He'd thought of it now and then, but in the end forgot.

He gave his little sisters the shoes and the other little things he'd bought for them. Of course there was great excitement and they were very pleased. Yet at the same time . . . at the same time he was too late here as well. The little girls had themselves been earning money and they could buy shoes and other little things for themselves at Gabrielsen's store. They had, in fact, already started to do so. No longer were they bare at the neck; they had little scarves around their necks, little blue silk scarves indeed. So what could they do with the blue silk scarves which their brother Edevart had brought? If only he'd brought red ones! "Yes, but mine were bought in town," said Edevart. And in depression, in despair, he added: "Wait! I've something else!" He happened to remember the little gold medallion. He'd wanted to give this away, too. It hadn't been his fault that Lovise Magrete hadn't dared accept it.

"I brought this for you!" he said to the older sister. Now there was a light in her eye and her lips trembled. His other sister sat there making pleased noises, but her lips were not trembling. Edevart drew his snake ring off his finger and put it in her hand: "That's for you!"

The little girl was filled with confusion and wonderment. A triple coiled ring, a snake's head, gold—what should she do with it? "It's to wear around your neck on a cord," he said. And he added what he imagined August would have said: "That's what they do in Russia!"

"Oh!" said the sisters.

Edevart realized that something was wrong, so he continued: "But if you would perhaps rather wear it on your finger, all you need to do is squeeze it together a bit, like this, and then you get four coils out of it!"

The sisters watched excitedly as he squeezed the ring. They tried it, and indeed it almost went into four coils. It covered the entire length of her tiny finger. But it was still too slack. "Then the best thing I can think of is that you two should swap," he said to his sisters. And they followed their big brother's suggestion.

But the presents had been a flop. The one thing that had meant anything had been the few daler he had given to his father out of the "extras." They came in useful. There was the cost of the funeral: the priest would want a daler for meeting the body at the churchyard gate and accompanying it to the grave, and another daler for the address. Anyway, Joakim insisted on paying for everything.

All in all, Edevart had found his homecoming a disappointment. He no longer found the old simple faith; the homeliness had disappeared; innocence was rarer. People thought differently. Admittedly, deep down the girls were genuinely pleased with their presents of gold. You wouldn't have expected otherwise! But they had thanked him without coming over and shaking hands with him. They'd always done that before. They'd held out their little hands, and there was a catch in one's throat. Now they merely said "Thanks!" His father had shaken hands when he got his couple of daler. He was old-fashioned and unspoiled. He said nothing, too overcome to say anything. But he shook hands. No, there was something wrong!

Edevart said to Joakim: "I think you've completely ruined the people here with this herring catch of yours!" What in fact had happened was that nobody in Polden had any inclination to earn anything from drying fish. No, they were used to better things. They had earned double from the herring.

No sooner did Edevart seek to have his cargo unloaded than Karolus and one or two others presented themselves with a demand for higher wages. "But we agreed on a price in Skroven," said Edevart. "Yes, but times have changed," they replied in their new prosperity. They demanded still higher rates this year because times had changed. Edevart then threatened to take his schooner elsewhere. "Where?" they asked, knowing that all the neighboring grounds were booked. "South," Edevart replied. "Do as you will!" said the people of Polden, for they were now so prosperous they had no objection to taking the summer off and not bothering to do anything. Joakim and his crew in particular were very unconcerned about fish drying. So Edevart had to telegraph his firm to see if he ought to sail south; and Knoff replied that there was a risk that all the drying grounds farther south were booked, but he nevertheless left things entirely in Edevart's hands. What happened in the end was that the sloop *Hermine* had to pay more in rent and higher wages in Polden, rather than run the risk of being turned away farther south.

No, Polden was not the place it had been before. The spirit had changed. Even Joakim had had too great fortune, and it was too much for him. Edevart offered him a place on his crew—he had sent home the two men from Fosenland and needed a man. He said: "You can have the same job as I had with August aboard *The Seagull.*" No, Joakim turned the offer down. He'd got a taste for being the big man who owned the seine net and made herring catches. That summer he was planning to go to Vesteraal with that end in view. He had already contracted for a boat and he was making thorough preparations. Edevart couldn't help getting angry at his brother, young hothead that he was, pretending to be a grown man. "How much money have you left?" he asked. Joakim told him. "Then it's best I put it away safely for you." Well, Joakim handed over as much of the money as he could spare; he would rather have had it in his own pocket, he would indeed; but Edevart was his big brother and had been in Bergen and everything. Apart from that, the net had come from him in the first place.

The work of cleaning the fish was slow going, and Edevart had expected more goodwill from his fellow villagers. Now that he had met their demands and increased the wages, what was stopping them? They came late in the mornings and finished early in the evenings; they came and went as though they were their own masters. Admittedly they were paid accordingly; they got so much and no more for every "fisherman's hundred" fish that they cleaned. But Edevart wasn't at all pleased to see the work dragging on like that. Delay cost money. He also felt that his personal status suffered.

He criticized them for dawdling. They replied that it was a foul job dealing with all that raw salted fish; it made their hands all swollen and made their clothes filthy. Edevart suggested that the work was no worse this year than last. But it seemed it was. It had got worse. For one thing, times had changed; for another, the fish were bigger this year, with a lot of cusk and ling, and heavier on salt.

"Ah, yes!" Edevart nodded, with all the solemnity of an elder. "There could well be seven lean years in Polden yet!" At this they became offended; and hinting at the fact that he had been turned down for confirmation the first time, they asked him maliciously how it was he could remember so much of his book learning, heh! heh! Edevart bit his lip and didn't answer; but he began to get an uncomfortable feeling that it was perhaps better at Fosenland among strangers than it was here at home in Polden. Surely it was better? There he had risen to the position of shop assistant and had eaten at a rich man's table.

If only August had been here! He would certainly have taught the men to obey orders, if necessary with a revolver in his hand. They wouldn't have got very far with him. Nobody knew everything about August. He was from the mists and from the deep. Perhaps he'd also studied at the School of Wittenberg.

Things might have looked bad for the fish cleaning if Beret hadn't stepped in. She was a good lass, sure enough—young and lively, married to a quiet-mannered little man. She brought Josefine along with her, the young widow from Kleiva; and these two set about the job really stoutheartedly, standing knee-deep in the sea and cleaning the fish. They earned masses, indeed they did. Edevart kept them liberally supplied with drams and salt biscuits; for did they not work all-out, putting the men to shame? These two young women, whose reputations were not of the best and who were indeed probably among the more wayward, proved to be the quickest and the cleverest at all sorts of work. Could this be in order to attract Edevart, this young skipper now in his eighteenth year? Was it so that they might be picked as stackers later in the summer when the fish was dry, and might find their way into the cabin and widen their experience? However it was, they certainly cleaned the fish and finished the job, and the sloop *Hermine* was sluiced clean.

Then began the routine work of drying the fish. From then on, the menfolk were less frequently seen on the drying grounds, and the work was taken over by the mothers and children. Edevart's younger sisters also took part. Edevart was the only man around to deal with things on board and on shore. He should have scraped and painted the sloop, but that had to be put off. It was more essential to get the fish dried. He should have had somebody to cook his meals for him; but he just had to make the best of it. He lived on dried foods and coffee and did not complain. Naturally his face became somewhat drawn and he didn't laugh very often, only when it was absolutely necessary. But it did him no harm to take things seriously. A heavy responsibility rested on him; he had a valuable cargo on his hands. All his knowledge of fish drying came from the previous year when he had worked with August. It did not amount to particularly wide experience, but it was a good basis at any rate, and he did not spare himself when it came to learning more. Many were the night hours when he lay awake; and even on Sundays he was ashore seeing to the fish.

The seine crew had gone out on spec since there were no reports of herring sightings. Karolus could safely leave his wife now. She had got over her sickness and was eating and sleeping. Spring had come, the days were lighter, and there was money in the house. Ane Maria looked young and pretty again. She had even been up to Gabrielsen's store and bought herself one or two things to wear. She appeared at the drying grounds, not because she had to, but just to be where the others were and show them that she wasn't "odd" any longer. And she had become so very pretty these last few weeks, had Ane Maria. Quite luscious, indeed. They talked to her as though nothing had happened and she answered them sensibly. She smiled indulgently when the others made some rather crude jokes. So she must have been quite well again.

Then something happened. Nothing much. A minor matter.

An old woman, Ragna's grandmother, had arrived at the drying grounds. She was old and shrunken about the face and had tiny hands. She had brought Ragna up as a child. This old grandmother wasn't much use in the work, and she hadn't been there last year, either. But this year, when she was even older, she appeared one morning and stood there saying nothing. Well, she was given a job to do—the lightest work Edevart could think to put her to.

One day he asked her: "Why doesn't Ragna come and work here?"

"No" was all the old woman said.

"Is she sick? Is she not at home?"

"Yes, she's home."

Since that was all the answer he was going to get, he said: "Ah, well! I was only thinking she might have been here along with the rest of us."

"No," said the woman, and shook her head.

There was probably something wrong with Ragna. God knew. But he was preoccupied with important matters of his own, so he didn't ask any more.

The following day was Sunday, and as usual he had rowed ashore to see to the fish. A woman came walking toward him. She had gone around the outskirts of Polden, a long way. That looks to me like Ragna, he thought. It is indeed Ragna! Once he'd been in love with her; she was the prettiest girl at school. And here she was. He busied himself with some of the fish so that he wouldn't have to stand there staring at her. But when she was near enough, he said: "Well now! Look who's out taking a walk!"

Ah, youth! They both turned scarlet.

She kept her face turned away for the most part and she didn't say very much. But he realized she had heard he'd been asking after her the previous day. Since they were both too embarrassed to know what to say to each other, he suddenly invited her with a kind of captain's pride to come aboard his ship. "You can make us a cup of coffee," he said.

She excused herself. No, she was only taking this little walk because it was Sunday; anyway, she wasn't properly dressed for it.

He looked at her, stupefied. Had she gone crazy? Not well enough dressed?

"No," she said.

Eventually it dawned upon him why she was holding back; and remarked offhandedly that things were in a pretty awful mess on board—he hadn't even had any coffee yet today.

That worked. She felt sorry for him and said: "You poor man! Well, in that case . . ."

He rowed out with her to the ship. She found it a little awkward climbing the rope ladder, which swung this way and that; but she managed to get on deck and waited till he had made the boat fast. He showed her the galley and set about lighting a fire.

"I should be the one doing that," she said, trying to speak lightly. She sat down on the box of firewood and let him see to the fire.

Yes, he saw the change in her. You couldn't help noticing. The saddest thing was that even her pretty little face had become altered and coarse. How she must have suffered!

"You can grind," he said, handing her the coffee mill. "That's what I'm worst at!"

At this she laughed. Imagine, she could still laugh! He glanced at her. Yes, there was some small resemblance to her laughing eyes of old. He wanted to help her feel that she hadn't come aboard for nothing, so he said: "What I say is true. When I grind coffee, I get it all over my lap."

Then she laughed a little more and showed him how to hold his knee against the drawer so that it didn't slip out; and he was very grateful for this instruction and promised he would faithfully remember it. She asked if he had any cream. He hadn't, but she could have syrup if she liked. Thank you, yes!

They drank coffee on deck and had buttered biscuits with it. "That was good!" said Ragna gratefully. She declined the offer of a drink.

This good breakfast put life into them both, and they became more communicative. Not that they became what they had been to each other before. Far from it. Neither of them was what they were earlier. They had both seen something of life. He had been in love with her at school, as well as later; but it hadn't ever been serious, just kid's stuff. Now they sat here together, and it was pretty irrelevant to him what she had been through; he wanted to spare her and did not inquire too closely into it.

"Wouldn't you like to see my quarters?" he asked.

She would like that, and she went with him. This betokened no threat to her; she was taking no risk with Edevart, and there was no danger in it for him, either. She represented no attraction the way she was now.

She sat down on the bench in the ridiculously little hole of a cabin: there was the bunk, there was the table, there the stove, and there a cupboard. And that was the lot.

"I'm going to have a drink now whether you want one or not," said Edevart, all manly, and produced a bottle and some glasses. Well, yes, she would have a little of his not very strong brandy, and she thought it didn't taste at all bad. They went on talking a while about nothing in particular. I wonder why she's come, he thought. She asked him what time it was, and he told her. Perhaps if she were to stay on a little longer she could cook some dinner, suggested Skipper Edevart. She smiled and shook her head at such greed, asking whether he was hungry again already? Not exactly, but it would take time to cook it. What was he having for dinner? Ship's food—peas, beef, and pork.

Suddenly it was as if she couldn't bear it any longer, and she burst out: "Oh, now you must tell me what I ought to do!"

"What do you mean?"

"The fact that I am as you see me," she replied. "And have to live with it."

He realized that this was why she had come, but he shrank from hearing more, so he asked foolishly: "What are you rambling on about? Can't you take your drink?"

This compelled her to continue. "He doesn't want to know. He just laughs at me," she said.

When Edevart realized there was no avoiding it, he said: "Who is this all about?"

"You know—that skipper," she replied.

"Skipper? No, I don't know."

"That skipper last year. When you came and found us in the bushes."

Edevart, thoughtfully: "It couldn't be him."

"Why not? Certainly it's him."

"But you didn't want to! You were pushing him away when I arrived, weren't you?"

"Yes. But it's him all the same," she said stubbornly.

"I don't understand."

"My dear man! Who else could it be . . .!"

"All right," said Edevart, giving in. "All he does is laugh, you say?"

"Yes, he doesn't believe it. He thinks, as you do, that it isn't him."

"Where have you met him since?"

"I've just been to see him. He's busy drying fish in Nordvaag this year."

"And he just laughs? Not that I'm saying anything about it!"

"What do you mean? Of course it's him!"

"How can you talk like that! Didn't I see you fighting to get away?"

Ragna was near to tears. "Yes, but that was when he wanted to do it a second time."

Edevart was silent for a long time. "So that's how it is!" he said.

So he had come too late that time! So why had he bothered! He recalled the events of the previous year: there had been a fire in Karolus's barn and he'd run down to *The Seagull* for water containers; when he came back from the waterfront, he missed Ragna and went out to look for her. He found her in the bushes. Although she was still only a youngster, there she was in the bushes. It had all happened during his brief absence down by the sea—she must have been willing. So why had he been in love with her? She hadn't thought of him, not for a moment. She had given herself at once. He remembered from his schooldays, too, that she hadn't cared much about him. He had been so bad at reading and had always sat there dreaming and he couldn't learn anything by heart; the others laughed at him and she laughed at him. Thinking the whole thing over now, he regretted he'd also made a fool of himself later and tried to save her—that was when Skaaro wanted her down in his cabin. Why had he bothered! August would have said: "Goodbye and good luck! Off you go with Skaaro!"

Perhaps there was some wounded pride here, but what of it? He'd been taken with her for many years, had sheltered her image tenderly in his heart. And it wasn't all that long ago, just a few months—and now she turned to him in her misfortune. He wasn't going to be made a fool of again.

"What are you thinking?" she asked timidly.

"About what? No!" he said in repudiation. "It's nothing to do with me."

"No," she said dully, not daring to pursue it.

But it wasn't long before he began to have second thoughts. Was he himself any whit the better? What if he were to tell her about his own love affair? He was worse, not better. Gently he said: "I don't know what advice I can give you."

She took hope and spoke again, her eyes bright with confidence in him: "Well, you might perhaps put in a good word for me."

"A good word? I don't know what use a good word would be," he replied. He suddenly felt angry: despite everything, it was as if some large and powerful dog had come and taken a bite out of the leg of a little child. That's how it seemed. Now as ever, Edevart didn't take long to make up his mind. Defiantly he thought of a solution and said: "With all I have on my plate right now, I haven't got a great deal of time . . ."

"No," she quickly agreed.

"But if you can wait until next Saturday night, I'll take a trip over to Nordvaag."

"May God bless you!" she cried, and held him with both hands. It was a gesture of helplessness. She stopped herself before it was half complete. Immediately he felt deeply moved. His lips trembled.

"And I don't think he'll be laughing when I'm finished talking to him," he said grimly.

"No! Oh, no!"

There she sat: Ragna, little Ragna from school, from playtime, from tending the goats. She had been so pretty, she had laughed so nicely. He remembered that every time he had come near her he had felt a sweet pang in his breast.

She sat there in a threadbare skirt, of green and brown checks, the colors faded. She hadn't been able to help with the herring, or earn any money like the others. Part of her petticoat was showing at the neck. He noticed the neckband was fastened with an old dark horn button sewn on with white thread. That button might simply have meant that she was slovenly, but it surely wasn't that. Simply that she didn't have anything better. It looked so out of place. On her feet she wore wooden-soled clogs of the kind they called "clumpers" in Polden.

He was overwhelmed with pity for this neglected child and he dragged out his sea chest from under his bunk. He'd been thinking about this the whole time, thinking about Ragna for the cape and the skirt as soon as he heard his mother was dead. "Look!" he said brutally, to conceal how soft he was. "You can have these few bits and pieces!"

He spoke firmly and clearly, but his words were incomprehensible. She tried to grasp them, looking first at him and then at the clothes. He piled them on her lap and explained curtly that he'd bought them for his mother, but she had died and had never had a chance to wear them. His sisters were too small . . .

Yes, but that she should have them . . . That's what she heard, and that's what she saw. She began to cry; then, to hide her tears, she laughed crazily until she became quite unrecognizable. When she held out her hand to thank him, she couldn't speak, only whimper. Her hand was large and puffy, but limp with no strength in it. Her emotion was almost immodest, was too blatant. She didn't care that her nose was running, that she dropped one garment on the floor while she looked at the other.

"Try them on," he said, and immediately checked himself. He realized that she wouldn't be able to get into the skirt as things were at present; so without further ado he raised her up from the bench and put the cape around her.

Ah, that cape! Exactly what she needed and had been needing for the past six months to hide herself in! She stood with it on and looked down at it, splendid, incomparable, with a silk cord around the edge. Nobody else had a cape like that! It concealed her shape, smoothed her bulging figure; it was as if she had already had the child. "If anybody had told me this this morning . . . ! she said, time after time. "If anybody had suggested . . . !" Then she sank exhausted on the bench, with the cape still on her.

Edevart: "Well then, next Saturday evening. I'll be there late that night. Then I'll see him on Sunday and I'll be back in good time on Monday morning."

"Really, you are too kind!" she murmured. But it didn't seem any longer to be important to her what he did next Saturday. She was only interested in the cape, in her bit of finery. She was just like a child again.

"What about dinner now?" he said.

But when they came up on deck, Ragna grew silent. She had to spit over the rail a few times. She pretended that nothing was amiss, that she was in good form. But he realized she wanted to be ashore. And he hurriedly rowed her back to the boathouse.

Things couldn't have gone better. He continued to see to the fish and he lived on dried foods and coffee. On Thursday morning Ragna's old grandmother brought him a message that caused him much thought. For a time it seemed as though he might give up the trip to Nordvaag that he'd planned. Give it up? Was it unnecessary? He brooded on the matter and finally came to a decision. Give up the trip? Not likely! The days passed, and when Saturday evening arrived, he sat himself in his boat and rowed off to Nordvaag on what was still an important and pressing matter. He arrived later that same night.

Sunday morning he went aboard to see the skipper. They didn't come to blows; they reached an accommodation acceptable to both sides. At first the skipper turned deathly pale at the lad's audacity: the young whelp, what did he mean?

Edevart: "I haven't come here to lie to you. The child is born."

The skipper laughed, baring his teeth. Child? That was rich! That was charming! Get off my ship! The young dolt! What child?

Edevart: "I have come here in the first place to get some help for her."

"Ashore with you!" the skipper ordered.

But that was little use when the lad clearly wasn't going. The skipper tore open his collar and a button came off. He could breathe a little easier, but apart from that, it didn't help much. He had a man in the forward cabin who must not hear of this affair. The skipper dared not speak too loud in case he attracted the man's attention. But he snarled to himself. "You were also in this thing yourself, and now you are trying to swing things onto me!"

Edevart gave him a look; it was as hard and as furious as a blow delivered by a fist. "No more joking!" he said. He clearly wasn't going to stand for any more of this. He turned pale and he clenched his jaws.

The skipper: "What authority have you got to come here and behave like this? I'm warning you! Take yourself ashore while the going's good! I've a man up forward."

"You'll be lucky if I don't take hold of you and tear your guts out here and now!" shouted Edevart, jumping up. "I'm not leaving here until I've got some help for her! Please understand that!"

"Ssh! Shut your mouth! Stop shouting!" growled the skipper. "The whole town will hear you!"

Trembling, Edevart demanded: "Bring out this man of yours! Call him!"

That was just what the skipper did not want. He must at all costs avoid implicating this man from the Bergen Line who was from his part of the country. The skipper was no coward. He could well have said to Edevart: "But, my young friend, while you are busy tearing my guts out, what do you think I'll be doing? Sitting looking on?" But he didn't want to risk provoking any further this crazy youth, who was quite capable of completely losing control of himself and dragging into this vulgar business anybody who happened to be around. He could have gone on repeating that it had nothing to do with him, that it couldn't be him, that it must be this wild lad himself, and in any case that it was far too early to come demanding assistance from him at this time—he hadn't seen any papers yet about the matter. Indeed, he might very well have raised objections such as these. But he wasn't very anxious to get a certain document someday from the sheriff of his district. That would really give him away. Everybody would know about the affair. And God alone knew, perhaps he had somebody in tow back home who mustn't at any cost hear about it! The skipper was now cornered, and he decided he'd better make the best of it. He put his hand in his pocket. When he held out a blue five-daler banknote he immediately halted this little contretemps and temporarily satisfied Edevart. But then they discussed the matter further, and the conclusion was that Edevart left for home with a ten-daler note.

Well done! Damned sharp piece of work! Especially as the child was stillborn.

When he got to the drying grounds on Monday morning, he heard from the women what had happened. He pretended ignorance. He could rely on what the old grandmother said—she who had brought the message. She hadn't much to say; aged and remote, she simply nodded while the others gossiped, and kept puttering on with her work.

"So, the child was stillborn?" he asked.

"Yes. And just as well!" was the answer.

Yes, Edevart had learned a thing or two. No doubt about that. He became progressively less scrupulous in thought, word, and deed. He had quite cheerfully deceived the skipper up in Nordvaag, and would happily have done it again if need be. Little Ragna wasn't going to bear the cost alone of something it had taken two to make. As long as she now spent the money sensibly and didn't just throw it away! She was already on her feet again, so the grandmother shortly reported. That day she'd gone to the store.

The following day she came to the drying grounds, a bit thin and somewhat blue about the face, but otherwise quite hale and contented. She had come in place of the old woman. Edevart looked her up and down. She might in one way be well again, but surely not strong enough to stand bent over and deal with the heavy fish. Moreover, she must be worn out after the long walk to the store yesterday. He gave her instructions to go aboard the sloop and make dinner for two. One of the young lads would row her out.

Ane Maria came up close to him and said: "You might have picked somebody else to do that. She's not well."

Edevart started. "What do you mean? That's the very reason I sent her off to cook some food—to give her some light work."

"Oh, don't talk to me about food!" Ane Maria whispered, suddenly furious. "It wasn't the food you were thinking about!"

Edevart gaped at Ane Maria. She was deathly pale. She can't have got over her sickness yet completely, he thought. He did not want to upset her further by answering. Shortly afterward he saw that she was weeping.

Damnation, but what an upheaval there had been in Polden, what mental illness, what misery! He could have borne it better in some strange place, but this was his home. This wasn't what he had grown up in; the place had become unrecognizable. What made it twice as bad was that they all wanted to teach him the art of living at home again. Here he was back after having seen something of the outside world and having been in Bergen and all that; he'd come with a sloop and cargo, come with work and wages for everyone, come as a force to be reckoned with—and all he encountered was perversity and resistance and ingratitude. They wanted to do things their way and not his. They grumbled. How should he take this? What did they mean? There was Ane Maria, the wife of one of his neighbors, sticking her nose into his affairs. He ought to sack her; he had the power to. Just wait! The day the fish was dry and stacked aboard, he'd sail. What about the wind? He wouldn't wait for wind, not even for an hour. There was always wind outside the fjord. Cost him what it might, he would have himself towed to Outer Polden. There was wind there.

Ragna shouted across from the sloop that dinner was ready, and he raised his hand in reply. He didn't hurry, did not go scrambling across. No, he was skipper and he'd come when he felt like it. It wasn't right that anybody should shout across to get him to come for dinner. They shouldn't do that. When his expensive pocket watch told him the time was right, then he would come. Who did these people think they were?

When he was about to row out, Ane Maria came up to him

again. "You mustn't give her anything to drink," she said. "It's dangerous."

He got angry and said: "Away with all your silly nonsense!"

"Well, I just wanted to tell you."

"Oh, yes! You've had so many kids yourself, you know all about it, I suppose!"

"No," she said, and gave him a peculiar look. "No, I've had no kids—and I won't be having any."

Was this meant as a hint to him, an invitation? Was she trying to tell him she was safe? Ane Maria was now red to the roots of her hair. She was no longer crying. She had a brazen, provocative look. At any rate, she confused him. He said: "I hadn't thought of giving her a drink. She'll be left in peace as far as I'm concerned."

He came aboard, feeling irritable. Ragna had done the necessary, but he wasn't very pleased with her. It was clear that she had already been out yesterday buying some fancy bits and pieces at the store; and she was wearing a bought petticoat from the town with lace around the neck. So where was her petticoat with the horn button? Yes, she was the right one to go shopping with a ten-daler note!

"Won't you sit down and have something to eat yourself?" he asked.

"No, I had a bite in the galley when you were so long in coming," she replied.

That didn't improve his humor. This was sheer disrespect and ingratitude. Very well! Here he was back in his home district; they spoke to him as a familiar; he had known the younger ones from childhood. But he was no longer one of their kind. Remember that, he thought.

He ate in silence, observing the refinements of knife and fork which he had learned at Knoff's table. "By rights there ought also to be water on the table," he said.

"I'll run and get you some!" she said, and dashed off.

He might have stopped her, because he didn't really want any water; but he let her go.

She came back and handed him the long, narrow tin scoop which always hung by a string from the bung of the water barrel. Well, he accepted the water; but not wanting to miss this opportunity of teaching her something, he reached up for a glass from the wall cupboard, filled it, and silently handed the scoop back to her. She took it as meaning that she was to hang it back in the water barrel again, and went. She remained on deck.

When he came up, she asked meekly: "What do you want me to do now?"

"Wash the dishes first, I suppose," he replied. "Then you can clean up my cabin."

She was on the point of going when he stopped her and said: "What a damned funny woman Ane Maria is! Isn't she supposed to be well again?"

"Yes. Why?"

"She didn't think it should have been you to come aboard and cook."

"So that's what she thought, did she?" said Ragna bitterly. "She wanted to do it herself, eh?"

"No, she didn't say that, but . . ."

"Yes, but that's what she meant, all right. She's like that now . . . Crazy, running after everybody. I wouldn't repeat what her own husband, Karolus, said about her the last time he went away."

Edevart rowed ashore.

In the late afternoon, when Ragna had finished cleaning the cabin, she again shouted across and Edevart sent a small boy to fetch her. She reported: "I've cleaned the cabin and scrubbed the stairs and washed the windows and I took the bedclothes out and shook them."

"That's good," said Edevart.

"And did you try them?" Ane Maria couldn't help asking.

"Try? Try what?"

"The bedclothes. Did you try them?"

"You swine!" said Ragna.

At once they began quarreling. Edevart tried exerting his

authority and ordered them to hold their peace, but that didn't help. They went on abusing each other without paying any attention to him. Many evil words passed between them; the women round about stopped work on the fish and stood and listened and sniggered. The children learned a lot in a short time. When Ane Maria continued to provoke, it was bound to end in trouble. It was inevitable. Grinding her teeth, Ragna screamed out what Karolus had said about his own wife before he went away: that all she did was go around with this great shrieking thing between her legs! And the women standing around nodded that that's what Karolus had in fact said. They could vouch for that! Nevertheless, when the slanging match was over and Ane Maria was weeping bitterly, one by one the women went over to her side, because she was more approachable than the other woman and not averse to lending them a spot of coffee when they were out of it.

Nobody had shown any respect toward Edevart; and he had it in mind to say to Ane Maria that evening: "Don't bother to come back!" Oh, how marvelous it would be to be able to say that! But he couldn't afford to turn a single worker away; all he must think about was getting finished and sailing away from Polden. One thing he did do: neither Ragna nor Ane Maria were allowed aboard after that day. He brought in a young lad to cook for him, and managed without the assistance of women. Things went not too badly. The lad was alert, twelve years old, quick to learn, Ezra by name, came of a poor family. This youngster now got enough to eat—something he hadn't known at home. Eating in the galley, he soon filled out. Moreover, he could now stand on deck and pretend to the lads ashore he was an admiral and spit over the rails like a man. They shouted to know whether he could go up the rigging, whether he could twist the weathervane. No, Ezra couldn't do that yet. Anyway, there wasn't any weathervane. But he secretly practiced. Since he slept on board, he could climb up in his bare feet at night and get practice that way. He was a tough little lad, was Ezra.

Now came a quiet period. The drying made good progress and the fish seemed to be good and white. Birch bark arrived for covering the stacks; and money arrived for the final payout. Only a few more fine days were needed while the fish dried during the day and lay under pressure from large stones at night, just a few more days and a bit of luck with the weather—and then they could begin loading.

Joakim arrived back with his seine crew. No, the fortune hunters had made no catch. All they had done was lie in Vesteraal all summer, consuming their provisions and wasting their days. They didn't regret it; they were still quite well off; but they weren't as cocky as they had been. But nobody showed any great appetite for work. Like Karolus, for instance. Now that he was back, Ane Maria wouldn't let him out of her sight. Nor would she herself come near the drying grounds. No, she would never set foot there again as long as Ragna was there, she said. Then there was the fact that Karolus had become district chairman, and all sorts of documents and accounts and miscellaneous problems had piled up which needed to be dealt with. This was the worst thing he'd ever known! Naturally he had called all the parish councilors together to a meeting in his cottage; but as he hadn't himself learned to write, he had to have Joakim there to help him. All in all, this meant the loss of many pairs of hands for Edevart; nor would Karolus loan out his eight-oar boat if he wasn't there himself. Sheer lack of cooperation and ingratitude again on every hand! Yet the fish had to be loaded aboard.

Without further ado, Edevart borrowed Joakim's seine boat and collected Teodor and one or two more underage lads to man it. Things went reasonably well, with Beret and Josefine doing the stacking and Ezra doing the laborer's work for both of them and working enough for two.

No question of Edevart not daring to take the seine boat!

One dinnertime, when work had stopped and they were all sitting eating, there was a commotion on the drying grounds. People shouted and pointed! In heaven's name—look! It was

Ezra up aloft aboard the sloop. He was already perilously high. He had let go the final rope and was holding on to the bare mast at the top. He clambered higher, shinning up with his hands and feet. The people ashore kept silent. One or two small girls threw themselves face down on the rocks. Then Ezra pretended to be turning the weathervane. He was climbing higher, the fool! Oh, what he needs is a good thrashing! He passes the weathervane, is above it, and now he's high enough to reach up with one hand to the masthead and hold on there and take a rest. If only he were safely down again! But Ezra didn't want to come down again. Tempting providence he was, the sinful young devil! He wants a thoroughly sound whipping, he does! Did he think he was climbing up to heaven? "Don't shout! For God's sake, don't say a word!" people said warningly on the drying grounds. Ezra hauled himself up inch by inch, hanging like a monkey on that slender mast and making it bend. Then he stood there in the air, his body from the waist up above the top of the mast. Several people moaned. "Be quiet! Be quiet!" others hissed between clenched teeth. Ezra had reached his goal. Slowly he bent his body forward and balanced on his belly on the masthead. There he stayed.

Edevart and his stackers had remained standing on deck, motionless. What else could they do if they didn't dare shout? Now Edevart in his quandary climbed a little way up the rigging and called out: "Ezra, come down now at once!" He spoke as one speaks to a naughty child, and his voice trembled.

"All right!" answers that rascal up there, hanging there head downward. Oh, a few strokes with the rope's end across his backside is what he needs! "All right!" he says, and raises his belly off the masthead. It didn't take him long to come down; the worst bit was past the weathervane. But when he got farther down and grasped hold of the ropes, he slid down to the deck in a moment.

And Edevart gave him a clip or two about the ear. Indeed he did. But so gently it was quite shameful. And at the same time he promised the stupid fool that he could come along and help to sail the sloop south . . .

On the morning of the last day of loading Karolus came along to offer his services—he hadn't been able to come along earlier because of committee meetings and all sorts of other important paperwork. Joakim accompanied him. Edevart was inwardly furious, but he did not dare refuse the offer of these gentlemen. He still needed men to help tow the sloop out to sea if there was no wind. Joakim he pretended not to see.

They worked sluggishly. They were listless after a whole summer of idleness, and they puffed and panted. That evening, just as August had done the previous year, Edevart announced that he would be paying everybody individually the following morning.

All night long Edevart sat doing his accounts. He was a pitiful writer, but he was hot stuff at mental arithmetic and juggled brilliantly with two accounts: his own and the firm's. Oh, he intended coming out of this affair a prosperous man! In the morning he sent Ezra off to telegraph his departure to Knoff. Ezra was also to read the weather reports.

When the workers assembled, he paid them one by one. Beret and Josefine got substantial bonuses because they had deserved them; and to his two little sisters he gave an extra daler apiece. All had been calculated beforehand and figured in the accounts under some item or other.

He was finished by midday. Ezra came back and reported on the weather: the outlook not too bright, drizzle and fog at sea. Good! They didn't particularly need clear weather tonight. They weren't likely to run aground crossing the broad Vestfjord.

"Now, what about towing me out?" said Edevart.

"Towing you out? When it's getting dark?" asked Karolus and Joakim.

"This very evening!" Edevart replied.

He took in the hawser and then went with Teodor and Ezra to the anchor windlass. When the men saw that he was serious, they lent a hand and raised no further objections.

The towing proved easier than expected. They found wind

some way out in the fjord and they set the foresail. This helped greatly, and they reached the open sea before the sun had set.

When the men had come aboard after the payout, they had lent a hand to raise the mainsail. Joakim had until the very last been expecting to be offered a place on the crew. He asked if they weren't short of men for the journey, with only Teodor and Ezra? No, Edevart had men enough. Not that this should be taken as meaning that Joakim really wanted to go along, for he intended taking the seine boat out again. He mentioned his money. Edevart gave him a few daler; when Joakim asked for more, his big brother answered that he would look after the money for him.

9 NATURALLY THERE WERE MANY DIFFICULTIES; AND IT was particularly hard work for the small crew across the stretches of open sea. But otherwise it was a speedy voyage and a voyage without mishap. They had no specific orders from the firm; and their original idea was that when they got to Knoff's they would simply hand over the ship there and sign off. But when they arrived off Fosenland things took a rather remarkable turn. In the middle of the day and with a fine breeze blowing they nevertheless messed about so long trying to find the entrance channel that they ended up by sailing right past it. Teodor began to suspect his skipper of having done this deliberately.

They arrived at Trondheim during the night and Edevart telegraphed in the morning. Somewhat astonished, Knoff answered, congratulating them on their trip and giving instructions about the cargo. LETTER FOLLOWS! Edevart heard from the merchant there that the schooner had not yet arrived. These were proud tidings. Youth and enterprise had beaten old Norem. He also heard the news that the bark *Soleglad* had gone down in the Baltic on her return voyage. The crew had saved themselves by taking to the boats and were already back home again; but they had lost everything.

Edevart immediately set about looking for August. He was not hard to find; he was installed in a hostelry, half drunk and short of money, his clothes unkempt, and he seemed to have aged. Edevart was a skipper and had money. He was given a private room where he and his friend could sit, and August told him of his misfortune.

"I have been shipwrecked before, but that was in decent fashion on the high seas. But this time I was shipwrecked in a duck pond," he said, and pulled a scornful face at the Baltic Sea. He talked and talked, rambling on disconnectedly. In the middle of one account he could easily switch to something quite different. But everything bore on his misfortune.

"What am I going to do now? Must a man suffer total ruination? I take it you got my letter, so you know just what has happened to me. There isn't a glimmer of hope left. I tell you nobody was onto such a good thing as I was. A few more days and I would have been sitting here on this chair a wealthy man. Yes! And I wouldn't have minded an honest, decent shipwreck— I'd have welcomed that! I've been shipwrecked plenty of times before and managed to salvage things both gold and silver. But this time I barely got away with my life."

"Didn't you save anything?"

"What could I save! I had five big cases full of jewelry and silks and other things. Do you think I could simply stuff them in my pocket when I jumped overboard?"

August shook his head dejectedly. He was in low spirits. He asked for something to eat and he ate hungrily everything that was put in front of him, and washed it down with beer. He kept on talking the whole time. "I might as well take some sustenance, though it won't do me any good. Save anything? Nobody saved a thing. When the captain stepped ashore he didn't even have his hat. We were all cleaned out."

"Didn't you even have time to grab your money, either?"

"What money? I hadn't any money left. I had spent it all, buying gold and jewels. Ten big cases . . ."

"Five, you said."

"Five? Yes, but you are forgetting I had five others! And those cases were even bigger, and they were stacked in a different place on board. What else would you expect? And in one of those larger cases I had put a whole wad of banknotes as well. The lot all gone to the bottom!"

Edevart probably didn't believe everything he heard; but he wanted to demonstrate his sympathy, so he shook his head sorrowfully.

"Did you ever hear anything like it!" August burst out. "But maybe you think I was insured? And had my ten thousand daler waiting for me on a plate when I got home? If I said that, I'd simply be sitting here on this chair telling lies. I was an idiot and didn't insure a thing. I was a fool and I swindled myself!" August spat, despising and reviling himself. It was as though he had turned his back on himself and walked away. "And if I had insured? The heavens could have fallen but I would have had my money when I got home. Well, I put my trust in the Lord and like a decent man put my goods and my valuables into those crates. But then He let loose that storm and those huge seas."

"Was it such a terrible storm?"

"Puh!" August snorted. "I have been out in worse weather, but then it was proper upstanding stuff. But you can't say that of a cesspool like the Baltic. The barometer had dropped right down and looked like a clock pointing to six o'clock. That gave us clear warning and we began to reduce sail. But do you suppose there was any time, any delay? It was like sneaking up and assassinating somebody so he doesn't even have time to turn around. Hurricanes? I don't give a damn for any of your miserable hurricanes. I don't at all, not when it is on the high seas and I have a stout vessel under my feet. I don't give a damn! But this thing! When both the foremast and the mainmast had gone in the first minute, we knew we were done for. A hurricane that starts way down around six o'clock is one which is on you before you know it. You can scarcely count five, possibly ten, before he's on you. He doesn't wait for you to finish what you're saying before he turns as black as night. That's it, and you don't know what he's up to, and you don't know what to do. *Waitress, a trifle more of that meat!* She understands English. I could nicely take a little more food, but in fact it would be wasted, indeed it would. You see, the trouble was that the vessel was rotten. She hadn't anything solid in her belly. She was carrying a cargo of rye and she couldn't even have survived a nail hole. But she got ripped open with gashes as long as this room. That's a deplorable thing, too: a ship that can't even carry a cargo of rye, with rye like a down pillow, as you might put it. Save anything? I don't know how you can talk about saving anything. We sank like a lump of lead. It was like lowering a bucket into the sea. What do you mean! The captain wasn't even able to save his log! He was an experienced captain and he will be given command of another vessel, so I hear. He stood by his ship until we were up to our knees in water. "To the boats!" he cried, and this we had already done and got the boats clear. But this was no weather really for taking to the boats. It was a close thing whether or not one of the boats might not be torn out of the davits. We remained aboard as long as we could and didn't leave the ship until the last and fatal moment. For a ship is still a ship, whereas a ship's boat is nothing. I suppose you got my letter?"

"Letter?" No, Edevart had received no letter.

"I sent a letter to Fosenland for you."

"But I have been up in Lofoten, and I came straight here last night with the sloop and its cargo of fish."

August was not listening to his friend. He was totally preoccupied with his own sad fate. "All those cases gone to the bottom!" he said. "On top of all that, I nearly went down myself, and a fond farewell that would have been. I didn't want to get in that boat. The captain was already in the boat, but I stayed behind. They took me by force, and I screamed. They thought I'd gone crazy, but it was the others who were crazy. They didn't understand that a boat means damn all. Once I was in a boat and we overturned and the sea was alive with sharks! A Negro was bitten completely in half! Yes! But they didn't know. In half! I'm scared in a boat, but standing on a ship's deck I'm not scared and nobody's going to think I am. But in a boat I'm scared. They had to take me by force. If you'd seen that Negro bitten in half! And then at that very moment he reached out toward me with his upper half, the half which still had his arms. But there aren't any sharks in that duck pond, you might well say. No, I never said there were. But I haven't been about the world for nothing. I know that a boat means damn all, and we would all have been sent plunging to the bottom like this beer glass if the storm hadn't abated that very instant. That's what happens with that kind of hurricane: it suddenly grows calm and the blackness rapidly disappears. When it grew light we were rescued by an Estonian ship. Of course I call it being rescued, but all we saved was our skins. There were those ten cases at least. And all that Russian I learned just to be able to speak good Russian when I was selling my stuff! Not much use that any more! When I have a bad head, I say: *"U menya bolit golova!"* When I want to sell anything, I spread out my things and say: *"Chevo vam ugodno?"* And if I don't make a sale because some wretch can't pay a decent price, I say politely: *"Proshu posyetitye menya zavtra!"* I tried it on the waitress here, but all she understands is English, so I can't talk to her. Anyway, I haven't anything left to say. But it's absolutely shameful: there, inside the Baltic, not even salt water and the Kattegat straight ahead, and we didn't even get as far as Skagen! I must say I have been shipwrecked before—I'm no stranger to it. I could give lessons in being shipwrecked. But this! No, the ship was rotten. No sooner had she lost her masts than she sank. And now here I sit with no more fame or fortune than what you see in front of you. Have you still got your gold ring?"

"Yes, but you shall have it back," said Edevart. "For now you need it more than I do."

"You are not going to give that gold ring of yours away!" August objected. But he took it quickly enough.

Edevart: "And now we'll go and get you some clothes."

August: "I'd be happier if you'd shut up and stop making fun of me. Do you think you're made of money?"

"I'm not exactly broke."

Both were moved by the other's words, and Edevart said: "I'm doing no more than you would have done in my place."

"Who, me? Don't talk rot! I've never so much as lifted a finger for you, as far as I know," the other protested. "But we've been friends now for many a long day and if I'd saved all those cases of mine you'd have had a pretty good share of that coming to you. Never doubt that! What have you done with the snake ring? Your sister? But it was too big for her. Too bad I didn't pick out three or four rings for her with real diamonds and precious stones while I still had them."

They went into town, bought some clothes for August, and then went aboard the sloop. "Lucky I got some decent clothes before Teodor saw me!" said August. "Now he'll think I'm still rich!" Nor could he refrain from showing off in front of Teodor, putting his hand over his vest pocket as if he had something there and saying: "I could buy this entire sloop with a single one of my diamonds!"

August quickly recovered. He already had a plan for giving a concert with his accordion in Trondheim and perhaps earning a few daler. If he distributed some posters announcing that he was a shipwrecked Russian, surely a mass of people would come. But then the Russian consul might perhaps turn up and look into things and find only a Norwegian? He abandoned the concert. After this he had the idea of building himself an incubator like the one he had seen in America and buying eggs by the tens of thousands and hatching them and raising the chickens and selling them to rich townsfolk. At any rate, August had begun using his brains again, and that was the important thing. Now and again he sorrowfully recalled to mind those five or ten cases of his—

however many it may have been—but he no longer talked endlessly about the shipwreck.

The sloop *Hermine* was now discharging; and Edevart and his men wandered about with nothing to do. He received a letter from Knoff with a long list of things he was to bring back so as to save freight costs. Edevart handed over the list to the relevant merchant and once again found himself at a loose end. When the sloop was unloaded, he had it cleaned and swabbed. He waited for the goods, but they did not arrive. He made inquiries. The merchant made excuses, saying that his men had not had time.

"How much time do they need?"

"We'll have to see," said the merchant.

August called on the lady who had had the dozen boxes of cigars from him last year and who had not paid up. "She couldn't manage payment this year, either," said August. "Of course I couldn't very well go and see her before I'd got these new clothes. But even though I was capable of all the Russian in the world and was never at a loss for a single word, I still got no money. No, she just offered me love instead, and that's the way it is every time I go. It's all very well, but I can't make a living that way. So I went and looked on her shelves myself, but *my* cigars had been sold long ago, for they were the czar's own personal brand, you understand. Well, I might have turned on her, been a bit rough with her, but what do you do when she starts kissing you every time and cries like a child? I just haven't the heart. Well, today she got the gold ring as well."

Edevart's eyes opened wide in amazement.

"Sure, it was stupid!" said August. "And I don't wonder you're angry at me. But what was I to do? Someday I'll learn. I'm thinking of getting a job with a butcher for a while, because I can slaughter and skin animals as well as the next man. Don't worry! I learned that in Australia."

The ordered goods still did not arrive; the difficulties seemed endless, and Edevart had to call on the merchant again. The merchant sent his apologies, saying that he was busy and couldn't talk to him just then. But from the people in the firm Edevart received certain hints which he began to piece together: Knoff couldn't simply expect delivery of all these goods—a big consignment of flour, together with much other merchandise—without further ado. Knoff had been telegraphed about security; and Knoff had referred them to the firm who had bought his cargo of fish. Yes, that was all very well. But this firm could not stand security for such a very large order—the fish had already been more than paid for by the advances Knoff had received. Indeed, it was questionable whether the schooner's cargo would cover those advances.

In heaven's name! Edevart was utterly taken aback! Was Knoff shaky?

That was the last and most astonishing thing Edevart might have expected. In the meantime, Knoff must have arranged for a loan or something of the kind. Edevart received instructions to take the list back and to go along with it to an entirely different merchant and get the goods. This he did. The new merchant bowed and scraped and let it be known that Knoff was good enough for him. He delivered the goods on board at once. So the whole thing was presumably only some stupid misunderstanding.

The sloop now made ready to sail. But what about August? Up till now he had had food and lodging aboard. But now that was over, and August was no further along.

"If only it wasn't so far to India," said Edevart. For he doubtless still believed those stories of India from his early days with August.

But for August himself those stories were distant, forgotten things, and he asked: "To India? What do you want there?"

"Not me. You're the one with a lot of money there, surely?"

"Oh, yes!" August remembered. "Someday I'll have to take a little run out there and see about my chests. I lost the keys when I was shipwrecked, but I reckon I can pick the locks. Twelve keys at least! What I was going to say was this: there's a marvelous man here who wants to write down everything I've been through in my life. Wants me to talk and he'll put it all down in writing. I met him on one of the quaysides, and I sat and talked to him for a long time. I'll think about it, I said. I've never seen a man who could write like that, though I've been all around the world. I can talk as fast as I like, but he still gets it all down. He says it will be a whole book with my picture and everything. We called at a printer's yesterday to see if he'd print it. He'd think about it, he said. We'll make a mint of money, this writer says. And I'd go out myself and sell it by the thousand all over the place. Well, we'll see. But why shouldn't we make something of it, said this writer. Just like Gjest Baardsen, who went and wrote a big book about all the things he'd stolen in his life. What do you think?"

Edevart didn't know what to think. He was neither a great writer nor a great reader himself. For him, books were an unfamiliar world. Faced with them, he shook his head. But he'd learned a thing or two by now, and here he scented danger. He advised his friend to be careful and not say too much or he might find himself in trouble and sitting behind bars for life.

August snorted: "Pshaw!" That would never happen! He was no fool! The thought of being in on the writing of this book greatly appealed to him, especially if his picture was going to embellish the book and be seen all over the country. Then the people back home in Polden and everywhere else would see where in fact his travels had taken him; and all the girls who had made fun of him would regret it. In short, it meant no small fame for him.

But already that same evening August had decided, after careful consideration, to decline the proposition. Might not this writer all too easily trap him into revealing some dangerous little detail of his life? And no sooner was it said than there it would immediately stand on the printed page. And then his picture would also be there, staring all the world's policemen in the face. No, thank you! He was no fool!

August again began pondering things, making plans and discarding them, weighing up one way of life after another, and finally deciding for a life at sea again. He wasn't without resources, indeed no. Edevart mustn't think that. A man of his kind could get himself taken on any time, don't fret! But it would have to be on a decent sea this time and not the Baltic, he'd watch out for that! Could Edevart lend him a few daler? He wanted to make for Bergen to find a berth.

A few daler? Sure! But couldn't he look for a berth here in Trondheim?

Perhaps. In any case, he'd first of all try finding a job on the land for the winter.

This was his final plan.

GREAT CHANGES at Knoff's place. Edevart brought the sloop in alongside an enormous stone-built quayside with hoists and other machinery, and rail tracks running into both warehouses. The place was still swarming with men and horses working to get the installation finished. A powerful overhead crane lifted a dozen sacks of flour at a time from the sloop, and the men just laughed—it was so easily and quickly done.

Knoff came down to the sloop, nodded to Edevart, and was generally friendly, but he was as usual greatly preoccupied in giving orders to his workfolk: "Coil up that rope! Roll all those barrels away! A lot of stuff from the sloop is to go there!" He turned to Edevart and asked: "Did you see anything of the schooner last night? You didn't? So he hasn't sailed on past. I suppose you haven't any idea where he might be? He's probably still at the drying grounds."

"That's not unlikely," Edevart replied. "All the vessels north of us were still at the drying grounds when I sailed!" He swelled with pride; he could tell from the boss's tone of voice that Norem, that old skipper, shouldn't have let himself be outdistanced by a beginner, a mere lad.

"You had a bit of messing around in Trondheim," said

Knoff. "But I taught that merchant a lesson! He could well have had that big order of mine. But when he behaved like that, I simply went straight to another merchant. You didn't have any trouble with the other man?"

"No, nothing of the kind," replied Edevart and laughed. "He nearly creased himself in two with his bowing."

Edevart realized at once that he should not have permitted himself this joke. The boss frowned and asked: "How many separate items have you?"

"Thirty-seven. Not counting the two hundred sacks of flour."

"And how many men have you?"

"Two men. From the north."

"Sign them off, and let them go home. But if they want to stay over and look around to see what a big place looks like, they can. When you've unloaded, you can have the rest of the day off. You can bring the accounts and the cash balance tomorrow."

Knoff left.

This was only bravado on the boss's part, a bit of showing off. Edevart had returned from a long and important expedition; he wouldn't have put his hand to any work that day even if he'd been directed to. He wanted to go around and see people and enjoy something of the respect they must surely feel for his exploits as a skipper. And the cash balance? Did the boss expect any cash balance from him? A few coppers left over, perhaps. But a cash balance—no.

He paid off Teodor and Ezra. They both wanted to stay over till the following morning, sleeping on board. Edevart finished unloading, talked to one or two people he knew, then went ashore and watched the masons and the planishers at work on the quay. Only one wing remained to be completed; the masons sang as they lifted the blocks of stone, singing as though they might be hoisting sail. There was general merriment, life, and gaiety. At the same time Edevart couldn't help being aware of an air of depression among Knoff's regular workers, something half concealed, a heaviness. The warehouseman looked around warily and said: "Yes, there have been great changes here since you left!" But he shook his gray head. A young man joined in: "Something will turn up!" The warehouseman said meaningfully: "Yes, it doesn't affect you young ones who are going to America. But I'm too old for that."

Edevart made his way up to the cooper's house and had a little talk. The cooper was not busy; he was pottering about on his own little bit of land. "Yes, there have been great changes here!" said the cooper, too. "God knows if it's all for the best! Won't you come in?"

"Won't I be keeping you away from your work?"

The cooper smiled. "From working my great estate? Oh, no! And I haven't any other work any more. The cooperage has been shut down."

"Shut down?"

"A lot has been shut down. The boat shop has also been shut down. The men are going to America. Soon the bakery will be shut down."

"But I've just brought in two hundred sacks of flour," said Edevart.

"Well, he'll keep baking for a while, and then he'll shut. You don't need just flour, you need wages as well. The tutor has also left."

Of course Edevart realized that Knoff was in difficulties. His brave face on the quayside was only a show of confidence. "Now he has a quay," said the cooper. "But what's he going to do with it? A huge stone-built quayside with machines and other equipment, and instant loading and unloading, but the steamers don't come." What did Edevart think the quay had cost? An enormous amount! Just think how much construction work there had been up till now, and those huge cash payments every single Saturday! One thing about Knoff's business was that it had many branches, and one branch could help another out when it was in difficulty. But this kind of large cash outlay, stretching over the whole summer, was too much to expect Knoff's business to carry.

So where had he got the money from?

"I don't know. A loan? A mortgage on the place? It's sad to think. And I still say the same: what in God's name did he want with this quay? He's just too big for his boots and wanted to show off. He wanted the scheduled steamers. But, anyway, he's not going to get them."

"Won't he get them?"

"No. Because the regular landing stage has also built a quayside."

"You don't say!"

"We'd hardly got properly started building here when things began happening down there. And it didn't mean anything to them. They had long-standing financial reserves. They could afford it. Moreover, they are building in timber, and wood's not expensive. To make the structure rigid they bought some second-hand rails from the Støren railway, and they paid only scrap prices. Ah, they are clever and prudent people! They don't over-commit themselves. Their quay was finished long ago. It isn't more than an eighth the size of ours, but they manage. The steamers use it."

"But can you possibly understand," said Edevart, "why they didn't want to have the landing stage here? For here, surely, is where it ought to be?"

"Ah, but as long as one particular director sits on the board . . . Anyway, when it comes to the point, they don't like Knoff. No, they don't like him. He's too grand. He laughs at them. Certainly the landing stage ought to be here, and everybody knows it—we're a big and busy place, and built up around three sides. But there's no point in talking about that. And as long as the shipping firm has that director—because it's said he once took offense when Knoff laughed at him at a big meeting a long time ago . . ."

The cooper finally intimated that he would probably have to leave the place soon. It wasn't because he wanted to. He'd been here a lot of years, had his cottage and a little plot of land . . .

"But I nearly forgot. The people from Doppen have been out here a few times asking for you."

"That crazy man. I suppose he was drunk again?"

"It was his wife. They are trying to get to America, I hear. They've been to Knoff trying to raise their fares, offering him their smallholding as security. But Knoff has enough on his plate as it is."

"So what did they want me for in all this?"

"I don't know."

When Edevart left the cooper, he was deep in thought. The thing now was whether Knoff was able to settle up with him and pay him what was owing! To think it was true, after all, that Knoff was in difficulty! This ill-starred quay had ruined him! It had been Edevart who had given him the idea; and even though he hadn't expected any reward exactly, he might well have felt like throwing out his chest a little and taking some of the credit. Now he daren't even hint at it. The people who had been turned out would simply have set on him. It was absolutely terrible. If only he had the place far behind him!

He ran into the housekeeper, Miss Ellingsen, once a sweetheart of his in a kind of way, a lively brown-eyed girl with whom he'd been friendly once or twice. She was the only one in the place who seemed cheerful and energetic; she laughed and talked and was warm in her admiration for his achievement. So he'd pulled it off! And come out of it alive! And the boss himself had praised him at the dinner table the previous week. It did not come averse to Edevart to hear this; and when, shortly afterward, he went into the bakery, he shouted loudly to his old roommate: "That's right! Keep it up! I brought two hundred sacks of flour for you!"

"Well, that'll last a little while," the baker replied gloomily. So the baker was gloomy, too. His wages had been cut and he was faced with unemployment. Now he was off to Trondheim at the end of the week to have a look around. Catch him staying on the deck of a sinking ship!

Wherever Edevart went, he found the same feeling of depression. Even the children who attached themselves to him were subdued, even the young boy Romeo, though he was rid of his teachers and had finished with lessons.

Edevart went to the store. "You've come with new supplies," they said to him. There was a little encouragement for the lads in this, even though they, too, had had their wages cut. "It'll be nice to have full shelves and cupboards again," they said. But Lorensen, the head clerk, saw further into the future and simply shook his head. He, too, had begun thinking about America. What else was there for him? Edevart suggested he might do better to find a little place nearer home and set up in business himself, but the other rejected the idea. He hadn't enough capital! You needed capital!

It seemed as if everybody had come to expect too much; they couldn't now accept any adjustment to their wages or their standard of living. They were prisoners of a hopeless dissatisfaction. Who the devil was going to accept lower wages! There was America, wasn't there? The whole thing seemed to people to be out of joint, not what they were used to. They had earned good money, and they weren't inclined to earn less. Why couldn't the good times continue? Why should building a quay turn them all into paupers? Lorensen, the head clerk, put it thus: "We're quitting the country, and that's all there is to it! We've become unsettled, and we're giving in to that feeling. We'll all land up in America." He turned to Edevart. "You'll see, you'll be following us."

No. That's the last thing he would contemplate. Never.

"What'll you do?" asked Lorensen. "Are you thinking of taking the sloop to the Lofotens for another winter? Maybe it can be done. So long as the sloop isn't sold by then, along with everything else. But don't say I said it!"

It was possible Lorensen was right. He knew the business, and took heed of lots of things. But all the same he didn't know

Edevart. America? Not if he had his way! He'd never given it a thought, and never would.

THE NEXT MORNING Edevart took leave of his crew. Ezra was no longer very brave; when he held out his horny little hand, he couldn't say "goodbye" properly because his lips were trembling so terribly. "One of my shoes is pinching me like the very devil!" he said, and bent over. But then he had earned a fair amount and had plenty of money in his pocket, and he quickly took comfort from this.

"Good journey home!" Edevart wished him. Then he added: "I might be following you before very long!"

Edevart went up to the office with his accounts and his small amount of cash, oh! so small! How could it have been any bigger? He'd paid for the fish in Lofoten, and for the drying back home at Polden; then there had been the provisions, the crew's wages, and the extra expense of the towing and of some necessary rigging in Trondheim. Furthermore, there were a number of more private items which were attributed to various heads elsewhere in the books, and which thus in a sense had disappeared, but which nevertheless swelled the account. So how could the cash balance be any greater?

A little grimace of impatience passed over Knoff's face when Edevart knocked and entered. It might just have been his usual pretense: that he was busy and had no time for minor matters just now. It could also have been that he was anticipating an embarrassing settling up and a small return.

"Perhaps I'd better come later?" Edevart inquired.

"No. But my accountant can look at the books later. You can hand in the cash balance. Is that it?" he asked, looking up from the few notes and coins at Edevart.

"That is the cash balance. That's what's left."

"From all that money? From what you got from Norem to buy fish as well as the thousand you got for the drying?"

Edevart had learned how to ride out a situation like this. He had learned it from many people, from August, from old Papst, from Norem, from all sorts of people. He said firmly: "That's all that's left. You can check it from the books."

Knoff was silent a while. He thumbed through the book, turning the pages back and forward, paused at the final entries, and asked: "All the wages are paid, I take it?"

Edevart: "All the wages, yes. Except mine."

"Haven't you included your own wages?"

"How could I? I didn't know what you were going to give me, did I?"

"What I was going to give you? Surely we were agreed on that—an ordinary seaman's wages was what I said."

"That was before I was appointed skipper."

"Skipper!" said Knoff, and shook his head pityingly.

This brought Edevart up short, but he managed to say: "I've had the responsibility, in any case."

"All right," replied Knoff patronizingly. "We might say that. But surely I am the one who has really borne the responsibility."

"And things didn't finish up too badly for us, either," mumbled Edevart.

Knoff remained silent.

Suddenly Edevart asked: "How much are you paying Norem?"

"Norem? On the schooner? Why do you ask me that? It's quite different with him. He has worked his way up with me, and his earnings have also gone up."

"All right," said Edevart, and nodded, his jaw clenched.

Knoff, tersely: "It's to be as we agreed—ordinary seaman's wages. So I owe you for six, getting on for seven months' work. But then there's that set of fishing gear!"

Edevart, bitter at this trick of his boss: "That was no set of fishing gear. It was an old seine net. Are you expecting payment for that?"

"I'll get my accountant to see what it cost me. I'll let you know the price later. An old seine net? Wasn't that the seine that landed that big catch up north that I read about in the papers?"

"What of it?" said Edevart. "As a net, it wasn't worth talking about, in my opinion. I just gave it away."

Knoff leafed through the book. "I noticed the sloop has not been painted."

"I didn't have time to paint her."

"But I see from the books that you have entered up wages for two men for the entire summer. What did these two men do, when you didn't even manage to scrape and paint the vessel?"

Edevart was silent for a moment. This was one of the weakest points in his accounts; it was only too obvious to him. In fact, he hadn't had two men aboard all summer; he'd been quite alone aboard the sloop, right up to the last month, when he'd taken Ezra aboard to do the cooking. But he had put in a claim for two men's wages for a whole summer and pocketed the money himself. Edevart had often wondered about this step: was it so very wrong of him? Certainly he'd done worse things than that! Hadn't he lived aboard the sloop all summer on dried food and coffee simply to put a cook's wages in his own pocket? And as far as this second man was concerned, didn't all the ships up north have another man on board apart from the skipper? The fact that Edevart managed on his own ought to be to his credit. The one thing he'd done wrong was this detail of neglecting to scrape and paint the sloop: a trifle, nothing at all. What about the fact that the sloop *Hermine* was all of two or three weeks ahead of the other fishing boats, and in consequence had saved its owner a lot of money?

"The thing is," said Edevart, "that I had to have *one* man aboard apart from myself. Or didn't you want me to have decent food to eat? He did the cooking and kept the place clean and stood watch alongside me as is usual on board ship. As for the other man, I needed him to see to one end of the drying ground while I was at the other end. We toiled and slaved. There was little or no male labor to be found up north to help with the drying, only women and boys, so the two of us had to cope with everything. Then for several days the tide was so tremendous that it came up almost to the fish and seemed ready to sweep them all away—what do you think I could have done there on my own? I didn't dare risk it."

Knoff merely sat there saying nothing. Edevart was into his stride, and continued: "But if you reckon that the sloop hasn't been scraped and painted, then I'm prepared to knock off half a month's wages, if you think that's right. And, moreover, if you really think that what I did last summer was nothing worth speaking of, then you can simply give me what you like."

A telegram was brought in. Knoff opened it and leaped up from his chair. It contained serious tidings, from which anything might follow. The schooner had gone down . . .

It occurred later to Edevart that it is an ill wind that blows no good. What had he seen in his boss's face at that crucial moment when he read the telegram about the shipwreck? Knoff uttered a remark or two: what a misfortune, the vessel and its cargo gone to the bottom, a disaster, a crash, ruination! But his face betrayed no concern—on the contrary. Whatever Knoff might or might not have done, he now began to chat to Edevart.

"Can you believe it? Sailing the schooner straight to the bottom?" he asked. "Wrecked and sunk. He was beginning to get old, was Norem. I don't wonder you thought he was a bit past it. Ha! ha! A fine old man, of course, but in fact a fool. Wasn't he? And there I was thinking next year I might send the schooner straight into the Baltic. There's so much bother with those middlemen in Trondheim—you really have to laugh. Well, that's over, sunk! Where was it? A little north of the Villa lighthouse, it says here. Well, it was good that the crew were saved. So old Norem at least doesn't have any lives on his conscience. What I was going to say was this: take a man with you and go and clean up the sloop. I don't want it tied up here at the new quay looking so filthy. No question . . ."

If only his boss had stopped there, Edevart thought later.

but he became almost confidential with a few concluding words. And what did they signify? Had the shipwreck made so little impression on him that he could talk so indifferently about other things?

"You didn't call in at the other landing stage yesterday when you were coming in?" he asked Edevart. "So you don't know that they've got a quay there as well? You should take a trip over and look at it."

"I shall."

"Only a thing of wood," said Knoff. "They say they just nailed it together. Well, they're welcome to it . . ."

It was the opinion of the cooper and all the others that Knoff would do well out of the shipwreck. It depended on how much the schooner and its cargo had been insured for; but if they knew their boss, he would have insured for at least double the value, if for no other reason than sheer megalomania, and so as not to seem a man with a mean vessel and an insignificant cargo. His innate vanity stood him in this instance in good stead. He didn't complain. He didn't halt any more work, and he paid every man his wages on Saturdays.

Strange! The fact that Knoff seemed to have regained his strength, that his warehouses were once again full of flour and his stores filled with new goods had its effect both on the firm and on the district. People grew more animated, and there was hope in their eyes. Edevart didn't pay much attention to the change; he busied himself cleaning up the sloop and even slept aboard at night; but one Saturday night his assistant, a young lad, told him there was going to be dancing again in the servants' hall. Didn't Edevart want to go ashore? Haakon Doppen was coming to play.

Edevart didn't dare ask what he would dearly have liked to. But he had learned from experience and didn't intend to get mixed up with the dancers. Not at all! It would only mean fighting again! He realized he had to be careful about the lad, otherwise there would be suspicions about him and the Doppen woman. But he could talk freely about Haakon. Indeed! So

Haakon Doppen had come? Come for his usual sackful of shopping? When did he get here? This morning? So he'd be drunk already by now? "No," the lad replied, "he hasn't anything left now for drinking." Edevart somehow had to ask about Lovise Magrete, indeed he had. But he used a different name, as though talking about somebody else. Was Haakon alone, or did he have any of the children with him?

The lad said: "I don't know."

"I meant, was he with that red-haired girl he was with last year—Severina she was called, I believe?"

"Don't be silly! He's got his wife with him," said the lad, looking at him.

Edevart remained on board. He had made a big enough fool of himself. There was a time when he would certainly have given his life for her. Now he told himself he had to grow up—just note that! How he had been messed about, had had all sorts of crazy ideas, and had wandered restlessly back and forth between Polden and Fosenland! She meant no more to him than some bush back home! She had two children—what would he want with them? Anyway, she was married . . .

The hours passed and he lit the lamp. He daren't walk about on deck, for they might see him from the road and draw conclusions as to why he wasn't in his bunk. More hours passed. The night was long and he couldn't face any longer sitting in the cabin like some prisoner. Of course he dared walk about on deck! Why not, he'd like to know! He could stump the boards—it was his own ship! But never had the hours been so long, never had his good old pocket watch gone so slowly, though he stumped and stumped around the deck. What about going ashore and taking a stroll up by the house? No, I said!

He ended up in the cabin again and settled down to doze.

Footsteps on deck. He could easily pretend that he wasn't expecting these footsteps. Indeed, he did that, and appeared surprised. Who could it be coming aboard so late? But in fact he had been expecting her. Hadn't she called at the cooper's and inquired about him!

When she came down the stairs and entered, he was surprised only by the fact that she seemed in no hurry. She didn't seem to have stolen away to see him. No, she shook hands and begged him to forgive her coming. "You haven't gone to bed yet?" she said solicitously.

He seemed tremendously surprised at her calling; and she didn't really wonder at this, she said. She took out a piece of paper from the bosom of her dress and held it in her hand.

First she spoke about him: that he was now quite a man, that he was probably the youngest skipper in the whole country. She looked about her and remarked how cozy he had made things. He kept his cabin nice. Clean lamp glasses!

"You're not afraid to come here?" he asked.

"No," she replied.

She was so gentle and quiet. It was a year now since he had lived at her place. She was perhaps even sweeter now, her mouth more tender, gently trembling. What was he to say? He asked after the children. A little later he put his arms around her and kissed her. She was as good to kiss as she had been before, and she responded openly to him. "Lovise Magrete!" he whispered.

She had a purpose in coming, she said, and he mustn't turn her away. Naturally he had known all the time what she wanted from him, but there had been moments when he had dreamed wild dreams of a different kind: that she wanted to leave Doppen and come to him, live with him, live and die with him. Wild dreams—and now here she was asking him to help her and her family go to America! She told him how things were: that it would be doing them an enormous favor. They had asked Knoff and everybody else, but in vain. Nobody on this earth had been so kind to her as Edevart had been! He would have security— look at this paper! They would fill out something like this in the morning, and they'd both put their names to it, both Haakon and she. They'd do everything. They were in such a bad way. Haakon had trained to be a tinsmith while he was away, and he could make the loveliest things—strainers and pails and ladles—but all they could do was hang them on the wall at home, for nobody came to Doppen to buy them, since it was so far off the beaten track. That's why they were in a bad way. And nobody on this earth had been so kind to her as Edevart . . .

She had said all this in one breath, as though afraid of an immediate refusal. Now he must decide. She took his hand.

There was no doubt he felt flattered that she thought him so rich and powerful; but he shook his head at what he had heard.

"Can't you?" she asked.

"No!"

Despondently, she crumpled at these words. "Then there's nothing more to say!"

He asked: "Why can't things be as they were before, with you weaving and him . . . well, he's never really done anything, has he?"

"The thing is," she said, "that everybody knows about it here. They all know about him. He can't meet anybody who doesn't know. And even though it was all for my sake he did it, and he was himself innocent, nobody thinks about that. But he thinks it would be a lot better in some new place where he wasn't known, for then he'd be a changed man. He's a useful worker."

"I left a crowbar behind at Doppen. Has he ever used it? Taken up any of the stones on your fields?"

Silence.

"Has he ever used that crowbar? I'm asking."

"No, because he's trained for something else now, and if only he could get to a new country . . ."

Edevart had an idea. "Then let him go alone!"

But despite her helplessness, there was some logic in Lovise Magrete's thinking. Edevart's proposal was impossible. She spoke, humbly and loyally: "The point is that Haakon wants me and the children to go with him. After all, we are married and have lived together. That's the way it is. And without us it would be difficult for him to lead a decent life."

Edevart gave his words a double meaning: "Yes, without you it could be difficult for others, too. But you don't greatly care about that, I see."

"Yes, yes, I do!" she cried, pressing her breast against him. "I am unhappy for your sake, and don't know what we are to do. Tell me!"

Edevart repeated: "Well, you can let him go and you can stay behind!"

Long silence. "How would things be then?" she whispered, shaking her head. "You know I'd do wrong, and we wouldn't be able to conceal it. No, it's not to be thought of."

Edevart: "So what you want me to do is help you to leave me?"

Silence. "I don't understand!" she murmured despairingly.

He undid a button on her blouse and she did not resist. But when he made to undo a second one, she kissed him tenderly and sat back on the bench.

"Haven't you time?" he asked.

"No. He knows where I am."

Edevart shouts: "He knows you are here with me!"

"Yes. He asked me himself to come to you. Oh, he's not as bad as you think."

"I think he's worse!" said Edevart, confused.

Lovise Magrete: "No, it's just that he is so depressed. We can't get any help anywhere, and we'd give the whole of Doppen for it. It's all written here, if only you'd read it. He said I was to come and try with you. And he never thought . . . about anything else."

"It's all the same what he thinks. Or isn't it?"

"I don't know."

A sound from on deck, faint footsteps. Lovise Magrete listens, looking terrified. Edevart pays no attention, but continues: "No, you don't care a bit about me!"

"I do, I do! I love you! There's somebody on deck."

"All you want is to go off with him. That's all you want."

"What am I to do! It isn't easy for me, three children and everything . . ."

"It's three children now?"

She answers with her eyes on the floor. "Yes. But the last one isn't his."

Although the shuffling on the deck had become louder and could betoken danger, he was totally preoccupied by her last words. He asked sharply: "How do you know the last one isn't his?"

With a distant smile, she said: "I know all right!"

This gave him something to think about. An expression of anger crossed his face, when a fingernail scraped across the skylight and interrupted him. He shouted impatiently: "Get away from there!"

"Who is it?" whispers Lovise Magrete.

"Doesn't matter who it is—she's got to go away!"

"She? Somebody coming to see you?"

"Don't know. Might well be Miss Ellingsen."

"Really! Miss Ellingsen!"

"I'll go up and find out. Sit quietly here, then she won't see you."

He went up on deck and found himself face to face with Haakon Doppen.

Haakon greeted him in a whisper and said: "I just wanted to . . . Is she still here? I'm sorry about last year! Sorry! Here's my hand!"

Edevart was greatly astonished by the man's sudden change. There he stood, like some beggar, a poor wretch, pleading, pleading. You could smell the brandy from far off.

"What do you want?" asked Edevart.

"What do I want? Is she still here? I just wanted to help her to plead with you. But don't for God's sake say I've been here! I didn't want her to be alone when she asked you. Didn't want to make it too hard for her. That's why I came. I'll be sitting playing up in the servants' quarters till she gets back. We're in such trouble! Help us to get away. You can have the whole of Doppen just as it stands. Have you read the terms? You won't regret it. She'll bring the papers early tomorrow morning. Don't for God's sake say I've been here. Say it was somebody else. I'll leave at once. I just slipped away for a minute. I want to say sorry about last year. Here's my hand!"

He scrambled back onto the quayside and disappeared.

The drunken sot. He just wanted to see if I was undressed, thought Edevart, and he went back down into the cabin.

"Three children?" he asked. "Did you say you'd had a third child?"

"Yes," she replied.

"When did you have it?"

She named the day and the month, but made no great fuss about it. She didn't try to hold it against him. She was more concerned about who had been on deck. She asked: "Did you get rid of her?"

"Yes, I got rid of . . . her."

"I was so afraid," Lovise Magrete whispered. "I thought of hiding myself in your bunk. So, she comes here to see you?"

"Yes, that's right!" he said. "Creep into my bunk!"

She paid no heed to this, and asked more questions about Miss Ellingsen. Did she usually come at night? Did she come often? There was no bitterness in her words. She hung her head, thoughtfully. He turned her questions aside. Miss Ellingsen had had a message to bring this evening. She never came at other times.

"Now, Lovise Magrete, please! Won't you take your things off? Look, lovely white pillows . . ."

Still she sat there thoughtfully, not daring to look at him.

"Very well," he said impatiently. "You don't want anything. All you want is to leave me."

"I . . . leave you!" she cried. "No, I want to be with you as long as I live. I do. Dear God, don't you understand . . . ?"

How sorry he felt for himself! And when he gave in and promised to help her leave the country, he didn't recognize his own voice. Yes, he'd had second thoughts. It would mean unhappiness and ruination for him, but she didn't care. So be it, then.

His fate had declined. He would help her. She should have every-thing he possessed. Did that satisfy her?

"Oh!" she moaned, and clung tightly to him. He felt her breast rising and falling, felt her kisses more ardent than ever before. Again and again she murmured her gratitude, calling him by many a pet name—dearest lad, my darling, may God bless you!

At this moment of high passion he tried to advance by undoing her clothes. But she was unwilling, gave him no assis-tance. She began to cry. Surprised and angry, he pushed her away and said: "All right! Have it your way!"

"But I do want to! I do!" she cried. "If only you'll help us to get away."

So that was it!

He said curtly: "I've said I'll help you. Look! You can have all my money!" He ripped open his wallet and slapped the wad of banknotes down on the table: "You can count it yourself!"

"Oh! How much is there?"

"Count it yourself, I tell you!"

"No, no, Edevart. Bless you! How much is there?"

He mentioned the total sum.

"In heaven's name!" she exclaimed, with that familiar ex-pression of hers. "I shall thank you, sing your praises as long as I live. This is much more than we ever expected to get for Doppen. You can't give all your money away, can you? Look, won't you keep some?"

"Take the money, I said!" he ordered harshly.

Did he now expect her immediate surrender? He waited some time, but nothing came of it. She handed him the docu-ments to read. He threw them on the table. She promised to bring the real documents early the next morning.

"I'm not worried about that," he said, and waited.

She understood what he meant. She again wept and began to undo her clothes.

"What are you crying for? That earlier time you didn't cry."

"No, I'm not crying," she said. "Look, I'm undoing . . . Any moment now and I'll . . ." More and more she wept, her eyes brimming with tears. But she tried to pretend she was eager and in the mood, as though she was entirely willing.

Edevart stood up, hurt to the quick, and brutally threw her clothes back at her. He seized her by the arm and raised her. "Take the money and go!" he said. "I won't do you any harm!"

She tried to placate him, mumbling words of tenderness. But he tramped angrily up the stairs ahead of her. They came up into the darkness. She said urgently: "Edevart, I couldn't!"

"Couldn't you?"

"No, not tonight. I'm very sorry."

"You couldn't? So you'd lined it up that way before you came?"

"No," she said. "I didn't want to. It was Haakon who wanted me to do it that way. But I regret it."

Silence. Edevart, at length: "Why didn't you say so at once down there?"

She: "I couldn't . . . it was so light."

10 AUTUMN WAS DRAWING ON. EDEVART HAD FINISHED working on the sloop and was back again helping in the store. Business was good for a time; but as the shelves and the bins emptied and were not replenished, everybody realized that the end was approaching for Knoff. Admittedly, the quayside installations were now complete and all the workmen and the horses were gone; but this merely served to increase the sense of emptiness and desolation in the place. Lorensen, the head clerk, had already left Knoff's employment, and was doing all he could to make ready for the voyage to America so as to make his departure before winter. He was taking two of the store assistants with him. And up in the village a lot

of young men were getting ready to join the voyage to America. They would make up a big group, a colony. The people from Doppen were also intending to join the party.

This was America fever!

Knoff poured scorn on this malady! It was pointless. These wayfarers would come to regret their going! But nobody listened any longer to Knoff. He had forfeited their respect. Even old Skipper Norem shook his head at the decline of his boss.

"He overreached himself building that quayside," he said. "Even my wrecking the schooner is not really going to help him!"

There was an air of dissolution and unease about this otherwise large and busy trading place which only the boss himself appeared unaffected by. The quayside had been a crushing blow, but he was still breathing. The head bookkeeper had been dismissed, the baker was leaving at Christmas, and Miss Ellingsen, the housekeeper, had to manage with one girl less.

Edevart languished; he wanted to get away. He felt empty; he was hard up. His wallet lay flat in his pocket. He hadn't only got through his own money but others' as well. His brother, Joakim, would be making his demands soon. Admittedly Edevart had got Doppen for his money; he had the deeds and the receipt in his pocket. But Joakim wouldn't understand that bit of business; indeed, Edevart hardly understood it himself. Doppen— what did he want with that? Previously perhaps, but now . . . ?

On the agreed day, the emigrants for America arrived. They assembled down on the quayside and boarded a boat that was to take them as far as the landing stage. All the emigrants had a fair amount of baggage. Haakon Doppen had a lot of luggage, to say nothing of a wife and three children. But there were a few bags he was particularly anxious nobody should sit on: they contained pots and pans he was going to try to dispose of in Trondheim. There were fourteen men and five women in the party, as well as many children. The boat was fully laden.

Edevart deliberately stayed away from the leave-taking. He stood and waited on the road by the warehouses; only when he saw the boat out in the bay did he walk slowly down to the quay. A woman stood up in the boat and waved. Edevart waved back. He felt numbed; her leaving didn't mean all that much.

Knoff and Skipper Norem were standing on the quayside. Edevart was surprised that the boss had turned up, but presumably that was so as not to seem to be hiding. Never seem to be hiding, indeed not! As he turned on his heels to go, he said casually: "I'm going to set up two big lights here on the quay so the ships can see to unload at night!"

Norem watched him go, shaking his head. They talked for a moment or two about Knoff. Norem was afraid his mind was beginning to go. "You heard what he said! He's going to set up two big lights here on the quayside! Well, he's quite capable of that kind of stupidity. But it'll cost money! And the moment before, he'd been asking me to endorse a note for him."

"Oh, you don't mean it!"

"What do you think of that! The ship's owner having to ask the ship's captain!"

"Did you do it?"

Norem: "Promise to endorse his note? No, I'm not stupid! If I had, I might just as well have left straightaway with the others for America! But I've enough here at home to keep body and soul together, thank God!"

"That's more than I can say," Edevart mumbled.

Norem asked: "You got your wages, I hope?"

"No. We haven't settled up yet. What about you?"

"Me?" said Norem. "Yes, I made sure of what was mine first of all. I dried my fish only for as long as I had money for."

Edevart fell back. "Then the fish weren't dry when you left?"

"No! Oh, no! Far from it! But why should they be dry when they were meant to go to the bottom, anyway?"

Edevart, almost in a whisper: "They were meant to go to the bottom?"

Norem: "That's what I understood. Don't repeat what I'm saying!"

One couldn't really be sure that Norem's account of the matter was honest. Edevart left him, feeling very uneasy. The old rogue was maybe saving his own skin first by implying that he'd sunk the ship on orders. For the first time Edevart felt that there was something corrupt about Norem. Even in his appearance. His gray shaggy neck was too powerful and evil-looking. Arrogant and shameless, he bragged freely and openly about his duplicity. I could honestly wish him dead and buried, thought Edevart. Last winter he gave me the idea of stealing a few skilling, and where has all that thieving got me?

Edevart's view of the boss, on the other hand, was very different, despite everything. In his days of prosperity he, too, had been a rogue and a cheat. Now he was floundering, in trouble; but even today his vanity betokened something lively and scintillating, high above the run-of-the-mill. Edevart wasn't clear why he was beginning to feel sympathy for his boss. Perhaps he felt a little to blame for his decline. Apart from that, he felt the pity which the common people always have for a great man brought low. He remembered from his childhood days at home how a certain sheriff had been dismissed from his post for drinking and Edevart had wept and prayed for him. From what he now heard on all sides, things must be going very badly for Knoff. Mrs. Knoff looked thin and poorly compared with what she had been, because now she had to help Miss Ellingsen in the house. Knoff himself still went about with his gold watch and his thick gold chain across his waistcoat, but soon they'd come and take those away from him as well.

Edevart began to feel seriously worried about his wages. It wasn't at all certain that Knoff would be able to settle up properly with him. And how would things go with him then? He had some good clothes, a pocket watch, and a new gold ring; but, apart from that, nothing. And then he had Doppen. But what could he do with that? Edevart could always return to Polden and go off fishing to the Lofotens as before. In any case, he decided that when it came to settling up he would show sympathetic consideration for the boss's difficulties. That was the least he could do. He owed this to the boss.

On Sunday he borrowed a boat and rowed off to "his place," to Doppen. The green bay now looked faded and gray; the cottage was desolate, all its contents gone. The one unchanging thing about the place was the roar of the waterfall. In the hayloft he stood a while dreaming, recalling the ecstasy he had once known there. Then he closed the door and went over to the storehouse: Lovise Magrete had left behind a woven wall hanging for him. Dear God, as though she hadn't had enough to think about as it was! Carefully he rolled it up and took it with him. In the woodshed stood his crowbar. He left it there. The fields were still dotted with boulders.

Here there had once been a home. Parents and children had put down their roots here, had known joy and sorrow. Now this home was deserted. Not a sound to be heard anywhere; only the roar of the falls up in the forest. The wanderers dragged their torn roots behind them wherever they went; but the noise didn't reach here . . .

On Monday morning when the store opened, Edevart went in and stood there a while. There were no customers. The other assistant, the lad called Magnus, busied himself by taking down a few miserable remnants of material from the shelves, dusting them off, and putting them back up again. Only enough work for one man here. There was nothing to do.

Edevart knocked on the office door and went in. He nodded a greeting and said: "It's probably best if I leave now . . . don't you think so?"

"I don't think so at all!" answered Knoff. "Am I to be left here on my own? What's the matter with people! The Christmas trade will be starting soon!" Nevertheless, Knoff immediately seized his opportunity and nodded. "So you want to leave? All right, let's settle up! We still have that seine net to sort out, but that's beginning at the wrong end. How long have you been at the store, and how long did it take you to clean up the sloop?" Knoff took a pencil and sat ready for battle. He was certainly going to make sure of looking after his own interests.

"I don't want payment for those two things," Edevart answered. And when Knoff looked up at him, he added: "No. That wasn't real work."

Knoff seemed to weaken. There was no need for belligerence. He smiled almost sadly and said: "This is the first time I've known any of my men to voluntarily refuse payment. Quite the reverse. They've always thought they were getting too little, my men have. Always too little."

At that moment Edevart would have given much to have been able to stand and face his boss, frankly and blamelessly. There was no doubt that his men had each in his own way exploited him, cheated him, played on his vanity. No wonder then that the boss for his part had had to be on the alert and play their game! Touched, Edevart forgave him. It wasn't so very long ago that this same Edevart thought it was great to know all the tricks and have all his wits about him; now he felt humble, defeated. What was the matter with him—had he become simpleminded? Knoff, that great magnate, had had to abandon more and more of his business; here he was, nearly all washed up. This last year had aged him. He no longer had the look of a big man. Today he was even unshaven, and Edevart noticed he had tufts of gray hair growing out of his ears. A pitiful boss. But he didn't give up. Suddenly it seemed as though he didn't want to smile that sad smile any longer. Certainly not! His face took on again the look of a busy man; he pulled out his gold watch, looked at it, snapped it shut, and said: "There's six, nearly seven, months' wages. Don't interrupt!" He did his sums and wrote it down. While still writing, he said: "That net . . . I don't know . . . the bookkeeper didn't manage to look up what it cost me at the time. What will you give?"

Edevart answered evasively.

Knoff: "Shall we say ten daler for the net?"

Edevart: "Yes. Thank you. If you can do it for that."

Edevart did splendidly out of the settlement. As they parted, the boss said: "I'm sorry to see you go!" Then, curtly and severely, he added: "You can come back to me when things have improved."

THE TIDINGS awaiting him back home were many. One item was savage and terrifying. Polden and the surrounding district were like a storm-tossed sea after what had happened.

Who would have believed it of respectable people like that? Going about planning such dastardly and murderously criminal deeds? It took people's breath away; they weren't used to it. For years they had sung that song about a gruesome murder way down in Strassburg and shuddered at the worst bits; they remembered Andreas Mensa, who had been executed in Lofoten ten villages away; they hadn't forgotten the girl Ellen, who had strangled her child, but even that had happened in the neighboring parish and not here. There had never been the slightest hint of inhuman or dissolute behavior in that poverty-ridden and peaceful place. Now it was Polden's turn.

Ane Maria had just been arrested and taken away.

From all sides Edevart heard the story of her tormented conscience and her confession. During the light days of summer she had been able to bear her heavy burden and even walk with her head held high; but when the dark days of autumn set in, her mind gave way. She began one night with a great scream that woke the neighbors. And when many people had arrived and candles were lit, she rose from her bed and stood in her shift in front of her husband, Karolus, and the others and took upon herself the blame for the death of Skipper Skaaro in the bog a year and a half ago.

Unbelievable! She has lain there and dreamed it, they all said. They thought she had only got a return of that old sickness of the previous winter, when she went about mumbling, her mind disturbed. But she gave so many circumstantial and plausible details that there was no doubting her guilt any longer. Later she repeated her confession to the priest and to the authorities. She did not waver. She demanded her punishment. Even then there was a kind of pride, of hauteur about Ane Maria. She was no woman of straw. She wept as though she were being flogged; but she did not snivel. When the authorities asked her whether she had had anything against Skaaro, she replied: "No. Quite the reverse!" And asked why she had done away with him, she replied frankly: "It was because he wanted me but didn't ask me enough and left me alone!" All in all, Ane Maria displayed such incredible brazenness on this point that the authorities could only shake their heads. Even Josefine, the widow from Kleiva, and young Beret, both of whom found it difficult to behave themselves when it came to men, were aghast at Ane Maria's frankness. If the matter hadn't been so profoundly horrible, they would have held their hands to their mouths and sniggered.

The authorities didn't actually know themselves how they ought to proceed with Ane Maria. She was an unhappy creature, with no children to occupy her, ruthless in her desires, self-indulgent, but strong and capable. She had got it into her head that she wanted to punish Skaaro; and in cold blood she had watched him sink deeper and deeper in that bottomless bog. On the other hand, it had been proved that she had ultimately gone running for people to come and save him, had run as though her life depended on it, but had returned with help too late. So she had delayed too long in seeking this help. The very fact that she believed herself justified in taking revenge on Skaaro must point to some disturbance in her mind; and what in any case must very clearly stand to her credit was her own self-accusation and confession. She was dealt with leniently by the authorities: a combination of prison and asylum.

But it took Polden a long time to settle down. After such frightful events had occurred right in the middle of the village, it was not unusual to find even grown men reluctant to be out late at night, and children not daring to go out to fetch water after dark. There might easily be cries from the bog!

And then there was Karolus. What about him? He started to be something of a problem himself. If the truth were known, all this great upset in the district was to Edevart's advantage. Nobody paid any attention to him. His brother, Joakim, for example, was one of those who kept watch night and day over Karolus; so he did not come along immediately to demand his money. Edevart gained time.

Yes, Karolus took his wife's fate very badly, nobody doubted that. He ate nothing and drank nothing, but went off into the hills and lived among the rocks and bushes, and lay there talking to himself. God save anyone from being so sorely tempted to put an end to his life as Karolus was.

While he was still reasonably sane, they went to him and begged him to come back home with them. No, he mumbled, he didn't want to! They scolded him, asking whether this sleeping out in the hills was any way for a man of property and influence to live. Well, that didn't worry him! But, they said, you need looking after! You're getting nothing to eat or drink! You'll freeze or starve to death! Well, he was quite content if it was all over for him. There was no salvation anyway! Finally they put it to him that it was tempting God to stay out here at night when at any moment a cry might come from the bog. Well, Karolus said, that's as may be! He was in God's keeping! They got nowhere with him and had to let him be.

But however things were, it happened one dark and stormy night that Karolus himself felt that he'd been long enough in God's keeping alone. He had presumably heard something from the bog. In the pitch blackness he stole back home and remained sitting outside the village; toward morning he sneaked a few loaves and other items of food from the storehouse and ran off again. Somebody caught a glimpse of him from one of the cottages and called out to him, but he hadn't answered. Oh, Karolus was in a bad way! He was living up in the hills and there seemed to be no end to it. They went out to him every day to reason with him; but one day when they arrived, he had become insane. He was lying on his belly. Not lying on his side, not behaving decently and reasonably. No, he was lying there prostrate, flat on his face, with no desire now to appear impressive or imposing. Moreover, he had been lying on his yellow sou'wester, creasing and crushing it, that brand-new sou'wester of his! And when they turned him over, he lay there curled up like a ball. It looked bad. They spoke to him, but he no longer answered. It must have been a deliberate and exhausting position for him, lying there on his back with his knees drawn up and his head between his knees; and people muttered to each other that he must have got cramp. But all of a sudden Karolus rolled over and began running around on all fours, spiraling around like an animal chasing its own tail. After doing this for some time, he lay down elbows first, like some animal lying down forelegs first. It was a sorry sight. Suddenly he takes a daler note out of his purse and tears it in two. It was his last. People now understood that things were serious; now they would have to take him home by force. Somebody ran off for a rope in case he resisted; and while the others waited, they agreed among themselves to take turns in keeping watch over him. Here was an extremely sad case of insanity.

But it wasn't necessary to tie up Karolus. They got him on his feet and he stood there without demur. "What happened to the pieces?" he asked. Pieces? What pieces? Ah, the pieces of the banknote. Yes, Teodor had taken care to save them. He would get them back! Then they led Karolus back home; he was weak, and Teodor held one arm and Joakim the other. He seemed to accept this, and indeed walked along in docile fashion. Perhaps Karolus himself in some lucid moment had come round to think that it was a dog's life he was living out there in the hills, letting his madness accumulate. Perhaps he had also come to think that by now he had mourned long enough. Sure, it was a terrible pity about Ane Maria, but—in God's name—she really had been a nuisance and a burden.

Now the whole thing might have sorted itself out, but an insane man doesn't recover overnight. By no means, nobody must expect that. And the warders couldn't be withdrawn. Hadn't Karolus in his insanity wanted to get his hands on the parish records themselves? Nice thing that would have looked! A man who tore up banknotes wasn't likely to spare even the most important official and government documents. He might even have taken it into his head to tear pages out of the minute book! It was Joakim who for the past year had kept the minutes, and he had no desire to see his work ruined. "It won't happen!" said Joakim, and kept faithful watch. In due time he would enter in the minute book that he ought to have some payment for standing guard. He was running short of ready cash.

One day he had to ask his brother if he could let him have some money? Yes, answered Edevart, and gave him a couple of notes. Joakim didn't think this was very much, but Edevart said he hadn't any more on him. All in all, Edevart lived from day to day in Polden. Naturally he did not enjoy the same esteem as he had had some months earlier. This time he had no sloop or cargo or other distinction to show; but he wasn't completely overlooked, either. When it was feared that Karolus would not be able to take his boat out that winter, some of the men turned to Edevart to take over in Karolus's place. They pointed out that they were worried about putting their lives in the hands of a lunatic. Edevart promised to think about it. One thing was that he didn't have the tackle for Lofoten fishing; but already the fact that he had been picked out made him feel a little more assured about the future. Something would surely turn up. It also helped to raise him in the general estimation when one day he was able to spread a new woven cover over his bed at home, a magnificent object, gaily colored and fringed, such as had never before been seen in Polden. People shook their heads in amazement and thought: Oh, there must be more where that came from! Edevart isn't all that badly off! But he was, in fact, pretty badly off; he had crippled himself buying that farm in Fosenland. He felt most sorry for his little sisters, for whom he had brought nothing this time from the big world outside. One of them had her medallion and the other her snake ring on a string around her neck; but they had now grown out of their Sunday clothes and badly needed Josefine over in Kleiva to make them some new ones. Edevart saw his sisters' need, and suffered agonies. He realized that what they had earned during the summer drying fish had gone into the housekeeping.

One day as he was getting ready to go to the store, he noticed in his sisters a mood of happy expectation. They seemed to be thinking: What do a few nice dresses mean to a man like our big brother! But of course it meant a lot for big brother, and he was uneasy about the outcome.

Gabrielsen's big new store was closed. Simply shut. Edevart went around to the kitchen, met Olga—the girl with the beaded belt—and got her to get Gabrielsen to put in an appearance.

"What do you want?" asked Gabrielsen, looking severe. "The store? All right, let's go!" All the way there, he went rambling on. Why should he stand there all day long in the store? he asked. Nobody came, and those who did wanted credit. He had no liking for that kind of customer. "And that reminds me! That's a fine district chairman we've got over in Polden! He who's supposed to be so much better than me—and now there's his wife a murderer and he walks about on all fours like some animal, so I hear. Well, you're welcome to him! What was it you wanted?" He made ready to measure and to weigh.

Well, Edevart twisted and turned, but eventually he managed to say that it was a matter of having some tackle for Lofoten fishing, but he wouldn't have the money until he returned in the spring.

"Oh, go away!" said Gabrielsen.

This could hardly be anything other than a refusal, but Edevart had to persist. He took out the deeds of Doppen and put them on the table.

"What do I want with them?" asked Gabrielsen. "That's no hundred-daler note. Tackle? A score and more idiots have been here before you trying to get winter tackle on the security of their farm. The whole village is on its knees. You won't find a single man with a daler in his pocket. Security? I've no use for securities. Money is what I've use for. If you haven't any money, you might as well leave."

Edevart muttered that he was good for a hundred sets of tackle. It was just that at the moment he was a bit hard up . . .

Gabrielsen: "I'm hard up myself. I went and built this great papal palace of a shop and overspent myself. One of these days the crash will come. I'm just waiting for the end. Am I to play God Almighty to everybody who is hard up? I've never heard of anything so stupid! Get back home! At once! What the devil have you done with that money you earned? Weren't you here last summer, skipper of a sloop and with a whole cargo? Tackle? Consider the thing sensibly for once: I have to settle my account for tackle within thirty days, and you are asking for four or five months. Yes. And maybe you'll never come back from Lofoten alive."

Edevart: "In that case you'll have a whole farm as security."

"Security, my foot! Don't you security me! Where is this farm of yours?"

"In Fosen," Edevart answered.

"Might as well be on the moon. I don't want farms! Not anywhere! I can't pay my bills with farms. Go back home, I said! It's no use hanging about here!"

"I see you have some dress materials on your shelves," said Edevart.

"Materials? Yes, I have. But why don't you just go?"

"You can give me a few yards of dress material on this ring of mine."

"Can I now? Your ring?" asked Gabrielsen, somewhat confused. "I haven't any use for rings, either."

Edevart: "It's gold. And if you are going to have the material lying unsold on your shelves anyway, you might as well have a ring doing the same."

"Is it gold? Let me see it!" Gabrielsen weighed the ring in

his hand, looked at the hallmark, listened to the sound it made when dropped on the counter, and said: "You could always have a few yards of material for it. What kind of material?"

"Dress material for my sisters. Wool. I know what I want," said Edevart, stepping behind the counter. "I've served in a store myself."

They agreed on terms. Gabrielsen must eventually have realized that gold kept better than cloth and was almost as good as money for making payments. He became more amenable and said: "That brother of yours, Joakim, should have been strangled. I'm telling you straight. He inflicted that herring catch on us last winter and drove men mad. We all found we had been somewhat corrupted, and I wasn't a whit better than anybody else. God preserve us from another time like that! Everything became dearer, wages went sky-high, everybody became filthy rich and bought everything in sight. We just threw our money around. That lasted a few months, then we were poor again and much worse off than before. We were left with our minds corrupted. I had a piece of fine imported cheese left. What was I to do with it? What do you think I did? I ate it myself! Yes. Just like that. Spoiled, I was! But otherwise it would have gone moldy, you might say? No, I could have given it away, given it to the priest and got some of my annual church offering waived. Yes. But I and my wife ate it up. And d'you think I'll live any longer for that? Quite the reverse, probably, for there were quite a few maggots in it. Oh, nobody lives longer by eating rich food rather than plain! But you can tell that brother of yours that next time he makes a catch of herring he needn't come to me to telegraph all over the place to find him customers. I won't do it again! That much I have learned!"

As Edevart started to leave, Gabrielsen kept him with more talk. "I can't help laughing when I think of the chairman we got. I am going to make sure that I run rings around him next time. That road—shouldn't we build a road and allow people to get around? That's just what we should have done when we had money, and if I'd been chairman, that's exactly what would have happened. You people over there in Polden—do you think that Karolus is simpleminded? No more than you or me! He! he! that's priceless! Sheer tomfoolery! He was absolutely delighted to get rid of a wife that gave him no peace. But it doesn't matter what you people over in Polden are served with, you take it all as gospel. Karolus as chairman! Just go home now and throw a bucket of cold water over him and give him a kick up the behind, and you'll find he's all right. All the same, he'll never make anything of himself. He's never been anything, and never will be. You can pass that on, if you want to!"

Edevart went. In a narrow passage outside, Olga intercepted him, wanting to talk to him. She was waiting for him; she had, in the manner of servant girls, left her work and taken up a position here. He was after all a young lad; she knew him; and there weren't all that many young men around the place any more. Olga had washed and tidied herself up for the meeting, but she no longer wore her beaded belt, or her cross, or tassels on her shoes. No finery any longer. She was simply a dark-eyed girl looking for a bit of fun. Were they going to have a Christmas dance in Polden this year? In which case Edevart must remember to invite her. Were those visiting skippers coming again next spring? Nice men they were—a whole daler as a tip for the musician was mere chicken feed to them. Then there was that business about Ragna having a baby—crazy, wasn't it? But Ragna was a bit of a fool; she was too young to know any different. It was a blessing from God that the child departed this life. They say it was the grandmother who strangled it.

"They say what?" cried Edevart.

"That's what I heard. The old grandmother couldn't see how they could manage to feed both the child and its mother, so she did it. Hadn't you heard? No, you've been away all this time, but everybody around here has heard it. What I was going to say was: where did you take that sloop of yours after you left here? Ah, to Trondheim! Well, you've been around, haven't you! I also

217

tried to get to Trondheim but it isn't so easy, as I've discovered. Do you think any of those skippers might take me along if they came back here? Because even though you might well be sailing your sloop again, you'll not want me with you—which doesn't surprise me, because you've got a sweetheart down south and you'll want her with you. No, you needn't try to deny it . . ."

Edevart arrived back home without his gold ring on his finger, but rich and much happier than when he left. He had two dress lengths with him; and when Josefine came over from Kleiva to make the dresses, she shook her head, so overwhelmed was she at the magnificence of the cloth. The young girls had of course known all the time that when Edevart went off to buy anything for them, it would be of the best.

THE ARRANGEMENT was that Edevart should take over Karolus's boat and his tackle to go fishing in the Lofotens. Karolus agreed to this. He had become much more sensible. He now understood everything that was said to him and a little bit more. He doubtless noticed that the crew no longer had any confidence in him; and he pretended therefore that he had no objection to remaining at home himself while his boat and his tackle were making money for him. Indeed, he was damned smart, because he finally announced that he couldn't spare any time from his official duties to go off fishing. From then on he sat thumbing through the records and the minutes without giving the slightest sign of wanting to tear any of them up.

Edevart was not satisfied with the arrangements, not at all. There he was with another man's boat and tackle, and thus he was little more than a hired hand; all he got was a little supplement for being in charge. Was that anything for a man who had once been skipper! But he had no choice. If the fishing went all right, he would do quite well out of it; and he needed some money. He had begun to formulate a plan.

It was nothing grand or remarkable that he had in mind; but

he had to get away from Polden. For good? God knows, maybe for good. No use staying here.

He had never imagined that his home village of Polden could ever have become so awful. Murder, madness, and corruption were abroad here; a gloomy hopelessness hung over the people; there was shrieking poverty; there wasn't even food for the children. A house in Outer Polden had been broken into one night and some dried coalfish had been stolen; and the prints in the snow were those of children. Oh, dried coalfish—which is without food value, like chewing wood shavings! The herring catch the previous winter had destroyed the people's good sense and finally ruined them. Polden was bankrupt. Was this any place to be? Edevart lived and ate at home, consuming the little money his father made out of the telegraph company. He didn't know how he would get provisions for his Lofoten trip.

Little Ezra was the only one who was still able to laugh and be happy. He hung on Edevart early and late, just as a few years previously Edevart had hung on August. Ezra wanted to work for Edevart again, so Edevart signed him on as a half-hand in his Lofoten crew. Ezra had his wits about him. He was not confirmed, but he had seen the priest and talked himself out of it. He acquired some tackle and some oilskins and still had some money left over. "You can lend me something," said Edevart. "Sure I can!" replied Ezra, and laughed and took it as a joke. Edevart had no option; he was compelled to borrow a few daler from his galley boy. Well, only because his own money was tied up down south and he couldn't for the moment get at it.

That problem was over. That left Joakim.

Ah, Joakim had a nose for things. He had known for some time that things were not well with his big brother's affairs. He had happened to catch a glimpse of his flat wallet. And when his brother had returned that day with the two dress lengths, he noticed he was lacking his gold ring. Joakim was no fool; he was a thoughtful fellow. Of course he, too, had to think about his winter provisions; and when at length Edevart came and talked to him and admitted the whole sorry situation, Joakim already had a solution.

"What solution?" Edevart asked.

"You don't have to know," answered Joakim.

Edevart was very depressed about what he'd done. He couldn't tell the whole secret of his having bought the farm, but he showed his brother the papers relating to Doppen and he described the place: good buildings, a fine mountain behind, a big clear river, a waterfall to take their water from, good growing land, pasture sufficient for at least two cows, the whole thing in a splendid green bay. The people there had wanted to go to America and were forced to sell for what they could get. The price had been daylight robbery. The place was called Doppen, a pleasant-sounding name . . .

Joakim sat listening. Basically things were not as bad as he had feared. Edevart could so easily have lost his money, or gambled it away, the way he had knocked about the world! But he had put it into property, and that was something. But Joakim still felt constrained to shake his head over the whole business. For had he not once been in charge of a seine crew? Did he not know a thing or two?

Edevart: "You shake your head, but you should see Doppen!"

"What'll you do with it?" asked Joakim. "Will you settle there?"

"I don't know. But it was dirt cheap. Wouldn't you like it?"

"I don't think so," said Joakim sagely.

Silence. Edevart was glad to have got this over with his brother, and glad that it had gone well. He said: "As soon as we begin fishing, you shall have your money, I promise you!" And although he was the older brother, he began to talk to Joakim as an equal in order to flatter him. Yes, he had a plan. He wanted to get away from Polden. Wanted to go away, perhaps never to return, God alone knew. But he wanted to get away. This was no place to be.

Joakim: "Where will you go?"

"Ah, where will I go? A fortune-teller once said I would go to America like the others, but I'll have to see . . ."

The weeks passed. Christmas was over, a barren Christmas without festivity. It was no time for dancing and fun. All men and all things had been brought to their knees. Edevart wondered what it was that made him wish to leave Polden. What had happened to him? Could it be that he had already drifted around too much and become a confirmed vagabond? One place had come to be for him just like any other, no better and no worse. Any feeling he had for home was beginning to fade. His roots in the earth were damaged. What did they mean to him any longer: those familiar places in the district, the hillsides, the paths, the distant mountains, the sea, Polden itself? What did all those childhood friends mean to him?

One Sunday morning Ragna came to fetch him. She asked him to come over to her grandmother's cottage. Please, he had to come, for she was so puzzled . . .

Edevart didn't care particularly for Ragna any more. She meant almost nothing to him. When he recalled their school days, their playing together, it was like some dream. He remembered he had once helped her hunt for a shining button in the snow, a pretty button of hers with a crown on it.

When he got to the place where she lived, the old grandmother was sitting at the table leaning against the wall; but she did not move. Edevart stared at her, confused.

"Yes, she's dead," whispered Ragna. "I'd been out to draw water, and when I came back in she was sitting like that."

The grandmother was very old and her face was white. Now there was blood in one of her ears, but her expression was peaceful, almost smiling. It was as if she herself did not know she was dead.

"I didn't dare stay here alone," said Ragna. "Now you must help me to lay her out, otherwise she'll stiffen up."

Edevart had never before seen a dead person and would doubtless have preferred to clear off straightaway. But he felt it would be shameful; apart from that, he had been appealed to for help and he must act like a man. August would not have drawn back; and anyway, it was broad morning daylight. He lifted the body and carried it to the bed like a child. He was strong and the grandmother was so thin and small, shrunken like a doll. She was still good-looking, with an open serene expression.

Ragna deftly arranged things about the corpse, closed the eyes, and tied up the chin so that the mouth should not gape open. Finally she spread a kerchief over the face. When they left the cottage, she upturned a wooden bowl on the threshold as was the custom.

Ragna was thereupon homeless and had to go back home with Edevart.

During those days while they were under the same roof before the grandmother was buried and before Edevart was to leave for the Lofotens, he had several talks with Ragna. Now and then it seemed to him as though she had an eye for him; but as he felt nothing for her, she merely irritated him and he avoided her. Until the day she told him that Teodor was to have her.

"What's that!" cried Edevart.

Yes, he'd asked her many times, and then last Christmas she'd said yes.

Did he feel a spasm of jealousy? Was there still life in his childhood love? "Teodor with his rupture!" he said.

"So I've heard," she answered. "I don't know what that is."

He didn't know very precisely either, but it was something bad.

"It can't be helped," said Ragna patiently. "I've nobody else to turn to."

"Good luck and goodbye!" August would have said and made ready for the next affair. Edevart said: "I think that's really awful."

"How?" Ragna asked.

Edevart stood up angrily, as though to leave, and answered: "Why should I care! Do what you like!"

"I can't live in that cottage alone," she said dejectedly.

"So you'd rather throw yourself away?"

Ragna didn't know what to say to that. It was a good start to have the grandmother's cottage, and Teodor would surely be able to earn enough to keep them as well as any of the others. He wasn't bad-looking—you couldn't say he was.

"All right!" said Edevart furiously. "If you think you're in love with him, then go ahead and take him, along with his rupture. It's no business of mine!" Clearly he was jealous, and he hadn't been man enough to conceal it. When he realized this, he tried to laugh and act superior. But the attempt failed; his mouth formed a grimace; his feelings were in an uproar. Imagine! Teodor! Well, he was good enough for her! Suddenly he wanted to wound her, punish her; and he asked after the child—that child she'd had in the bushes, had she forgotten? Well? But of course the grandmother had strangled it, hadn't she?

Deathly pale she stammered: "What are you saying?"

"That your grandmother strangled it."

"No, no, no! It's not . . . I know nothing about that . . ."

"Then you're the only one who doesn't," he said.

She sat bowed, listening to him. He went ranting on, bitterly, stupidly. He'd always been a hot-tempered lad, as quick to do evil as good. Before he left, he snorted: "So you don't know anything about it? You must have lain there watching. I can well believe it of you."

Naturally he regretted his behavior afterward. What was she to him? It all came as a result of her never having set her cap for him. He had been mistaken. She had never really had an eye for him. No, she had ignored him. At school she'd paid no heed to him, and it had been the same for her ever since. He was bad at his lessons, and nobody thought very much of him.

Some days later, just as he was preparing to leave for the Lofotens, he saw her again. The whole crew was gathered down by the boathouse: Joakim, Teodor, Ezra, and an older man.

They were taking their boxes of provisions aboard, and attending to various things, when Ragna arrived.

She was no longer dejected. She was lively and in high spirits. Little Ragna was in the best of spirits and joked with Edevart about his crew. "Babes in arms, nearly all of them," she said. "Only one grown man in the boat!" The grown man was of course none other than her sweetheart Teodor, for old Martinus had become shrunken with age.

They all laughed at her joke and nobody took exception to it. But Ragna went on to speak maliciously to Edevart. Did he remember last summer when he was skipper and she was to make dinner for him? He'd been so grand he wouldn't drink water except from a glass.

Edevart might have responded to this in many ways, but he kept silent. It was in any case rather ungrateful of Ragna to ridicule Edevart for last summer. He had, after all, helped her quite a bit with that skipper of hers. And suddenly Ragna, too, seemed to realize this. She covered her face with her arm, turned, and left. Her back was bent with weeping.

A CHANCE EVENT which is good is considered providence; one which is evil is fate.

Here in the Lofotens it was Edevart's fate to have fallen to the level of an ordinary crew member aboard an eight-oar boat— he who the previous winter had been skipper of the sloop *Hermine* and able to entertain his friends from Polden with drinks and salt biscuits. A considerable comedown for him, both in his own eyes and others'! Last year he had aroused admiration, made himself a reputation; this year there was no trace of that. The men had no more respect for his words than for their own. Martinus, the old man of the crew, could call on his long experience and join in the talk about fish and about prices, about fishing weather and shore weather; whereas Teodor might as well have kept his mouth shut, though he talked the most. He was nothing.

At weekends and when they were inactive, they would sit in their fishermen's shelter talking about this and that. And what the man in charge said counted no more than what any other man in the crew said. Martinus was an even-tempered and wise old man, ignorant as a beast of the field, but not without understanding; moreover, he was of a religious disposition. Joakim, who was a great reader, would often go ashore and bring back with him some song sheet or a newspaper with which he entertained his friends. Edevart might of course have talked about Bergen and Trondheim, but Teodor had been there, too, and, it seemed, had had much more significant experiences.

"Yes, you others go sailing off seeing all the glories of the world and mankind," said old Martinus. "Yet I don't know, I'm so ignorant and unimportant . . ."

What did he mean by that?

"Nothing much, really," he said. "It's just that it's so strange the way people like you play around with life doing all sorts of things. God created each one of us in his proper place. And here we are. But you all go sailing away from it. I've lived all my life in Polden, like my father before me, and my grandfather before him, and his father before him. We all lived long. It must be getting on to three hundred years that we've been looking at the same sky and the same earth. One cottage after another has rotted away and fallen down, and then we've built ourselves a new one to live in. Providence was with us. We didn't go sailing off around the world. We lived in Polden and went fishing in the winter and lived as well as we could from year to year. That was good enough for us. We had no cause to complain to God. He kept us alive and did not forsake us."

Well, that was all very well, but to the younger men it was just so much talk; and Teodor began to whistle.

"You heard!" said Joakim to his brother. "You don't have to go away!"

"He was talking as much to me as anybody," said Teodor, pushing himself forward.

"Take Edevart now," the old man went on, unruffled. "He's sailed many a sea and been in many places and many parts of the world. And last year there he was lying offshore as skipper in charge of a great sloop. And so well known did he become that even Karolus, who'd been elected chairman for the whole village back home, was nothing by comparison with all that. But let anybody try flying higher than he has wings for and he'll take a mighty tumble."

Edevart: "Is it taking a tumble to come out fishing again?"

The old man: "Ah, you may be right there! But what did it all add up to for you? You sailed off and became a great man, then came back again to be no more than the rest of us. You didn't have providence on your side."

Edevart: "In God's name, providence can't be everywhere. It had to keep a hand free to hold over you!"

"Ha! ha! ha!" Laughter filled the shelter.

"Ah, yes!" said the old man tolerantly. "Have it your own way! But when you came home again, Polden wasn't good enough for you any longer. It was no place to be, you went around saying. Was it all that better where you'd come from? So why weren't you there? I don't know. Yon August is another one of your kind, who sails and sails and doesn't belong anywhere, and when he finally dies he'll be buried in foreign ground. What's he doing all that sailing around for? He could have been at home. He was a nice, bright lad when he was growing up. He could have been a good man in the boat . . ."

"No! no!" interrupted Edevart. "August was frightened to death in a boat."

"How can you sit there and say that?" cried Teodor. "I've sailed with August and I've never seen him afraid."

"Shut your trap, you clot!" growled Edevart. "I know what I'm talking about!"

Things went from bad to worse. They turned to abuse and they became very offensive to each other while the conversation lasted. But it passed over when they sat down together to share their bowl of stew, dipping their bread into it in turns. No, they were none of them cannibals. They were all poor, but this they had been used to from birth. When things were going reasonably well, or given a good catch, they were as pleased and encouraged as though great fortune had smiled on them. More they didn't want.

After a spell of fishing, Edevart paid back Ezra his loan. And in time he was able to do the same for Joakim. "How much was it?" Joakim wasn't sure. Well, the money's there! Joakim didn't want to take it. It led on this occasion to conflict between the brothers. Both were angry; neither would give way.

"What kind of money is that?" asked Joakim, pale with fury. "Go away and buy a plate of porridge with it!" Edevart called Joakim a louse and a pauper who couldn't afford to turn away money like this. But Joakim retorted that he could perfectly well afford to, and that *he* hadn't had to borrow money for his winter provisions like certain other people.

Oh, so in that case he must have stolen it somewhere? Perhaps he was the one who had stolen the dried fish in Outer Polden that time?

No, Joakim retorted that he was a bit better off than that. The district council itself had paid what was owing to him for his secretarial assistance and for standing watch over the chairman.

"The devil they did!" Edevart burst out. "But you'll take the money before I lose my temper!"

"You can put it into that farm of yours," replied Joakim, leaping up. "And now if you don't shut up, by God, I'll run you through with this bread knife!"

Edevart looked at him and gave way. Joakim had the same excitable temperament as himself. "So our dirty little brat can swear!" he said. There was nothing sentimental, nothing lovey-dovey between the brothers. They meant well by each other, but took care not to demonstrate it. Of course, Joakim was not some young upstart throwing his money around; he knew that his brother needed everything he could scrape together for his expedition. Apart from that, Joakim still had his Lofoten earnings untouched. The fishing was good, and in consequence the earnings, too.

Winter was now well advanced, and Edevart had come to an arrangement with one of the fishing vessels to come to Polden and had signed a contract. It was a new skipper who was to come and dry his fish in Polden this year, a man who was himself owner of both the boat and the cargo, an elderly man from Ofoten, dependable and serious-minded. He would supervise the drying himself. Joakim was to act as pilot for him across Vestfjord to Polden.

One day in late April, Edevart had a confidential talk with Martinus, the old man in the crew, and told him he was thinking of taking a long voyage.

"I knew it!" said the old man. "I was afraid of it. Who's going to sail the eight-oar home now?"

Edevart couldn't help laughing. "Sail the eight-oar? A child could do it. You shall take the helm yourself."

"No," said the old man, and shook his head. "I'm not taking any helm. I've never handled a boat. I've been a deckhand and sat there on the gunwale—and that I've been happy to do all my days. Good Lord, how you go tripping around! Where are you off to?"

"Well, where do we all want to go! It's off to America. Even though you've only got daughters, you know that one of them left for America."

"Yes, she went with her husband. Then she died. And now she lies buried in foreign soil."

There was no other way. When the fishing was over and the boat was to return, Edevart was gone. He had looked after Karolus's tackle very carefully, and had stowed it properly to be sent back home. He had left his oilskins hanging there, but he himself was gone. He had taken leave of nobody.

Part Two

Part Two

1

ON THE STEAMER A FEW PASSENGERS WERE SCATTERED about below deck. It was cold; they sat huddled in corners. Some were occasionally seasick but tried to conceal it; others, who were better sailors, bragged about it to anybody who cared to listen. Edevart came down from on deck.

Three men were playing cards for small stakes. They laughed and talked and banged the table. They sat on sacks and packing cases and their table was an empty upturned cask. Now and then they would drink from a bottle.

A young woman with several woolen scarves wrapped around her head moaned with seasickness and lay there as though lifeless. "We'll soon be in calm water," Edevart said to comfort her. She looked up with dead eyes and did not answer. He sat down beside her, looked down at his boots, and pondered. The ship's movement began to abate and the woman revived somewhat. They fell into conversation. She was on her way to Bodø to have an operation; there was something wrong with her throat. "Where are you heading for?" she asked. Edevart answered evasively that he hadn't fully decided; perhaps he might be going some considerable way. The woman had enough of her own problems to think about and asked no more. Time passed.

The card players called over to him and asked whether he would like to join the game. No, he didn't think so. Was he seasick then, perhaps? Edevart smiled and shook his head and said he was an old sailor. "Come and have a swig!" they said. He went over to them and took a gulp from the bottle. It was a mild kind of brandy, nothing to make you drunk. The men were from the south, discharged seamen from ships that had bought their fish in the Lofotens but which were now fully loaded and about

231

to leave for the drying grounds. The men had their earnings in their pockets and were in good spirits. They were heading for home; they were happy. Where was Edevart heading for? For the second time he answered evasively.

Aye, where was he going?

He had left his oilskins hanging in the fishermen's shelter as an indication that he didn't really have any further use for such things; but within himself he felt very unsure. To depart thus, to travel far—but what road should he take? Certainly, he had thought of leaving; and he had even said he would. But when it came to the point he hesitated. Apart from anything else, where would he get the money for a long journey? Since everything was so indeterminate, it was natural that he hadn't taken proper leave of his comrades.

What was the matter with Edevart? His hands were big and strong, his sinews in good trim; but his mind was split. Here he was, sailing away empty and homeless; he had gradually ceased to belong anywhere; wherever he went, he was dragging roots behind him.

The card players had nothing to show for their kindness toward him. He didn't want to play cards and wasn't much of a drinker. Finally they formed the impression that he must be religious and they made appropriate comment. "There are various views about playing cards," they said. "Some people think it is a sin." "Some people think it's also a sin to take a drink," they said, and looked fixedly at him. Edevart had no wish to be a wet blanket. He laughed out loud and said it was good to have a drink. And he wanted to thank them for letting him take a swig of theirs! He took a leaf out of his friend August's notebook and exaggerated somewhat: how he'd certainly taken too much on more than one occasion, but it left you with a terrible hangover. Huh! At this the others laughed and nodded and slapped him on the back.

"Have you got a watch to swap?" one of them asked. Edevart shook his head. But they persisted and asked him point-blank: "But you do have a watch?" Edevart unbuttoned his coat and held up his watch. His intention was to shut them up, but that wasn't so easy. The others also had watches, and these hadn't varied a minute in years and had never needed repairing.

"Where did you buy your watch!"

"From Papst," replied Edevart.

"From Papst?"

Yes, Papst was all right. He had watches costing from one daler up to two hundred. He only swindled wealthy people.

"I also bought mine from Papst," one of them said. "The best watch he had. Guaranteed for life. Let's see your watch!"

Edevart held it up to their ears so that they could hear how splendidly it went; but he would not allow them to open it. At this they took offense and said: "That's no gold watch!" They muttered among themselves, withdrew, and closed ranks against him. They began their three-handed game again, and Edevart looked on. Then there happened what usually happens: they quarreled about a few coppers. Edevart asked: "Shall I tell you what I think?" Yes, they all said. Edevart, like a fool, adjudicated; but he simply made enemies of the losers.

Time passed.

The ship made a stop. The seasick woman was sufficiently recovered to be able to get up; she shook her skirts, tidied herself up, then opened a box and began eating waffles. Edevart fetched her a cup of coffee from the galley, saying it would do her good. She thanked him kindly and offered him waffles in return. There followed a long conversation.

Yes, she was going to be operated on in Bodø. Her husband was going to meet her there, coming from the south. He was a traveling salesman, selling from door to door, a peddler. He'd been many months away. Dreaming, longing, she couldn't bear it any more. They had only been together for a few weeks after the wedding; then he'd gone back to his job, traveling all over the place and exposed to all kinds of temptation. He'd taken his wedding ring with him, but God alone knew if he hadn't hidden it

233

in his pocket—forgive my sinful tongue! Now he was planning to come up and meet her . . .

While she was talking, she had loosened the scarves about her head and neck; and now she sat there with her face open to view. She was young and pretty. No faults. Even her teeth were flawless.

Edevart looked at her in amazement. "I'm not sure, but I think I know you!"

"Mattea!" she said, and nodded.

It was Mattea from Stokmarknes Fair. August's sweetheart for a day.

Edevart was at a loss for words. "Fancy meeting you here . . . it's two years ago now . . ."

"Three years," she corrected him. "I recognized you at once. That's why I wrapped all these scarves around me. But then you brought me coffee, and you were nice to me. And anyway, I have nothing against you. Where's your friend August?"

"I don't know. On one of the seven seas somewhere. He's everywhere—now rich, now poor."

"Was he angry with me?"

Edevart replied: "We went looking for you that last morning. We went all over Stokmarknes, but we didn't find you."

"I looked for him, too," said Mattea, "but I hadn't time to do more than I did. Well, that's a long time ago now! What I was going to say was: where are you heading?"

Edevart: "Don't ask me! 'I go lost in a thousand thoughts,' as it says in the song."

" 'And love the one you cannot have!' " Mattea added with a smile. "Has she made a fool of you?"

"She's gone away."

"Poor lad!" said Mattea sympathetically. "But don't you go worrying about her—a nice, good-looking lad like you."

Edevart was flattered. "What's wrong with your throat? I can't see anything."

234

"If only you knew!" she replied with a sly smile.

"So it's a secret?"

"Yes, it is," she replied. "There's nothing wrong with me. But I had to think up something, so I wrote to him to say I couldn't face having an operation on my own without him."

Edevart was struck dumb. He stared open-mouthed as if he didn't know what to believe. "That sounds pretty devious!" he said.

She tried to play it down. "Well, it's not just a wild-goose chase he's coming on, not entirely. For I did have a pain in my throat when I wrote. And I really will go to the doctor and have myself examined. But the main thing was to get him to come and meet me, and I can't be blamed for that. And all the neighbors said the same—that I had to have an operation."

Edevart felt more at ease with her now, and allowed himself a joke: "Well, I must come along and watch you being cut open."

"You mustn't joke about it. I might be worse than I think."

"How can you talk like that! A good-looking healthy woman like you. If I was your husband I'd be very satisfied."

They talked animatedly. Inside the skerries the sea was smooth, and she was relaxed and happy. They told each other where they were from. He explained that he'd bought a farm to the south and showed her the deeds. In the evening they sat together until they fell asleep. When he noticed that she had slipped her hand into his, he leaned over and kissed her. A faint light showed dimly from a distant cliff. Here and there, passengers sat about dozing.

Edevart and Mattea woke several times during the night, whispered together, and nestled closer. He had his arm around her, and that warmed them both. By morning they were very well acquainted.

When they got to Bodø, she saw her husband in the distance standing on the quayside. "There's my husband," she said. "I think you'll recognize him. It's Nils, the one I was engaged to.

You met him at the fair. He's the son of a wealthy skipper in Ofoten. Ha! ha! When I think how worked up August got, I can't help laughing!"

Of course! It was the young lad who had had August brandishing a bread knife and flinging a stool at the ceiling. Ah, that had been a tremendous moment! And Mattea, the little witch, had denied being in any way to blame, and subsequently had taken a solemn oath that she would belong to August for life.

"Are we never going to meet again, do you suppose?" she asked Edevart.

It was doubtless only a polite inquiry without any deeper significance; but at the last moment she slyly felt behind her back for his hand. This was not without its effect on him. He was thrown off balance and said: "I might just as well get off here as well!"

He had no plans. His thoughts lacked any firm shape or direction. He was not reversing any decisions by obeying a sudden chance impulse. Carelessly, without any deeper intent, he quickly handed in his ticket and stepped ashore.

It was a matter of indifference—it seemed to offer a way out of things.

To BEGIN WITH, Nils was a bit embarrassed at meeting Edevart again. "At Stokmarknes? Ah, *that* time!"

"Yes, don't you remember?" said Mattea. "That crazy man with the gold teeth? Ha! ha! He was really worked up!"

They walked up to the town, talking as they went. They stopped outside a lodging house and went in together. They ran into each other again later, and indeed often met, living as they did in the same house. Mattea saw the doctor and—praise be!— did not need an operation. She was given some drops and some good advice; and at this she was very relieved. Nils thought of a plan: Edevart and he could join up and go into business together.

Edevart had that farm of his down south: they could raise all sorts of credit on that. He himself had a wealthy father up in Ofoten, though it was difficult to get anything out of him.

Edevart was by no means against the plan. It didn't seem a bad idea. It also felt good to sit there, seemingly well-off and solvent, and be able to say yes and no to things. Mattea looked at him, and spoke enthusiastically about the idea. It was as though she would like to have him near her, as though she was well disposed toward him.

"I'll think about it," he said.

He thought. But, all things considered, why should he join up with somebody else just to go off selling from door to door? Nils had complained about his lack of credit; his stock was nearly all gone; he was scraping the bottom of the barrel. What had this to do with Edevart? Couldn't he exploit his little farm for his own benefit? Use it as security for goods and go into business on his own? That would be another way out. Mattea made the point that Nils had experience; he had been traveling for two years. Edevart smiled at this and indicated that he was no novice either when it came to business. He had served in a good school—with the great Knoff at Fosenland, no less.

But Nils had his regular route, said Mattea. He knew everybody in all the places and how to handle them. He also had his father.

That afternoon Nils went to call on the merchants of Bodø to try to raise a few more goods for his nearly empty pack. While Mattea was alone with Edevart she managed to talk him round— persuaded him so convincingly that he was unable to get out of it. She was very determined. But this time Edevart did not lose his head, did not do anything stupid; this time he wasn't in love. When Nils came home and heard the good news, Edevart shook him by nodding and saying: "We'll draw up a contract!"

"Contract? Why?"

Edevart merely nodded again.

They went to a lawyer and drew up a paper. Edevart stuck

237

to his guns. It was his farm, and it was he who was raising the credit. Nils came in on the deal simply as an assistant.

Ah, Mattea! Determined Mattea! She turned pale with fury. "You just go and burn that contract!" she said to her husband.

Edevart had no objection. Mattea wearied him with her relentless persistence. He remembered how, three years ago, she had run off with August's watch and gold ring.

"Go ahead and burn it! Doesn't matter to me!" he said.

No, no, Nils wouldn't do that. They would remain friends and let time take care of things. Perhaps it wouldn't be too long before he would be able to buy himself out of their arrangement!

So the two traveling salesmen stocked up in town; then each went his own way. Edevart took the regular steamer southward along the coast of Helgeland. He went ashore with his pack and his yardstick at one of the smaller landing stages to see how he got on. It was early morning, a bright day; the ground was covered with snow. A footpath led up from the quayside at the little trading station, then a broad road continued up to the village. He stopped at a little brook, saw the throb of the water beneath the ice crust, and heard its sad little gurgling sound. Later in the day he noticed catkins already beginning to sprout on the osiers standing in the snow—these were things he understood, things familiar from his childhood, things which spoke to his heart. He had not been wholly corrupted!

Things did not go too badly with his business. He worked his way south, selling cloth, shoelaces, combs, and other necessities at the various places, and earned enough to keep him and a fair bit more besides. The pack grew lighter; he hadn't such a heavy load to carry. It was work that appealed to him; he could wander along or stop quietly just as he felt like it. In some larger village he might stay several days and do business with the entire neighborhood. And bit by bit his wallet grew fatter with banknotes. The young good-looking lad met no hostility; he was well-behaved and polite, quite ready to knock a bit off the price, and thus paid almost nothing for board and lodging. In truth, Edevart had never known better days than these, not even when he was skipper of the *Hermine*.

He sent a remittance to the merchant in Bodø and still had some ready money left. At reasonable intervals he sent a daler or two back home to his father. From Nils he heard nothing.

He wandered on from place to place. Signs of spring were everywhere; the going underfoot became difficult, the roads muddy and impassable. He thought of getting himself a boat, then realized that would have to wait until he could better afford it. When, by early summer, he had got as far south as Fosenland, he considered making a little detour by way of Doppen; but this, too, he put off. It would be no novelty for him to see the place again, nor any pleasure either while it was mortgaged and the mortgage still unredeemed. That fine fellow Nils ought to be sending money. Why hadn't he? By this time he must surely have sold the greater part of his stock; Edevart's own pack was as good as empty. He no longer carried it slung over his shoulder but as a bundle under his arm.

His road led past Skipper Norem's place. A dog barked. Somebody was already standing at the window, so he couldn't pass by unseen. He made a quick decision, wiped his muddy boots in the snow, and entered. A cry of recognition, many questions and answers, great astonishment, much friendly jocularity. What was he up to now? So! He'd become a peddler! Open up the shop! His wife very badly needed four yards of calico for another christening dress—couldn't he see how big she'd become!

Norem himself had a great shaggy mane of gray hair, and looked as self-satisfied and as wicked as ever. Neither he nor his family knew that that tiny white speck on the end of his tongue betokened any danger. It meant death. But they didn't know that.

Edevart heard all about the way things were in the village, about Knoff and his place, the quay, the store, the workers and servants he had dismissed, the sloop *Hermine*, which was away, and all the business interests which had been abandoned.

239

Edevart: "So that's the way things went. Was Knoff bank-rupt?"

No, but crippled, said Norem. As good as ruined, you might say. But not absolutely flat. It was like a fairy tale, and the devil alone knew how it happened, but the son had managed to lay hands on some money. Romeo, that fifteen-year-old lad—there's a bright spark! When he left school he pulled himself together, got confirmed, then suddenly he was a grown man! He set to work. Nobody had seen anything like it—fifteen years old and a grown man! He had a trustee and had to seek advice; but he was so exceptionally clever that he always managed to get his own way. "You remember him? He wasn't particularly bright before."

"Where did the money come from?"

"From his father's brother, they say. A big landowner down south. All the Knoffs are big people. This one was a bachelor farmer, something of a miser. He's believed to have refused help to his brother here more than once. Then last year, when things got pretty desperate, Romeo was sent down south to beg for help. But no, he still wouldn't. Far from it. He couldn't afford to. But Romeo himself must have appealed to his susceptibilities. He gave the lad both money and presents; and when he died last March, he left his nephew everything. They're busy now trying to sell the large farm and sorting out all the other assets."

So many things to hear about!

Norem had news of the emigrants to America; letters had come from many of them, and a little money, too, for some of the old people left behind. It seemed they hadn't done too badly in America; they had found work in the towns and on the land, and they weren't complaining. They wouldn't be returning home until they were rich—indeed, why should they? They remembered how hard it had been to get half a pound of coffee on credit when they were hard up; and now they had silver dollars jingling ceaselessly in their pockets. "Well, good luck to them with their American money," said Norem. "I wouldn't swap! Look at Haakon Dop-pen, now! He writes to one of my sons that he'd just been playing his accordion at a wedding and got eight dollars for it. Eight dollars for a single night's work! I've never earned that sort of money. Anyway, where does it get him! When, at the same time, one of the others writes about Haakon Doppen that every time he makes easy money like that, all he does is drink it—he never puts any on the side for the future."

Edevart: "He has a wife and children."

"Yes, you know them, don't you?" Norem continued. "He's just the same as he always was—hasn't changed a bit. Didn't he spend several years inside, and it didn't do him a bit of good! He'll run into trouble in America, too, I declare. And things don't seem to be going too well with Lorensen, either. You remember Lorensen, Knoff's chief clerk? He's complaining that he put so much money into the crossing. Well, Lorensen was never the kind of man to show off. If there was ever anything he did, it was to complain. Now I suppose he's heard that Knoff has laid hands on some money, and now he's regretting that he ever left. For there's no doubt that Romeo's going to make the business pick up again."

"And what about yourself?" asked Edevart. "Have you packed up for good?"

Norem: "Packed up! What do you mean? But what can I do without a vessel? I'm just waiting. I've spoken to Romeo; and it surely won't be all that many years before he has vessels of his own again, and then I'll be taking another trip to the Lofotens. Why should I be giving up? Don't you believe it! Perhaps you and I might again be sailing to the Lofotens for the same firm. You surely aren't thinking of spending all your life wandering around with a bundle under your arm selling christening materials, are you?"

"I don't know. I like doing it."

"But you haven't any stock?"

"I'm sold out. I shall buy new stock again. And I've been thinking of buying a boat."

Norem was seized with suspicion: this lad wouldn't be looking for a guarantor, would he? "A boat?" he said. "You'll get that from Romeo. He's selling out. And if you haven't ready money, he knows you to be an honest man."

"I have the money," said Edevart.

Norem was relieved. "Ah, so you have the money? Then what's holding you back? I didn't want to ask, but they say you've been saddled with a little farm near here?"

"Yes, Doppen. That's right."

"Then you can't have all that much money left. Not that it's any of my business."

Edevart somewhat evasively: "Well, not all that much exactly. A few thousand, maybe." Whereupon he looked about the room negligently to give Norem a chance to respond.

"A few thousand?" he asked. "Did I hear right?"

"I'm not just running any small business," Edevart deigned to reply. "I have a few assistants acting on my behalf up in Nordland."

"Is that so!" said Norem, and capitulated.

EDEVART WANDERED down to the store. He was familiar with the place; he had himself stood behind the counter here and sold things and taken the money. The young assistant was still Magnus, but he had grown, was really grown-up, a big man. Edevart had thought of getting him to write a letter to Nils demanding money—for he was greatly superior to Edevart when it came to forming his letters—but Magnus proved to be very odd and cool in his demeanor, so much so that he barely managed a nodded greeting. Edevart bought some little thing to justify his call, then left the store.

Outside he ran into Miss Ellingsen. He prepared to stop and shake hands with her, but she walked past him. Of course she nodded slightly in recognition, but she walked on past. This caused him considerable astonishment; but it didn't upset him. He had rather dreaded this encounter. He watched her as she went, but she did not turn around.

He made his way to the bakery. Yes, the bakery was working; the fire was burning in the oven, and two men were preparing the bread—the baker himself, Edevart's old roommate, and an apprentice. All was as it should be. The baker told him that he had in fact gone off to Trondheim and found work there, but some months ago he'd been recalled by Romeo and was now back here again. Changes for the better! Things were improving around the place.

Edevart asked after the cooper. Yes, he was still living in that house of his; the cooperage was no longer active, and the cooper himself had gone over to something else. He was a handyman around the place, and worked mainly on cutting firewood.

Edevart prepared to leave and said jokingly: "Ah, well, I just thought I'd look in and hear what you had to say. And whether there was anything you wanted—whether you had enough flour."

"I have flour," replied the baker.

"If not I could easily come back with a few hundred sacks."

He went to the cooper's, found the wife at home, and asked if she could put him up for a few days, as she had before. That she could. They talked to each other; they discussed how things were with Knoff, she from her own point of view as a woman. No, Mrs. Knoff wasn't to do the housework any longer; they were to have a couple of housemaids again, because Romeo didn't want his mother to wear herself out. Oh, Romeo would surely restore things to what they'd been before—he was so wealthy! And Miss Ellingsen had got engaged to Magnus . . .

"What?"

"Exchanged rings and all, everything fixed. Of course she's somewhat older than he, but she's a very capable woman. You remember her? They say she made a dead-set at him, hanging around his room early and late. But people say all sorts—please don't repeat what I've said. Are you staying on here?"

"No, I just want to get hold of a boat."

He went back to the store somewhat better informed. As

things stood, he did not wish to ask any favor of Magnus. Instead, he went straight to Romeo's office.

"Well . . . !" said Romeo, surprised, and held out his hand as he did when he was young. "So, you've come back to see us again!"

Romeo hadn't exactly grown more manly. He had grown tall and thin and remarkably long-armed, which made his sleeves seem rather short. "What's on your mind?" he asked. "Why are you traveling around? I hear you have become the owner of a little place in the district. Now, what's it called?"

"Doppen," replied Edevart, who nevertheless did not pursue the question. Instead he explained that he had gone into business, as a traveling salesman—he had to try something—and he ended up dropping a hint about a boat.

Romeo: "A boat? Sure, you must have a boat. Four-oar or six-oar?"

"Six-oar. With sail and anchor and complete tackle. But that isn't the prime reason I've come to see you today. But it's a shame that I come here asking things of you and taking you away . . ."

"What is it?"

Edevart made further explanation. He had a man up north working for him who had stocked up with lots of goods but since then had sent no word about money matters. Now the greater part of six months had gone by. Would Romeo write an urgent letter of demand to him?

Romeo agreed at once; he wrote a formal letter, phrased in businesslike fashion. Romeo certainly set out to do his best; perhaps it appealed to his young heart that Edevart—to whom he had clung as a child—should now address him so respectfully. "Yes, come whenever you like," he said finally, "and we'll go and look at the boat. You can stay here and sleep at the baker's as you did before."

"I've fixed myself up at the cooper's."

"Why have you done that?" asked Romeo. "My father

won't like that. He's talked about you. He said you were a useful skipper. Have you looked in to see him?"

"Not yet."

"Come up with me to lunch. You are sure to meet him then."

Edevart excused himself. He wasn't dressed for it; the condition of the roads was very bad and he was dressed accordingly. Thanks, many thanks, all the same!

He stayed at the cooper's and took things easy. After a few days he began strolling about the place in the evening, pretending he was looking for his friend the baker; but his thoughts were elsewhere. Actually he thought it rather shameful that Miss Ellingsen had gone over to Magnus—a downright miserable thing to do. Not that Edevart really deserved any better of her, all things considered. But, all the same: a shop lad! Young Magnus! If only Edevart could manage a meeting with the lady on her own; it would be odd if she didn't show him a little of her old affection!

He did not succeed in catching her. She was doubtless lying low, staying in her own room or in her young man's and not showing herself outside. In one way this could only increase his respect for her: she didn't play false. She kept to one man at one time, and wouldn't be moved. Well, she had tried her wings a little—what was her name again? Karoline? She had indeed tried her wings, had given herself, had jumped in with both feet. And, damn it, how tight she could cling! Ah, yes, but she was faithful —and faithful now to Magnus.

There was no denying that he was worked up. The hunt also wasted a lot of his time. He delayed his departure on its account —and how could he afford to do that! He stayed for over a week.

One day he had a message to say that a letter had come for him, a registered letter. This was something extraordinary—what could it possibly mean? It was from Mattea, a sharp and offended letter, a mixture of lies and truth, but otherwise direct enough, devastatingly direct. Here was the money which Nils owed him.

Thank God, Nils need no longer be a mere assistant. He was not his father's son for nothing, wrote that go-getter Mattea. Moreover, she now made so bold as to ask whether Edevart had at any time given any account of his movements or left an address. For if he had not, it was clearly impossible for Nils to send money to an itinerant peddler of no fixed address. The money had now been in her hands for a long time, she lied. And she added, in righteous indignation, that he'd better not think of reporting Nils to the authorities if he wanted to avoid unpleasantness!

Mattea, the go-getter!

Good! Edevart settled his accounts with the merchants in Bodø down to the last penny, and still had money in his pocket. He sent a couple of five-daler notes back home to Joakim and still remained well-off. If Romeo had gained the impression that he wanted that boat on credit, he'd been mistaken; and he would go and tell Romeo so.

He met father and son in the office. The elder Knoff drew himself up, did not offer to shake hands, but nevertheless greeted his one-time skipper in friendly and familiar fashion. "I am glad that you remembered what I said to you when you left—that you had to look in on us again when conditions had improved. I don't know whether I can make very much use of you at this moment, but it doubtless won't be long before I can."

Romeo explained that Edevart was now in business for himself, that he was now working his way south selling his goods, that he had men working for him in the Lofotens and was doing good business. Now he wanted to buy a boat.

"Yes, it was that boat I've come about today," said Edevart.

Romeo: "Just so. I said that you could take the boat."

Edevart looked at him and smiled. "Yes, but I wasn't exactly thinking of borrowing it."

"No?" said Romeo. "Of course not. You shall have it any way you want." And like a flash our young lanky Romeo showed the kind of man he'd grown into and how quick-witted he was. "Have you any stock?" he asked.

"No."

Romeo: "It so happens that we are having a clearance sale just now. And Father and I were thinking that you might just as well stock up from us as from anybody else."

Old Knoff nodded but looked distant, as though he were hearing this now for the first time.

Edevart: "I had thought of stocking up in Trondheim."

"Why do that?" asked Romeo. "We can offer you a good price and load up your boat here."

Old Knoff spoke up. "My dear Andresen, so you doubt my ability to undersell those small merchants in Trondheim?"

"No, please don't misunderstand me . . ."

Romeo: "We have surplus stock which you can have at rock-bottom prices: materials, garments, and other necessities. They are as good as new, but they have been lying there a long time. You can sell them at a good profit. We can't get rid of them here, for people recognize them from one year to the next. Come with me into the store and look at them. You'll remember many of the things from the time you were here yourself."

They went in and looked over the shelves. They began negotiating. A great pile of goods was laid on the counter. Edevart was overwhelmed. He had to resist, to restrain himself. "I can't afford to buy your entire store. No, no, not twenty rolls of twill— ten, maybe. How on earth am I going to sell all this? The boat won't take it all!" He pondered more than once. The prices were not exactly rock-bottom, but they were unexpectedly low, and Romeo never seemed to tire of repeating: "Go on, take it! We'll never sell it, anyway. You can pay us later."

Once Magnus pushed himself forward, doubtless wishing to help his master. He flushed and said: "No, that would be too stupid! That's less than half price! If you look at the invoice . . ."

Romeo did not answer him.

They were still not finished when the elder Knoff emerged from the office, opened the gold case of his watch, snapped it shut again, and announced: "Lunchtime. Come along, Andresen!"

Edevart again tried to excuse himself, but Knoff uttered only one word: "Come!"

Once again Edevart found himself standing in a splendid room, enjoying a glimpse over the fence into a world far removed from his own. He greeted Mrs. Knoff and her daughter, bowed low, and was often rendered quite speechless by their kindness to him. No place had been set for him at the table, but Miss Ellingsen blushed and went to remedy the deficiency. He felt very small and wished himself far away; but Romeo came and sat at his side, and old Knoff now and again turned to address him. "Are you thinking of going into business for good, Andresen? If so, you can always use me for a reference!"

What concerned Edevart somewhat was that Miss Ellingsen couldn't avoid serving him at the table, pouring out his soup, removing his plate. He was annoyed with himself for not being better dressed, for not even wearing his gold ring. What must Miss Ellingsen be thinking of him? That he was just some ordinary peddler who still got his stock on credit from the local store? On the other hand, no run-of-the-mill peddler would be likely to get invited to Knoff's house and dinner table. And this gave him a lift, made him feel grander. Who knows but what Miss Ellingsen wouldn't soon be regretting that she hadn't hung on to him! A casual remark also helped. Old Knoff, happening to hear that he'd been here several days, said: "Oh? I haven't seen you."

"He's staying at the cooper's," Romeo explained.

Knoff: "At the cooper's? Why aren't you staying here?"

Edevart, evasively: "It happened to fit in . . . I thought . . ."

"You thought what . .·. ?" said Knoff, hurt.

Romeo: "You hear that, Edevart? I told you my father wouldn't like it!"

All this Miss Ellingsen found herself having to listen to. Perhaps it might lead her to break with Magnus!

After the meal he saw no more of her. He continued making his purchases in the store, made his choice of boat, paid what he could of the total, and made ready to leave. Magnus was made to help load the boat. He did it on instructions, without chatting and joking as he had in the old days when they worked together.

"When are you sailing?" Magnus asked, his face averted.

Edevart realized that he was in a bad mood and wanted to see the last of him. He hung on the answer to the question. Once again Edevart hesitated. Suddenly he had no strength of will left. He saw in front of him a tormented and jealous youth whom he could frustrate and torture. Magnus had always been a nice lad— why should he now be nasty to him? A thought occurred to him that weighed heavily with him: what blessing could he expect for his great expedition with that laden boat if he behaved as badly as this? Was he to show himself so utterly godless?

"I'm sailing at once," he replied. "There's nothing more for me to do here." There—it was said! So he had, after all, wasted a good number of days trying to effect a meeting with a certain lady. August wouldn't have given a damn about matters of conscience and simply thought of the excitement of the moment. Edevart felt himself incomparably more righteous.

Relieved, Magnus said: "So, you're sailing at once? Are you more or less ready?"

"I just have to go and settle up with the cooper. What do you think about this business of mine, Magnus?" Edevart asked, wanting to be nice to the other and hear his opinion.

"What do I think?" answered Magnus. "I'd be very happy if I had all your stock at the price you paid."

"You think so? Well, now let me say thanks for all your help!"

They parted. Edevart went to settle up with the cooper and sailed immediately afterward. It was like leaving with a floating shop.

Of course there were disadvantages traveling by boat. He had to tie up at certain fixed places which he judged to be right and then work the surrounding district; and when that was done, he had to make his way back to the boat again and continue on to a new district. He might have made more rapid progress on foot. The one good thing was that the boat served him as a base where he could store things he couldn't carry in his pack.

He worked his way south, selling his goods at reasonable prices and yet still making a good profit. It became clear that he had bought at very advantageous prices. As early as St. Olav's Day, he was able to send a hefty remittance to Romeo and still have money left over. But the pleasantest thing for him was the free-and-easy manner of his work. He was his own master, he could move on or stay put just as he wished. It was truly a drifter's life, and matched the irresolution and lethargy of his present ways.

He sailed up the Trondheim Fjord, raked over the whole of the western side, went on past Inderø, pressed forward into Namdal, and then turned back again through the inland villages. Summer was over. Autumn was well advanced. The snow had arrived.

At a farm up in Frosta he ran into August.

2

AUGUST HERE?

He was working on the farm, and hadn't gone to Bergen after all to sail the seven seas. He had wandered on from place to place in Trøndelag taking casual work. He came in for supper quietly and humbly, tucking his cap under his arm and looking around for a place to sit. A hired hand.

Edevart had just been promised a room for the night and was sitting there looking about him. There were also two girls, each busy with her own work, and a number of children in various parts of the room. The table was set with two large bowls of porridge and milk to go with it. A lamp was burning over the table.

When August caught sight of Edevart, a foolish grin came

over his face and he leaned forward in order to see better. Edevart, for his part, stared back at him. "What in the world . . . ! Is it you, August? This is unexpected!"

The man of the farm came in with ponderous tread. He was a heavy man, slow in his movements, dressed in working clothes and knee boots, young and powerful, with a full blond beard and a pug nose. He looked in astonishment at the two friends who had found each other and were talking together.

"This is a peddler who is staying here," the wife explained. "He can sleep in with the other man."

The husband said nothing but sat down at the table and picked up the spoon. One by one the others also sat down at the table, and finally August, who stood there dubiously for a moment or two.

During the meal the little girls quietly made joking remarks to August, and seemed to be making fun of him. He wasn't upset by this; indeed, he went so far as to laugh a little at their remarks. He acted as though he was used to it. In this Edevart recognized his old friend from back home, from Polden, where he would sit and laugh good-naturedly when people poked fun at him—a very different August from the one who had stood on the deck of *The Seagull* issuing orders like some great admiral. August sat here cowed; he put up with a great deal from the girls and the other children, and they for their part went rather further than usual because this visiting peddler was sitting there listening. They went to extremes, asking him if his gold teeth were meant to crack porridge with.

"Little fools!" replied August, and laughed, but he looked across at the husband in case he had said too much.

They mimicked his Nordland dialect, correcting it for him— these brats from a region with Norway's most hideous dialect!

Edevart felt indignant on behalf of his friend.

After supper the wife asked: "Where did you two know each other?"

"Back home," Edevart replied, in deliberate support of his friend. "We are from the same village. I was once his first mate."

August: "So it's true, isn't it, that I was once skipper of a sloop."

"Perhaps you were," answered the woman shiftily. "Makes no difference to me."

"None of you would believe it," August continued.

Silence.

"Hm!" The farmer cleared his throat. "Surely we've the right to think what we like about your stories."

At this August fell silent and hung his head, but Edevart said provocatively: "I wouldn't have thought you needed to invent anything, August. If you were to tell everything you've actually done, there'd be more than enough to astonish the people of Frosta."

Silence again. The farmer, too, was silent, but he wrinkled his brow.

The young girls now felt they wanted to smooth things over. One of them remarked that at all events August played lovely music.

"Marvelous!" the other agreed. If only you could get him to.

August: "I don't play every day."

"Every day? You've only played once."

"And there'll be no more," said August.

The girl, angrily: "Oh, well, please yourself!"

August and Edevart went over to where they were to sleep, and Edevart said: "What kind of a shit hole is this you've come to?"

"Don't talk so loud!" said August.

"Let them hear it—I don't give a damn! Are you thinking of staying on here?"

"No, not long. Just a couple of weeks, till my time is up."

Edevart: "As I told you, I'm on a trading trip. You must come along with me on the boat."

"What's that? . . . No . . ."

"You want to stay here?"

"Don't talk so loud. No, I don't want to stay here. But there are a couple of weeks still to go. I don't know . . ."

"Don't you think the man will let you off those two weeks?"

"Perhaps. If you were to speak to him. But I can't come with you in the boat."

"Oh?"

"No, because I'm no sailor. I'm frightened of boats."

They talked the matter over. At least he would be all right for as long as the boat remained in Trondheim Fjord. Edevart asked: "Are you worse than you were before?"

"No, but I'm no better. I'll never be any better."

They talked half the night. August told about his life since they were last together in Trondheim, and about all the farms and other places where he'd worked. "But it never came to anything," he said. Enough to buy him something to wear now and then, otherwise nothing but a few odds and ends. "Are you all that well stocked with goods?"

"No, I've sold most of the things. But I've enough left to take us both as far as Trondheim."

"I'd rather go by land," said August.

The next morning Edevart spoke to the farmer. He was mulish and self-interested and turned away without replying to the question. August went off with him into the fields with the horse and wood sledge. Edevart waited till they returned for dinner and brought up the matter again.

"I don't know about that," said the man.

"You should just let him go," said the wife. "What use have we got for him here with winter coming?"

There was disagreement when it came to settling up. During his stay August had had various things from the local store which the farmer had paid for and kept note of. He'd also had one or two small cash advances.

August questioned the very first item. "Coffee? I've never had any pound of coffee. What would I do with that?"

The girls, who were listening, laughed.

The farmer: "Twice it says here: half pound of coffee. That's a pound."

"It wasn't me. It must have been one of the other casual workers you had this summer."

"No, it's against your name!" the farmer insisted.

"Oh, all right," said August, and gave in. "I never bought two half pounds of coffee. But never mind. Put it down to me."

Edevart pretended that he heard nothing of this disagreement. He settled up with the wife for his lodging, and for the roast meat he had had for breakfast. He carried his pack outside into the yard and came back in again.

There was now an argument going on about a head scarf.

"I didn't buy that, either," August protested. "You must have entered it on the wrong sheet."

The farmer pounded the table and shouted: "Watch what you say!"

August apologetically: "I didn't mean . . . I just wanted to ask you to make sure that that was my sheet . . ."

"See for yourself!" commanded the farmer in a loud voice, holding up the paper. "What does it say here? Can't you read your own name?" But suddenly the words died on his lips. He stared at the paper himself and didn't seem to know what to make of it. Finally he managed to say: "Oh, well, I think this can't be your sheet. It doesn't look as though it is!" He at once began rummaging among his other papers.

August was happy to be proved right and laughed triumphantly across to the wife and the girls: "What did I say! Ha! ha! ha!"

"Here it is!" said the man, holding up a piece of paper. "It was a mistake. But there's no need for you to go showing off that gobful of gold teeth."

That same moment Edevart shouted across to August: "Why don't you give him a poke in the nose and flatten it a bit more?"

The man craned his neck. He couldn't believe his ears. August held his breath in terror. The man leaped up from his chair and took a step forward; Edevart came to meet him; the two men stood face to face, each deathly pale. "Please, you mustn't, Edevart!" August pleaded.

The man saw himself trapped between the table and Edevart. He called sharply over to his wife: "Go and open the door!" When this had been done, he pointed and shouted: "Out! Out of my house!"

Edevart: "I'm not going. I am a witness to this settlement between you."

What action could the man now take? His wife, who was standing over by the wall, tried to take a hand. "It was just a mistake, wasn't it!" And August again tried to mediate: "Let it go, Edevart! Let's not worry about it!"

"Witness?" said the man. "I don't usually need witnesses when I settle up. This was a mistake."

"Yes, that's what I say!" said the woman.

"Yes, but that man there needs to have it knocked into his head!"

Edevart: "Go ahead and try knocking something into my head!"

"No," said the man. "I won't. I wouldn't lower myself."

Edevart had the last word. "I wish it had been me in your place, August!"

The settlement proceeded in orderly fashion.

Ah, but August! It turned out that he'd found himself a sweetheart among the girls about the place. Perhaps she didn't care all that greatly about him, seeing that she made fun of him, and like the others tried to make him look a fool. But afterward she would embrace him and generally make it up to him again— or so it seemed to August. He took it that she felt compelled to behave as she did so as to divert the others' suspicions. They were undoubtedly sweethearts in their fashion. But for his part August had had to endure this miserable treatment from everybody on the farm, had had to demean himself, had put up no defense, simply in order to be allowed to stay the winter. So what wouldn't August do for a girl? And now that he was leaving the

255

farm at Frosta, he was sad. She was completely faithful, he said to Edevart, and always looking after my interests.

"How's that?" Edevart asked. "I thought I saw you giving her money when you left?"

"A few daler, three daler, out of my pay. It's not so good to be left behind here without anything at all. Didn't you see she was weeping?"

It was good weather as they rowed away from Frosta, but August wanted to be ashore on the mainland. He was given a pack and a huge load of goods to make his way on, given instructions as to his route, some good advice, and a measure of warning. They were to meet in Trondheim at an agreed time.

AUGUST PROVED to be a splendid salesman on this trip, and arrived in the city with his pack as good as empty and his pockets full of money. As he made his way along, he had often called in again at the various places where he had previously worked. The people recognized him again and were glad to see him. He had never been dismissed but had always left of his own free will, had merely yielded to his own wanderlust, his restlessness, and had taken his leave. Now he reappeared as a kind of traveling shop; he greeted people with a laugh, and was recognized—it was August, the man who played his accordion once and then no more, the man with the gold teeth, the man from Nordland who had been shipwrecked and lost everything. Here he was! People bought from him; they liked him and did not turn him away.

And the business went well. He had learned to ask high prices and then reduce them to a reasonable level. That's the way things had to be in this business. There was much lively talking and disputing about things; there were many clever witticisms; and when he left the place, they wished him luck on his journey.

Yes, August was all right! He had talent and a sense of the job; he was a born peddler.

In Trondheim, the two friends each bought a gold ring and

some good clothes to wear; after which they went sniffing around the various stores and bought suitable goods to see them through their trip north. Edevart paid off his remaining debts to Knoff and now stood there firmly on his own two feet as the prosperous possessor of a boat and cargo. A decent career after only a year. Added to which was the pleasure of a life of easy vagabondage.

They traveled back north again: one of them overland by the inland roads, the other along the coast. Edevart again looked in on Knoff at Fosenland and bought a number of goods from Romeo. Once again he made a good bargain and stayed over for a few days' rest.

The cooper's wife gave him the news of the village. The emigrants in America wrote less often now; they had settled in those foreign parts, had become Yankees, had adapted to the life over there, and their pockets were full of chinking silver dollars. The young ones who had gone over became less and less ready to send money home to support the old folks who had remained behind. In some of the letters there were complaints about bad times in America, too; the wheat crop had suffered after a long drought, and the tobacco crop had partly failed because of hailstorms. Lorensen, the one-time head clerk, had resolutely written to Romeo asking if he could have his old job back in Knoff's store. He wasn't able to support himself where he was. So everything can't be all that wonderful in America, either, concluded the cooper's wife.

"Exactly what Norem said last year." Edevart nodded. "He wouldn't swap for America."

"Ah, Norem!" the wife began again and shook her head. "Yes, he's also got his troubles now."

"What troubles?"

The woman again shook her head. "Operation. Cancer. It doesn't bear talking about. They took him to Trondheim and did all they could for him. But it won't help, they say."

"That's awful! Is he bedridden?"

"I don't know. They've still got him in Trondheim."

"How's he taking it?"

"How's he taking it! He can't even talk. They've removed his tongue."

Edevart threw up his hands and let them fall again.

"Yes," said the wife. "First they took half of it away. But then a little while ago they cut everything out. They say there's no saving those who have cancer."

"There we have it! There we have it!" said Edevart, and was well pleased that he had neither gone to America nor come into any other sort of trouble. "Norem was telling me last year that he wanted another vessel, wanted to go to sea again. Ah, man's lot is uncertain!"

They talked about Knoff, that eternal topic of conversation. They talked about Miss Ellingsen and Magnus. They were going to be married in the spring and live in the little house meant for casual visitors. They were going to keep their jobs with Knoff.

Edevart smiled. "Is she still going to be 'Miss' after she's married?"

"You mustn't say things like that."

"And how will she have children—have them on her arm?"

The wife: "They say she'll have no children."

At this they both laughed slyly and made no secret of what they thought.

Again Edevart sailed away from Fosenland with a well-laden boat. Once again he avoided calling at Doppen. In the north of Helgeland the two friends met up once again. Again August had sold out. He was a masterly salesman and, as Edevart's assistant, worth very much more than his wages. He filled his pack from the boat, agreed to the next meeting place, and was off again.

They came to Bodø in late autumn and were then more or less home. Edevart did not want to show himself in Polden without a full boat, so he was compelled to make up his stock from some of the smaller stores in Bodø. It was not greatly to his advantage, but it couldn't be avoided. He now saw the necessity

258

of making some permanent arrangement with one of the Trondheim firms, which could send him goods at any time and wherever he might happen to be.

INNER POLDEN was ice-bound. They had to tie up in Outer Polden and cover the long road to Polden on foot. They did not hurry, but let the news of their arrival run ahead of them. They were carrying a heavy burden of goods and they were forced to make only slow progress, chatting to each other, swinging their yardsticks, and occasionally stopping to rest.

Both were dressed in their best clothes and both wore their best finery. Dear Lord, they were no ordinary lads from the village. They wanted to look their best when they arrived, wanted to appear nice and prosperous and have a bit of money to show. More than anything Edevart wanted to give lots of treats and presents to his father and his brother and sisters. They were so grateful even for little things—so wouldn't they be absolutely speechless when they saw this mass of stuff!

It was rare and cold; and they constantly had to blow clear water from their noses, then they dried them with the gaudiest handkerchiefs they had in their stock. August had lavished great care upon himself, dousing himself with scented water and parting his hair in the middle. He had no father or sisters to show off to, but he didn't want to be left behind. He couldn't exactly start speaking Russian in a village where they didn't even understand English. But this didn't mean he had to appear like some tramp. He was an experienced connoisseur of the splendid ways of foreign lands; and in obedience to his taste for expensive exhibitionism he had wound a blood-red sash around his waist like a belt. This was the height of fashion in South America, he explained. "What do you think they'll say when we get there?" he asked Edevart.

As they approached the village, he asked that they stop and get their breath back and not appear on the scene exhausted. He took out of his pocket a cigar for each of them, bought in Bodø for just this occasion, and he cautioned Edevart about smoking it too fast and finishing it too early. "But as we go past Karolus's cottage, you must puff as hard as you can!" he said.

"When we get home, you must go in first," said Edevart.

August: "Why?"

Edevart replied bashfully: "I can't face it!"

The village lay silent and dark, poverty-ridden and decaying. Nothing remained of the wealth that had followed the great herring catch; no fresh paint on the houses; no dancing or merriment. What had the whole thing meant! People had had their day, but since then nothing. They had been given a taste of something, they had grown proud and careless, had become accustomed to extravagance, had learned to smoke tobacco and spit arrogantly. They'd known their day, but nothing since. What had the whole thing meant!

On this wretched winter's day, these two extraordinary village lads came along and brightened up the place. The people had virtually eaten up all they had earned from last year's fishing in Lofoten and were scraping the bottom of the barrel. They shuffled from cottage to cottage, exchanged news, and shook their heads sorrowfully. They were good kind people, but they were lazy and they were poor. No earnings, no herring catches, no work, only winter and darkness. Some of them kept up appearances. Gabrielsen, the storekeeper, had gone bankrupt, but he had kept his home going and still sported a white collar around his neck. Johnsen, the sexton, was not brought so low that he couldn't still smoke his pipe on his way to church on Sundays. What sustained him was that he had a steady income and he didn't have to worry if there was nothing in the church collection.

The two friends came puffing into the village, past old Martinus's cottage, past the cottage Ragna had inherited from her grandmother, where Teodor stood in the doorway looking out, past Karolus's big house with all the faces in the window, and along the road to Edevart's home.

"What's this . . . I don't understand," said Edevart as he walked along. "Things have changed. Where's the hill?"

August also stared. "You're right. There used to be a hill there. I remember it well!" And when they got to the house, he half turned to Edevart and said: "Just look at this! Stone steps!"

The entire family was at the cottage. The news of the impending arrivals had gathered them together. Several neighbors had also found their way there. Ezra, that funny little hound of heaven, was there, as well as two women from the neighborhood, and Karolus and several others possibly. When August opened the door and made to enter with his pack over his shoulder, he saw at once that it was impossible. The room was full of people. They left their packs outside and went in.

Four people got up and offered them seats.

"Don't get up! Don't get up!" they shouted, waving their hands to demonstrate their modesty and politeness.

They took the seats left vacant by Joakim and Ezra, who sat on the table.

Embarrassed silence.

Finally Joakim speaks. Freckled and facetious, he sits on the table dangling his legs. "Had you thought you would get into the house with those bundles of yours?"

Timid smiles among the company. The old father says, lost in thought: "Aye, they're enormous bundles!"

Joakim, full of juvenile wit, says in a loud whisper to Ezra: "We'll have to pull all our buildings down and build bigger ones!"

Karolus, very much the district chairman, says importantly: "That shouldn't be necessary. My place is quite big enough."

The others thought the same, and hastened to assure the chairman: "*Your* place, yes . . . We needn't talk about that!"

The conversation became more general. Karolus asked if they had come by sea or over land; and they told him. They hadn't been looking for herring? No. How was the wind out there? Northeast. August had to unbutton his coat in the overheated room, and in so doing he revealed the South American sash around his waist.

But such was homecoming. It wasn't the custom to go and meet people on the steps as they arrived, or to show the least sign of joy or bid them welcome. That was considered foolish affectation. How easily that sort of thing could turn into emotional sentimentalism, even tears—the most shameful thing of all! Edevart had been dreading that his father's feelings might run away with him, and then drag Edevart along with him—it was in all ways a good thing that so many others were present to reduce the tension. He spoke across to his sisters without feeling he might make a fool of himself. "How big you've grown! I hardly recognized you again!" At which their cheeks burned and they busied themselves with the stove and the coffee pot.

Only after some considerable time did the neighbors begin to leave. Right up to the end they had hoped to see what was in the packs, but neither of the two men gave any sign of wanting to bring them in and open them. They were given plenty of hints. The curiosity among those present was only too obvious. Even Karolus said before he left: "I imagine there must be all sorts of things in those packs of yours?"

"Oh, yes!" replied Edevart.

"Ah, well, you'll look in soon and see me?"

"You can depend on that!"

But already the things they had seen meant much. People ran around telling each other what great characters Edevart and August had become—they both had pocket watches and gold rings, they had good dark suits, wore their hats at a rakish angle, and on their feet they had high boots with patent-leather trimmings.

The days came and went, happy days in that little home, festive days. Josefine in Kleiva was immediately given the job of making some new clothes for Edevart's two sisters; the old father found himself wearing a new duffel coat, which even had a few banknotes in the inside pocket as well; and the debt to Joakim was settled in full. Edevart now owed him nothing. And Edevart was the sole owner of Doppen.

The settlement between the brothers was not achieved without argument. Both became angry, for they both had their pride to defend. It was also fitting that Josefine should be sitting there listening to them and offering her opinion. Why should the older brother want to settle this matter in the presence of a third person? Simply to ensure that he would be heard—and Joakim had every intention of standing firm. There sat Joakim the creditor, freckled, rather thin and untidy, pretending that he found this shameful offer of money from his brother quite incomprehensible.

"What do you mean?" he asked.

"That's what I owe you."

"Don't be a fool!" said Joakim.

"Take the money," said Edevart. "It's what's left of the money I borrowed from you."

"You haven't borrowed anything. I got that seine net from you. And besides, you sent me that money order from Fosen."

Edevart pushed the money over to him and said: "I'm not sitting here like a monkey any longer trying to coax you!"

And Joakim finally took the money, but he had the look of a man about to be sick. He did not mean to lose as easily as that. He cogitated. Suddenly he says caustically and without warning: "Welcome back from America!"

That struck home. Josefine bent over her work and smiled.

Everybody in the village had of course heard that Edevart had been planning a big voyage. And it had come to nothing, eh? It had just been so much showing off, a bit of boasting? Or what then? Josefine looked up from her sewing and listened.

Edevart bit his jaws together, though he had nothing in his mouth. "I turned back," he said.

Joakim: "Yes, you turned back. You didn't dare go on."

"I didn't dare? Don't you believe it. But I think I did the wisest thing."

263

"What was that?" Joakim asked uncomprehendingly.

"Well, you've seen what I had in the pack. And I have more in the boat."

Josefine felt it was time she ought to mediate. She said: "I wonder if you have any reeds for my loom?"

Edevart: "I have plenty of reeds in the boat, coarse or fine, any size you care to mention."

"Oh, you are a wonder, Edevart!" she exclaimed. "What a blessing it is you've come. Now that Gabrielsen's gone bankrupt, you can't get anything here."

"I've a four-oar boat loaded to the gunwales," said Edevart. "I think I've enough to satisfy Polden's needs for some time to come."

"Where did you get them?" asked Joakim.

"Get them? The articles?"

"I hope you haven't gone and broken in somewhere and stolen them?"

"I'm not paying any attention to you!"

"For then you'll be arrested," Joakim continued. "And a pretty bouquet you'd look then—sitting there with your handcuffs on!"

Josefine laughed and once again interposed: "I don't suppose you've got any sieves, Edevart?"

"Have I got sieves!" he replied. "Just you come down to the boat!"

"You are marvelous! I felt so helpless, because that cow of mine has calved and I haven't any sieve . . ." And then Josefine felt she wanted to do what she could to help Joakim out. He had lost, and sat there beaten and looking angry. She said: "Well, Joakim has also accomplished a thing or two."

Edevart: "I suppose he's been lying out in Vesteraal with that rotten old net of his."

"No. He's taken all the flat stones from the hillside and made stone steps of them. That's the latest thing."

"So, that's what's made him so fat and round-cheeked!" Edevart said derisively. "He must have done well out of it!"

Josefine refused to give in! "And when spring comes and the snow goes and everything turns nice and green, you'll be able to see all the things that Joakim has done. He's cleared all the stones from that field of yours, turned every bit of it over and made it all into usable land . . ."

"And sowed salt?" Edevart asked.

"Don't pay attention to him," Joakim advised her.

But Josefine wasn't stupid, far from it. Like the capable and hard-working woman she was, she had noticed over the past two years the rich returns Joakim was getting from his newly won land; and she praised him for this, expressed her admiration for him, and held him up as an example. Starting from nothing, he had succeeded in growing on that little patch of land enough fodder to keep yet another cow. "I don't understand what gave you the idea," she said to Joakim.

Joakim: "I read about it in a paper in Lofoten."

"Yes, you read books and papers, and you study and examine things and go deep into them," she said. "You just listen to that, Edevart."

To this Edevart replied that he could not afford to waste his time on things like that; he had other things to do. And Joakim, bringing things to a close, said as he left the room: "Why do you bother to talk to this numbskull, Josefine! He can't even read a book . . ."

The two of them switched to talking about village affairs. Josefine knew everybody and everything. What was that—Ragna? Hadn't he heard? Yes, she was married to Teodor and they already had two children. Things were pretty hard for them; their little cottage had no land with it, and they had no animals, not even a goat. But the days had passed, one by one. Yes, they were struggling along quite well up at old Martinus's place, now that there were only three of them. It was a pity that their cow went barren, but it was fat and sleek, and they were going to send it to the parsonage for slaughter in exchange for a good milking cow.

"And you want to know like everybody else how things are

with Ane Maria. All we hear is that she is all right and being kept under observation. She doesn't write very often to her husband, but they say the parson gets letters from the priest at the prison to the effect that she has become extremely religious, reads the Bible from cover to cover, and sings every hymn in the hymn-book. What does Karolus have to say to all this? That you must ask your brother Joakim about. He reads and writes for the whole village, you might say. But one thing seems clear: she wants her husband to be with her. She longs for him, she writes; and she maintains that man and wife should be one. But, bless you, Karolus can't be taken and locked up with her. He hasn't killed anybody."

Edevart: "What do you think she wants with him?"

"Wants with him? Don't you sit there laughing!" said Josefine, laughing herself. "She probably just wants to convert him. But now let me tell you something you might find funny. Did you know that your sister Hosea is to have Ezra? No, you didn't know that, either. Yes, they are engaged. And I dare say I'll be making the wedding dress if you can provide the material."

"Ah, well!" said Edevart. "She might have done worse than Ezra."

"Yes, it could have been a lot worse. And now he's bought a piece of land from Karolus. He must be meaning to build there. Let's only hope they have good luck with it!" Josefine nodded portentously.

"What do you mean?"

"No, I'm not saying any more. The only thing is that the bog where the skipper sank lies on that land."

Edevart: "Ezra was a fool to buy it."

Josefine: "He wouldn't have bought it, only Karolus wouldn't sell the land unless the bog went with it. He wanted to get rid of that bog. And he couldn't be blamed for that, when it had brought his wife all that misfortune."

"Do you know what he gave for it?"

"No. But they say Karolus sold it cheap."

"He could have bought from me," said Edevart. "I have a farm down near Trondheim."

Josefine shakes her head. "My goodness, Edevart, have you got a farm as well?"

Edevart swells with pride: "And it's not all that little, either, though I do say so myself."

THROUGHOUT THAT WINTER the two men peddled their wares around the district and in the neighboring villages, selling a few odds and ends. The desire to buy was great, but money was short. They had to let a good deal go on credit until the men returned from the Lofotens. For a time there was a lot of to-ing and fro-ing out to the boat in Outer Polden; but when spring showed signs of starting and the ice began to break up, they rowed their floating shop right in as far as the boathouses in Polden and made it quite unnecessarily fast with two anchors and an extra line ashore. When the men returned from Lofoten, Teodor couldn't resist making a disparaging remark about the mooring: "Look at Edevart's great schooner there—he must be expecting Atlantic storms here!"

And now the two peddlers went and collected their money. They got most of it; and their breast pockets once again bulged with the thickness of their wallets. Edevart was doing well; no complaints. He sent a remittance south and ordered more goods. His business was growing. But when two huge cases arrived from Trondheim, he was at a loss to know what to do with all his stock.

"You ought to build yourself a store and go into business here," said August, who had the ideas.

"You don't say!"

"I do say. Far better you having a store here in Polden than Gabrielsen trying to run a business in that out-of-the-way place of his and going bankrupt. You ought to go right ahead and build a store!"

Edevart answered that he had no intention of listening to any such fanciful ideas.

His home began to become an assembly point. The people of Polden didn't have so very many diversions to choose among. The only one now was that old man from Ofoten who tied up in the bay and dried his fish, but he had been coming year after year and he was no longer a novelty. Otherwise the days passed uneventfully. Joakim worked his land, and Ezra diligently cleared his piece of territory, leveling the site and building his foundations. It was more entertaining to be with the salesmen. Well, Edevart's father was a quietly religious man, but he was tolerant and seemed to have no objection to seeing strangers about the house. Especially did they come crowding in on Sundays after the service—decent folk, all of them, from the neighborhood, who just dropped in to talk over the bits of news they had heard as they stood around after the service. They wanted to know what the two lads thought about things—they were men you could question about the new star which had been discovered in the heavens, or about the war between Germany and France. As far as Edevart was concerned, he was a man of some property; he had money and possessions; he had commanded a sloop and been in charge of many things. And as for August, he'd been all around the world. They were both splendid fellows, not least August. When Teodor—the one with the hernia and little else— began sneering at one or another of August's stories, he was quickly brought up short. Edevart always brought his friend to the fore, boasted about him, sought his advice in the presence of everybody, and created a sense of respect for him—Teodor had better not try picking a quarrel!

Edevart encouraged his friend to tell things about his life, backing him up with nods and interested questions and never interrupting him even when he was telling the most outrageous stories. There was enough to last a whole summer of Sunday evenings. It was certainly worth it to come along and listen! One thing, however, remained obscure: and that was where August had learned to play the accordion. And he did nothing to dispel the mystery that continued to surround him. He talked about trees with leaves of silver, about manna absolutely pouring down from heaven, about ships with twelve masts, about men with green faces who lived to be four hundred . . .

"Did you see them?" asked Teodor.

Had he not! August had seen far more than that! Name any country or kingdom in the world and August knew it. Edevart had himself held in his own hands a bunch of eight keys which came from India. Wasn't that so?

Edevart nodded.

"Yes," said August. "And you saw me that time I'd been shipwrecked and had lost everything and was cleaned out, but not many days later there I was on my way to Levanger Fair with a huge consignment of pearls and diamonds and was received in honor by the priest and the authorities. You remember that, Edevart?"

Edevart nodded.

Teodor: "I don't understand where you get the money from."

August maintained a mysterious silence, but one of the other listeners spoke up. "Yes, you would like to know, wouldn't you, Teodor! But that's no business of yours or of mine!" And August became expansive. He opened up that tremendous gold-filled mouth of his and let his imagination flow forth. Dear God, that was something to listen to! And Edevart allowed him his triumph.

"What was the name of that king in India?" asked Edevart. He asked merely so that the people of Polden should have the chance of hearing an incomparable Indian name.

But August pondered. "Wasn't it King Achab? I don't remember. How can I be expected to remember the names of all those kings and all those different kinds of people I've met! It's too much for any one man to carry in his head. But you remind me of something—something that happened one bright moonlit night. It was where the Pretoria and the Colombia meet . . ."

"Where what meet?" asked Teodor.

August: "I can see you don't believe me . . ."

"Can't you keep your mouth shut, Teodor!" one exasper-ated listener shouted.

"I was just asking what met what."

"The Pretoria and Colombia," said August. "That's what met what. They are two rivers, like two great oceans both of them, and they rush at each other furiously like butting animals. You can hear the roar fifty miles away up country, and the spray hangs so high in the air it's like a permanent eclipse of the sun. Now, Teodor, you might well ask what do they do for light? And in a way you'd be right. All they have is moonlight. But it's moonlight of a different kind from ours. You can't begin to com-pare the two. Because it's like the brightest sunshine here."

"What were you after there?" asked Edevart.

August pondered. "I was forgetting the point of my story. That was the place I found myself walking through gold, wasn't it?"

"Gold?" shouted Edevart, himself interested.

"Gold, my dear fellow, gold pure and simple. I couldn't understand it, but when I looked down there were my boots absolutely covered in gold. I stamped my feet, but I couldn't get it off. Then I knew what I had to do. I ran up along the river as fast as I could, managed to get aboard, and informed the captain. Nobody would have believed me if they hadn't seen it on my boots."

August paused. The audience waited tense. What then? What happened?

"What happened? What happened was that neither the cap-tain nor any of the others wanted to turn out that night and go back with me. But the next day we immediately went straight back, but by then the gold was gone."

"A bloody likely story!" exclaimed Teodor vehemently. "So you had nothing to show for it."

August looked hard at Teodor and replied: "That's what you think!"

"What do you expect us to think?" the other asked, misled by the speaker's assurance.

"Well, you see, I'm not the silly fool you take me for," said August. "When the others wouldn't turn out and go straight back with me, I lay there the whole night thinking. And in the morning I went and showed them all around, but I didn't show them the right place."

"You don't say!" exclaimed his listeners.

"Oh, don't I? It was my gold. I didn't have to share it with all the others. No, thank you! Not on your life!"

Some of his audience said he'd done right: they would have done the same. But the tireless Teodor objected. "Then why did you inform the captain?"

August replied earnestly: "It was my duty."

Long silence. Everyone sat thinking his own thoughts. So *that* was where August got his money when he was on his knees and required it. That explained how a shipwrecked sailor could go off to Levanger Fair with a consignment of diamonds! August, the old devil! So he had this place in some part of the world where he walked around in gold. That was the absolute truth. He had given himself away.

"But did you find the place again yourself?" they asked.

"Don't you fret!" replied August.

Ah, August, that incredibly cunning old devil! There was more to him than met the eye! Nevertheless, his story did not leave them absolutely and totally convinced. If only he'd been able to produce those boots! "What happened to the boots?" they asked.

"The boots? The captain got them. 'Let me have the boots!' he said to me in English. 'Wear them with my compliments!' I replied, also in English. But from that day on I didn't have to do a hand's turn aboard that boat and I ate every meal at the captain's table."

Long silence again. August himself had fallen deep in thought and sat with folded hands. Suddenly he shook his head as though overcome by his memories and said: "He later sold those boots in Sacramento and got a mint of money for all the gold that was on them. What a pair of boots! All the goldsmiths in town had to combine in order to buy them."

"In what part of the world did all this happen?" they asked.

August looked around at them all and asked slyly: "Now wouldn't you like to know?"

No, he couldn't be expected to deliver up this secret. For then anybody at all who wanted could go there and tramp about in his gold. Teodor, for instance, might find his greed too much for him and make his way there, the scoundrel.

"But do you go there regularly, or haven't you been back since?"

August: "I've been back once since then, and I'll go there again if I need to. But you also have to take into account that you can't go there at any old time. You just can't do that. It's not a country with ordinary decent God-fearing people like us. The forests are swarming with headhunters and wild beasts, and you take your life in your hands with every step you take. And terrible though it is to talk about, it has to be said that they have the habit of attacking and killing any Christian man they come across. And afterward they eat him."

"Eat him! Eat the man!"

"Cook him and eat him."

"Have you seen them?" asked Teodor, getting up. He seemed disturbed.

August: "Since you ask me, I'll tell you. Yes! One of my comrades and I went ashore from the ship. We were taking on a cargo of pearls, and there were palm trees and fig trees and all sorts of other fruit trees round about. But then, if you please, they made a move to capture my companion, and at least a dozen of them surrounded him. They didn't touch me because I stood there with a loaded revolver. 'What do you want?' asked my friend. 'Hoo-wah, hoo-wah!' they replied, and this meant they wanted to kill him. 'You're a lot of rogues and scoundrels,' he said, for he wasn't afraid of them. He punched one of them and drove his nose right back into his head, so there was only a hole left. I stood there and watched. But they couldn't help but overpower him. They kept clubbing him over the head with handspikes, and it didn't much help for him to keep on telling them that they were bandits and swine. So I shot one of them. But that didn't worry them, because there were still plenty of them left. My companion shouted to me that they were hitting him hard. He was hurt, he screamed. So I shot another one. But then they got him down on the ground and they were all over him, and I daren't shoot any more in case I killed him as well. Shortly after that he was dead. The savages then danced with delight, hopping and leaping, and the only way I was able to save myself was by walking backward, pointing the barrel of my revolver at them, until I reached the ship. But then the whole crew went ashore armed and in a terrible fury and attacked the savages' camp. But it was too late. They had already cut up our companion and put him in the pot."

The listeners shuddered. The old father asked uneasily: "But did you shoot them, August? Surely you didn't shoot them?"

August: "What was there to do with savages like that? They were heathens."

"Yes, yes," said the father. "But they did have immortal souls."

"The devil alone knows what they had—I don't. Anyway, I didn't shoot them dead, I only shot them in the hands and fingers and feet, so they had no cause for complaint."

"That's what I would have expected from you, August!" The old man nodded, satisfied.

Edevart must have realized that his friend needed support. He noticed that both Teodor and Ezra and even Joakim had certain doubts about the story. Edevart said: "It's amazing all the different things you have been through, August! It's not for us to try to figure them all out!"

August clasped his hands behind his neck and yawned indifferently. He answered deprecatingly that it was nothing very much to boast about. He had grown accustomed to it by now. The suggestion was that if murder and death and other acts of violence occasionally interrupted the monotony somewhat, it wasn't altogether out of place. Any time now and he'd probably be taking a bit of a trip around the world to see to his possessions in one or two places.

3 THERE WASN'T MUCH MONEY ABOUT IN POLDEN AND the district that summer, and the two young salesmen should have left long ago. But one week followed another and they made no move to go. They were well content, surrounded as they were by friendliness and respect. In new and strange places they would have needed to be more on the alert about holding their own. As it was, the old skipper from Ofoten was now there drying his fish. In the autumn he would settle up and people would once again have money. Things would right themselves in time.

The one thing was that August began to feel restless. The days did not have sufficient variety. He was not one for lying in bed and sleeping half the day; instead, he wandered about the village mingling with the people working on the drying grounds and chatting to them. He also paid a call on Ezra out at his new place and commented on the site and on the newly begun buildings.

Ah, yes! August had seen much worse in other parts of the globe, indeed he had. A lot of good sense was already evident here. Ezra was having to dig a drainage ditch along the upper side of the house, otherwise water would get into the potato cellar; he would also have to see that the foundation stones for both the house and the little barn were dug in deep, otherwise the frost would displace them. It was these foundation stones for the barn that Ezra was busy working on.

August said: "The barn will be too little."

Ezra replied that he could never expect to have very many animals.

"It's not a dog kennel you are building. Make it twice that size, then in time you can put four cows in your barn."

Ezra laughed loudly. "Where d'you think I'm going to find fodder for four cows?"

August cast a glance around at the attached land and delivered himself of an impromptu idea. Ah, August, how often had he not had to use his wits to save the situation, and this was just such another instance. "You must drain that bog there!" he said.

Ezra looked up, startled. "Are you kidding?" he asked.

August was not kidding. His idea was not a joke. It needed much talk to demonstrate to this little local lad Ezra just how right he was, and even then Ezra wasn't convinced, far from it. Though it was fun to listen to the arguments of this widely experienced seaman.

When all was said and done, what was the point of Ezra doing all that work?

Couldn't he see that? He had a nice big bog on his property which he could turn into usable land any day he liked simply by turning over the turf. There were no stones in the bog. It was virgin soil, wet swampy earth which he could cultivate the first year it was ready. "Come on, let's go down and have a look at it!" said August.

They went, picking their way among the junipers and other trees. August pointed and chattered; he became excited; the frozen blue of his eyes warmed. They halted down by the drying grounds, over whose rocks the water from the bog rippled ceaselessly. They saw the whole bare and treeless extent of the bog, and Ezra again said with a laugh: "I'd certainly have to dig deep here!"

That wasn't so certain, August thought. There was only that

one point in the middle where the bog was bottomless. He would have to dig a trench around the bog, then put in a deep trench straight across it, and finally divide the whole bog up with oblique trenches all running into the main central channel. There was plenty of fall, and a river of water would run straight from the hills and down to the sea. "Think of all this as green fields!" concluded August. "At least enough for three cows."

"Have you ever seen it done?" asked Ezra.

"Many times, and in many countries."

"And seen them dig a body out?"

August, uncertain for the moment. "A body? I don't know exactly. Why do you ask?"

"I'm asking if you think I ought to disturb the man who's buried in the bog. You can't mean it?"

"Ah!" said August. In fact, there was nobody who had more to fear from that body than he himself. He had at one time swindled him greatly over the accounts, and he had misappropriated the pocket watch, the high boots, and other clothes belonging to the dead man. So what? Hadn't he also given the dead man a gold ring? August paused to collect his thoughts, then asked Ezra: "What can Skaaro do to you?"

"Nothing, I suppose."

"And isn't it the case that he keeps crying from the bog asking to be brought up again? He terrifies the whole village."

"It's been quiet since Ane Maria went to prison."

August concluded: "It would be better if we could take him out and give him a Christian burial in the churchyard."

A week later something dreadful happened to Ezra. One Sunday afternoon, just about the time people were returning from church, there came a cry from the bog—a cry! Oh, God, it was so long-drawn-out and sad and unearthly! A girl herding the flocks up on the hillside heard it and ran home distracted and fainted on the doorstep. The churchgoers from Outer Polden also heard it and ran for their lives. The whole village was in dread. Ezra came running, his tongue lolling from his mouth—he had heard the cry from his new place. All evening long people discussed the event. It was no small matter if the wailing from the bog was going to start up again. Poor Ezra, he couldn't very well build a place to live out there now, not after this. And what about everybody else? What about the whole of Polden? Could anybody pass a peaceful night after this? It hadn't been Karolus's bull bellowing. Nor had it been the grating call of the grebe, a lone bird call in the silence. So it was presumably an uneasy soul lamenting. All thoughts turned to Skipper Skaaro.

"I think we should drain that damned bog," said August. "What do you think, Karolus?"

Karolus took his time. He had little desire to speak about the dead man and thus rake up again all the business of his wife's misdeeds. "I don't know whether we ought to disturb the dead," he said.

August: "If we can find him and bury him in the churchyard, he'll have consecrated ground to rest in, and nobody will hear a whimper from him again. That's my opinion."

Some people nodded in agreement. Others thought it risky to dig up a body. What right had they to interfere with God's purposes? There the matter died. It affected the whole of Polden's peace and quiet—but it died. Even Ezra, whom it affected most, couldn't live forever with his tongue lolling out of his mouth. His frenzy abated. He began work again on his buildings —and strangely enough, he now followed August's advice and made his barn twice as big as it was before. What did he mean by doing that?

But now something sad happened to old Martinus. He had this new cow of his from the parsonage. It was called Fagerlin, was well behaved, and gave a little milk every morning, noon, and night. Everything augured well. Admittedly, the other cows were nasty to her, butting and charging her out of their way; but that was always the lot of a new beast to begin with. It would soon wear off. But then Fagerlin went down in the bog. It was very sad, but there was nothing one could do. She was unfamiliar with these pastures, had not learned as a calf to keep away from that bottomless bit of the swamp. Who knows, she might even have been butted into it. At all events, she was lost. So what about Martinus and his family now? He himself accepted the catastrophe patiently, comforting himself with the thought that he didn't have all that long to live, anyway. Nevertheless, people came flocking together to hear what it was thought should now be done.

"Are we still not going to dig out that bog?" asked August.

"Would Martinus get a living cow in return for that?" they asked.

"Well, do we leave Skaaro lying beside a cow?"

They all shuddered and thought that was bad, but there was nothing to be done about it. What *could* be done about it? The matter died. Ezra had now gone over to August's side and argued strongly in favor of draining the bog, that hellhole, that glaring abomination! In vain Ezra argued. So what else could he do but continue building his barn big enough for four cows, now that he had got the foundation stones in place for that size building.

But finally something happened that swung public opinion over to August's plan. On Sunday afternoon there was again a shouting from the bog—this time two cries in succession.

Now there was no getting away from it! Something had to be done. The shouts were heard at exactly the same time of day as the previous time. People became aware that it was the very same time of day at which Skaaro had gone down. Now he was crying out for release. It was him! It couldn't be anybody but him! The fact that he called out twice today could be explained by his being in deep despair and disgrace now that he'd been joined down there by a cow.

The goat girl rushed home. The churchgoers from the village itself heard the cries this time. Ezra came rushing across, threw himself down on the ground in despair, and admitted that now he really must stop work on his new place. He couldn't think of living his life amid all that loathsomeness.

Karolus, as district chairman, at the same time took a serious view of it and went to ask the priest for advice. He took Joakim with him in case anything should need to be put in writing or prove too difficult for him in general.

MANY MEN are at work on the bog. All the men of the village. It is broad daylight, a summer's day, and no danger. They are there on a necessary task. August is in charge. He has run a line from the sea straight up to the hill pasture to show the path of the trench, and he allocates people to different parts of it. He is himself hard at work and doesn't spare himself. Ah, this is not the August that wore a red sash around his waist and had a cigar in his mouth. The sweat pours off him. It is as though he feels some compulsion to make good something relating to the late Skipper Skaaro. This is why he is so active. He blows his nose with his fingers and wipes them on his trousers. And he cares not a jot about his fine high boots with their patent-leather trimmings.

They don't talk much on the job. And when they do speak, it is in a hushed voice, for this is a solemn matter they are engaged in.

As they approach the fateful spot, they drive in their spades rather more circumspectly. They can never be sure what they might strike. Ezra is first in line and takes off the top turf. After him follows a whole line of men; they are lost more and more to view the deeper they dig, until the last one is almost lost in the depths of the trench.

Ezra is very near the spot. He puts out stakes and planks ahead of him to stand on; the whole bog heaves as he drives in his spade. He glances back to see if help is near in an emergency; whereupon he straddles the place itself, then stands on it. He strikes nothing but slime with his spade; he pushes the treacherous tussock to one side, but the slime fills the hole almost instantaneously. His spade leaves no sign behind it. It's like work-

279

ing in porridge. He steps over the spot and works his way over to firm ground. At the end of the line he steps away and allows the next man to relieve him as leader. Ezra himself then goes back and takes over the last place in the row. This is how August has arranged for it to be.

By midday a broad black track could be seen running across the bog, and by evening pretty well half the work had been completed. The men went home chatting among themselves. They were now four spade depths down at the fateful spot without striking anything but slime. Already the water was running merrily along the trench.

In the morning they started anew.

Then something happened.

The man who happened to be first in line for the moment let out a cry and jumped up out of the trench. Had he come across something? they asked.

"Yes, something solid, with the spade. Something like clothes."

Teodor, who was the next man in line, sneered scornfully and offered to take over the lead. Ah, that was just like Teodor! He dug in his spade a couple of times and came upon a round sort of thing. "It's just a tree root," he said as he took hold of it and tried to throw it up out of the trench. But it wouldn't come; it was stuck fast. Teodor let go, and began cleaning the slime off it—and what he then saw sent him reeling backward. He'd taken hold of a dead hand.

Teodor felt very unwell. He began to rid himself of everything he had inside him. It came both ends at once. He lay there devastated. August came striding up and stepped past him.

Of all these men he was the only one prepared to dig around the body and bring it out. August was man enough to look a corpse in the eye!

It was remarkable how well preserved the dead skipper was. The mud had protected him. There was no smell from him other than that of the bog. Even his clothes were undamaged. His gold ring was there on his finger. The outstretched arms had to be carefully bent back into position. He had lost one shoe. The body lay on the underlying rock that was shaped like a kind of witch's caldron and lay only three fathoms below the surface. The water bubbled up from a crack in the caldron. It was a natural spring.

They got the body over onto firm ground, rinsed it clean of mud, and covered it over. August took two men out of his team and sent them home to make a coffin.

Now most of the tension was over and some of the men began talking about giving up the work. Ezra was anxious to continue; he of course had special reason for so doing. He went to August to complain. "What's that?" said August. "Stop work? Not likely! Far from it. The dangerous bit must be completely drained so that it can never again suck down any living thing!"

So they worked until the evening of this second day, by which time they had driven an enormous trench right across the bog. The water ran like a river; it was flat bedrock for nearly all of the way, and only the witch's caldron remained constantly full of mud and water. They never found old Martinus's cow, but they did find Skaaro's missing shoe.

When they finished for the evening, the question was who would stand guard over the body. All of them declined this dangerous duty—even if it wasn't exactly dangerous, it was felt in another sense to be rather hair-raising. Ezra was willing to keep watch if he could have another man with him; and Teodor, who was back to his old self, volunteered. He needed to make up for his miserable showing a little while ago. He'd been down to the sea and cleaned himself up.

It was summer and a light Nordland night. The two men paced up and down on their lonely vigil; they weren't afraid, far from it; they had taken over their watch out of the goodness of their hearts, so there could be no blame attached. The only thing perhaps was that Ezra felt a secret delight at getting his fine bog drained—whether or not this delight could exactly be called God-fearing.

They sat and dozed. The sun went behind the hill, and it grew dark. They buttoned up their coats. The last thing they said to each other was that neither of them had any account outstanding with Skaaro, so what evil could possibly befall them? Indeed, no. But a corpse is a corpse, all the same, and not a living skipper. Well . . .

Teodor woke with a start. He must have been dreaming.

"What is it?" Ezra got up at once.

"It's nothing. But look over there. Something seems to be moving!"

"What's moving?"

"That cover over him. We must go down and look."

"Yes," answered Ezra. But he hesitated.

It was now past midnight and only half light. They stood staring. "It's something reddish. It's an animal," said Teodor.

Ezra: "It'll be a fox. You'll see."

"Yes," said Teodor also. "It might well be a fox, but . . ."

"We must go and see," whispered Ezra.

"That we must. Hm! But what if it's Old Nick?"

"What are you saying?" asked Ezra, shuddering. "You don't mean it?"

"Well, I don't know," said Teodor. "But you know as well as I do that Old Nick goes about in all sorts of shapes looking for whom he can devour. So why can't he be a fox? I've heard about that kind of thing before."

Ezra became uncertain. "It's many years now since Skaaro went down, and for all that time he has been a soul departed. Why should Old Nick come along after him now?"

Teodor did not answer.

"What do you think?" asked Ezra.

Teodor: "What do I think . . . ! But there is something curious about that animal. Skaaro wasn't exactly the man he should have been, believe you me. He was guilty of many a sin in his day, that I know. It could well be that Old Nick is after him now."

But, all the same, Ezra was something of a daredevil; he picked up a fair-sized stone in each hand and began to walk down.

"Are you going?" Teodor called out after him, and followed him down reluctantly.

At that moment an animal streaked away from the body, like a flash. A red fox flew through the air. Ezra threw. A little squeak came from the fleeing animal, perhaps only a cry of fright, but a squeak nonetheless. And it gave Ezra great satisfaction to hear it.

They walked over to the body. A smell of putrefaction came from it now. They held their noses. Teodor had become more courageous; he now felt certain of things. It was just some miserable earthly fox. Had it been Old Nick himself, he wouldn't have been the sort to run away; instead, he'd have vanished into nothingness, or else turned himself into an ant.

"Just take a look at what that bloody animal has been up to!" he said.

The fox had tried to rip open the clothes on the corpse in an effort to get at the body. It had left the face untouched, but it had clawed and bitten the clothes, tearing apart buttons and buttonholes, and making a gash in one of the pockets. What a fiend a fox can be! They quickly arranged the dead man's clothes in some sort of order and covered him up again. They agreed they wouldn't fall asleep again.

"It was pretty marvelous of me to wake up like that before any serious damage was done to the body," said Teodor, and assigned to himself alone the honor of having saved the body.

In the morning some of the men returned and some did not. Some were tired of digging trenches. They had exerted themselves to the point where the body had been released and thus those uncanny cries had been silenced; more than that they had no desire to do.

"But what about Martinus's cow?" asked August. "Shouldn't we try to find it and remove its valuable hide? And what about the next time some animal or person is in danger of getting lost in the bog?"

He went over to the body and lifted the cover, but an evil stench forced him back immediately. Luckily for those who had been on guard, August noticed nothing untoward about the body. He made his way up to the bog, staked out two oblique trenches which ran from the witch's caldron right up to the hillside, pointed, commanded, and generally gave directions. In the left trench, the cow Fagerlin came to light. She was still in good condition; they rinsed her clean of mud and set about flaying her. In the late morning the two men arrived with the coffin and took away Skaaro's body. It was high time they did, for it wouldn't keep much longer. In the end it was only the clothes that held it together . . .

August had been quite extraordinarily active. Edevart, his friend, had by contrast done little. He had frittered his time away, lazing indolently and dallying with the ladies. For instance, he had played no part in trenching the bog. Although it was something which would benefit the whole village, he didn't do a hand's turn with the spade. He excused himself by saying that he had no working clothes. In any case—as he indicated—he had little interest in village affairs. What did they mean to him? Admittedly it was his childhood home; but he no longer belonged there, not exclusively, in any case. He had many places he could belong to. If he was going to dig any ditches anywhere, it would be first and foremost on his own place at Fosenland. Nor would there be any dead men to dig out there, either.

It was with August's support that the draining of Ezra's bog had been given such a splendid start. One could say that pretty well half of the undertaking had been accomplished with this huge central trench and the two diagonal ones. Already the swamp was beginning to settle and dry out. But then there remained all the work lining the trenches with stones—the work of months and years. All this remained.

But a start had been made, and Ezra had tasted blood.

August encouraged him by word and deed. Ezra also collaborated with Joakim. They both had an innate sense when it came to working the land. When Joakim needed help in dealing with large boulders, Ezra would be called in; and in return Joakim would put in a day's work on the bog. They made small but steady progress in this way. The two lads got on well together, as might have been expected. It was no secret any longer that they were to be brothers-in-law. Joakim's sister Hosea already wore a gold ring to stop her getting away.

But now August found himself with nothing to do and was sniffing about for something to occupy him. He had again approached Edevart about building a store in Polden—look, the boat was still tied up by the boathouses laden with goods and couldn't stay there throughout the winter all iced up. This time Edevart gave in. He had himself thought things over in the meantime.

In that case he ought to start at once before the winter came. What was he waiting for?

Well, said Edevart, he would have to get hold of the building materials first.

Very well, a letter this very day, this very hour. So many battens, planks, boards of such and such dimensions . . .

Joakim wrote the letter.

And now even Edevart seemed to get his spirit and initiative back again. He was up early in the morning and worked on the site till late at night. Edevart was not without understanding, and the things he had seen and heard at Knoff's business establishment down in Fosenland stood him in good stead. Together with August and Joakim he built up a cellar suitable for taking a barrel of lamp oil, a small keg of tobacco leaf, a tub of soft soap, and whatever other items he needed to keep in a cellar. August also objected here that the foundations were too small, but Edevart wanted to begin in a small way and make sure of keeping going.

When the building materials arrived, it was no great time before the two coffin makers had erected the building—a shed attached to the cottage, half-timber construction, with panels inside and out, no stove, no frills, no special carving. That same autumn Edevart was able to acquire his license and begin selling from a permanent place of business. Things went well. By now the old man from Ofoten had dried his fish and settled up. And people once again had a little money.

But what about August now? He was once again at loose ends and he became more than usually restless, peevish, even ill-tempered and difficult to deal with.

"What's wrong with you?" asked Edevart.

August wanted to be off. Edevart suggested he might take a trip northward peddling his wares. He could easily go as far as Tromsø, and goods could be sent to him as he needed them. August shook his head. What did he want, then? He wanted to cut loose, he said. How? Well, the thing was, he didn't want to go on in the retail business any longer . . . Edevart didn't want to lose him and offered him a partnership; they would each have a half share in both the shop and the peddling business. August declined.

No, August simply had to have a change. He couldn't get the idea out of his mind. He had become accustomed to moving around, going from one job to the next. He had now reached the end of his tether in Polden for this time, and he was consumed by his old restlessness.

"You could have had a great time," said Edevart. "Gone up to Tromsø and back, then down south again, staying over wherever you fancied and managing your own affairs!"

"Yes, and come back along the same route!" said August.

"Why not?"

"And meet the same people, talk about the same things, slap your boots with your yardstick and try to keep lively!"

"You once said you liked that."

"Did I say that? But now I want to cast off."

"What will you do?"

August answered with his usual phrase: "Don't you worry about me!"

But he pretty certainly had no plans for the future when he left.

So it comes and goes. Indeed it does. Everything comes and goes, but some things go under. It cannot be otherwise.

Edevart went into business in Polden. He had built his shop against the gable of his cottage in order to get by with only three walls; but this made the old house twice as long and almost as big as that palace of the district chairman, Karolus. Edevart did not object to people having respect for his place of business, so he had the whole building painted white, just like the parsonage; and things became so splendid at his home that he had the yard swept clean of the straw from the packing cases. His old father was guilty of the sin of being secretly rather proud of his distinguished son. Occasionally he would say: "If only your mother could see you now!"

In the winter the place was dead. All the men were off to the Lofotens, and there was no money about in Polden. Edevart's days were quiet; he ate and he slept. This was a good thing, something one couldn't value too highly. Nothing happened after nine o'clock in the evening either inside the house or outside. Everybody went to bed; and nobody needed to lie awake listening.

He continued to be a goodhearted lad. In the difficult winter months he would help the poorer people out with a couple of stones of flour or half a pound of coffee on credit. And little Ragna, who was married to Teodor, might get some white loaf sugar for her coffee, and that sugar wasn't always very carefully entered in.

"Then you must come over and have coffee with me," she said.

"I'll come this evening!" he said.

There are no two ways about it, that was both stupid and bad. But he went and called on little Ragna, who lived in her grandmother's cottage, went there on dark nights and stayed there long. Everybody in the village knew, but he needed no excuses. He was a man of means; he was rich. Perhaps they should all go to Edevart and be helped out with a couple of stones of flour and half a pound of coffee! And in Ragna's case, it was quite a feather in her cap to be picked in preference to both Beret and Josefine. That's the way things were.

And Edevart himself? Things came and went. All things come and go. He had become less and less particular about what he did and how he did it. Little Ragna was not the same as Lovise Magrete. No, nobody was quite like her, and he would never forget her. But "Good luck and goodbye!" as August would say. Ragna was at hand, and she had such a pretty mouth when she laughed. His soul was torn. He felt no compelling pleasure with her, yet he would not leave her in peace. Lovise Magrete was perhaps never for a day out of his thoughts, but he had of course given her up. What else could he do? But again, what else could he do but remember her? She had left a deep and lasting mark on him; now a period of years lay between. She had left him weak and divided that last night aboard the *Hermine*; and weak and divided he had continued to be. He could easily have got hold of her address when he was down south; but he deliberately hadn't. He lacked the courage and the initiative for that. Now, at home, he found himself composing letters to her in his head—letters that never got sent, never even got written. He no longer knew gaiety or fun; he had forgotten how to laugh. He was a young man with a bowed soul, even though his body was physically strong. August had once said to him: "You are just like a corpse—simply that you haven't been buried!"

But he was not completely dead, not stone dead. When the men came back from the Lofotens, he helped Martinus to get a new cow by standing surety for him. Great joy for old Martinus. But at the same time Teodor was struck dumb with astonishment to find that Ragna was expecting a child.

"Where have you been to get that?" he asked darkly.

"Ha! ha! Where did I get it?" replied Ragna. "Here at home!"

"Who's the man responsible?"

She laughed even more, and repeated: "Man responsible!"

"Who did it? I'm asking."

"What a weird question," she replied. "Weren't you back for a visit at Easter?"

"Yes, but that's only three weeks ago. And look at you!"

Silence.

"I mean to know!" he shouted, and jumped up.

But Ragna had been clever at school, and she'd remained clever. She could do sums in her head, and she wasn't at a loss for an answer. "Well, then it was the time before. You left for Lofoten in February, and now it's Holy Rood Day. Just count up!"

She confused him. Like the fox, she had two exits from her lair. He was getting nowhere and had to sit down again. And subsequently she in fact joked about it with Teodor, and made fun of his dark suspicions. Little Ragna was very assured.

Things came and went. All things come and go. In the long run, not even Teodor could be annoyed. All the others were happy with what they had made from the Lofoten fishing; they had earned good money and they could call at Edevart's store with cash in their hands. When Teodor came to pay what was entered against his wife's name, he was agreeably surprised to see how little she owed and how cheaply she had managed during the winter. Oh, Ragna was a clever wife, there was no denying that!

And now, for a few weeks, there was money about in Polden, and Edevart built up his stock and did pretty good business. He needed an office, nothing very grand; just a little office with a little glass pane in the door leading from the shop. Actually, he could also do with a little room of his own where he could sleep at night and not take up room in the old cottage, which had been full enough even before. Edevart would have to build on again. And more than once his old father said: "If only your mother could see you now!"

All in all, an unfamiliar air of activity in Polden. The village gradually awakened and began stretching itself. In certain heads thoughts began to quicken. Ezra was a good example. Tough little Ezra was a card; he continued draining the bog the way August had shown him. For as long as his Lofoten money lasted, he hired a horse for carting stones, and things went well. He was able to line the first of his oblique trenches with stones and then fill them in again. He now looked out over a little drained stretch of land. This he carefully dug over, then harrowed it and manured it and sowed barley, more or less as a test of faith. Three weeks later the field was green. A miracle and a blessed event for that one-time swamp!

A thousand thoughts ran through Ezra's head as he worked. He realized that in time the land would need more manure than he could beg from people in the village. So he would need animals. But to keep animals, even if no more than a single cow, he would have to have a barn. Yes, but did that take care of everything? Who would look after the cow while he was away earning money in the Lofotens? His wife! Ezra's wife! Bless you, he wasn't even twenty yet! And even if that strapping lass Hosea said yes to all this, where was there for her to live out on this remote bit of land? You couldn't expect her to live with the cow. So the very first thing he had to do was to get a little house built. But that was a hideously big job! And all for the sake of some manure! Ezra sometimes felt overwhelmed by all these thoughts.

On Ascension Day he was going about his work and turning over in his mind various solutions to his problems when he noticed that Joakim had been up to something unusual these last few days. He had spread seaweed over his field, seaweed from the shore, ordinary bladder wrack. Joakim, the old devil! He seemed to know what he was doing. He buried his nose in any reading matter he could lay his hands on while they lay waiting in the Lofotens; his head was full of knowledge, and soon he would probably know more even than the priest who had confirmed him. But seaweed spread over the fields, over the hayfield . . . ?

"Yes," said Joakim. "And that's not the worst. I have put

seaweed in every furrow of my barley field, dug it in and sown on top of it."

"Is it a fertilizer?"

"So they say. But you shouldn't believe that just yet."

"Where did you get that idea from?"

"I read about it last winter. It's supposed to be an ancient practice, and known in this country for over two hundred years. I just wanted to try the experiment."

"I'm glad to hear about it," said Ezra, and at once began to ponder. If Joakim's experiment was a success, it would change all Ezra's plans. He could put off building until he could afford the time and money; he could let the cow wait; he could put back the wedding. Why had Joakim kept silent about his discovery until now? He said: "You read about this last winter and did nothing about it?"

"I didn't want to commit you to the idea. I wanted to wait and see how things went myself. Anyway, you mustn't think you can manage with seaweed alone on your land. You need to add it to other things."

Ah, that was how it was done! This again changed Ezra's plans. He said, discouraged: "I knew it was so much nonsense. I can't understand how you can spread seaweed over your field. You'll get it in the hay in the autumn."

Ezra went off, still with a thousand thoughts running through his head, and none the wiser. But following this, and to be on the safe side, he concentrated on building his house, a place to live. He got a man to help him and he went hard at it. The roof had to be on before the snow arrived.

THEN SOMETHING HAPPENED which was a little thing in itself but which had big consequences. Edevart got a letter from America. The people who had been to church brought it back with them from the post office: a yellow envelope made of strong leathery paper and lots of stamps, and readdressed from Knoff's at Fosenland. Edevart read the letter in his new office; and when eventually he had finished reading it, he went into his bedroom and placed it under his pillow.

It was a very old letter which had been lying in Fosenland a long time. Ah, well! Edevart was not one to worry about leaving an address behind. But all things come and all things go. Now here was this letter from distant America. The words were simple and restrained—so like her in every way. She hadn't forgotten him, but wanted to see how things went first. It was very different from Norway. But they had their health, those who had been left behind when Haakon went west and never wrote. The boy and the girl were both big now after all these years but not confirmed, which they didn't do here. He was working in a *factory* and earned good money, and the girl too who worked a *spool machine*. Pardon these words if some of them are hard to understand, since we speak only English in this town and the children never speak a word of Norwegian. But the littlest one I told you about, she's a little girl and called Haabjørg after Haakon, who wanted that. As for me, there isn't much to tell from all the years which have gone by, except that I don't get on here and have never got on, not for a day, but I did it for somebody else's sake to give him a chance to change his ways in these foreign parts. Yes, I long to see you again and Doppen, which was my home and where you now live, and that's very strange. But the children are now big and grown-up and don't want to leave here, but I want to bring little Haabjørg to see you and Doppen again. Let me know what you think and if I should arrange it? But perhaps you are married now and living at Doppen, and then I won't come. I just happened to think of you this evening, and I am writing this. Loving greetings from us all, but most of all from me. Lovise Magrete Doppen.

What was Edevart to do now? Answer! Answer at once! August would surely have telegraphed. He was always talking about telegraphing to America now that the Great Eastern had recently laid a cable across the Atlantic. But for Edevart that was just a fairy story and nothing for him to use. Since he was reluctant to get Joakim to answer the letter, he tried writing it himself. Had he not kept the fishing accounts, and did he not keep his own books? But this was remarkably different. He spoiled many sheets of paper, then gave up. Feeling despondent, he happened to think of his little sister—not the older one, but Pauline. She had been most recently at school and was very clever at writing and spelling. He would give her a lot if she would write this letter for him—and then keep silent about it.

This brother and sister felt shy of each other. It was shameful to show any emotion, to allow one's face to betray any feeling. They would rather die! He got Pauline to write, but he sat the whole time with a wry look on his face, pretending that this Lovise Magrete over in America was a bit cracked but he wanted to humor her and be nice to her. Anyway, she wouldn't come home. He dictated the letter himself, told her where he was living, and that he was in business in his native village. He hadn't been to Doppen apart from one time when he found a woven blanket from her, which he thanked her for. It was so sad and lonely to stand there, hearing only the sound of the waterfall and not seeing . . .

"Her?" suggested Pauline.

" 'Her'? No!" Edevart replied. "Well, all right! Put that. Then you'll make her happy."

Pauline wrote. Oh, little Pauline was no fool. She sat there pretending nothing was going on, but this youngster had a good nose for things.

"It was nice to hear that you are coming back," Edevart dictated, "and I shall go and get everything ready for the day you can stand again in your old home."

Pauline: "Don't you want to say that you are longing to see her?"

"No, are you crazy! Unless perhaps you do it for a joke. Yes, put that! She'll surely know it's a joke."

Pauline wrote, and then asked: "And 'loving greetings' to finish up with?"

"Well . . . after all those other things you've written!" replied Edevart, tossing his head. "But I'm sure she'll go all around the town showing it to everybody. She is pretty cracked."

He gave his sister a silver coin for her work, and enjoined her to be as silent as the grave about the letter.

THE SUMMER PASSED. Joakim's land gave a higher yield than ever before. Ezra noticed to his astonishment that there was no seaweed in the hay. Well, it must have been raked away in time, he thought suspiciously. Ezra was wrong; the seaweed had rotted away. The remains showed brown about the roots. Naturally, they had to rake the hay with a rather light touch. The field of barley stood there, tall and heavy. "Never saw anything like it!" Ezra admitted.

But then Ezra hadn't had such a bad summer, either. His little barley field on the bog seemed more and more of a miracle to the people coming over to church from Outer Polden—and wouldn't their eyes open when someday they saw the entire bog taken over! In addition to his work on the land, Ezra could also point to his buildings. Didn't his house stand there already, with a door and three windows and smoke coming from its chimney at dinnertime when he made himself coffee! Indeed, and hadn't that selfsame Ezra, in a mad rush of pride, thrown himself straightaway into building his barn! There was no holding him. He became all skin and bone, but never seemed to tire. But he only managed to complete a couple of stages of the timber work when he had to stop. Clearly it was altogether too big a barn, an enormous barn, large enough for four cows and a horse—a horse!—as well as some smaller animals. It was stark staring stupidity and arrogance! Even Karolus, the district chairman, hadn't more than four cows and a horse. And think of the amount of timber needed for a barn like that! Ezra hadn't reckoned with this, and would surely run into trouble getting material. He worked incessantly and in his excitement neglected to think things through properly. Even when the barn itself was ready, he would still be short of a whole mass of material for the hayloft above it; and until the hayloft was up, he would have no roof on his barn. It was a knotty problem!

One evening he went across to see old Martinus, who was a wise and simple man who had lived all his life without wealth or great possessions. Ezra came to him and said despondently that he wouldn't get any further with his buildings this year and he'd have to stop work.

"Well," said Martinus, "you've come a long way in a short time."

"It's not all that short. It's now over two years since I got that land and started working on it."

"But you are still no great age yet. I remember the day you climbed the rigging of the sloop and balanced yourself on the masthead. That was practically no time at all ago. And now you are a grown man with a house and land and everything. You aren't telling me that counts for nothing!"

"The thing is," said Ezra mildly, "that I could have put in a good deal more work before Lofoten if only I'd had the materials."

Martinus thought this over. "The first thing is to thank God for your health and strength. After that, there's bound to be some way or other. When I lost my cow, I got a good cowhide, and then this spring I got a new cow. I haven't paid everything off on it yet, that I haven't. But if God gives me my health and strength, I'll pay what's left after Lofoten. But I must say Edevart was very good and stood security for me, and the three of us in this house bless him for that."

Well, well, talk and more talk. Everything the wise old man said, Ezra could have said himself. But he didn't. He had young blood, and he was in a hurry. Early one morning he was seen leaving his house and trotting off through the woods. He was away a long time, and when he came back his face was dripping with sweat. He had been to call on Gabrielsen, the storekeeper, and had run all the way there and back. He had young blood; and he was in a hurry. Gabrielsen was of course now bankrupt and his place was either to be sold or vacated. It had many good outhouses and Ezra wanted to buy one of these buildings, pull it down, and transport the material back by boat for use on his new barn and hayloft. That was the idea. But was it, or was it not, the case that Ezra had neglected to think things through? Ha! he had thought it through, all right. He cut through all the chatter and thoroughly worked the thing out in his mind. Indeed he did. After a sleepless night of plotting and planning, he leaped up in the early morning and acted.

Gabrielsen couldn't sell any of the buildings as and when he wanted. In any case, he was furious that anyone should come looking over his buildings. "Go to the sheriff and talk to him," he said. "But he'll just throw you out! I never saw the likes of it—a Poldener coming looking over my buildings!"

The answer Ezra got from the sheriff was that he didn't want to sell any of the buildings off separately, but instead wanted to dispose of the place complete.

"Who do you think's going to buy it?" asked Ezra.

The sheriff didn't answer.

Ezra maintained that it was no place to have a store. There was no village there. The village was Polden and the district round about, and Edevart dealt there.

"There is something in that," the sheriff admitted. "Have you got the money for the building?" he asked.

"No," answered Ezra. "But I'll have some after Lofoten."

That wasn't wholly certain, the sheriff remarked with a smile. It depended on Our Lord.

Ezra: "It depends a little on me, too. If things go wrong, I can always split fish for other people or sign up on some other ship. I won't come home with an empty purse. If it's difficult in Lofoten, I'll go on up to Finmark."

"You'll do that, eh?" said the sheriff. "But are you sure you'll live that long?"

"Live?" Without a smile and without hesitation, Ezra answered: "Yes."

Whereupon the sheriff laughed loudly and said: "I do believe you must have that building!" He greatly liked this young fellow, who was so self-confident and spirited, who was no stick-in-the-mud. "Could you provide any security?" he asked.

Security? Ezra could provide any amount of security! He had a house and land, and the sheriff ought to see his field on the bog. Nobody had seen anything like it. "If you would like to come with me and take a look," said Ezra, "we could walk where it's driest and I could carry you over the muddiest parts."

The sheriff again laughed out loud, shaking with mirth at the thought of this young fellow, who wasn't properly grown up yet, carrying him: "You're not exactly useless, I can see. Well, what had you thought of giving for the building?"

"I'll give the price you put on it after you've valued it yourself."

The sheriff was touched. He brought out some papers and said: "I have in fact a valuation for all the buildings. By rights I ought to let it all go at auction and sell to the highest bidder. But I don't know."

Ezra: "It would mean waiting a long time for me, and I'm pushed this autumn."

"We can't very well sell in advance below the valuation price," the sheriff murmured to himself. "But it could be that I have valued that particular building too high. It could well be. Altogether too high, especially if the place probably has to be abandoned and all the buildings pulled down one by one . . . Give us a day to think about it," he said to Ezra. "I'll talk to the other assessors. I'll send you word . . ."

Yes, Ezra got his building and borrowed Karolus's boat to bring it back home in. He began building at once. Two men in the village came along and helped him out as a favor. Things were going ahead.

4 EDEVART RECEIVED A VISIT FROM THE OLD OFOTEN SKIP-per; he had now finished drying his cargo of fish and was ready to load it aboard the sloop. He wanted to settle up with his workers and feared he might not have enough money. He wondered if Edevart could lend him a few daler?

He was given them.

They began talking. The old skipper was rather depressed. Things hadn't gone too well for him this year, he said. During the first month in the Lofotens, when it looked as if the fishing was going to be bad, he had been afraid he wouldn't have any catch at all, so he had bought at high prices. He should have waited about six weeks before starting to buy. Now when he saw what dried fish was bringing at Rønneberg's in Aalesund and at Nicolai Knudtzen's in Kristiansund, he was dreading the journey south.

He was a decent, steady old Ofoten type, and Edevart had a lot of sympathy for him. "But you've still got a vessel and a cargo. You ought to be able to stand a bit of a knock?"

"I don't know," said the man thoughtfully. "I've a son who has been going the rounds as a peddler. He has cost me a lot of money. I don't know exactly why things have gone so badly for him. Perhaps he hasn't worked hard enough. Whatever it is, I've had to pay his debts several times."

"What's he called?" asked Edevart.

"Nils. But he's now given up that business and he's started work back home with me on the farm. I needed it, too."

Edevart realized they were talking about his one-time assistant Nils. He also saw at once where the money had come from which Mattea—Mattea the go-getter!—had sent him with that arrogant letter. He tried to cheer the skipper up: it was rather a tricky business being a peddler, much less straightforward than dealing in fish. The thing for him to do now was to sail down the coast and get paid in cash—it might be more or it might be less, but at least he would have it.

The skipper looked down. He wouldn't pretend to be better

off than he was, he explained. In fact, he didn't own the whole cargo but about two-thirds of it. Wouldn't Edevart like to come in with him over the fish this winter?

Edevart shook his head, but he was flattered at the proposal. Fish trading and shipping was an integral part of the trade of Nordland; and without it he could never be considered much more than a small shopkeeper. Edevart hesitated before answering: "No, I haven't the resources for that."

"I've heard it said that you have a house and land farther south?" said the skipper.

"Yes, I have."

"So you can at least bank on that. I merely mention it . . ."

Edevart immediately came to his senses and replied: "No, I couldn't think of it. I won't do that."

"No, of course not!" said the skipper. "It was only a suggestion. And as far as the money you've lent me is concerned, I'll send it straightaway before I pay anything else."

Perhaps he was letting a good opportunity slip by; but Edevart no longer hesitated. Mortgage Doppen again! When any day or hour now he might have to hurry south and get the place ready! Had he gone crazy! Doppen with its green bay and the delightful sound of the waterfall! Where once in the mountains behind it he had risked his life—and only because a certain somebody was standing below looking up at him.

But hours and days turned to weeks and months. It was a quiet and dreary period. The menfolk in the Lofotens; no business to speak of; only sleeping and eating; the village lifeless. The only people around were the old folks, women and children. Last winter he'd allowed himself a few modest transgressions with coffee and sugar over in Ragna's cottage, but that no longer had the right appeal. No, no! Not that stupid kind of fun again! Not at any price. He had nobody to talk to. He was too lowly for the grander people of the village, and too grand for the lowlier. He received no more letters from America, and became angry and sick of waiting. He heard nothing from August, either. He felt so deserted that it seemed to him he could easily have died and nobody would have known. He took a trip up to the Lofotens just to get away for a week or so, but he didn't feel exactly cheered by it. The fishing was bad; the buyers were complaining; the fishermen were complaining. The crew of Karolus's boat had lost a man in the last gale—old Martinus.

Ah, yes, they said, he had served his time, sitting at the tack all those years. Now God hadn't wanted him to return home to Polden, broke and penniless like the rest of us!

That was all very well. But Edevart had stood security for the cow.

He returned home full of bitterness, wasted the whole winter, unable to concentrate on anything. There was no right or justice in this world.

Karolus and some of his crew came home for a visit at Easter: Joakim, Teodor, and of course Ezra. Ezra who wanted to see his buildings and his sweetheart. For some time now the fishing had been quite decent. The Ofoten skipper had made up his cargo and was meaning to come to Polden again as in previous years. Martinus might just as well have lived—he would certainly have been able to pay off what remained on the cow.

When Easter was over, Karolus wanted to leave again with his men, so there was little respite. They were at church also on Easter Monday, but that was all. But that same Easter Monday the churchgoers brought back with them a letter for Edevart. A yellow letter, a leathery letter, a heavy letter, bulky and ponderous, with a photograph. Was there then no right and justice in this world?

He left home at once, although there was far from being any hurry. Along the coast southward he recognized again every feature from the time he had sailed the sloop there; and he slept only occasionally. He was as excited as in the days of his youth. Already aboard the steamer he heard that the landing stage had now been moved to Knoff's magnificent stone quayside—that had been inevitable after the wooden quay at the old landing stage was blown into the sea during a gale. The director in Trondheim had in fact wanted them to use boats again to unload the ship, but the captains opposed this and a certain district council stepped in. Moreover, a young man by the name of Romeo Knoff came up to see the director, spoke frankly and sensibly to him, and made a very good impression. The boy did not have his father's pomposity; and never once did he laugh at the director's ideas but treated them with great seriousness and was almost persuaded by them. A good-natured lad, a born negotiator, a good business sense, a real merchant. The people aboard said: "He got the landing stage, sure he did! He should have had it long ago."

Edevart did not grudge the young Romeo his victory.

They tied up at Knoff's quay in the evening, with lights burning aboard ship and on the quayside. Magnus, the store assistant, came aboard with charts and documents and saw to the formalities. There wasn't a great deal from the north to be unloaded; on the other hand, there were various goods which were destined for the towns farther south: butter and hides and wool and empty barrels and carcasses of beef. The whole district was waking to new life.

From the deck Edevart spotted several old acquaintances, among them one whom he looked at incredulously several times —one of the stevedores on the quayside. August . . . ? August!

Edevart couldn't believe his eyes! August, too, was surprised, and it took a little time before he opened his gold-filled mouth. "What on earth! You here?"

"Yes. And you here?"

"Yes."

Magnus came up and nodded to Edevart, made himself important, and in a loud voice ordered people about. As the ship pulled away from the quayside, he went walking up the road with the mail.

"What a baboon!" said August, laughing at him as he went.

"So you don't like Magnus, eh? But tell me now what you are doing here."

"What am I doing here?" said August. "I just happened to stagger ashore here and I've been here ever since. I remembered all the things you had told me about this place, and I saw from the ship that it was an impressive place, so I came ashore, even though I had a ticket to Trondheim. Goodbye and good luck! That's now more than a year ago, much more than a year. What do you want here? You'll be wanting to see to that property of yours you were telling me about? Well, everybody here knows you, and I never hear anything but good about you."

"Why didn't you write?" Edevart asked.

"Write? No. But I forwarded a letter from America to you last year. I was the one who did that. Otherwise it would still be lying here, for Magnus is a fool. What was in it?"

"In the letter? A lot of nonsense."

"Well, I saw it was from a woman," said August. "They must surely be having better times in America than they are here. I'm thinking of having a run over there myself some time. Now, what's the point in me writing? This is no place for me, and I don't mean to stay a day longer than I have to. I'd thought of telegraphing you to that effect soon. So you've come down to look over your place? Well, I suppose it needs a few things done to it now with the spring coming on. Why should I hang on here any longer? That Romeo is a splendid fellow—as indeed all the rest of them are in there: old man Knoff and his wife. But Magnus is a twit. Scared to death of mice! Let's go up to the house."

"Can you leave here now?"

"Yes, the others can do what little is left," said August carelessly. "I can't be bothered."

August was clearly fed up with being a stevedore, it seemed. He was ready for a change. "Don't you worry about me!" he was in the habit of saying. Well, he was no stick-in-the-mud. He was ready for anything. He was no scholar, no learned professor; but he could turn his hand to almost anything. And since he was never lazy, he always gave a good account of himself. Free as a bird, a bird on the wing, at any new place he could always begin from scratch.

As they walked he talked. "I've never spoiled things for you here, believe you me. First I talked to Romeo and told him all about myself. That I'd been all around the world and had been in charge of a sloop and could speak Russian and all the rest of it. Romeo didn't take too badly to me and promised me I could stay on. But he asked me to go into the office and have a word with his father. And this I did. This was the next morning. I washed and rinsed myself three times, and I was wearing my watch and my gold ring when I walked into the office. The old man also quite took to me. He was friendly and said: 'Good morning, Captain!' But I realized that Romeo had been talking about me, and I wanted to put things straight and deal decently with him. 'Let's not use impressive words like that,' I said. Perhaps I *had* been a seaman and a peddler and knew a lot of languages and had been all around the world as well as working on the land in Trøndelag, and all the rest of it. 'But,' said I, 'captain I am not.' 'You have been in command of a ship,' he said. 'Only a sloop,' I replied. 'That's all the same,' he said. 'So you want to stay here a while? That's fine. It's a big place here, and it so happens I need somebody like yourself to be general foreman and supervise things both down at the quay and in the warehouses and also up at the store when things get busy. So you can start in at once.' And I've been here ever since. But I have to tell you that that little twit Magnus became jealous of me because I'd been appointed at that level which made me foreman over him and all the others. And since that day he hasn't been able to stand me. The baboon! A store assistant, and scared to death of mice! I'll settle with him one of these days. I believe he took my watch."

"That's not possible! Is it?"

"It looks like it. Though . . ."

"And the ring?" Edevart inquired. "I see you're not wearing your gold ring."

"Oh, that," answered August, hesitating somewhat. "No, I know where that is. But he must have taken my watch once when we were out fishing."

"You went fishing?"

"Once, just for fun. It was last summer. Lovely weather, calm as a millpond. We were to go out and catch a boiling for the people up at the big house. While we were fishing a wind sprang up, and you know I'm not much use then in a boat. The wind freshened, there was some hail, and the weather got worse. Then I became scared. But that twit Magnus just sat and laughed at me. Can you beat it? And when I threw myself down in the bottom of the boat and held on tight, he just howled with laughter. I'll settle up with him, he can depend on that! But it was on that trip that I missed my watch."

"It must surely have slipped out of your pocket?"

"He would know that best! But then it would surely have been found in the boat. But no! On the beach? No! . . . Let's go in and find out where you are staying."

"I'll stay at the cooper's, as I usually do," Edevart replied.

"So you'll be staying at the cooper's. All right. As for me, I stay in the baker's little room. I get on well with him—as I do with everybody, in fact. But that twit Magnus . . . ! And if that wasn't enough, he goes around telling people that I'm scared of the sea and have never been to sea. What do you think of that!"

So ONCE AGAIN Edevart found himself going along to the cooper's and got fixed up there. The wife bade him welcome and said it was nice to have him. She sat there alone all day now that the cooperage was in operation again, and she'd almost forgotten how to talk.

"Where is your husband?"

"Need you ask! He's working in the cooperage. They're terribly busy. They are working overtime to finish a consignment that has to go to Finmark. I go across with my husband's supper at eight o'clock. He eats it there and starts work again. He comes home at ten o'clock. Oh, it's a great life."

Edevart heard all the gossip about people and what was going on. No, the cooper's wife had not forgotten how to talk. Romeo had got the landing stage and was now rich. His mother, Mrs. Knoff, again had as many servant girls as she had fingers, and was getting fatter and fatter. Even Knoff himself only put on a show of being busy, pulling out his watch and hurrying off somewhere else . . .

"I suppose you know that Magnus, the store assistant, is married? You didn't? Yes, he got his little miss in the end, but at one time there was a bit of difficulty about her. Who knows but what she didn't have her eye on Romeo herself at one time? But of course he was just a child, and his mother tried to get Miss Ellingsen sent away. It was then that she accepted Magnus, and she's still housekeeper here. They live in the guest house."

"Have they any children?"

"No, they've only just got married. What makes you ask? They say she can't have children—I don't know whether that's true or not."

"By the way, that reminds me. Have you heard anything more of the people who went to America?"

"Yes. Some of them have come back since things got going again here at Knoff's. But the others are still over there. They don't write any more and never send anything home. Perhaps things aren't going too well with them. Or else they're dead. But Lorensen—you remember him, the head clerk?—he came back and got his old job back. The store is full of workfolk and stock. They've also got a new office manager. Very elegant fellow he is, with buckles on his shoes and gold-rimmed spectacles. They say he goes for walks with Juliet in the evening."

"How did things go with Norem?"

The woman grimaced. "He died. They cut away more and more of his mouth. First they took out the whole of his tongue, then later they cut even deeper. But I don't suppose it would have helped if they'd cut his entire head off—God forgive me for saying so."

"How did he take it?"

"They say he was obstinate to the last. I don't mean that he lay there laughing, or tried to make light of the danger, or put on a brave front. That's not what I mean. He lay there with clenched fists and an angry look on his face as though he just wouldn't loosen his grip on the world. He lay bedridden a long time, but in the end death got the better of him. It cost a great deal of money, and they say that his wife had to mortgage the house and land. Who would have believed it—he who was so rich and had saved so much! But that's the way it goes: 'Thou fool, this very night thy soul is craved of you; to whom shall then belong these things thy hand hath gathered.' He must have known that it was death; but he just lay there and roared angrily and beat on the table when they brought him his soup. He wasn't a human being any longer. I shudder when I think about him."

"I ran into an old friend of mine here this evening," said Edevart. "He's called August."

"August—yes, he's been here a few times and he talked about you. He's got a funny mouth."

"He's got a set of gold teeth. He and I come from the same village up north. He's a rare fine fellow. Knocked about the world a lot, too."

"Yes, he's told us as much. They say he's scared of the sea."

"August! Scared of the sea! Then he wouldn't be likely to have sailed the world's greatest oceans, would he? But he *is* scared in little boats that lie right down near the water. That comes from his having been so often in peril on the sea and taken to the lifeboat with sharks and sea lions and serpents all around."

"I only know what I've been told," said the woman humbly.

Edevart's temperature rose. "It's all lies what you've been told. Put him on a deck and you'll see how scared of the sea that lad is! I've sailed with him myself when the going's been hard."

"He's said to be a master of the accordion. Better than anybody here. Better even than Haakon Doppen was. But they can't get him to play. Only once did they get him to."

"Better than Haakon!" exclaimed Edevart scornfully. "Haakon had better not try! When August plays it's sheer magic."

"Ah, yes! Haakon Doppen! He's another one," said the woman reminiscently. "Nobody would have dreamed of that happening to him."

"What d'you mean?"

"Well, the whole thing. Fate. Everything. Things went wrong for him here. And when he got to America, he left his wife and children and has never been heard of since."

"Never been heard of?"

"Never. He's considered dead. His wife is separated from him and is free to marry again. Anybody she wants to."

Edevart moved closer. "How do you know? Has she written to say so?"

"Those who have come home say so. Anders Vaade says so. Lorensen says so. Everybody knows. She was declared free by the courts. That's the way things must work over there. She's had a lot of trouble with that husband of hers, what with him being in prison and everything. She has three children, but two of them are grown up now. She seems to be doing all right."

Edevart had a suspicion that the cooper's wife was trotting out all this gossip just to please him. She knew about his having stayed at Lovise Magrete's place and about his fight with Haakon. She doubtless also knew where the couple had got their passage money from. He had to be on his guard, so he said indifferently: "I'm on my way to Doppen now. I'd be happy if Haakon or his wife were to come and redeem that place of theirs."

"Of course, that's right! You knew them well!" the woman suddenly remembered. "Fancy me sitting here and forgetting that! So, you want to sell?"

"Yes, if there's an opportunity. I've settled down at home up in the north there. I'm in business."

"Well, well! And you're on your way to Doppen?"

"To have a look at it, yes. To do a few jobs on the place, and in case any of the windowpanes are broken. I haven't been there for several years."

AT THE STORE.

Edevart had had some difficulty in getting past the cottages without being seen. He no longer had any desire to run across Miss Ellingsen and perhaps be accosted by her. Nor was he even very anxious to meet his old friend the baker just yet. He wasn't safe in the store, either; he might meet old Knoff and perhaps again be invited to live in the big house, an invitation he would once again have to decline. Edevart was preoccupied; an important matter was in the offing. He meant to put things in order at Doppen, both inside and out, and he needed several things from the store: kitchen utensils, chairs, bedclothes. He might not have enough money.

He asked for Romeo. He was not there. Lorensen gave Edevart a friendly greeting and was quite ready to talk to him. There he now stood: a head clerk who had quit the country several years ago and had tried both good things and bad things in foreign parts, but he seemed not to have tried hard enough. Wasn't he glad to be back home again, then? Oh, yes! he replied. Oh, yes, he had no great objection. But then he'd had no great objection to being over there, either—America is a magnificent country! So why had he come back?

Well, people like to move. Why had Edevart come here?

Edevart had a little place here that he wanted to see to.

But surely Edevart also had a place up north, where his home was? Lorensen asked.

Oh, Lorensen was never at a loss for an answer. He had come back in order to try what it was like to come back, and he wasn't sure but what he might not go abroad again. This matter of coming back did not correspond with what he had imagined it would be. And there were many like him. Look at Anders Vaade —you know him? You don't! Well, there's this man called Anders Vaade. Pretty well off. With an old father who wants to give up the farmstead: six cows, a horse, a bit of forest. Anders Vaade thinks and thinks and twists and turns. He no longer thrives back here at home. Everything is so limited and restricted, he says. He can't seem to adjust to it. That's the way it is. Here a worker on the land goes along and gets things from the store on credit, but when a *farmer* in America runs out of money, all he does is drive into town with a load of wheat and he's in the money again. And the way they live over there! Hot meat meals three times a day!

"But do they live any longer?" asks a bystander beside Edevart.

Lorensen: "I don't know exactly. But they live better."

"In what way better? Are they healthier? Are they happier, more contented?"

"I think they are. It makes a hell of a difference to your state of mind if you can dive into your trouser pocket for a fistful of heavy silver dollars instead of fingering around in your waistcoat pocket for some miserable coin that's as thin as a wafer."

"Ha! ha! Lorensen! You know how to put things!" one of the women exclaims.

Lorensen feels stimulated. "That's the way with everything! Timber in the forests, wheat in the fields, hundreds of head of cattle grazing on the prairies. Everything in abundance, while here you find only the bare necessities. America can afford to throw things away. The supply is endless."

"But what about living better? How is it better?" asks the indefatigable bystander.

"It just is!" Lorensen answers shortly. "All those cakes every day! The puddings! The sweets!"

"Lots of sugary things, you mean!" says the bystander, disappointed. "Like goodies. And raisins."

Lorensen becomes impatient. "Let me tell you, Karel, that

you don't know what you're talking about, because you've never tried it. How many cows have you?"

"Two cows."

"Two! There you are, you see. And how big is your family now? How many children?"

"Five."

A laugh ran around the store, and Lorensen laughed out loud. "Just keep it at that!" he said.

"We manage," said the man. "The two oldest boys are big now. We also have goats. Apart from that we have land. We sow corn and plant potatoes and have red-currant bushes. We have firewood in the forest and water in the brook. Smoke rises from our chimney. Would we do any better if we left all this behind?"

"Well, Karel, you are content with things as they are, and that's a good thing!" Lorensen admitted. "You live in your little bay and know nothing else. What are you here for today?"

The man: "Today I've come to get a couple of hoes and a spade."

"So. For you, these are good things to have. But in America they dig and hoe with machines."

"But there's something I can never get out of the likes of you who have seen so much of the outside world—are people more content there?" the man asked.

"I've already answered that," Lorensen said dismissively. "They have these heavy silver dollars and they can buy anything they like, they are so rich. But don't pay any attention to me, Karel. Stay there in that bay of yours, and come along in spring-time to the store and buy your hoes and spades here. And we'll go on selling them. You are a good customer. You can manage."

The man: "Some years ago my neighbor sold up and went off to America with his wife and children. Was it all that much better for them? I wonder. I don't know. I heard many different things. Haakon went missing, didn't he?"

"Yes. And there's your new neighbor," Lorensen indicated. "He's the man who bought Doppen."

The man shook hands with Edevart and said: "Well, well! I didn't look particularly closely at you, otherwise I'd have recognized you. I remember when you used to serve in the store."

"I did once," Edevart mumbled.

The man said: "I rowed over to Doppen one Sunday and borrowed your crowbar. I hope you don't mind!"

"That's all right."

"Glad to hear you say so. The crowbar stood there looking so lonely and the whole place was deserted, and I wondered whether I dare borrow it for a bit. I had some stones. But I'll use it carefully and put it back in its place again. How strange that I should run into you today!"

Edevart explained that he was in fact on his way to Doppen and asked what it was looking like. Only so-so, it seemed. None too good. The land unworked just as it had been in Haakon's day. Various other things needed seeing to. The man hadn't wanted to go snooping around another man's property, but it seemed as if wind and weather had done a fair amount of damage.

"That's not the way I've got things looking at home exactly," boasted Edevart. "House and store all painted white. Can I come with you when you go back, Karel?"

"I'll row you right into the landing place, with pleasure."

Lorensen resumed his lecture. "As far as Haakon Doppen going missing is concerned, the thing is this: America is a big country, a whole continent, and some people just get themselves lost. I myself was in many different parts of the States. I was too restless to remain at one spot. But as to Haakon—has that man really ever done anything else but go missing? Here he was away for years. And over there he straightaway disappeared. But it wasn't to the detriment of his wife and children. They actually did better. They did splendidly, earned good money, and rose in the world. Marvelously clever woman the wife! She adapted very quickly to the unfamiliar conditions, moved from place to place, and found out where it suited her best. What would she have made of herself if she'd sat on at Doppen weaving rugs? She was cut out for more than that. It took only a couple of years for her to become separated from her husband. And no matter whether he is alive or dead, that was no more than he deserved."

THERE CAME busy days; days of great activity.

Edevart was unused to work, and his whole body felt bruised. Nor was he any great master of the domestic arts. He could cook after a fashion; but he had got out of the habit and disregarded mealtimes. He worked to no plan. He forgot about food until he was trembling with hunger.

But as time passed, he became less tense and he went about things more sensibly. He realized that in fact he had no need to rush. Lovise Magrete did not come, had perhaps not even set out. How could he know? He received no more letters. He replaced windows, washed down the main room and the kitchen, repositioned doors that weren't hanging straight on their hinges, and repaired the roof and the wooden boarding. He was quite useful with his hands and his work was well-finished. Inside the cottage he painted the doors and windows; outside he carefully cleared and raked the yard. He had help from Karel in clearing some of the bigger stones from the fields.

"Aren't you going to sow?" Karel asked. "There's manure enough here for several fields."

"I don't know," Edevart replied. "I suppose yes, now that you mention it!"

He dug over a good-sized plot and sowed. He dug over a piece of sloping ground, manured it, and planted potatoes. He had never worked on the land before, but the rudiments remained with him from his childhood days in Polden.

Then he was finished. Whitsun was over. The summer itself was now working on his fields and meadows.

He was often across at his neighbor's. Karel and his wife were understanding people, nice to meet, and helpful in any way they could be. Their place was like all the other places in the bays along the coast: usable land running down to the sea; the house and buildings up on a slope; and forest and outlying land behind the buildings. There was no waterfall here as there was at Doppen, no roaring sound hanging in the air, and no rocky cliff rising abruptly behind the cottage. Doppen was prettier.

Edevart wrote home to Polden asking if there weren't any letters lying there for him. He did have some letters forwarded, but they were business letters and the like. There was nothing from America. His sisters sent him the takings from the store and asked if he wasn't going to return soon. As for news, his sisters were able to report that Ezra had now got the roof on his barn and had bought a cow called Rosemor in Outer Polden. Ezra was now coming round to the idea of getting married and would not take no for an answer.

But whom Ezra was to marry, the sisters didn't mention. Hosea was too shy to say.

Edevart felt homeless and rowed alternately over to his neighbor's place or to Knoff's—to see the cooper, the baker, and August. What could he turn to? Naturally he couldn't go back home. The corn was now well on and the potatoes were showing at Doppen. The fields were green. But Lovise Magrete did not come. The photograph was not the same as having her.

One Sunday Edevart wanted August to come out with him to the Norem place, but August couldn't—he was expecting the northbound mail boat and was working on the quayside. Edevart was tired of coming to meet the mail boat and returning disappointed. Nor did he dare to stand down there watching very often. Some of the men began asking each other whether he was expecting anybody, and who it might be. Anyway, she wouldn't be coming today, either; and even if she did, she would doubtless wait. He would look in at Norem's place and have a word with the family. It looked odd that he hadn't been there before now.

It took a fair time to get there, and more time talking to the widow and hearing all her troubles. She was left there. Two of her sons had gone to America and sent her money to meet the interest and installment payments at the bank. Her third son was at home still, but he had started talking about their selling the place, and about them both following the others to America. What did Edevart think about that? She was now old and was fearful both of the long journey and of the strange life she would encounter.

On the way back he heard a blast from the steamer. He had no great hopes, but he felt restless and pressed on faster. The ship already lay alongside; baggage and freight were coming ashore. August was working. Some distance away stood a lady holding a little girl by the hand. She was talking to a man in a linen jacket, with his hat at an angle. Could that be her? Edevart didn't want to go any nearer. He turned to August and asked about the woman and the child. August listened. "They're talking English," he said, and he moved across the quayside to them. August was never one to hang back; he took the chance of showing that he, too, could speak English. Shortly afterward Edevart saw the lady and the child walking quickly toward him. His eyes grew misty; he felt her hand in his. He saw her face, smiling and happy. He heard her speaking as though from far off.

Later it struck him that she hadn't even said goodbye to the man in the linen jacket.

She asked how they were going to get away from there.

"By boat," he said.

"Oh, you have a boat! That's good!" She looked around for her baggage and pointed it out. Edevart piled one case on top of another and carried them down to the boat. "Look how strong the man is!" the mother said to the little girl.

He took his jacket off and rowed in his shirtsleeves. All the time he kept stealing glances at her. He listened to what she said, and answered her questions, shyly. He felt an infinite tenderness in his heart. But tenderness is not exactly the best thing for rowing a boat.

"This is Haabjørg I wrote to you about. She speaks Norwegian as well as I do. We have been practicing it a long time, and teaching each other, because we were coming home. She has been such a good girl on the journey. She was seasick only for the first few days, then she went around the ship making friends with everybody. Are you sleepy, Haabjørg? See those big light-colored birds? They are seagulls. I remember their cries—how nice they are. That's the way they talk to each other. Have you waited long, Edevart? I didn't want to write again. Or telegraph, either. I just wanted to arrive, without any . . . How do you say it? Out of the blue. How tall and good-looking you are!" she said suddenly, and Edevart dropped his eyes and smilingly shook his head. Lovise Magrete also felt embarrassed at her words.

"Yes, I'm much older now," she then said. "Many, many years older. How many I dare not think. You know, I almost feel as though it's not really you I am talking to. It's so strange. I don't suppose you'd have recognized me again if you'd been on your own? I was standing there talking to somebody I knew and telling him I was making for Doppen, when one of the men on the quayside came over and heard me say that. And he told me in English where you were and that you were the owner of Doppen. But I don't think you recognized me at first, did you?"

"Of course I did," Edevart answered. "Because I'd also had your photograph."

"That photograph . . . well, it's many years old. I didn't dare send you a more recent one, for I look even worse now than I did then."

Again he laughed and shook his head as though he'd never heard such stupid nonsense.

"Even worse," she repeated.

"You're not to talk like that," said Edevart.

Of course she was not the same; neither was he. There she sat in a well-cut dress, a hat on her head, wearing tall laced boots with patent-leather caps, a silk scarf about her neck, and white cuffs at her wrists. It made her look different. Her face showed the passing of the years; and the voyage had clearly also taken it out of her. What more? Nothing more. Much less than might be expected. She was lovely. She spoke tenderly and sincerely, and to him it was like the sound of singing. He was moved to the depths of his soul by a new love, a new happiness. It was Lovise Magrete again, his dearest one, his first kiss, his first embrace. And one hot and overwhelming June night.

As she sat there, did she also recall all they had once been to each other? And yet was still able to face him openly and frankly? Edevart was less at ease; no doubt he still felt some slight sense of guilt. He hung his head uncertainly. Again he wondered, as he had so often done over the years, whether on that occasion he perhaps hadn't behaved like some callow and inexperienced young fool! What must she have thought of him all these years. It didn't bear thinking about! And what about now, at that very moment? Was he sitting properly at the oars? Were his legs too wide apart? Was he rowing sufficiently hard? He mustn't overdo it, of course, and give her reason to smile.

She clearly felt much more at ease than he did. She seemed much more natural and composed. When he took his hat off because of the heat, she gave a spontaneous cry: "Oh, what wouldn't I give to have hair like yours!" He couldn't let this compliment to his hair pass without a joke. "Do you want to pull it all out?"

"I wouldn't want to go as far as that!" she said.

Little Haabjørg was also wearing a hat and city clothes. She lay trailing her hand in the water. It was fun, something new for her. The cool water ran through her fingers. She was a bright girl. She asked if there were fish here? Big fish? How big? She caught a jelly fish in her hand and shouted with joy.

"It'll sting her!" Edevart warned the mother.

And the mother rinsed the child's hand and said: "You'll see plenty of those on the beach at home, but you must never pick them up."

"Why not?"

"They sting! You'll get burns on your fingers!"

316

"What are they called?"

"Yes, what do we call them again?" asked Lovise Magrete.

"Up in the north we call them 'seal spit.' "

The words "seal spit" were repeated several times. Then Edevart said: "They aren't really spit, but then they're not fish, either. But they're alive. They're some kind of animal."

"They're alive and they're a kind of animal," repeated the mother to the child, letting Edevart instruct them. "Jelly fish!" she cried suddenly. "We called them jelly fish here. I remember we also used to call them 'slobs.'

Silence.

"Isn't Haabjørg big for her age?" asked Lovise Magrete.

"Yes," replied Edevart, and looked down.

"And so bright and lively! You mustn't think she's always as quiet as she is now."

"No?"

"No. And she knows her letters and can read already. We brought some things with us to read, using the sort of letters they have over there. She sings as well. Won't you sing us something now, Haabjørg?"

"Tomorrow," replied the child fretfully.

"Yes, you are tired. Soon you'll be able to come to bed with Mama and sleep."

"But I've fixed up a bed of sorts for her."

"You have! You beat everything!"

"The cot was still there," he said.

"Yes, but the bedclothes and everything! You think of everything! But that's splendid, because she isn't used to sleeping with me. Nor, for that matter, am I used to sleeping with her," said Lovise Magrete, laughing . . . "Oh, there's Karel's place. He was our neighbor. I often used to look in there when I went to the village by road. Have you been there, Edevart?"

"Yes, often. I've also made an arrangement with Karel and his wife . . . because the problem is what to do about food when guests come, like yourselves."

"We've brought some food with us," she said. "What arrangements have you come to?"

"That you should eat here this evening to start with."

"Here? No, no! I don't want to!"

"The child can have milk here."

"She's not specially used to milk. No, let's go home. I'm sure you'll have enough food."

"Of a kind," he explained with a smile. "I've brought in food for you several times, but it always started going bad, so I had to eat it up myself."

Lovise Magrete herself laughed at this, but immediately afterward she said sympathetically: "You poor man!"

He shrugged it off. "No, I didn't mean it that way. And I can get more food tomorrow."

"So you haven't a cow?" she asked. "You have no animals?"

"No."

"Of course, you don't live here. You wrote and told me. You've just been wasting your money on us, since you don't live at Doppen. It's very sad, it really is!"

Edevart became angry and embarrassed: "What are you prattling about!"

"All this time you've wasted being here just making things ready for me to come home."

Edevart shipped his oars. "I'm not rowing another stroke if you go on talking like that!"

"That man's angry," whispered Haabjørg.

Her mother laughed. She explained that the man wasn't angry but kind, altogether too kind. "There—now we can hear the waterfall. We'll soon be there."

"Waterfall?" Haabjørg asked, hearing this unfamiliar word.

"A big river that falls straight down. Lots of water. Lots of white foam. Oh, it's very special, believe me! We'll go and see it tomorrow . . ."

When they came into the bay, Lovise Magrete exclaimed: "How little it is!" She shook her head and stared.

"Is that where we're going?" asked Haabjørg.

"Yes. But how little it is! Dear God, how strange it is to see it again! There it is!" She counted over to herself: the cottage, the barn, the shed, the well, the meadows. "But some of the land is dug over?"

"Yes," he answered. "A few potatoes and some corn."

"This is where I used to walk, in among the buildings, doing my work and knowing nothing else, looking up at the mountains, looking at the sky, looking across the bay, seeing to the animals, doing all the things I was used to doing, and so the day passed. Can you hear the waterfall, Haabjørg? The roaring of it . . ."

"It's nice here," said Haabjørg.

Her mother put her arms about her and exclaimed tensely: "You think so? Oh, yes, it's nice here!"

And all the way up to the cottage she murmured to herself, preoccupied with her little memories, sometimes with tears in her eyes, sometimes smiling. "Look, this is the very place I got a splinter in my foot. I was very supple, and I just had to sit down and pull the splinter out with my teeth . . ."

Not a word about her husband.

5 IN THE MIDDLE OF THE NIGHT HAABJØRG IS STANDING outside in the yard calling for Mama. She has woken under a strange roof and feels lost. Now she stands under the open sky in nothing but that white night-gown of hers which comes down to her ankles. The dew is wet on her feet. A faint bluish light shows dimly in the night.

"Mama!"

"Yes!" answers Mama from the hayloft. "Go back to bed, child! I'm coming now!" And Lovise Magrete hurriedly throws something around her and tucks the rest of her clothes under her arm.

Edevart, taken aback and embarrassed, remains where he is. He hesitates for an instant to stand up and let himself be seen undressed; but he learns boldness from her, jumps up, and takes her in his arms, kisses her and fondles her breasts.

"Was I good?" she asks.

It was not at all his nature to talk about such a thing, to admit it. But in his embarrassment, he says: "Yes, thank you! And me?"

"Oh, *you!*" she replies rapturously, and smiles.

"I am so much in love with you . . ."

"Mama!" a voice cries outside.

"Heavens, is she still standing there!" whispers Lovise Magrete and rushes off . . .

Early the next morning Edevart rows off to get food and comes back later in the morning with all sorts of good things: salted, smoked, and fresh food. Lovise Magrete is again in raptures; she unpacks and is even more enraptured, thanks him and calls to Haabjørg: "Come and look at all this!"

Edevart swells with pride at this praise, but is still somewhat embarrassed. "It's nothing compared with what you two are used to."

"Oh, but this is home! It's the finest and best I've ever had in this house!" replies Lovise Magrete, and gives way to tears. "Biscuits, spice cake, goat cheese! Heavens above, I haven't seen goat cheese the whole time I've been away, so you must understand! I had a taste of goat cheese at Karel's just before I went away, and that was the last time. We never had such things ourselves, because we were so poor. The children and I never had anything; around these parts we almost never had enough to eat. Surely you must admit . . . I've remembered so many of the old things this morning," says Lovise Magrete, and begins to cry again.

"Well now, Haabjørg, have you seen the waterfall?" Edevart asks, changing the subject.

"No, we waited," Lovise Magrete replies. "I thought you

might like to come with us. But I must see to the cooking now," she says, and hurriedly dries her eyes. "We'll go to see the waterfall this afternoon . . ."

Edevart and the child go down to the beach. Something about the child moves him; and if Lovise Magrete hadn't been able to see him from the window, he would have sat down on a stone and sat the child on his knee and chatted to her. She is a pretty little girl, with blue eyes and thick plaits.

They find shells and little silver mussels, and these are unusual delights and treasures for Haabjørg. She cries out with delight and says she thinks they are even prettier than Mama's rings.

"Does Mama have rings?"

"Yes, she does. Haven't you seen them? Two rings, one of them with a pearl. But these are even prettier!" She asks Edevart to help her find lots and lots of shells and mussels. She carries them in a fold of her dress and says she is going to rinse the sand from them and make them look pretty.

"What will you do with them after that?"

"You'll see!" she replies. And her little head nods as an indication that something will come of it.

A clever and well-behaved little child. Edevart had lots of fun with her. He finds a spot where they can't be seen from the house. It is a stretch of white sand, and Haabjørg very carefully and conscientiously marks out a big square, which she then divides up into smaller squares of different sizes. It was a child's drawing.

"What's it going to be?" he asks.

"Can't you see? A house."

He sits down on a rock and wants to sit her on his lap, to hold her and talk to her. He feels moved; there is a kind of tenderness, of sweetness in his heart. Perhaps she could also tell him who Mama got her rings from.

But Haabjørg has no time for such things. She is so occupied with her house that she eventually empties all the shells from her dress and leaves them lying on the sand. "Now you must wait here while I run in and get my dolls," she says. And away she has gone.

A lovely child. Dear God, how near she seemed to him sometimes, quite unafraid of this strange man. She comes back with a big doll and a little boy doll. She says: "This is the mama and her baby. Now they are going to have a nice time."

"What's the mama called?"

"We used to call her Mrs. Puck in America. But here I don't know . . ."

"And what's the boy called?"

"He's called Johnny."

"But what are you going to do with them here?"

"Here? They're going to sit in their house and have a nice time. That's why I made it. Here's the best room—please come in, Mrs. Puck and Johnny. This is your new home. Sit on the sofa! Wait a bit, Mrs. Puck, I forgot the bedroom!" Haabjørg marks out a bedroom, and with a profoundly thoughtful look she marks off a tiny square and makes two holes in it.

"What's that?" asks Edevart.

"Can't you tell? That's their privy."

"So it's their privy! But what about the kitchen? Where's that?"

"Here, of course. You thought I'd forgotten the kitchen, but I hadn't. Well, now I'm going down to the water to wash my shells. Do you want to come?"

They go down to the sea and pick the sand out of the shells and rinse them. The work lasts a long time and he cannot persuade her to stop and sit on his lap. She hasn't time.

Eventually, after some time, Lovise Magrete calls them to dinner and they have to leave their work. He gathers up all the shells and carries them higher up the beach.

"Why are you doing that?" she asks.

"If I don't, the tide will take them."

"The tide?"

"That's when the sea grows and comes up over the beach. Bring your dolls back home with you now!"

"Does the sea grow? Is it alive?"

"No. It just grows once every day and once every night. That's just how it is. I don't know any more. It comes up over the land."

"How far does it come?"

Haabjørg keeps asking one question after another all the way back to the house.

THEY EAT THEIR dinner, wash up, and walk to the waterfall. It is up in the forest, along little paths and animal trails. Haabjørg goes in front, darting this way and that among the trees, sometimes right and sometimes wrong, eager and impatient. Occasionally her mother has to shout directions to her.

"Which of us do you think she takes after?" asks Lovise Magrete.

Edevart looks down, embarrassed. In Polden, unmarried parents didn't talk about such things. He wasn't used to it. But here he was forced to answer. "Well, I suppose she's like her mother," he says.

"Perhaps me for the greater part. Oh, I don't know. Perhaps you mostly. About the eyes and the hair. She'll be pretty."

Edevart sought to avoid the subject. He says: "You must call her back at once, otherwise she'll get too near the waterfall."

"Haabjørg!" the mother shouts.

"Yes!"

"Wait for us! . . . But it's still quite a way to the waterfall, you know."

"In fact, I don't know," Edevart replies. "I've never been there."

Lovise Magrete stops. "Never been there? No, of course not. This isn't your home. As for me, I know every stone and every mound. It's all still here, but everything seems to have become so small. Even the boulders seem to have shrunk."

That's because the earth grows up around them, all those leaves and rotting branches—so Edevart had heard knowledgeable folk say.

"That could be. Look at that anthill—no life in it now. In my day it was huge."

Again Edevart has an explanation. "That's because the ants have found a better place and moved. Some years you come across whole columns of ants in the forest. That's the ants moving."

"That could be," says Lovise Magrete, and starts to walk on. "But there isn't a single animal here. I used to meet our sheep around here when I came. They knew me and used to follow me. Nice sheep, with lovely wool. If only they were here now!"

"Sheep aren't hard to come by," said Edevart.

"What with one thing and another," she replied, "a great deal has changed. And fancy you've never been out to the waterfall! When it's your own place!" Lovise Magrete seems a little hurt. He hasn't even looked over the property he acquired. He has despised it. She walks on for some time in silence; then she says: "If I had the wherewithal, I'd buy Doppen back from you!"

Edevart smiles. "You shall have it!"

That didn't make things much better; though finally it became all right. "Do you care so little about Doppen that you want to give it away?" she asks.

"Yes, to you," he replies. And after a cautious silence, he ventures to ask: "Don't you think we might have it together?"

She stops, looks down at the ground, and answers: "Yes."

That settled it. He puts his arm around her, blushes, and lovingly kisses her there and then. Uneasily she glances at Haabjørg and whispers: "She can see!"

"It's a pity we're not alone right now!" he says.

At this she smiles and replies: "You're just as crazy as ever!"

324

They call to Haabjørg and walk the last bit of the way to-gether with her. At the waterfall they all stop. Haabjørg stands open-mouthed, saying nothing; not that she would have been heard, anyway. She stands silently facing the miracle, tense and bending forward. For safety's sake, Edevart takes her hand and holds it.

The waterfall comes pouring from above as from some enormous spout, cascading down, beating against rocks as it falls, and plunging into seething foam in the depths. Spray rises up from below; rumbling, heaving, quaking, it is as though thunder itself were locked there in the depths, endlessly reverberating.

Edevart looks down at the child; her hair is wet. He tries to draw her back, but she resists, pointing forward, wanting instead to move nearer the abyss. He has to use a fair amount of strength to hold her back.

Lovise Magrete has gone back into the forest and Edevart is left alone with his little girl. He cannot forbear to stroke her hair, indicating to her that it is wet. She shows no concern. He rests his cheek against hers; and then, the moment being right, he kisses her. She looks at him and takes this to mean that he is entreating her to listen to him and stand back. And she resists no longer.

They move a few steps away, and now they can speak to each other and be heard. "Wasn't that marvelous?" he asks. And again he asks, but she does not reply. The experience seems to have been too great. He sees Lovise Magrete sitting on a mound, her hands in her lap; just sitting. The child runs to her mother, and Edevart is terrified she will embarrass him by telling what he did. "Hello!" he cries, putting on a bold front.

Lovise Magrete nods to him and smiles. "She tells me you kissed her," she says.

Edevart, blushing, said cravenly: "She wanted to go where it was dangerous, and I didn't quite know how I was going to . . ."

Lovise Magrete: "Yes, it was a good way, and I've told her so."

On the way back, Haabjørg again runs on ahead and the

two of them follow behind on their own. They walk slowly, chatting casually about this and that.

She says: "Isn't that a marvelous waterfall you have?"

"Yes, indeed. We have a marvelous waterfall."

"I didn't want to stand there any longer looking at it," she says. "It all seems so deserted for it there."

"For who?"

"For the waterfall. It just goes on and on. It's so deserted there. I knew I would just cry—so I left you there."

Edevart understands nothing of this enigmatic remark, and he makes no reply. Nor does he understand the significance of it when she picks a star flower and puts it in his buttonhole. They didn't do things like that in Polden; he isn't accustomed to it. But he responds naturally and spontaneously when she holds him close, when he senses her face near his and feels her breath. His heart is aflame and he holds her in his arms, his one and only, his irreplaceable. They both breathe heavily. Then again she becomes anxious and looks around for Haabjørg.

That evening they putter about at home. He chops firewood; she prepares supper, lays the table. She calls to him, standing there young and beautiful, speaking to him as though to a lover, to a husband. Miraculous moments for them both! They go into the house, hand in hand.

And after supper Haabjørg grows sleepy. She is weary after all the events of the day and goes to bed. The grown-ups are free . . .

That was the first day.

OTHER SIMILAR days followed. Weeks that brought much happiness, much love. Edevart fetched food from the store, able to pay in cash from the money his sisters sent him. It was a gloriously relaxed life; he couldn't want for anything better. He got hold of August and rowed back with him to Doppen to give his friend a chance to comment on the place.

"Well, yes!" said August. "I've seen worse. I've seen people living in bamboo huts, round as a ring, with the roof coming down to the ground. But they managed to live. But what are you going to make of Doppen? You can never feed more than a couple of cows, and you'd never make the place any bigger."

August came and greeted Lovise Magrete and spoke English to her. It all went splendidly. Neither of them would be put in the shade by the other. They both knew something of New York, though to be sure August knew only the waterfront. For Haabjørg he was an immediate curiosity—such a remarkable person, with such extraordinary teeth, she had never seen. She positioned herself eagerly in front of him, waiting for him to open his mouth. Her mother was quite upset by this and said: "All she wants is to ask you to come with her to see the waterfall. That's all she wants! And Edevart and I are tired of that!"

"Come along!" said August in English.

"Don't let go of her hand!" shouted her mother after them.

Of course August did not make this trip to the waterfall without getting a new idea. "You should have had a massive water mill there, with five millstones," he said to Edevart. "You could grind enough there to keep ten parishes supplied. You could be a rich man."

"I have enough to do keeping things going in Polden," Edevart replied.

In this he was right. He'd become a little concerned recently about how things were going back home. He had had a letter from his younger sister asking him to come back. Pauline was sending him hardly any money now; there was hardly any custom, because most of the regular stock was now sold out. Why didn't he return with more stock? Now that things were as they were with Hosea, his sister. For Ezra had the place he had been building, had cows and harvest, but nobody to help him out. Joakim was at home working on the land; but the father was off seeing to the telegraph line in Nordvaagen. The worst thing was that they were out of flour, coffee, and tobacco. So nobody came any longer to the store; and rumor had it that Gabrielsen was thinking of starting up business again in his wife's home. Surely Edevart didn't intend them to shut down the store: for it was a great disgrace to go bankrupt and be no better than Gabrielsen . . .

Edevart was thus reminded that he was still a businessman in his native district; and that it was up to him to find a solution. He took August into his confidence. And August took thought. "If only I'd had all those packing cases of mine that were sunk!" he said. And he began to elaborate great plans of what he would have done.

Edevart kept his feet on the ground. He declared: "You would have had other uses for your money than helping me!"

"What are you saying!" August shouted, taking offense. "Wouldn't I have given you at least half of it! Didn't you do as much for me! So shut up! At least half!"

"I wonder if Romeo will let me have a bit more than what I've had?" Edevart says humbly.

"What have you had?"

"Various things. Kitchen things and bedclothes for Doppen here. All sorts of things. Three beds and bedding . . ."

"Are you thinking of staying here?" asked August.

"That I don't know," Edevart replied. "It's just that she was over there in America and she came back and wanted to see Doppen."

"Will you take her?"

"It'll probably come to that."

"You could sell Romeo the waterfall," said August.

"The waterfall?" said Edevart in astonishment.

"So that he can put up a huge mill here. He's a fool if he doesn't."

"He won't."

"Doesn't he need a mill?" asked August. "He buys two hundred sacks of flour and they get mites in them before he's got rid of them. They've been ground by steam mills, fired by imported coal, and that makes for expensive flour. Here at the waterfall he could run his mill free, gratis and for nothing. All he has to do is build the building. He can also start a sawmill if he wants. It doesn't much matter what, so long as he gets something going. Ah, you wouldn't find them having a waterfall like that in Canada and not using it . . ."

Edevart shook his head at this great plan and hinted that, even if Romeo did do it, he wouldn't pay much. There wouldn't be very many daler in it.

"You just don't know!" said August. "Anyway, why shouldn't *you* be the miller and run the thing yourself, seeing that you're the one that lives here. There's many a worse thing than that you might do."

This last remark made Edevart prick up his ears. He'd grown sick and tired of selling things and everything else he'd been doing. He was not averse to thinking of some new way of earning a living. "But I could never run a concern like that even if I did have it," he said. "To tell the truth, the only mill I've ever seen is a coffee mill."

"I could teach you in a week," replied August in lordly fashion. "Don't worry about that!"

They talked it over and both became interested. God, how August seemed to have an answer to everything! The one disadvantage was that the waterfall wasn't sold, the mill hadn't been built, and Edevart hadn't been appointed to run it. This realization was borne in on Edevart after his friend had left; and he became somewhat subdued again.

In the morning he set out to row across to see Romeo and ask about credit. Lovise Magrete needed a few things from the store and made ready to go along. All three of them set out. Mother and daughter were dressed in their best.

It must have begun to be rather lonely and monotonous for Lovise Magrete. She still had the noise and bustle of New York in her ears. She complained that there weren't even any animals around the place. Edevart repeated that it would be easy to get some animals, but Lovise Magrete merely answered as before: "What with one thing and another, a lot has changed here!"

As Edevart sat there rowing, a vague thought came to him

—perhaps his two ladies shouldn't have been wearing hats? It wasn't certain that that was the right thing. Well, the child perhaps. But the mother? It wasn't like her. A hat had never suited her in the past. She was prettiest when bareheaded, and not wearing clothes like these, but simply skirt and blouse. And such tiny bare feet . . .

August approached him on the quayside and said: "I think the old man wants a word with you."

"With me? What does he want?"

"I don't know, unless he wants to buy your waterfall."

"Not he! Now if it had been Romeo . . ."

August: "I mentioned it to the old man. Spent a long time talking to him and explaining it all. Marvelous man to talk to, he is! Great! Finally he slapped me on the back and said, 'August!' he said, 'I'd always thought of that waterfall if ever it were to come to setting up a mill!' His very words. He'll tell you himself."

Edevart met father and son in the office. They were both friendly. Romeo shook hands with him and asked how he was. But neither of them mentioned the waterfall.

Instead Romeo inquired: "What brings you here today?"

Then it was Edevart's turn to speak: could he be helped out with a few things on credit? Groceries, flour? They were sold out of these things in his store up home.

Romeo immediately picked up his pencil to note the order. It was yes from the start. He entered in even more items than Edevart had asked for, and said frankly: "It's a great pleasure both to my father and to myself!" There wasn't the slightest trace of guile about Romeo. He gave the precise price of everything, and Edevart found them very reasonable. Done! Edevart went and telegraphed home: LARGE CONSIGNMENT OF GOODS UNDER WAY!

He found his two ladies in the store. He was in good spirits following his success with Romeo and he greeted all the store assistants.

"We are talking about America," says Lovise Magrete.

"Sure! Go right ahead!" Edevart replies agreeably.

She was talking in English to Lorensen and seemed to have much on her mind. Lorensen had placed a stool on the other side of the counter so that she could sit there comfortably. It proved to be a long and animated conversation. Edevart listened to it for a while with a polite but rather idiotic smile; but as he didn't understand a word of it, he eventually left and went down to the boat and sat down to wait.

She didn't come. Didn't come for a long time. Little Haabjørg had had the good sense to take her hat off and was carrying it in her hand when they arrived.

"We were talking about America," says Lovise Magrete as she steps into the boat. "Lorensen wants to go back again. He doesn't thrive here at home. And that doesn't surprise me."

"Why?" asks Edevart frostily.

"You ask why! He'd grown accustomed to the country and to the life there, and it was so very different. He only came home on a visit to see how things were."

"And what about you? Are you also back here only on a visit?"

"Me?" replies Lovise Magrete. She realizes she must be gentle and kind to him again. She says: "No, it's different with me. Poor man, were you waiting long for us? He had so much to tell, and about all sorts of things, and we stayed much too long. And you sitting here in the boat waiting!"

"That didn't matter."

"I'll make it up to you," she says with a roguish look . . .

All well again. But as they come into the green bay and Lovise Magrete again catches sight of Doppen, she cannot help exclaiming: "Good Lord, how little it is! I never believed it was so little!"

Edevart pales and asks bitterly: "Again you say it's too little?"

She looks at him in alarm and begins to whimper: "I didn't

mean that, Edevart. I'm just being stupid. It will always be big enough for me. It's just that from here, from the boat, it seems . . . I didn't mean . . ."

Oh, there was nothing wrong when she was gentle and kind. What wasn't so good was that she kept wanting to go over to the store more and more often to talk about America. She also met Anders Vaade at the store, and that made three of them to chat. Anders Vaade, the man in the linen jacket whom she'd met on the quayside on her arrival, was of the same opinion as Lorensen about the home he had come back to. He did not thrive here. He had become listless and dissatisfied, did only what was strictly necessary on his piece of land, took a hoe to his potatoes, chopped wood, but otherwise spent his time walking around in his linen jacket.

Yet another vague thought occurred to Edevart. What was Lovise Magrete doing talking to these returned emigrants? What kind of beliefs and inclinations were they putting into her head? Each time she returned from her visits to the store, she was still preoccupied by what the two men had been talking about. She was thoughtful and glum. She needed deliberately to remind herself about her household duties, saying: "Here I am forgetting that we have to eat!"

When they returned from their third visit to the store, Edevart felt it was high time he had a talk with her about it. He asked: "This Anders Vaade—what sort of a man is he? Is he another one of those you knew over in America?"

"I knew him both here and in America," she replied. "We grew up in the same village and we traveled over together. It's the same with Lorensen. We were in touch all the time we were over there. We saw each other both at *picnics* and in each other's home. I do believe they were both a bit in love with me, ha, ha, ha!"

Was the tone just a bit too light? Was this the same sweet

innocence as before? Edevart felt embarrassed for her; and felt depressed himself. When she looked at him, asking whether he couldn't take a joke, he had to smile and ask: "So they were in love with you, eh? And what did your husband say to that?"

Evasively she said: "My husband . . . ?" She says to Haab-jørg: "Out you go and fetch Mama an armful of firewood." And when the child was out of the door, she continued: "My husband . . . Well, he left us and seems to have got into some kind of trouble. We don't know. But he certainly disappeared."

The tone continued light. It was without sympathy, without pity now, quite unlike the tone in earlier days when she had stood by her husband through thick and thin.

"I heard that you are divorced from him," says Edevart.

"Indeed, I am divorced from him. There was no sense in it any longer. Nobody thought I shouldn't. Do you think it was wrong?"

"I . . . !"

"You sound undecided."

"Good Lord, what are you saying! If you weren't divorced from him, how would we manage things now? For you and I are going to live together at Doppen, aren't we? Isn't that so?"

Little Haabjørg came in with the firewood and was told to go into the other room and set the table.

Lovise Magrete thought for a long time; then she said: "At Doppen, you say? But we can't stay here the whole time, not this way, I mean. People would begin to talk."

"So what do you want, then?" asked Edevart.

"What do you want yourself?" she replied.

"I want us to get married. It's as simple as that."

"Yes," she said softly. "That means: I am here and the children are in America. You don't want to go there with me?"

"Who? Me?" he almost shouted. "That's the last thing I'd think of, that I must say!"

"There you are, you see!" she said.

"What do I see? I don't understand . . ."

"I merely mentioned it."

"Do you want to go back?"

"I don't know," she answered. "Sometimes perhaps. But I'd also be quite happy living in some town in Norway, or wherever you wanted."

"In a town?" Edevart gave voice to a thought he had had now and then. "What about you coming home north with me? What do you think about that?"

"No! Oh, no! Home with you?"

"You wouldn't come up there?"

"No, I . . . What would I do there? What are things like at your place?"

"That's where I earn my living. I have a store."

"Yes, but I mean accommodation. Have you a house?"

At this Edevart felt almost afraid of his own proposal: to return home to Polden with her and the child was clearly impossible. For the conditions there were even more straitened than they were here. Above all: he really didn't have any house room. He had to say exactly how things were, and conceal nothing: a little store; a little office of sorts; a kind of small room within that. Oh, no, it would be cramped and miserable, worse than here at Doppen, but . . .

"Then it's not to be thought of," she said, shaking her head.

"I can build," said Edevart.

"Build? Yes, but it takes time!"

No, everything was impossible; and nothing suited her any longer. They couldn't even stay at Doppen very well now. Where then? Some other place; perhaps several other places would be best. Lovise Magrete's roots had been torn up from their native soil, and now she belonged everywhere, belonged nowhere. Edevart said in his uncertainty: "I don't understand it!"

Lovise Magrete's mood changed. She was sorry; she too was bewildered. At once she became his kindest, sweetest darling, caressing him and comforting him. "You mustn't take it so hard," she said. "We'll find a way!"

What way would that be? A few weeks ago they had agreed

they would marry and live at Doppen. Now that seemed no longer to be so sure. By no means sure. The passing days had brought a change. She had become indecisive, and dropped hints about living in a town. What in the world was there about a town to attract Lovise Magrete Doppen! She even began talking about her children in America, about whom earlier she'd never spoken a word and who in any case were grown up. She had had letters from them; they wrote in English, but said they were getting along fine and had had salary raises and they were very happy. These American youngsters needed their mother no more now than when she left them. Anyway, did she not have a child with her here?

So what way was to be found? The reasons looked as if they would no longer hold.

Yet strange, strange it was! Edevart did not give way. He stood up well under all this painful uncertainty. He had himself been undermined by his rootless wandering, had lost concentration and drive. He had become listless; nothing seemed of vital importance to him any more. It wasn't easy to know what Lovise Magrete would finally think of doing; but then the worst she could do would be to leave the country again. In any case, this would be the worst she could do . . .

He went out. Shortly afterward little Haabjørg called him in to dinner; but he said no thanks. Had he been waiting for Lovise Magrete to come out and call him herself, so that they could have gone in hand in hand? She had not come. No, lots of things were different from before.

He'd been well beaten. Was he just spineless? Was he prepared to put up with anything? That wouldn't be like him. It was his feelings that now felt numbed. But in things of the mind he was no more a fool now than he'd been before. As he followed the sheep track into the forest, his mind was clear and his resolution firm. He could not live on what little Doppen could provide; but neither could he settle down here and yet earn his living in Polden. His life was in a twist.

Were things any better for Lovise Magrete? He was no

335

dunce when it came to working things out in his head—he knew how many beans made five! He went over her behavior from the day she arrived home until now, from the moment he rowed her over in the boat and she was overflowing with sweetness toward him, and then afterward that evening, that first overwhelming evening. Everything about her was lovely—but it was all *calculated*. What else could it have been, when it hadn't lasted? It was calculated in advance. It had been an attempt to resurrect the old Lovise Magrete he had loved years before. She had sat there in the boat knowing that she was a different person, but she had wanted to please him. She had tried her best to be as she had been before. Heavens above!—as she used to say—why shouldn't she? There he had sat in the boat, so expectant and so trusting, how could she—God help me!—disappoint him! Just wait till we get ashore! But, poor Lovise Magrete, the task proved impossible. In no time at all, the task proved impossible . . .

He came straight down out of the forest and began talking to her anew. She was still sitting in her best dress.

"What are we going to do?" he said, throwing himself on a bench. "What do *you* want to do?"

"Oh, why do you take it so hard?" she replied. "Now listen to me! You obviously don't like me coming over with you to the store. So I'd rather not do it any more."

"Oh?"

"No. It makes no difference to me. What do I want there? If old Knoff comes along, he doesn't see me. If Mrs. Knoff or her daughters come along, it's the same. They don't even so much as nod. It's just as though they were gods and not people. The only *gentleman* in the entire place is Lorensen. If he'd had any say, they'd have invited me. But no!"

"They would indeed," muttered Edevart dully.

"Yes, they would. They'd have invited me in and talked to us and been nice to us. I'm sure it's because they can't speak English but don't want to admit it. I don't care a damn about it. But I'm dressed nicer than Juliet and I've seen more of the world than all the Knoffs put together, because I lived in many different places in America. Little Haabjørg wears clothes such as Juliet and her mother had no idea of when they were young. But look at me now . . . on top and underneath . . ."

With two fingers she lifted up her dress enough to reveal to him the hem of a white petticoat.

"Do you remember," he said, "the time when you only had a blouse and nothing around your neck and you went around barefoot in a little skirt . . . ?"

She looked at him in astonishment. That he should want to remind her of the days of her poverty! To humble her! "No, I didn't have many clothes at that time," she said, hurt.

"No, but don't you remember how pretty you were? That's what I meant. I felt it immediately—how incredible it was!—my love for you, I mean. I saw through your clothes how your body moved. It was so beautiful. I fell in love. I went down to the boat, and as we towed out the sloop, I just didn't know what I was doing."

"You wouldn't want me to go about like that all my life?" she asked.

Edevart was silent.

No, his words made not the slightest impression on her. She repudiated a train of thought which had become quite foreign to her. She said: "But this much is certain. I'll never come with you to the store again."

"Very well. But, tell me, what are we going to do?" he asked in desperation. "Do you want to leave me again?"

No pretense. She was herself frankly undecided and unhappy. She began to weep. "How do I know?" she said. "Leave you—oh, no! But we can't stay here."

Edevart: "I'll go straight home and start building. Will you come to me then?"

"Yes," she answered. "Perhaps that's the best, I don't know."

No real decision. No firm, irrevocable terms. No, she began

again saying how kind Edevart had been to her, what an expense she must have been to him, and couldn't she do something for him in return? She grew quite hysterical, threw herself into his arms, crying and laughing. She kissed him shamelessly, on the lips and with her tongue, and she whispered to him how good she would be to him that evening . . .

Oh, Lovise Magrete! She had never been immodest like this before!

It never became a serious talk. Only the preliminaries. She shifted her ground; she regained her cheerfulness; she moved about the room again. She began poking fun at the loom which still stood there in the room. "Ah, old friend! Still standing here! We couldn't take you with us when we left, and we couldn't sell you, either. So you had to remain. Isn't that funny?" She turned inquiringly to Edevart.

He didn't understand. "Funny? How? Did you never weave over there?"

"Not on your life!" she replied. "Where I was they never used hand looms."

"You used to weave such beautiful rugs."

"Oh, yes! They were good enough for us over here, but . . . No, I could never bring myself to sit here weaving in one thread at a time. I've completely forgotten how to . . ." And, just for fun, she sat down at the loom and moved the beater a couple of times and smiled pityingly at a loom such as this.

Lovise Magrete was spoiled! He remembered the time she had shown him her treasures in the storehouse. She had lots of things, and she was proud of them. There were rugs, a number of fleeces, a woven dress for Sunday wear, a little butter in a wooden tub—oh, a great many things, and Edevart had expressed his admiration, saying that it was all marvelous. For dinner she had given him porridge and milk, and that was good food. He remembered the day clearly.

Was it right to poke fun at a loom which had kept her and her two children alive for so many years? It couldn't happen except where there was stupidity and superficiality. Edevart felt upset by her behavior. He observed the manner in which she had stepped into the loom, with her legs together to make it look refined—she who without any shame had just promised him a torrid night. She had acquired artificiality; she had learned affectation. When she had shown him her petticoat she had lifted her skirt as though with tweezers. How had she stepped into the loom before? One leg at a time, straddling it naturally in two movements, one for each leg, her thin skirt taut across her loins, with a double movement of her body, and there in her youthfulness she would sit as on a driving seat, wholesome and beautiful . . .

He sought advice from August, saying that he had run into something that disturbed and pained him. But August was himself greatly occupied; he couldn't leave his job with Knoff for some time yet. He was working on something, but he lacked the capital. "And can you guess what it is I'm working on?" he asked.

Edevart thought only of himself. "It looks as though I'll have to return to Polden and do some building on," he said.

"But this thing I've gone in for now—I don't suppose you can understand it," August continued. "Look here!" he said, and he took a piece of brown rock out of his pocket.

Edevart wasn't in the mood for jokes at that moment. He pretended not to see the rock, and repeated his intention of returning home to do some building.

"Building? Can you afford it?" August finally asked. "In that case, you can lend me a little, I'm absolutely broke!" Oh, August! What a damned remarkable man! Clever, unreliable, wild—but clever.

No, Edevart had nothing to lend. He could not really afford to build, either. But however things turned out, he would have to try.

"Pick up that rock!" said August. "Take it in your hand!"

Edevart picked up the rock, then put it down. And when August burst out laughing, Edevart mumbled, embarrassed: "Bloody heavy that rock! Amazing!"

"Metal!" August announced.

339

"Well, what then?"

"What then? It might just as well be gold or silver as anything else. Now, for instance, take hold of this in your hand!" And August held out another piece of brown rock.

Edevart: "That's heavy, too. Same thing."

"Yes, it's metal all right, don't you fret. Whatever else it might be!"

"What are you going to do with it?" Edevart asked.

"You'll see when the time comes. I've sent a boxful to Trondheim, and now I reckon they're working night and day and they'll inform me when they've found out what it is. I'm no fool, working here on the quayside for Knoff. One Sunday I stopped and looked up at the mountains, and then I went up there looking for metals. Well, it didn't take me long. Not many blows with the hammer, either. Metal, did I say? The whole mountain is made of metal, heavy like this. I know what I'm talking about."

"What then? It presumably all belongs to Romeo?"

"You think so? I wish you'd talk sense! The mountains are open to all prospectors. Even so, I had to go and stake my claim with the sheriff. Then I dare say it'll go to the king."

"Now if only it was gold!" said Edevart, unconcerned. He had no interest in these rocks and began talking again about going home.

August: "Don't you go and leave before I've heard what's in these rocks! If it's valuable metal, I'll help to finance your building work. What do you want to build for? Isn't the store big enough?"

"The thing is," said Edevart, "that I can't arrive back home with her and the child if I haven't a house to accommodate them in."

"Of course, it could be that there's only lead and rubbishy stuff like that in these rocks," August murmured reflectively. "Then I'll have had all that effort for nothing. It was expensive sending them, too. It was a heavy box. If it hadn't been for my getting them sent free by one of the steamer's crew, I'd be sitting here with those rocks still."

340

Edevart did not follow. He said: "In that case they weren't expensive to send?"

"Weren't they? I had to give him my watch for it!"

"Your watch!" cried Edevart.

"What do I care about that!" August replied. "If there is gold in these rocks, then I've got a whole mountain of them. And then I can present watches to every single person in the country and kingdom of Norway. I won't say any more."

Talk and more talk about rocks, brown rocks, heavy rocks. Edevart realized that his friend was himself a bit short at the moment and wasn't able to help him out. He nodded and left. After he had gone a short way, he stopped and turned. He remembered something. He went up to August and said: "What do you mean? Hadn't you lost your watch?"

"Lost it?"

"Out fishing. You said Magnus had taken it."

"Ah, yes . . . I found it again. I'd locked it away from him."

"So you didn't have it with you on that trip?"

"No. What I was going to say was that you won't go shooting your mouth off about what I told you, will you?"

"About Magnus?"

"What do you mean 'about Magnus'?" snorted August. "I mean about what I've found up in the mountains. You won't say a word about that, will you? If any of them get wind of this, they'll just come running to me for loans. They'll want loans of five daler and more. The women are the worst—they won't take no for an answer. I went and loaned my gold ring to one of them, but do you imagine I got it back? Good luck to it! But feel this! It feels just as though they were a bit greasy," said August, holding out the rocks again.

"What about it?"

"That would mean they are the right kind. The greasier the pieces are, the more metal there is. I've been to lots of places in the world, and many and varied are the pieces of knowledge I've picked up."

"Yes, you certainly have."

"I got hold of a magnet. But these rocks have no effect on a magnet. So it's not anything rubbishy like iron."

"What do you think it could be?"

"I don't know. But gold has no effect on a magnet, either. You can try with your ring."

Talk and more talk about rocks. But Edevart no longer ignored his friend's words. He asked: "So you really do think you've found something up in the mountains?"

"Found something!" cried August. "Bless you, my dear man! Do you think I'm blind and stupid? Can't you see yourself? And let me tell you this, Edevart! You are not budging an inch in the direction of home until I've had word back from Trondheim. I won't hear of you leaving me empty-handed, remember that. You said something about building? You're going to build something big straight off—no fooling about!"

Edevart rowed back to Doppen and resumed his life of puttering about. His meeting with August had made him easier in his mind. His friend's faith in his remarkable specimens of rock also made him hesitate uncertainly. He thought: Who knows, he may have found gold. For there's more to August than meets the eye! But above all, Edevart had put things off. It was nice to feel that he didn't have to leave tomorrow. It was difficult and upsetting to reach a decision; and he told Lovise Magrete that the trip would have to be put back a little. He was waiting for something.

6 LOVISE MAGRETE HAD MADE A PROMISE TO HERSELF AND to Edevart to stay away from the store, but she couldn't keep it. Not in the long run. It had been a firm and sincere intention on her part, and at the time this had pleased Edevart. Later he grew less particular about it, and even helped her himself to abandon her resolve. "It's beautiful on the sea today," he would say. "You ought to come with me and bring the child." What did it matter to him if she had her

342

bits of English chat and took what pleasures came her way? Admittedly she was pensive and rather silent when she got back home afterward, but it no longer tormented him as it had before. As for Lovise Magrete herself, there was a turn for the better. She came to look more kindly on the Knoff family after Romeo one day had greeted her as he walked through the store, and begun to joke with Haabjørg. Romeo was not so bad. He gave the child sweets, and asked if she wouldn't like to stay with him. Yes, she would, Haabjørg replied, because there were lots of funny things to see in the store, and there were doves and chickens and cows and other animals around the place. Her mother smiled indulgently at this talk. Haabjørg was quick and gave bright answers. Romeo laughed like a young lad. As they were leaving, he said to the child: "You will come again soon?"

"Yes, please!"

"You're not fooling me?" he asked.

"No, you'll see!" Haabjørg replied.

In truth, this trip was certainly not wasted as far as Lovise Magrete was concerned. And she said about Romeo that he was better than she had supposed.

Nor did many days pass before Haabjørg wanted to be off again, and Edevart readily agreed. He himself hadn't got from the child what he had hoped. He hadn't dared kiss her again, and he avoided being alone with her. She herself never came and sat on his lap or put her arms around his neck; but in little secret ways she was all the time close to his heart. He could not say no to anything she wanted; and together they persuaded her mother to come along on this new trip to the store.

It was some time before Romeo showed himself this day. They made their small purchases; Edevart bought provisions and Lovise Magrete talked to Lorensen. The child had disappeared. Suddenly Haabjørg walked through the office door hand in hand with Romeo, who laughed out loud and said: "She came looking for me!" And as Haabjørg continued to hang on to him, he explained that she had asked to see the calves.

Her mother put her hands together and exclaimed: "Really! That child!"

"Splendid!" said Romeo, for was he not himself young at heart? "Come along, Haabjørg!" And the two of them went to look at the calves.

They were away quite some time; and when they came back, they had seen lots of animals. They walked the whole length of the store, chatting and wholly absorbed in each other. "Would you like to come up and see Juliet?" he said. She certainly would, and again she took his hand.

"Really! That child!" said the mother again. "We must be going home!"

"Couldn't she stay till tomorrow?" asked Romeo.

"Yes, please!" answered Haabjørg herself, and made the whole store laugh.

A few further remarks were exchanged. "She hasn't her nightdress with her," said the mother, wanting to show how refined they were. Nightdress? Romeo imagined Juliet might well have something of that kind left over from her own childhood days. He didn't even know that such things as nightdresses existed, ha! ha! ha! But in any case Juliet still had some of her dolls left, he said. When Haabjørg heard this, she clung tightly to him and wanted to be taken at once.

"Let her go!" Edevart whispered persuasively. "I can row back for her tomorrow."

On the way back Lovise Magrete sat in her boat looking through some American magazines. They were both pleased that the child was staying at the Knoffs'; it could also be interpreted as a gesture of approach toward the mother. "Not that I care anything about that!" she said. "But I don't mind them showing common decency."

"What are you reading?" Edevart inquired.

"Something Lorensen gave me from Anders Vaade," she replied. And she immediately became excited and explained: "It's about Florida in America. I've never been there, but it must be

344

the most marvelous place on earth. It's a pity you can't read it, because it tells all sorts of things about the country and the lakes and the railways and what they grow on the farms. Just look at these pictures here, and at all the colors, the red apples and the green grapes and the yellow wheat and the blue plums—oh, all kinds of things grow there. That country could never be poor and wretched as it is here. Look at this picture! It could well be Anders Vaade himself sitting there on that big machine with two horses to pull it. Look how the wheat falls in rows behind him. Afterward he takes it and binds it into sheaves. Good Lord, he probably has a machine to do that as well!"

"Yes, it's marvelous!" said Edevart.

"Have you really no desire to go to a country like that?"

"I don't know about 'desire'—I haven't really thought about it."

"But you should!"

"Yes, but . . . I thought the idea was that we should live at Doppen," shouted Edevart, annoyed.

"Oh? But I thought the idea was that you should build on at home and we would go and live there?"

Edevart was silent.

"It won't work, you'll see. I'll tell you all about what's in these books; then you can see whether you've still no desire to go to a country like that. Anders Vaade is going back again. Lorensen wants to go back, but this time he wants to go to Canada. He wants to live in a town. They're leaving this autumn, and a lot of people from here are going out with them. What about us joining them?"

Edevart shook his head.

"Promise me you'll think about it, anyway."

"I've got a small business and my living is here in this country," he repeated.

"What future is there in that? We skimp and scrape from one day to the next. Look at our neighbor Karel! Fat lot he makes!"

"Karel. He gets along all right. He has all he needs. His lads are strong and capable. His land is in good shape. I can't understand why you pick on Karel. He's probably quite content."

"That's only because he doesn't know anything different. Can't you see that? Does Karel have a machine like this one in the picture? And two horses? No, he knows nothing of such things. It's true what Lorensen says: It's good enough here at home for those who don't know any better."

Edevart looked fixedly at her and said: "There was once a time when you yourself found it good enough here at home."

She smiled, because this was easy game. She was able to answer: "Yes, precisely because I didn't know anything else."

"Don't let's talk about it any more," he muttered. "You are so changed."

Ah, that was just the impression she had tried to avoid giving ever since she arrived. Had she gone and spoiled everything? She was doubly sweet to him when they got home. She immediately changed her finery for her everyday clothes, cooked the dinner, and now and then came across and pressed close to him and whispered words of endearment. He had made up his mind not to go anywhere near her that evening. Of course he wouldn't. Certainly not. But he did so, nevertheless. She wouldn't hear of his sleeping in the hay barn that night. Not at all. On the contrary, she hinted that there was room for him in the house. Tonight there would just be the two of them. And just to be sure she hung sheets up at the windows. Who could then resist?

They both found much to give each other: love, promises, and lies. She was his greatest joy, lovely beyond words. There was nobody like her. A star had led him to her. It had been a great stroke of fortune for him. He felt it could only be something of that kind . . . he felt it so strongly, he said.

"Don't leave me!" he pleaded. "I love you so much, more than ever!" And, deep within, he didn't really object if she in fact believed him. In which case she would be the executioner and he the sacrifice, the martyr.

"It's the same with me," she replied, pitting lie against lie. "I could never love anybody else."

They both felt riven, carried away; nothing was as before. It was a moment when they could lie together and talk. The night was hot; they kicked away the covers; it was light. They could see each other and their kisses were not misdirected. And again she could say: "Am I as you want me to be to you?"

"Yes."

"As you want to have me?"

"Yes."

The moment came when they couldn't keep from each other, when the talking stopped. But scarcely was the ecstasy over when Lovise Magrete was again talking, there and then, her head close to him on the pillow. "Leave you, did you say? No, that I won't! I'll never leave unless you come with me. Nobody will get me to do that. And apart from that, there's Haabjørg—I can't really take her away from you, can I?"

"No."

"But couldn't you come with us as well, and all three of us go?"

"I don't know," he replied. He was reluctant to deny her anything after she had been so good to him. She hadn't employed that trick he'd seen others use—exploiting his rising excitement from the very start to get what she wanted. So he mustn't respond badly! "Do you want to go across so desperately?" he asked.

"Yes. If only to get away from here," she answered. "Yes, perhaps over there would be best. I'm getting more and more restless here. I don't know what's happening to me. And since I got these American books . . ."

"I'll think about it," he said.

"Oh, Edevart, I'd be so grateful to you!" she exclaimed, and threw herself over him, wild with joy. She drew him along with her, talking far into the night, saying again and again how kind he had always been to her and what she would do to show her thanks—yes, in heaven's name, indeed she would! She turned

347

him over, lay on his broad chest, and inflamed him to new passion and new promises. By morning he had promised her everything she asked for.

He sits in the boat rowing to fetch Haabjørg. At bottom, he is fed up with himself. His promises of the night had been irresponsible. He to America! And was his business back home in Polden just to go bust? For his aged father to see? He who had been overwhelmed by each extra bit built onto the cottage and who had said: "Your mother should see this!"

On the quayside he runs into August. His news is not good. A reply has come from Trondheim to the effect that rock samples from August's mountain have been analyzed several times before; borings have also been made in the mountain; the place has been known about for generations. "I came too late," said August.

"You don't say!" exclaimed Edevart, appalled.

August stood for a moment as though weighed down by cruel fate; then with a superhuman effort of will he straightened up and remembered Edevart. "Now I can't help you," he said.

Edevart felt sorry for his friend on his own account. "Fancy being so unlucky!"

"Yes," August replied. "And my watch and everything. Still, I can't bring myself to worry about it. Good luck and goodbye!"

"How so?"

"Because the whole mountain was nothing but a heap of rubbish."

"What are you saying?"

"Of course, I was neither blind nor stupid. I did find *something*, they don't fool me there. But the report only talks about sulphur and pyrites and that sort of muck. What am I expected to do with that? And even that is so thinly distributed it's not worth extracting. Did you ever hear anything like it! It looked as if the whole mountain was made of the same sort of stuff, then it turns out it's only here and there, and even then it's mixed up with five or six other kinds of junk."

Edevart stood there, disappointed and speechless.

"No, damn it, it wasn't gold!" concluded August. "What are you going to do now?"

"Me? I'm going up to the store to fetch that little American girl. She stayed the night up at the house there."

"I meant, how are you going to set about building now?"

"I can't build. The only way out I can see is to leave the country."

"If only I'd been able to do the same!" wished August. "I wouldn't have waited around! But as things are now, I'll have to put in a bit more time on the quayside here and earn myself a few daler."

"Are you absolutely cleaned out?"

"Absolutely. But I have my revolver."

"You can have the loan of a couple of daler," said Edevart. "I've just had some money from home."

"Don't talk drivel. You are not made of money!"

"And then we can see," continued Edevart. "If I scrape together what I've got here and what I've got back home in Polden, I might be able to help you. Then will you come with me?"

"Any time, any day!" replied August . . .

Edevart rows home with Haabjørg. She has bags of sweets and other things to eat. She's got a doll in a silk dress given to her by Juliet; and she is to get another one, which is bigger, but she has to go and collect it herself. Romeo has given her a ring with a red stone of the kind on sale in the store.

"Have you had a nice time?" asks Edevart.

"Yes. And I have to go back again soon to collect the other doll."

"What will you do with so many dolls?"

"They'll be mother and daughter, won't they!"

"What did you do all the time? Play?"

She answers these questions a little reluctantly. Now as always she holds back from him, looking at him as though he were an outsider. Suddenly she laughs and says spontaneously: "I have to laugh at those two kittens!"

Little Haabjørg is full of her experiences, and now and then she laughs. When she got home, she showed off all her presents and began to tell her mother all about her visit without being asked. Juliet had played the piano—clunk, clunk, clunk!—and that was marvelous. They were in the kitchen, and there was this man sitting there eating, the man with the shiny teeth, you know. "I sang for them, and he talked English, but there were two kittens running all over the floor and a big mother cat who quietly went after them every time and watched them playing. I'm going to have one of them and take it with me, because they were so funny."

"Was it a grand room?"

"Yes, it was. But in the bakery they were all white from the flour, and they had flour on their noses and sticky stuff in their hands. Ha, ha, ha! You should have seen them! Then we went and gave something to the chickens, and then we went all sorts of places."

"Who went around with you?"

"All of them. Well, not Mrs. Knoff, because she was so fat and stayed behind. But Juliet and Romeo and the big boss. And the boss showed me his gold watch and let me listen, and then he went away. The housekeeper also showed me the pantry. There were all sorts of things on the shelves and in the drawers, and I was given some cakes. Really, it was lots of fun there with them, I can tell you."

"Did they ask you to come back?"

"Yes, when I go to collect the doll, you know."

"Did Juliet have any night things for you?"

"Yes, she did. But it was so short, a kind of jacket."

"Ah, only a jacket," said Lovise Magrete. "I thought as much! That's what they have. Did they ask after Mama?"

"Yes. No, I don't think so. They asked after Papa. I saw the calves again. They didn't really want to bite, they just wanted to lick my hands."

"They didn't ask after Mama?"

"No. But I said you had two rings, one with pearls."

No, THEY hadn't asked after Mama.

There was a new disappointment for Lovise Magrete the next time she went with the child to the Knoffs. They didn't take much notice of her; it was little Haabjørg they took pleasure in and made a fuss over. Her mother was not even invited in. Fortunately, Anders Vaade was in the store wearing his gray dust jacket; and he and Lorensen entertained her without pause. They fixed the date of their departure and discussed other details. Edevart stood and listened; but when the discussion was conducted in English, he didn't understand a word.

A girl came with a request from "them in there" as to whether Haabjørg could again stay the night. No invitation to the mother. She looked at Edevart and said: "I don't understand what they want with the child all the time."

Lorensen was standing by with a sly look, and he softly answered: "It's just because Romeo's got the idea into his head. They want to please him."

"Why can't she stay?" Edevart whispered.

"I don't rightly know," said the mother. "But as it happens I've brought her night things this time." She handed the maid a paper parcel and let her go.

But the girl was hardly out of the store when Lovise Magrete gasped and uttered a little cry. "Run after her!" she whispered, seizing Edevart by the arm. "Get that package back. It's the wrong one!"

Edevart, rather slow on the uptake: "The wrong one?"

"Yes. It's my own night things. Look, this is hers! Hurry and change the packages!"

Her own night things? Edevart was puzzled as he ran off. He knew his way about the place and he put on speed, but he didn't catch up with the girl until he was standing in the kitchen.

In no time they had exchanged the packages. But Miss Ellingsen, the housekeeper who was married to Magnus, happened to be in the kitchen just then busy with something. She recognized him at once and colored, but looked straight at him, looked long at him, unflinchingly; and when he came up and greeted her, she smiled. Miss Ellingsen had not changed, although she was married and wore a large gold ring on her middle finger. She was just as she had been before; her sleeves were rolled up and her arms were youthful and rounded. Nothing had left its mark on her.

"A man we rarely see!" she said.

"Why should I show myself around here? You are married, aren't you?" he replied teasingly.

"And you? Aren't you married?"

"No, I haven't gone in for anything so stupid."

"Nevertheless, I've heard it said that you've found that wife of Haakon Doppen's again."

"Well, in one way that's right. She came back wanting to see her old homestead again, and I couldn't deny her that," he answered cravenly.

"Well, it means nothing to me."

"How are you getting along?" he asked.

"As usual, living from day to day. And you?"

"Oh, don't let's talk about me. What it will probably come to is that I'll have to leave the country."

"You've been doing something wrong, eh?" she said jokingly.

"Yes. To myself," he answered.

His self-pitying sigh achieved nothing. If he wanted to give the impression that he had been maltreated, that he was to be pitied, that he was a victim of fate and had been led astray, he found in Miss Ellingsen somebody who could nevertheless smile in his face, with a touch of irony that annoyed him.

"Are you laughing at me?" he said.

"Perhaps you think I should cry?" she replied. "Things are what we make of them. You mustn't go blaming others."

This of course he hadn't done, and he answered firmly: "I don't know what you mean. Have I blamed you?"

"Not me! But let it go. I just thought I'd mention it."

She was not very sympathetic; a bit too unbending. Edevart prepared to leave, but she would not let him go. Maids were going hither and thither in the kitchen busy with their tasks, seeing to the stove, laying the long table for the work people, washing and scrubbing. Miss Ellingsen quickly opened the pantry door and said: "Come in here. I want to tell you something!"

"What is it?" asked Edevart, following her.

They stood facing each other behind the closed door. Nothing happened.

"What is it?" she said at last. "It's nothing."

Edevart gaped. "What . . . ?"

Her bold air had left her. She gave an embarrassed smile, a dejected smile, and looked down. "I just wanted us to have a little talk . . ."

"I haven't time for that just now. Look, I was sent to collect this package, so I've got to go back with it. They are waiting."

"Who's waiting?"

"The people I'm with."

A bitter expression crossed her face and she murmured: "Then I'll not keep you. I just thought you might like to sit down and have a little talk over a cup of coffee and some cake."

"Thank you very much, but . . ."

He really felt rather sorry for her. He was not hardhearted. He wanted to be friendly, and he took her hand. "This is a big heavy ring you've got here."

"Yes."

"Why do you wear your wedding ring on your middle finger?"

"Because it was too loose."

"Yes, Magnus did you proud and made it a big one."

She made no answer to this. She drew her hand away and busied herself at the far end of the pantry. She opened a drawer.

As far as Edevart could see, it contained flour, white flour. What was she doing there? Probably just covering her embarrassment.

"Am I just supposed to stand around here?" he exclaimed impatiently and left.

She followed him. She was gray in the face and looked as if she could kill him. As he went out of the door, he felt her hand on his back, pushing him . . .

Lovise Magrete was on pins and needles, waiting for him.

"I was delayed," he said.

She at once examined the package, and breathed a sigh of relief. "Yes, that's it! Let's go home now! Are you ready?"

"Yes."

They hadn't bought anything and there was nothing to carry down to the boat. Outside she suddenly stops and asks: "Have you been in the bakery?"

"In the bakery? No."

"You've got a white hand on your back," Lovise Magrete says, dusting him off. "Where have you been?"

"In the kitchen."

"A white hand," she says. "Five fingers. It's flour. I can't get it off."

Edevart twists his jacket off there and then, brushing and rubbing it. He is angry and embarrassed. It runs through his mind that he might return to the kitchen, take her hand again, and thank her so ardently as to crush her fingers against that huge ring.

"I suppose it's that housekeeper of yours who has had her arms around you," says Lovise Magrete, her lips pale.

"She did not put her arms around me."

"That old flame of yours—the one on the sloop."

"Ha! ha!" laughed Edevart.

"So she did have her arms around you?"

"I wish you'd shut up!" Edevart put his jacket on again as it was, and they left.

"She might have got rid of the flour first," continued Lovise Magrete.

354

Edevart remained silent. That shameful woman, that she-devil! She had deliberately avenged herself upon him! He was also angry at himself for having taken his jacket off right in the middle of the yard and brushed it off. The little devil might well have been standing at one of the windows watching the whole thing and exulting.

"I should have run over with the package myself and changed it," said Lovise Magrete.

"Yes, that would have been best."

"But I couldn't. I didn't want to show myself. I'm not going to have them say that I was hanging about their kitchen hoping to be invited."

She continued nagging Edevart on their way home until in the end he told her everything. He was blameless; he could give an account of himself without lying; he was clearly innocent. It was at once apparent to Lovise Magrete that she was the one upon whom the housekeeper meant to avenge herself, not Edevart. But she took it all very well and said to Edevart as a rather sad joke: "I can't really let you row over to the store by yourself after this!" A joke with a smile, a rather poor and joyless smile. It hung over her for some time, prompting her to pay eager attention to Edevart early and late as in their first days together. Eventually it all passed over. She had other things to think about.

She asked Edevart: "Shouldn't you go back home and settle your affairs?"

"Yes," Edevart replied.

But days and weeks passed, and still Edevart hadn't left. He made no move. Things weren't in fact going so badly. He again received money sent by his sister Pauline following the sale of the new stock of goods from the Polden store. He was able to buy provisions from Knoff which kept them going.

After some time Lovise Magrete again asked: "Shouldn't you be making ready?"

"Yes," Edevart replied.

"Because there isn't much time left."

355

"How is it? Have you got your ticket?"

"Ticket? I didn't think I was going over there again. I thought I was to stay here."

"That's what I thought, too!" said Edevart darkly.

"But I can't stand it here. Don't let's talk about it. I must try once more over there. Some place or other. Perhaps out West."

"So you aren't certain what you want to do over there?"

"I don't really know," she answered. "I'll try everything possible. I won't think of anything else. You may well laugh! You think I'm undecided. But the fact is that I have children over there."

"Have you the money for your ticket?" he asked.

Silence.

"Have you the money for your ticket?" he asked.

And she answered frankly: "Yes. Anders Vaade is going to lend me some."

They were no longer very sensitive in their dealings with each other. A few months ago and Edevart would have considered it offensive for her to accept a loan from anybody other than him; a few months ago and she would never have bypassed Edevart. Ah, they were both over that blissful rapture; both were reduced and fragmented. There was no longer any complete surrender. Things which she had earlier denied herself, clearly out of regard for him—now she indulged herself, wearing her rings (which were beautiful, after all), and why shouldn't she? He watched and said nothing. It didn't particularly upset him. He didn't know what the origins of these rings were, and didn't inquire. What was more: when occasionally she was reminded of the affair of the five white fingers on the back of his jacket, she would laugh out loud at that monkey business and ask him if he didn't feel like going back and having it done to him again.

"Yes," he answered. "Next time Anders Vaade looks into the store, I'll pop up to the kitchen so that you and he can be alone."

"Well, Anders Vaade isn't all that bad, believe you me!" she said in his defense. "He was also perhaps a bit in love with me. He's the one who gave me this pearl ring. That was one Christmas in America."

Edevart replied: "Not that I might not have had one thing or another from my Miss Ellingsen."

No, they weren't very sensitive in their dealings with each other. Their romance lay in fragments behind them, and they had nothing secure to look forward to. They had also become wayfarers in love.

"There are two weeks left," said Lovise Magrete.

"What do you mean—two weeks?"

"That's when we leave. Now you must get ready."

"What about coming home with me and looking things over?" asked Edevart, testing things out. "Perhaps you'd feel like staying there."

"You haven't built on?"

"Built . . . built. Do you expect miracles, Lovise Magrete?"

"No," she said humbly. "God knows I don't. But you suggested it yourself. That's all I meant."

"Yes, I'll build. It will take time, but I'll build. I'll put up a nice little place for the three of us. Shall we set out and look at the site?"

"I'll come with you," she replied.

That was decided. But she made haste to be off at once. It was as if she had no great faith in the outcome of her journey and wanted to be sure of being back within the two weeks before the voyage to America was to begin. Edevart, too, was uncertain. He had the same fear that she had: that their trip might be in vain. And what was he to say to the people in Polden when he arrived there with this woman and this child? And what would people say?

No matter . . .

A little sadness for Haabjørg. She had now got the two dolls from Juliet Knoff, and was to go a third time and stay overnight

357

and eventually get her kitten. But now there would be no kitten. Edevart had to promise her lots of kittens when they got there.

They locked the doors and rowed away. Once again the place was dead. Nobody watched them go. Only the roar of the waterfall followed them over the bay. They dropped in to see their neighbor Karel and arranged for him to keep an eye on Doppen until further notice.

THEY ARRIVED by boat in Polden.

Edevart was not in particularly high spirits. This time he was coming home with neither a fishing vessel nor a rowing boat heavily laden with goods for sale. He was coming with two strangers. What would his father and his sisters say? Above all, what would Joakim say?

As they came gliding in toward Polden, they saw people working on the drying grounds; astonished, curious people who straightened up and stared. Edevart cringed as he sat there on the thwart. Ah, yes. Once again this year the skipper from Ofoten had put in to dry his fish. He hadn't paid back the money he had borrowed from Edevart the previous year. He simply hadn't been able to, for his son Nils, the peddler, had drawn too heavily on him. But he'd scraped together everything he could and spent it on fish again this year.

They came ashore near the boathouses and walked up to the village. Edevart carried their baggage. How would it go?

By no means badly. No, not at all. Lovise Magrete had found the trip stimulating. It had been a change, new surroundings. It was not like walking all day in your own footsteps as in Doppen. She was pleasant and good-looking, and she captivated Pauline. Haabjørg got along well right from the very first moment. She immediately took over the store cat and several kittens. Moreover, she made friends with the old father and told him about America. Joakim was not at home.

Indeed no, things didn't go badly. The mere fact that the

houses were painted white excited Lovise Magrete, and she said: "But this is a big building you have here, Edevart! A home with stone steps and everything!"

"No, anything but big," he replied. "But we've managed!" Embarrassed, he showed her the store with its few shelves and bins, then the little office, finally the even smaller bedroom. Everything was clean and tidy, but minute. He asked: "Do you think you could be comfortable here in this room?"

"Yes, of course!" she replied. "Why shouldn't I be?"

He: "Only to begin with. Later I'll build on."

"Where will Haabjørg sleep?"

"We'll think about it," he replied. "What about with Pauline? They are already good friends."

"What about yourself? Are you to be homeless?"

"Me? Don't worry about me! I can sleep anywhere."

They went walking around outside, then into the little barn. Lovise Magrete sniffed the smell and gave a cry of recognition: "Lord, how it all comes back to me! When the cows come home this evening I'll do the milking!"

Edevart went through the store, with Pauline reporting what goods were sold out. "I suppose we can afford to replace them," he said. "Where is Hosea?"

"Hosea? She's at Ezra's. What do you think they did but run away last summer and get married!" said Pauline, laughing. "It was a matter of life and death for the lad, ha, ha! And I didn't dare write and tell you. Well, never mind! They're getting along all right. Ezra knows how to look after himself. The whole summer he spent coping with that bog of his, and it's a sight for sore eyes to see how he's got things growing there. They already have two cows . . . What I was going to ask was: is this the lady you and I wrote to in America?"

"Yes, that's her. She came pretty promptly, don't you think!"

"Has she been married?"

"Yes. Her husband disappeared."

"You said she was a bit crazy. I don't see it."

"No, she must have got over it. It's not a thing I worry about. Where is Joakim?"

"In Kvae Fjord. He wanted to try the seine net out again. I dare say it'll only be a quick trip during a break on the farm. All the same, he's already made a catch."

"Made a catch!" Edevart cried.

"Yes, twice, so he writes. Top-quality fat herring, expensive! Nothing in quantity like the catch he made in Outer Polden, he says, but because they're good quality it will mean a fair return for the summer."

"Marvelous!" Edevart murmured. "Our Joakim's born lucky!"

"He needed a bit of luck at the moment," said Pauline. "That's why he went. He wants to build on his barn."

"Isn't the barn big enough?"

"No. Not since we put in another cow. And in the coming year perhaps another one. You've no idea what he's been getting out of that land since he began clearing it and treating it with seaweed."

"Marvelous!" Edevart murmured. "Who's with him on his trip?"

"I don't know them all, but he's got Ezra and Karolus and Teodor . . ."

That evening Lovise Magrete milked the cows, and afterward she laughed through her tears, complaining that her hands had got cramp as a result of this unfamiliar work.

This was the first day.

But more days came, and it was no longer all pleasure. Pauline had a serious talk with Edevart, and showed him that they were sold out of the more important things, and people were making fruitless visits to the store. You see, with time people had grown more and more used to finding everything they needed at the one store. They demanded not merely coffee, whole grain, and syrup, but also asked for axes, which the smith had previously provided, and for ropes for their boats, which at one time had had to be brought back from Bergen. Now it was St. Olaf's Day in Nordland, and they were asking for scythes for the reaping—in the long run they couldn't afford not to stock such things.

"No, of course not," said Edevart.

Then there were the office books. Pauline showed her brother the books. See here! She had not given more credit than what would be covered the day the Ofoten skipper finished drying his fish and paid off his workers. And such cash as she had taken she had already sent him in installments.

Silence. Edevart seemed unmoved. Well, then, Pauline would have to break it, have to tell him. She wouldn't keep silent any longer. Gabrielsen had set up in business again!

"So!" said Edevart. "He's started up again!"

"In his wife's name. She got financial backing from her family. They're going into business in a big way, I hear. And practically nobody is going to come shopping here."

Edevart sat on the edge of a drawer which had been pulled out, listening. After Pauline had waited a while, she asked: "So what are we going to do?"

"We must get in more stock," Edevart replied.

"It would be fine if we could!" she said.

"What do you mean?" he asked, with pretended surprise. "Just write me a long list of all the things you want, and when you've done that, hand it over to me!"

"As you say!" she said, her eyes glowing. Ah, this big brother of hers!

Edevart persisted. "Ah, you're a good girl, Pauline. Did you think I was bankrupt? I'm good for more than any list you could draw up. I have a farm down south, and a house and buildings in good shape, and several fully equipped beds. And apart from that I have crops growing in the fields, and a boat moored there . . ."

No, Edevart was not depressed. Could things be going better than they were? Wasn't Lovise Magrete delighted with this new place, and with the people and the animals? And not a single soul in Polden had been disagreeable about his having come back with two unknown ladies. So what could be wrong! His spirits rose, and he began looking more cheerfully on life.

He took his two ladies to call on Hosea, his sister married to Ezra and living at their new place. There was still no road there, just a path through the marsh and over the hill. He had to carry both mother and daughter over the worst places. But if he knew Ezra, there'd be a road pretty soon.

From far away they catch sight of a solitary woman working in a field. It's Hosea! Dear God, it's Hosea! There she was, giving the potatoes a final hoeing, looking after them well. When she caught sight of the visitors, she ran in and quickly tidied herself up and changed into something which concealed her corpulence.

Lovise Magrete said sadly: "Just the way I used to work in the potato field all by myself at Doppen!" But she did not allow her memories to get the better of her. She clapped her hands with joy to see how bright and new everything was here, with two windows in the main room and a bedroom under the eaves and everything new. From the windows she could see far past the green strips of land drained from the bog right down to the fish-drying grounds, where people were working, and from there right across Polden to the mountain pastures on the other side of the bay. She commented that it was a lovely and demure landscape.

Edevart: "So you've run away and got married, Hosea?"

"Do you think I could get him to leave me in peace?" she answered with a smile.

They looked at the cow byre. It was new and big, with stalls for two more cows than Hosea actually had, and a place for a horse sometime in the future. A great deal of importance had been attached to the outbuildings. The barn had a threshing floor. Doppen's little hay barn seemed no more than a shed by comparison, so big was it.

Ezra, the little devil! But he'd had to borrow heavily to get his buildings, there was no doubt about that. He was always ready to take a risk. Hosea was very content. They weren't badly off, she said. Ezra worked all hours and was always cheerful. It was marvelous to watch him digging ditches in the bog and running off the water like some great waterfall. "Ha! ha! When he's going to breach where he's dammed it up, he shouts for me to come and watch. He's a great lad!"

"Does he not have any help with the bog?"

"Off and on. Joakim sometimes lends him a hand, but Joakim has plenty to do on his own land. And when it's a matter of working the fields, there's only the two of us," Hosea replies proudly. "Ezra cuts the turf and loosens it, and I stand there with a big hook and turn it over. He's very particular about having nice straight rows. And so am I. Because then we get a nice straight black strip as we go along. It's pleasant work. Then late in the evening we go home. Perhaps you'd like to walk down to the bog and take a look at the fields?"

Edevart had long ago lost interest in farming matters. He was bored by his sister's chattering. "No, I don't think so," he said.

"No?" said Hosea, and let it pass.

He motioned to the two who were with him and explained: "You see, those two there have come from America and they've seen much more impressive things with horses and machines."

"That could well be," said Hosea. "We could also plow with a horse, for that matter, but we'll have to wait until we've got our own horse. We can't afford to rent one. But things are all right as they are. We already have two cows."

Hosea was proud of what she had—just as, many years ago, Lovise Magrete had been when she showed off her sheepskins and her woven rugs. That was many years ago . . .

They had milk and waffles, but said no, thank you, to coffee.

On the way home, Lovise Magrete was all sweet and charming again, really happy with what she had seen. And Edevart took this to mean that she now wanted to stay in Polden, settle down quietly in Polden. So content was she.

7 EDEVART HAD BEEN GIVEN THE LONG LIST OF ARTICLES
which they had sold out, and for the present carried it
about in his pocket. But he was not depressed. Things
continued to go well as far as Lovise Magrete was concerned. And he was moved to go and call on one or two
of his neighbors to avoid seeming stuck up toward old friends. He
no longer feared embarrassing questions about the two strange
ladies: they were a widow and her daughter, and they were the
people he'd bought his farm from down south. They'd come all
the way from America to see their old home, so how could he
chase them away!

He set out to be friendly to people, and spent long hours
chatting with them. Not because he was particularly concerned,
but because he had to follow the conventions. Lovise Magrete
did not come with him on these visits to neighbors. He thought
she was too fine, dressed as she was in her city clothes and her
hair curled with tongs. That was not Polden's usual custom. But
one or two women from the neighborhood came and looked in on
her; and as she was pleasant and patient with them and chatted to
them about America, they thought kindly of this widow woman.
She had, after all, traveled the world and was able to offer advice
about all sorts of things.

Edevart took another trip up to see Hosea. He was afraid in
case he had hurt her feelings by not wanting to look at her fields.
Poor little Hosea, who not so long ago had been such a little
thing and had thanked him by holding out her thin child's hands.
Now there she was doing all that heavy work in the fields, and
laughing just the same. This was how it was to be content with
one's lot in life. This time he went out alone to see her, taking
with him several yards of good cloth from his own store. And
Hosea, who wasn't blessed with many clothes, happily thanked
him for the present. "You are the same as you always were!" she
said, touched.

They walked up the hill to look at the potatoes. They
walked down to the bog—an extensive area with many ditches,

large and small, and with patches under cultivation with waving corn. Edevart pretended to be more impressed than he really was in order to please his sister. And he asked stupid questions to make her laugh.

"But how is it now? Are you left in peace?" he asked.

Hosea knew what he meant. "I haven't been troubled," she replied.

"No more cries from the bog?"

"No," she said, and smiled slyly. "No ghostly wailing!"

"All the same, you took a bit of a risk getting married and coming to live out here far away from neighbors."

"I never think that way about it any more," Hosea replied. "During the day I have so much to do, and at night I put myself in the Lord's keeping."

"I don't know whether I would do that," he said earnestly.

"Why? Because of the corpse? It's down in the churchyard now."

"Well, yes. I don't want to frighten you, but one night there might be cries again."

"No," she said with a laugh. "Because it never was the skipper who uttered those cries."

Startled, he asked quickly: "Who was it, then?" But when he noticed that she was reluctant to answer, it suddenly dawned on him. "Ah! Now I understand!" he exclaimed.

"Ah! What a lad!" she said. "But it was August who put him up to it!"

"Ah, August! So it was he who put him up to it?"

"To help him. He wanted a good start on the bog, so they dug out the body and also old Martinus's cow. Look, here's the big trench they dug!"

Edevart began to laugh. "So he lay here—this other fellow —lay here in the bog on Sundays and howled. That's the funniest thing I ever heard!"

Hosea: "But, bless you, you must never say a word!"

"I'll never say a word. How did you yourself get to know?"

365

"Well, the thing was that I said I wasn't going to marry him and live here with ghosts and cries from the dead and such things all my life. So then he confessed."

"Did he laugh?"

"Yes. He put his hand over his mouth and laughed. I could have hit him I was so angry. Because he'd scared the wits out of everybody. But he didn't care if I was cross. And he said so many funny things I just had to laugh as well. And anyway, the body ought to be in the churchyard, so it was a blessing for us all. Just look at those cornfields!"

"Wonderful!"

"I'm beginning to get a bit worried about those meadows over there," she said. "He ought to be coming home now to mow them. Haven't they produced a marvelous lot of grass! Enough for two cows! What I was going to ask was: are you going to marry her?"

"I don't know. What do you think?"

"She's terribly pretty. And I hear she's not too grand to milk the cows. I think you should."

"Well, worse things do happen!"

EDEVART WAS GOING to go to the post office, and Lovise Magrete sat in the office writing letters to her children in America. She was as bad as he was when it came to writing. She who was so clever in other things was hopeless at writing letters and made all sorts of mistakes. When it came to the spoken word, on the other hand, they both managed very well; and it wouldn't be wrong to say that occasionally she had the best of it and Edevart was reduced to silence.

Yes, he meant to go to the post office. He wanted to give the impression that he really was sending that long list of goods to the merchant in Trondheim. But before he left, there was one thing he had to say to Lovise Magrete. Just let her finish her letters, and then he would raise it. He'd been thinking about it a long time. Surely there could be no harm in it?

366

"H'm! I've been thinking!" he said. "How was it you came to talk to Anders Vaade about money?"

She was a little taken aback, and stammered: "I don't know. It just happened."

"You should have mentioned it to me."

"Oh?"

"Yes, you should. Anyway, it's all the same now. Or isn't it? You're thinking of staying here, aren't you? You don't need money for any journey?"

Lovise Magrete did not answer.

"So how is it?" he insisted, and looked at her suddenly. And his look implied that he found her silence hard to bear.

"I don't know," she said. "Let me think about it. If we settle here, we are committed. We'll be here till we die."

"What of it?"

"Just that I have children over there and everything . . ."

The same old thing again. Back and forth. She was by no means over her restlessness. But once again she was kind and dutiful to him; and she opened her letter to add a postscript saying that she was still uncertain about something. Back and forth—and finally she reminded him of his promise, made on a certain night, that he would come with her across the sea. To this Edevart had no reply.

He came back from the post office with two letters for her. One was from Lorensen about the journey, she said. The other was from the children in America. She read both letters and fell silent.

From now on Lovise Magrete found nothing to please her in Polden; and she no longer offered to milk the cows. All that mattered for her was to talk Edevart into coming with her. And Edevart hemmed and hawed and let the days pass.

They never actually quarreled. They talked to each other about America, and discussed things endlessly. Had Norway become so unbearable for somebody who, after all, was only from Doppen!

Yes, Edevart. Because although at one time she was only a

girl from Doppen, now she was also from lots of better places. America was so big. If you didn't want to stay in one place, you could simply go somewhere else. She had never been to Florida; and after reading those books . . .

But what about the children? Weren't they firmly settled in New York? Didn't she want to be where they were?

For a while, perhaps. Of course she would want to see her children and stay some time in New York. Anyway, her children were now grown up and no longer needed her. And she'd already lived two years in New York earlier. That was in the beginning.

Had she then left her home there?

Yes. Moved to another place. Was that so strange?

No, replied Edevart, himself a vagabond and rather like her at heart. But that was all right, he then suggested. They could shift around from place to place in Norway, too. From Polden to Doppen.

"Oh, don't talk about that again!" she pleaded tormentedly. "I can't ever think of that. Couldn't you see how things were with your sister Hosea? She was a slave to her smallholding and her cows. It makes me shudder!"

"Hosea!" he cried. "She's happy with what she's got!"

"Sure. She's happy, same as Karel. She doesn't know any better."

Silence.

"I took it you liked it here and felt at home. You didn't seem to have any cause to complain."

"I couldn't very well start complaining about things when I'm here as a guest," she replied. "It's nice to be here for a short period, just as it is at Doppen. Now let's not talk about it any more."

All right. He wouldn't press her. Things were bad enough as it was. He had indicated that she should have approached him for money instead of going to Anders Vaade. Now she was ready to take him at his word. Only one other thing did he remind her of. "Didn't you write and tell me that you hadn't taken to America, either? Not for a single day?"

"Yes, I found things difficult there, too. What I said was true. That was the very reason I moved from place to place, trying them. But it was better there than here."

Back and forth. But she stuck to her argument.

The following day things came to a head. She quietly asked him first to take things seriously and be ready to leave the next day. Time was short, and they would have to call in at Doppen.

By tomorrow? The rope was around his neck. So she was determined to leave the country again?

Yes, she *had* to leave.

She *had* to ?

"I didn't want to tell you before," she replied. The remark probably just slipped out, but now she staked everything on this one card. Oh, she threw everything into this one attempt to win over this stubborn lover of hers, perhaps without realizing that this would finally decide things and she would have to take the consequences. "The children have written to say that their father has been found," she said.

A cry from Edevart. "He's . . . What are you saying? . . . He's been found?"

"That's what they write."

That roused him. In truth, he now became interested. No matter whether it was some desperate device of hers or the simple truth, she now had the satisfaction of seeing him disturbed.

"Surely it can't be true?" he asked.

"Indeed, who would have believed it!"

"But however it is, you are divorced from him, aren't you?"

"Yes. I'm that, all right, but . . ."

"But you want to go back over to him?"

"What can I do? I can't very well let him be there alone."

"So!" he said, nodding and thinking. But in reality he wasn't greatly depressed. The news did not shatter him. Not at all. On the contrary, he felt relieved. The uncertainty was over.

"So you see, we can't wait any longer," she said.

Edevart, in confusion: "Yes, but . . . then I can't very well come with you."

369

"Yes, you can. Why can't you?"

"Well, how? What do you think?"

She immediately tried to find a way of retrenching. She showed how quick-thinking she could be. "Well, Haakon hasn't actually returned home to the children. All that's happened is, they've managed to trace him."

"But when they find him and bring him home . . . I don't understand. Do you intend being married to two people?"

"What am I going to do?" she sobbed, and tears came to her eyes. "But I *must* go back. They've written to say that!"

"Was that in their last letter?"

Again she was quick to find an escape. There was a risk he might want to see the letter and perhaps hang on to it and get it translated by his friend August, who knew English. She anticipated him and said: "It's too bad I burned the letter, otherwise you could have had it."

"You burned it?"

"Yes. So nobody should see I was married. It was chiefly for your sake."

They both thought for a long time. If the whole thing had been invented by her on the spur of the moment to help her to gain her ends, the effect was certainly decisive. She couldn't now take it all back.

"Well, then, it's all over!" he said.

"Oh, God! I suppose it is!" she replied. Naturally, she was now tender and sad. She spoke almost inaudibly and wept a little. But she, too, seemed able to endure it . . . yes, Lovise Magrete, too, seemed able to do that.

"So this is the end!" he continued.

She placed her hand on his and was silent.

"What about Haabjørg now?" he asked.

"Don't you think I've been thinking a lot about Haabjørg! She's still very young, so she'll have to come with me. You won't join us, I take it?"

"No!" he replied firmly.

"Poor Edevart!" she said, even more tenderly. "Are we both going to leave you!"

"It looks like it. I'll row you both to the steamer tomorrow."

"You'll come with us as far as Doppen, won't you?"

He answered as though deeply wounded, as though terribly rejected and hurt. "Yes, if it means anything to you."

If it meant anything to her! How did he have the heart to say things like that? They must spend their last few moments together at Doppen . . .

HE DID NOT go with them to Doppen. There was a last-minute change of plan. He had had a bad night, without sleep or rest. He no longer found the thought of losing her easy. Moreover, he fretted because he was unable to put up the money for her journey. He was absolutely destitute.

After he had rowed his two ladies to the landing stage, he tried to hide himself away until the steamer came, craven and sick at heart. But he was unsuccessful. Little Haabjørg looked high and low and eventually found him on the top floor of the warehouse. There he sat, shrunken, looking at his hands.

"So this is where you are!" said Haabjørg. "Mama's looking everywhere for you."

"Is she?" he replied, and followed her.

The child produced him triumphantly. "I found him up there, Mama. Under the roof! Ha, ha!"

Lovise Magrete probably understood something of the situation. She treated him kindly and indulgently, and told the child that Edevart had lots of things to think about. Edevart should have been left in peace. "Come here, Edevart, and sit on my cape!" she said, spreading out the cape.

Why couldn't he have been there to support and protect her till the end? It was painful; it cost him much pain now to part from her altogether. Not for nothing had she been the first profound love of his youth. At that moment he would surely have followed her all the way to Florida if only he had had the money.

Did she understand how he needed her? God alone knows. "You are so pale," she said, thrusting a friendly hand in his.

"I don't feel well," he replied.

"No, you aren't well."

"I'd take a drink if I had one."

"Can't you get one here, don't you think?"

"Oh, no. And it wouldn't really help, either. Lovise Magrete . . . Lovise Magrete . . . Lovise Magrete," he murmured, as though in memory of something. And he shook his head.

She was herself moved and turned pale; she wanted to be nice to him, help him. "You are too unwell to come with us," she said abruptly.

"I feel a little low. It just came over me."

"You weren't able to bear it," she said sympathetically. "You'd best row home and go to bed."

"I ought to be ashamed of myself."

"No, no! Don't take it like that. We'll be back at Doppen already by tomorrow evening."

At this Edevart broke down. He turned away and replied: "Yes, and I'll not be there!"

To comfort him she went out of her way to be nice to him. She promised to write to him. "The fact is that I'm in love with you," she said, standing on the gangway. "I love you more than anybody in the world. I want you to know that."

"But that hasn't really helped us. We're parting just the same."

"Yes, but listen to me," she said, as though in good spirits. "I don't know whether I'll take to it over there, either. Not at all. In which case I'll come back to you. Yes, I'm almost certain to. Or perhaps you'll come over to join me? That could also happen."

"Well, nothing's impossible, I suppose," he said more cheerfully.

372

"There, you see! So we're not parting forever. There's only one thing—I might become too old for you."

"You, too old? I'm older than you are."

"Yes, yes, I know. It mustn't be too long before we meet again. Now, see you get home safely!"

"Well," he said out of politeness. "I really will try to come with you."

She spoke as though thinking chiefly of herself. "You mustn't, Edevart. It will make things worse for both of us. Perhaps I won't always be as hale as I am now."

"If you are taking the steamer, please get into the boat!" came the loud warning voice of the ship's agent.

There came the steamer, already sounding its horn. There was general commotion. Everybody began picking up baggage. They seized each other's hands in quick farewell. There was no time for a kiss. Where was Haabjørg? Oh, that girl, always wandering off! "Haabjørg!" shouted her mother. "Here I am!" answered Haabjørg from somewhere. Yes, indeed, Haabjørg had kept a close eye on things. She was already in the boat, standing there bailing out water with a huge ladle, with her hat hanging down her back. What a girl! But she livened things up considerably, and the company couldn't help smiling at her . . .

Edevart sat in the boat rowing home. He felt now he didn't really count for very much. Lovise Magrete hadn't mentioned the travel money and Edevart had also kept silent. Appearances had perhaps been preserved, but nothing more than appearances. There he sat. What would August have done in his place? Drawn himself up and not given a damn. Edevart crumpled.

But everything passes.

The days passed; time passed. He had a letter from Lovise Magrete to say she was now sailing, but she would surely come back. That's what it said. Oh, a sweet and gentle letter, a little hurried and incoherent, but that was just like her when she wrote. Blessed creature, she wasn't leaving him like some fugitive. She had thought of him, had wanted to arrange things to his advantage, but it hadn't worked. But now I must tell you! Romeo again made a great fuss of Haabjørg and gave her lots of things and didn't want to let her go. Finally Mrs. Knoff herself had come and asked whether Haabjørg couldn't remain behind in Norway and stay with them and have a nice time. Well, Lovise Magrete had hemmed and hawed, and thought it might be nice for Edevart not to be left so alone. But do you think those people had had the common decency to invite her in? What do you think? For if they wanted to get her to agree to something as big as that, they should surely have shown her some respect, the child's mother. But, no, all she was expected to do was hand the child over to them, her own flesh and blood. And as if that wasn't enough, if they got Haabjørg now they might never give her up, and when she grew up Romeo might well want to marry her, so the child would get out and about and see something of the world. No, thank you! "What do you think, Edevart? Should I have done it? I leave it to you. But I'm seriously afraid that if you had come down and wanted to see her, as you have every right to, they wouldn't have let you, for they are all so proud and behave just like gods in their dealings with the rest of us, yet they haven't proper manners, though I've seen a lot more of the world than they can show . . . Everything seems empty and gloomy here at Doppen without you. I hope you got home all right, although you were as pale as death. Don't worry about Haabjørg and me. We got to Doppen all right, for Anders Vaade rowed us and helped us to get things in order, but Anders Vaade I never think about for a minute, I must tell you this, for then I could have done it already in America when they were in love with me, but never so much as a sign from me. I tell you the truth when I say that nobody will take me away from you . . . When you come here there's some food left, but I've taken away everything that might go bad and tidied up after us. I don't wear rings any more and I've left one of them behind for you in the table drawer even though it's no use to you, but give it to Pauline from me . . . Tomorrow we leave here to go aboard. You mustn't worry about us. I've traveled plenty and changed trains and driven night and day. Goodbye for now, it won't be for life, and I'll write again later . . ."

Not a word about the traced husband.

THE DAYS PASSED. Edevart began to worry that Joakim might return from Kvae Fjord, and he wasn't anxious to meet him. He was in general in such a bad way, felt so miserable, that he tended to creep away and avoid other people. Pauline had become impatient and nagged him about the goods which hadn't come. What had become of them? It was a long list, and lots of items on it, and still no word that they had even reached the landing stage. So where were they? Edevart said he would go south and look into things. He scraped together what was in the till and left.

Naturally there was nowhere else for him to go but Doppen. He could eat up the food which had been left there, and squat there and twiddle his thumbs.

At any rate he didn't get that far. August stopped him on the quayside and said: "So you didn't go to America with the rest of them?"

"No, I couldn't afford it," said Edevart, which was true.

August nodded. "That's what I thought!"

"I didn't sell a thing in Polden. You couldn't even find a king's shilling there. Of course I've got a good deal on credit outstanding, but I won't collect that until that skipper from Ofoten pays off his work people. The skipper has also borrowed money from me."

"What'll we do now?" said August.

"Ask me another."

"Yes, but what did you come here for? You must have had some reason. I stood here on the quayside as they left. She's gone."

"I know."

"There was a whole crowd of them. I counted fifteen going aboard. What did you say you came here for?"

"I just felt lonely and there was nothing for me to do. I came to see you."

"If only we could both get away from here," said August thoughtfully.

"I don't know how I'm going to get away," replied Edevart. "I haven't a thing."

August: "You have a watch and a gold ring . . ." But August himself wasn't in the best of moods just now, either. He muttered darkly about having been stupid, and having been made a fool of.

Edevart took comfort from the fact that others besides himself had been stupid, and he questioned his friend further. He didn't actually discover anything. But he gathered that it was not for nothing that August had hung around this one place for over a year. And there must also be some connection here with the fact that he had disposed of his gold ring. He went straight to the point and asked: "Where's your gold ring?"

August: "Where is it? I know where it is."

"Can't you get it back?"

"Doesn't look like it."

"Don't you ever see her?"

"I see her every day. What are you asking for?"

"No, it isn't really my business," Edevart admitted. "But who is it?"

"I'm not saying!" August replied.

"All right."

"No, because she's too high up, so I'm not saying anything. But it's the very devil of a mess, and it's been going on now for nearly two years."

"I'm aware of that!"

"But one thing I'll tell you, Edevart. The way I got caught up in it was all very innocent."

"I know all about that as well. Because I, too, got caught up very innocently."

"No, you could see what you were doing. But I had the wool pulled over my eyes."

"How?"

"How? How was I to know she was married when she didn't say so? I didn't find out till afterward, when it was too late."

"She was married? Can't you tell me who it is?"

August shook his head. "She's too high up."

Then it dawns on Edevart. He remembered a heavy ring, worn improbably on a middle finger and in evidence in all manner of company. "I know who it is!" he said.

"Then you don't need to ask."

"She's a right bitch of a woman. However did you get caught up with her?"

"Don't ask me! I had a through ticket to Trondheim, but I only got this far and no farther! Goodbye and good luck to that ticket! But it must have been fate. When I stepped ashore off the boat and ran into her, I knew nobody here. She asked me where I was from; and when she heard, she wanted to know why you hadn't come back and all that sort of thing. And then all I had to do was write to you and tell you she was now my girl friend, she said. That's all I had to do, she said. And she was extremely lively and good-looking. If I had realized she was married . . . But she said she was the housekeeper here, and what a nice gold ring you have there, she said. 'Would you like it?' I said. That's the way it happened."

"But when you discovered she was married . . . ?"

"Exactly! But then it was too late, you see. Because I'm not exactly made of stone, and I'd fallen for her straight off. All this time I've been waiting for her to give, but no. Apart from that, she's married to a real drip, the sort who'd run away from a mouse. As if that was anything for her! She's a real good-looking woman, you know. One of the most elegant I've ever seen in all my travels. So it's no wonder I'm after her. But every time she just laughs. The thing is that I can't give her up now. Because when I fall in love with somebody, you never get me leaving her. But it's never happened before that I've been two years in love with anybody. But then you must also remember that she's a lady, and that's never happened to me before, either. And as for my gold ring, the way I see it is that I'm quite content if she wears it for the rest of her life as a reminder of me. For she's wanted to give it back to me many times, but I've said no."

"So it's not really that she is holding on to the ring?"

"No. I only say that when I'm mad at her. On the contrary, she's a fine person and terribly pretty. She's slipped me many a tasty morsel while I've been here, so I can never forget her."

"Ah, yes," said Edevart, nodding. "I can understand why you are in love with her."

"It's only natural," August replied. "When I see her in the mornings I walk about in a kind of daze until dinnertime. Then I eat my porridge and think it's meat. Damned if I understand it!"

Edevart: "You must try to get away."

"Yes, I must, mustn't I? If it hadn't been for her, I'd have been away from here long ago. What is there here for me? Romeo did actually raise my wages a tiny fraction, but what's that to me? Kiss my . . . foot!"

The friends pondered the matter, discussing it earnestly. Finally August came up with an idea. "We'll break out of this place," he said. "We'll take the first boat south. That's in a week's time. There's nothing to keep us here."

"South, did you say? Where shall we go?"

"South. It's better than north. What is there for us to do up north in Polden? We'll go south as far as we can find money for. I'll take my accordion."

EDEVART ROWED over to Doppen. When he got there he was hungry, and he at once began looking for food. There was no bread, but there were plenty of biscuits, ship's biscuits; and there was cured meat. But no butter. Good.

It was lonely and desolate. The beds were tidy; everything

had been scrubbed and put straight, but there was now nobody in the house but him. The walls were silent. If he had had a bottle, he'd have had a drink.

Outside and round about, everything was green. The meadows should have been cut, but the corn grew high; and Karel had weeded and hoed the potatoes. To think that Lovise Magrete had had the heart to leave all this behind!

He wandered about this place of his until late in the evening, and finally lay down to sleep in his own bed in the hay shed. It grew darker and darker. The rush of the waterfall was in his ears. He felt lonely, the loneliest soul in the world . . . a great strong fellow who gave way to self-pity and began sobbing quietly.

The next morning he found the ring in the table drawer. What surprised him was that it was the pearl ring she had been given by Anders Vaade, and not the other one, which she might well have bought herself—though he never asked her. Lovise Magrete was so marvelously kind that she perhaps wanted to give him double pleasure by leaving Anders Vaade's ring behind, who knows? This was also a thought that touched him and he began to sob.

He looked for a scythe but couldn't find one. There was no scythe hanging in any of the buildings. Well, Haakon Doppen had probably never used a scythe—and his poor wife had doubtless had to get a neighbor to mow her meadow. That's how it had been.

He rowed over to Karel's to borrow a scythe and a whetstone. These he got. Karel said that he could nicely have sent his lads over to Doppen to mow, but he didn't know if he should. They had, however, seen to the potatoes.

"Your lads can have the potatoes for looking after them," said Edevart.

They got into conversation, and talked about various matters: of the crops that promised not too badly, and of all the new emigrants to America who had upset Karel by leaving. "That Anders Vaade has never really wanted to do anything," said

Karel. "He doesn't take after his father, who worked for everything he's got. All Anders ever wanted to do was walk about in a long coat and look important. But the worst thing was that he took a group of others with him, some of them young able people. My own brother-in-law was one of them. And then there's Lorensen, who worked at the store. He's done nothing else but moan about Norway ever since he got back. Why didn't he just stay away? But he talked lots of people round, he did. Well, let them now try it. Not that I don't wish them well, but it's not at all sure that they're going to be happy. 'Live better,' Lorensen kept on saying. 'Better in what way?' I used to ask. Then he had to admit that he meant sweeter food. Can you beat that! They don't get enough raisins and sweets here at home, so they quit the country! Deserters, that's what they are! Let them quit!"

Edevart, who would have emigrated himself if he had been able to afford it, merely nodded now and then. He said: "I've just remembered that I need a rake as well. There isn't one back at my place."

He got his rake.

Now Karel put a question to him: "I hear you've decided to sell Doppen?"

"What? I don't know," replied Edevart, surprised. "Who says that?"

"Then there probably isn't anything in it. Romeo said he wanted to sell it for you, and asked if I didn't want to buy it for my lads."

A strange look came over Edevart's face. He sensed trouble. Romeo was planning to sell the place one day to recoup his debts! "I haven't thought very carefully about it," he said, "but I remember I did once mention it to Romeo. He's got a good memory, that fellow!"

Karel: "He offered it to me. But excluding the waterfall."

"Ah! Excluding the waterfall . . . Well, yes, that's right."

Edevart rowed home feeling lower than ever. He had had a warning. Still, what did he want with Doppen now that he was on his own again? For God's sake, let Romeo have it and pay off his debt to the store!

As soon as he got back, he started to mow. He felt all worked up and upset, and he drove himself hard. The sweat dripped from him. The scythe bit well into the dew-drenched grass and he made evident progress. So long as it did not grow too dark over the next hour, he would finish off the first section. Tomorrow he would spread the hay, turn it at noon, and stack it in the evening. He was not the ridiculous novice at farming his young brother Joakim thought he was. No, he knew what he was about.

He went to bed at the end of the day, dozed an hour or two, then leaped up again.

The day was bright and promised to be hot again. Why not mow again, mow some more? It would be something like seven hours before the dew was gone. He'd show Joakim, by God! Tired and worn by the work of the previous evening and without any food in him, he made straight for the meadow again.

He was big and strong and he again showed his capabilities. The scythe sang, the grass fell in layers, leaving a broad swath behind him. Of course he was taking a risk cutting the whole of his meadow without being sure of several drying days, but he didn't stop.

When he was finished, he went indoors and found himself something to eat: some biscuits and cured meat. He made coffee and drank it with syrup. By ten o'clock the dew was gone, and he began to spread the heavy hay, twenty loads of it. By the end he was ready to drop, and no sooner had he sat down than he fell asleep.

He woke with a clear head—with a mind now crystal clear after all the turmoil. A number of things which previously had only been smoldering in him he now faced up to boldly. He no longer felt he would be unjustly done by if Romeo were now to sell Doppen. It would serve him right. He had cheated old man

Knoff over the Lofoten fishing several years ago. And now all those little "extras" were returning to their rightful owner.

That was that.

But now what about Lovise Magrete? That was a different matter. For the first time a feeling of resentment against her flared up in him. In a way she had deserted him and run off with Anders Vaade and the others. All right. And was it not her fault from beginning to end that here he was now—a grown man reduced to nothing, living on dried food as in the poorest days of his childhood? He had a whole catalogue of things against her. And it was incredible—chillingly incredible—how much she had changed. He excepted the passion and tenderness she had shown in their moments of ecstasy—and yet even those moments had been accompanied by immodest words and exclamations which had merely coarsened the occasion. And how was he to explain the fact that she never showed the slightest fear of any consequences? She must have learned certain practices out there in foreign parts which he only heard hinted at and which shocked him. She had done other things which went against the grain. There was he, brought up in a religious home, whereas for Lovise Magrete it meant nothing to profane the Sabbath by taking out her sewing at the very hour when the preacher was in the pulpit. Oh, she had become so emancipated, so sure of herself. This was all right in its way, but at the same time it was far removed from her original shy innocence. What did wantonness have to do with love? Was she any better for it? Did it suit her? Did it make her any happier, any more content? Certainly, it wasn't what one would call depravity; it was an acquired boldness. Those curls in her hair which didn't even become her, that hat she wore, those neatly laced boots, that city dress—yes, and she also wore something around her neck that simply made her look older and harder about the face and not nearly so pretty—all these things conspired against her. Yet she persisted; this was what she had learned, and this was what she would have. And what was all this nonsense about having wintergreen in his buttonhole? That's what they used to do on *picnics*, she had said. She embarrassed him by that; he had never experienced that before. And then it happened occasionally that she would be stuck for a Norwegian word and say: "What's it called now? I know it in English!" It was doubtless genuine, but sounded so stupid from a woman who came from Doppen in Fosenland. English, what was that! August could speak Russian, and he never got stuck for a Norwegian word. Then she'd gone on and on talking English in the shop with Anders Vaade and Lorensen until you couldn't stand it any more. But then, on the other hand, had she ever taken the trouble to get little Haabjørg to sing an English song for him, for Edevart? Never! Off you go then, and yap English all the way across the Atlantic! Go ahead! But he, Edevart, would by now have been an entirely different person if he had never laid eyes on Lovise Magrete . . .

That, too, was that.

Fortunately, he managed to bring in all the hay, carrying it in on his back. And this despite the fact that he very foolishly had mown the entire meadow at one go. Things went all right. Luck was with him. His whole body ached, so that he alternately felt sorry for himself and then laughed at his own feebleness. But his soul took no hurt; rather the reverse. In the evening he would make barley gruel for himself and sweeten it with watered syrup. This wasn't bad food at all, and he thanked God for it.

After he had finished taking in the hay, he rowed back to Karel's to return the implements.

Finished at Doppen. Finished *with* Doppen? At once. He simply walked around and took leave of everything. He was a bit sad, doubtless, that things had gone so badly for him; but there was nothing to do about that now. In the woodshed stood his new ax. He didn't want to leave it there all forlorn, but neither did he want to take it with him. Oh, he wasn't going to keep as much as a nail or a wood shaving from Doppen in his possession. He drove the head of the ax into the block, and left it like that. Thereupon he went in to take leave of the cottage. His eye fell on the bed; memories seized him and he broke down. A sob or two, a little cry of pain broke from him. At that moment he took back all the bad things he had thought about Lovise Magrete, regretting them with tears in his eyes.

AUGUST WAS READY.

"I've only one thing to say to you," he said to Edevart. "And that is, if I happen to come and ask for a delay of an hour or two so that I can make better preparations, you mustn't give in to me."

"All right!" Edevart replied, without really understanding what was meant.

They had the greater part of the night to wait for the southbound mail boat, and August continued with his preparations. Edevart glimpsed him now and then running back and forth among the houses as though he was in a hurry.

In the evening he came and said: "I'm not going to be ready in time for this boat."

"What do you mean?"

"We'll have to wait for the next one going south."

"We'll do no such thing!" said Edevart.

August, curtly: "Then you'll have to go alone."

Edevart couldn't. He needed his friend for all sorts of reasons. "What's keeping you?" he asked.

"It's my wages," August replied. "I can't find Romeo."

This certainly could not be the truth. Edevart himself even had had difficulty in avoiding Romeo, whom he didn't want to meet in the state he was in now. Indeed, he didn't want to meet anybody; he made no calls and slept out that night.

"I think you've already had your wages," Edevart said straight out.

"Yes, but this is something else," August replied and walked off.

Toward morning the mail boat whistled and Edevart turned

384

up on the quayside. August was nowhere to be seen. Nobody had seen him. Magnus, who was on duty, couldn't refrain from saying: "He daren't go aboard, he's afraid of the sea!"

Edevart sat on a packing case and slept.

Some time later August appeared. He was in a black mood, trailing along with a shapeless sailor's bag under his arm.

"You shouldn't have let me go," he said to Edevart. "Nothing came of it."

Edevart: "What have you been up to?"

"You mustn't ask," August replied. "But would it have been better if I had shot him?"

Edevart gaped, not understanding a word.

"At any rate, here I am. I've got my bag with me and I'm ready."

"I can't hang around waiting here for another week," said Edevart disconsolately. "But we could take the northbound steamer, which comes in tonight, you know. What do you think?"

August thought. "All right," he said. "We'll take the northbound."

All that day August scurried around and seemed much occupied. He came with food for Edevart, and joined him in the evening. They sat sheltering behind a tan vat. Finally they fell asleep.

When the time approached for the northbound steamer to arrive, the two friends woke as if by instinct.

They spoke no more than was necessary. August was thoughtful. Suddenly he says: "When the ship whistles, just you go aboard, and I'll be along immediately."

To this Edevart replied: "We are going on board together!"

"It's just that I want to say goodbye to somebody," August murmured. And a moment later, when the boat whistled, he leaped up and said: "You can laugh or you can cry, but I'm not ready to take this boat, either."

Edevart held him back and said: "Now we are going on board!"

"Let me go!" August demanded. "I have another good chance now! Magnus is on duty, and she's in bed there alone . . ."

When Edevart finally realized what these words meant, he unceremoniously took hold of his friend and didn't let go again until they both stood on board.

"Did you get your ring?" asked Edevart.

August: "Ring? I didn't want the ring. I'd be happy if she wore it in her grave. No, I got nothing else from her, either. She wouldn't."

"Have you tried before?"

"Have I tried before!" retorted August. "But I thought that since I was leaving . . . I'm sure if I'd gone back again tonight . . ." Suddenly he became bitterly angry and asked: "What the hell do you mean dragging me by the arm like that? Have I ever done that to you? You say I asked you to? Yes, but I didn't mean it that way. But you've never been in love with anybody, and you don't know how it feels . . ."

8 IN POLDEN AGAIN.
Great changes in this last fortnight.
While still on board Edevart was astonished to read his own name on a packing case standing on the freight deck. He looked around and found several cases with his name on, a whole pile of cases, bales, and barrels. They must be replacement stock. It was fantastic. Edevart called August over to see what he thought.

"They must be from her!" said August.

"From who?"

"That woman who left. These goods are from Trondheim!"

Edevart felt in his pocket; and, sure enough, there was the long list which Pauline had drawn up. Lovise Magrete couldn't possibly have got her hands on it . . . and, anyway, where would she get money from to spend on such goods? Damn it, it was a complete mystery!

When his ticket was being made out, and the ship's mate heard his name, he exclaimed: "Ah! So it's you! We've got a mass of things for you." Edevart was about to reply that he knew nothing about it all, but August intervened. "It's not the first occasion that this fellow has ordered a whole storeload at one time."

They were well looked after on board, and treated with great respect, even though they were traveling only as deck passengers. It was doubtless to be put down to a whim on the part of this big businessman.

The mystery was solved when they arrived back home. They saw that Joakim and Teodor had turned up to meet the boat in Karolus's eight-oar and take the goods back home. Here was the explanation. Joakim had returned from Kvae Fjord having made lots of money out of the herring and he had come to the rescue of the store.

August understood the situation at once, but was not overwhelmed by it. He was not brought to his knees. When the agent estimated that there must be goods worth about ten thousand there, August replied: "Yes, he's fighting against time in Polden!"

The agent: "I suppose the idea is to topple Gabrielsen once again?"

"Yes, there's no other way it can go!" said August.

Edevart did not have the nerve to take part in this conversation. He felt humbled, and could not conceal it. August talked to him, tried to cheer him up. Edevart and he had arrived last time as important men, great personalities, hadn't they? They shouldn't come like tramps this time. "We'll think of something. Don't worry!" said August.

Joakim met them, looking somewhat embarrassed. "We were sent to collect all these cases of yours," he said to Edevart. "Our Pauline wouldn't give us any peace!"

August was quite equal to the occasion, laughed good-naturedly, and asked innocently: "How did you know we'd be arriving with the goods today?"

"You imagine Pauline didn't get a telegram about it!" Joakim replied.

Edevart was totally lost.

They traveled back in the eight-oar. On the way Joakim had the chance to report that the old skipper from Ofoten had left without paying. He had promised to send the money from the south. All the workers had been left stranded with long faces and no money to show for their summer's labors.

"The fact of the matter," said Teodor, raising his voice, "is that if we herring fishermen hadn't made a packet in Kvae Fjord, nothing on earth would have saved Polden!" Teodor swelled with pride. He had himself made a packet and didn't conceal the fact. He had bought himself a pair of high boots with red edging around the tops. He looked very grand. August totally ignored him.

The fact that Joakim had had to spend his money on the store instead of on a new barn was rather painful; but the pain gradually wore off. Edevart presented the pearl ring to Pauline so that he should not be seen to be returning empty-handed . . . And in God's name, surely something would turn up that would stiffen his backbone again! Joakim pretended not to notice anything. He borrowed a horse, carted the goods up from the boathouse, broke open packing cases, prized open bales, and rolled barrels down into the cellar, joking all the while with his older brother that he would expect good wages for his labor. Pauline filled the drawers and the shelves and moved about with great dignity behind the counter.

"You've certainly bought a lot of stock," said Edevart.

"It was Joakim," replied Pauline by way of an excuse.

"What could I do?" Joakim asked. "She wouldn't leave me in peace."

"I wouldn't leave you in peace?"

"I tell you, Edevart, she lay here in the middle of the floor and screamed."

"You little liar!" cried Pauline with a laugh.

"She threw a fit," Joakim continued imperturbably.

Good-natured fun the whole way; never a sour face. When Joakim was finished dealing with the goods, he went back to his fields. He went by the doctrine he had learned as a child. He said: "One man to his fields, the other to his business—and I don't want to change places!"

There was nothing unresourceful about Joakim. His hay barn was full to bursting; he couldn't get another forkful in, and he wouldn't be doing any building this year. Ah, well! But he worked hand in hand with an even more resourceful young man called Ezra. *He* had room both for the hay and for the new cow Joakim had bought. Thus everything turned out for the best.

What about August? Did he sit there darkly in some corner, crushed, not saying a word? Not on your life! After two years Polden had become a new place again for August. Driven by a great urge to be active, he went around giving a hand wherever it was needed. He first helped out Joakim for a while, but when he heard that Karolus still had his mowing to do, he went to him, seized a scythe, and mowed manfully for two days. August was and always had been a remarkable character, capable, plenty of initiative, a liar supreme among liars, well liked by all, loyal and helpful often to his own detriment, but in a crisis unscrupulous to the point of criminality. Here he was back again. He no longer had those boots with their patent-leather trimmings; his clothes were threadbare and all the baggage he had was an ill-filled sailor's bag. What did all that mean? August let it be known that he'd left all his suitcases down south and only brought bare necessities with him.

He took a trip over to Ezra's place to inspect it. It was August's audacious ideas and advice that had led to this new place out in the wilds becoming the important development it was—and which in time was destined to become the miracle place of the entire district. August was therefore received with great honor and respect.

"You have worked marvels here!" said August, looking

round and nodding. "I couldn't have done better myself in the short time available. What are you doing here, Hosea?" he asked, as though astonished to see her there.

Ezra adopted the same tone. "She is just getting in my way, that's what she is doing."

"I hear you two are married?"

"She just wouldn't leave me in peace!"

Hosea broke in. "Now you just shut up, and let me tell August exactly what happened. I didn't want him, not likely. But then he asked me if I'd prefer it if he went and hanged himself. Ha! ha! I've seen better heads than his on nails!"

"Yes, I'm astonished that you two ever wanted each other," said August.

He was invited in and offered refreshment. He found the cottage very comfortable. "But," he said to Ezra, "you were a fool not to make the cottage bigger right from the start. From what I see of Hosea, there'll soon be several more of you."

"No," said Ezra, innocently shaking his head. "It's just that she's grown so fat and lazy out here."

Hosea pulled his hair. "I'll give you fat and lazy!" she threatened.

They walked up the hill to the potato patch. Ezra dug down to the roots and showed them how big the immature potatoes were already. "Just look! Huge half-grown potatoes!" They went down to the bog—that great glory and blessing. The stalks were three feet tall and the ears were already hanging heavy. Here and there they lay flat, but there was no danger now; ripening would take its course until cutting time came.

August was amazed. He nodded and cleared his throat, but remained silent. He stepped farther into the bog, and jumped up and down to see if it shook. No! The water ran merrily down the huge main trench; the many side ditches had dried out the bog to make firm ground. The whole area was now covered with sprouting bushes which had taken root in the drained land.

August had great respect for the enormous and patient work that had gone into this. But a man who has seen the world

390

obviously must have seen something better. "This reminds me of a place in Australia where I was once," he said. "But the area of wasteland was greater and there was more water. The central ditch was like a canal, and we used the water to drive a mill. Yes! And in the autumn we didn't harvest the grain. We milled it right on the spot and brought it in as meal. Perhaps you are wondering what we did with all that meal? We fed it to thousands of pigs, and then we sold the animals by the cartload."

His audience shook their heads in wonderment.

August reassured them that they had enough land and plenty of water in the ditches. "From what I see here—and which I can of course measure at a glance—I'm left speechless by what you two have achieved, all the things you've done. That I must say!"

The young couple were too proud to show tears in their eyes. But they were moved, and Ezra managed to say: "You think so. Well, we certainly went to work on it!"

"How many cows have you?"

"Two. And one calf."

"So next year it'll be three," said Hosea.

Ezra: "The thing is that a woman wants a lot of cows, while a man wants horses. I don't know what we ought to do first."

Hosea muttered what she had probably said a hundred times before: "You don't get butter or cheese from a horse."

August gave thought to this. Although he didn't exactly guide the fish through the seas or determine the path of the heavenly bodies, there was nevertheless nobody like him for giving advice. Ezra ought to have a horse.

"How are things now?" August inquired. "Any more cries from the bog?"

"No," Ezra replied. "It's been quiet since that Sunday when he cried out twice."

The two scoundrels looked at each other in total innocence. Hosea stood there beside them, full of dangerous knowledge and not daring to look up.

They walked over to the buildings. August inspected the

cow byre and the barn, expertly measured the width of the cow stalls in hand spans and nodded, measured the barn door against the height of a hay load and nodded, jumped on the barn floor to test whether it would bear the weight of a horse, and nodded at everything.

When he was about to leave, Ezra was still uncertain. "What do you think about a horse this year?"

"This year? No, you can't feed three cows and a horse on the land you've got under cultivation so far."

"No," they both said.

"But," August continued, "a horse you must have!" And with this he went.

August was still filled with the urge to work, and he infected others with it. Polden was still a new place to him, and Ezra's new development stuck in his mind. He went to Edevart and said that Ezra ought to have a horse this year.

"Well, if he must have a horse, he must have it."

Yes. And now August and Edevart were to take a spade each and turn over just enough of Ezra's marshland as would feed a horse. Agreed?

Edevart hung back. Joakim came along and listened with interest to the scheme; but Edevart, now putting on weight and becoming a bit fuller around the waist, hung back.

"You aren't a cripple, are you?" said August. "From what you said, you mowed the whole of Doppen in one night. Ezra has the money to buy seed with. He'll feed one cow for you, Joakim, and get enough manure from it for the new field. He earned enough money from the fishing to buy himself a horse, isn't that so? And you'll be able to borrow this same horse here for carting goods up to the store with. You understand? Here's the spade!"

So the two friends set about the bog, working like men possessed when it came to the point. They used simple brute force; they drew on all their reserves of strength. It was marvelous to see what they accomplished in a day. All Ezra had to do was to follow behind with a hoe and break up the lumps left by these work demons; and Hosea was kept busy all day making food for them, the way they ate. Never had Ezra had such fun with his bog; but the funniest moment of all came the following morning when Edevart yelped about his aching back before he'd got the stiffness out of it.

AUTUMN WAS APPROACHING, and the two friends did odd jobs in the district without earning a penny. Was that any life for lads like them! Both of them fretted. Pauline stood behind the counter selling things. It wasn't too bad as long as the herring fishermen had money to spread about the village, for it all eventually landed up in the store. But what good was that to the two friends? None. Edevart had to be associated with Pauline's business at least in name, but he claimed no responsibility for it. Always he would say: "Do what you want as far as I'm concerned." August, for his part, was also the kind of man who would not accept any payment for the work he did. "I don't need it," he would say with pride.

But in fact they were both in need. For many years they had moved about freely. Never a regular roof over their heads—no sooner a new one than they had had to relinquish it. There they stood. It hit Edevart the hardest: the skipper from Ofoten had gone off from Polden without paying back that old cash loan; he owed more to Knoff in Fosenland than he was probably worth; and finally they were now coming to him and asking for payment of the balance on old Martinus's cow, which he had stood guarantee for. It couldn't have come at a more inopportune time. "All right!" he had to say to the messenger, putting a brave face on it. "Wait a moment!" he had to say.

He got hold of August and they discussed the problem. "You must refer the messenger straight to the store," August thought, "and write out a note!" What, write out a note on his own store? But write it he did. He made out a kind of receipt on himself: Item, received from the store in cash and merchandise such and such a sum. Edevart Andreassen.

If he ran into any more trouble now, he wouldn't be able to survive it.

"You look so depressed," said August.

"I could sink into the ground," Edevart replied. He sat brooding, brooding. Winter was coming. He couldn't very well take on another fishing trip to the Lofotens. So what should he do? Set out with his pack again? That held no terrors for him; but it was greatly insulting for a businessman who owned his own store. He sat brooding, brooding. He said to August: "I could begin peddling again, set out with my pack again. But I don't know how I'd get started. I've no goods to sell."

"I've been thinking the same thing," August replied. "As for goods, you can bring out your old remnants and other such things from the store and fit us both out."

Edevart shrank from the thought of stripping the store still further. He said: "We haven't any money, either."

"Money?"

"A few coins. We can't go absolutely empty-handed. If a woman comes along with a daler note and needs change, we're stuck. We must have some small change."

"There must be some way," August replied.

Well, then, August had no objection to setting out again as a peddler. Far from it. He'd been thinking about it. It had a re-newed appeal to him as an occupation. The vagabond life was calling. The following day he said to Edevart: "That fool Teodor wants to buy a gold ring."

"You don't say!"

"He mentioned it to me."

Edevart, wonderingly: "But you haven't got a gold ring, have you?"

"Oh, yes, I have," August replied. "You don't understand, because you're not very bright, and never have been. But I can get some small change for us if only you'll help me tonight."

Edevart sensed thieving and skulduggery and shook his head.

"Don't you go thinking we're going to steal any ring," said August. "All you have to do is stand watch in the road and see that nobody is coming."

"I don't know if I dare join you," said Edevart doubtfully.

"Would you rather rot in Polden!"

The night was good and dark when they set out. August was carrying a spade and a hand ax which was used for breaking open packing cases at the store. Edevart walked along in silence.

They took the road leading to the church, with August slightly in the lead, eager and determined. At the various farms he made a slight detour around them.

"Where are we heading for?" Edevart asked.

"We mustn't talk," replied August.

They walked on for about an hour, through the whole of the inner parish, farm after farm, in and through the parsonage woods and onto the parsonage grounds proper. August stopped at the churchyard gate and spoke softly: "Stand here! If anybody comes, just come and follow me into the churchyard. Nobody will dare follow you there. But you must move incredibly fast and appear to swoop over the graves."

This is sacrilege, thought Edevart. He's going to break into the church. But what's he brought the spade for? He said: "I'm frightened you're going to break into the church."

"You fool!" said August. "The church is safe from me."

"So what have you got in mind, may I ask?"

August, curtly: "Shut up! I know where his grave is. I'll take the top turf off, then put it back on again."

"Are you going to open a grave?"

"Exactly. He's buried there with my ring on. A heavy gold ring. I gave three daler for it. I know which hand and know which finger, so I won't need to root around."

Edevart shuddered and whispered: "Don't do it, August!"

"Shut your mouth and stand there!" August snarled back, and left him.

The night was dark. Edevart could see very little; but he listened and heard August digging in the ground. Apart from that, there wasn't a sound. To begin with, he was exceedingly nervous and trembled every time he thought he heard somebody on the road. Whatever else, here he was a party to a sinful deed, violating the peace of the grave. But as the minutes passed, then a half hour, then an hour, he was able to breathe more freely, and even sat down for a while by the gate. In the darkness he glimpsed something even darker: a mound of earth which August had thrown up. At length he heard a creaking sound: that must have been the nails giving way as August forced open the coffin. Edevart, tense, stood up.

Neither of the two men forgot that night, even though no misfortune befell them. But it was clear to both of them that they were on a godless path; and even August, who behaved so boldly, had sleepless nights for some time afterward. He wasn't very practiced at robbing graves, and he was worked up. He knew he would have to work quickly and silently—no loud talk to set the church windows vibrating. Nor was it a particularly appropriate moment for swearing to himself if he scratched himself on a nail. He must simply be stern-minded and not listen to his friend's objections.

The job was not finished with opening the coffin. He still had to find the ring in the blackness of the night, the most difficult thing of all. August could well have found the hand and the finger blindfold on a fresh corpse. But this was different. The coffin contained only clothes and bones; and moreover, the corpse had doubtless been bumped around somewhat in the coffin during its long journey from Polden. What had become of the hands? He concentrated his search on the center part of the corpse. No . . .

The search took an eternity. Edevart couldn't stand the waiting any longer. He left his post and went into the churchyard. August had only one end of the coffin open, the lid propped up by the spade standing inside. He groped about in the coffin with one arm.

Edevart whispered down into the grave: "You must come now, August!"

August stood up. He answered desperately: "Get back! Get back, before Old Nick himself comes and gets you!"

"You can have my ring to sell instead."

"Your ring, eh? And let the sexton find my ring and keep it? Shut your mouth!"

Edevart was compelled to go back; and August again began to grope about in the coffin. He realized there was no point in simply feeling here and there; he would have to begin at one end and explore every inch. Oh, it was a painful business having to finger everything he got his hands on: clothes mainly, often a bone, several times a button, and sometimes something disgusting that stuck to his hands. The buttons often fooled him because they were small and round; the corpse lay fully dressed in the coffin, and there were jacket buttons and trouser buttons. August kept at it. When he finally found the ring, he couldn't refrain from whispering out loud across to his friend: "I've got it!" Thereafter Edevart heard him struggling to get the lid back on; and again there was a creaking of nails.

Naturally, August's work at this point was not exactly neat and precise. He couldn't find the old nail holes again, and he did not dare attempt to hammer. He pressed the lid down, stepped on it, and bounced up and down once or twice. Then Edevart heard him again shoveling earth and tramping on it to pack it down.

What was now left for him to do was very important: to remove all traces. Edevart heard him tidying up after himself, smoothing things with his hands, and finally replacing the turf. He labored at this a long time. The thing was to try to make the cracks as inconspicuous as possible.

At length August came. "Feel this!" he said.

Edevart felt. It was the ring. Edevart said: "Let me carry the spade and the ax!"

They walked silently back through the parsonage woods. It began to rain . . .

Yes, it was autumn rain and it lasted three days. August regarded this as a good sign, an act of providence. That blessed rain would keep people away from the churchyard; it would wipe out the cracks in the turf covering the opened grave, and all the soil would be washed down into the grass. That rain was a blessing which contributed to the success of the expedition . . .

So they took their packs and began their wanderings again, about the time people began lifting their potatoes, in October, at the approach of dark autumn days. August wanted the southern route; and Edevart suspected him of wanting to make his way back to Fosenland, where he was in love with a lady who was one of the high-ups. It made no difference to Edevart, so long as he didn't go shooting her husband, as he had hinted. "I'm expecting you to be sold out before very long, so then you can fill up your pack again by buying in the nearest town!"

"Don't worry about me!" replied August.

They parted. They weren't to see each other again until they met next summer at the Stokmarknes Fair.

Edevart sailed his boat north into Kvae Fjord before starting to do business. He was hoping that there would still be some money about in those parts after the big herring catches of last summer.

SEVERE COMPETITION developed between the store in Polden and Gabrielsen's store. One of them would surely have to shut eventually. Gabrielsen was said to be very powerful by virtue of the security provided by his wife's family. People didn't expect Pauline to be able to hold out against him. But she was a shrewd person who knew what she was doing; she worked out what people wanted most at the different times of the year, and stocked up accordingly. This was cleverly calculated; she did not buy lamp oil at the approach of summer with its midnight sun;

nor did she buy tobacco at the coming of winter, when all the men went off to the Lofotens. She operated with intelligence and prudence.

Joakim saw that the business was going well; and now that he had once got caught up in it, he began to develop a certain ambition—the ambition not to give in to Gabrielsen. He kept a strict check and never let his orders exceed his cash in hand. The two of them made the decisions together: sister Pauline came with her list and Joakim put in a firm order. The merchants in Trondheim could do what they liked: either sell at the buyer's price and terms, or have nothing to do with it.

Oh, sister Pauline had become a very capable person. She did not go out of her way to be pleasant; and people couldn't always count on her mercy when they came claiming to be in difficulties. No, she was not the softhearted person Edevart was behind the counter. Edevart simply gave things away when the occasion seemed to require it; Pauline held her ground, weighing things carefully and calculating things precisely in a businesslike way. If a demand was outstanding for too long, she was quite capable of calling the debtor's attention to the matter. Some customers took offense; some promised never again to set foot in her store. And indeed, they might stay away for a time, but they came back. What else could they do? They might shop at Gabrielsen's, but he was even worse, and abused the people of Polden for daring to support a shop in their own village. They only did it to ruin him, he said. He had no desire to do business with people of that sort. Anyway, they never had any money. They could damn well keep away from him, and he'd show them in the end that he could demolish that miserable little store over in Polden . . .

Gabrielsen was embittered by the fact that it was taking so long for Pauline and her brother in Polden to go bankrupt. But was there, then, any sense in his abusing his customers and in a way showing them the door? The consequence was that Gabrielsen's business was immediately undermined and began to go into decline. It also began adversely to affect the man himself. Sheer neglect led him to give up wearing that white collar around his neck; he shaved himself on Sundays only. Was that proper for a businessman? Look at Pauline now—how was it with her? A nice girl who more and more became a young lady. She always wore a white frill around her neck and a pearl ring on her finger. Moreover, to church she would wear a gold medallion which her big brother had given her and which must have cost a fair amount. Indeed. And Pauline wouldn't have been able to go about dressed like that if she hadn't been able to afford it. How the devil had these children of the telegraph lineman managed to become so affluent and powerful! People also knew that they had meat for dinner on Sundays.

All in all, the store in Polden survived. Of Pauline personally it could certainly not be said that she wept with pity every time some housewife came pleading poverty and asking for half a pound of coffee, for she didn't. But she was a good and sincere woman, that one couldn't deny. She was prepared to overlook a few raisins when the children of the neighborhood came into the shop. And furthermore, wasn't she still helping to support the dependents of old Martinus, even after she'd paid off for the cow in response to Edevart's note?

Then Old Nick himself must have got into Gabrielsen. He determined to have a showdown. He staked everything on one throw and bought in goods in huge quantities, great piles of goods, goods of the most incredible kind, delicate pieces and everyday ware, right up to heavy things like grindstones and round heating stoves of American design. Yes, indeed, Gabrielsen might buy in these things, but it must have been obvious to him that he'd never be able to sell them all. It was an act of desperation; he wanted to show his power. Good. There was a lively run on his store; he swept the village clean of ready cash, and for several weeks the store in Polden stood empty. So did Pauline and Joakim grow weary of the battle and shut up shop? On the contrary. Nevertheless, Gabrielsen was doing splendid business. He stocked things which even the finer people of the village and the neighboring district came to buy: silk and velvet dress materials and ladies' hats and watch chains and factory-made boots and splendid tablecloths with fringes and books of sermons with gilt edges—why should people write off to the towns for these things when they could get them at Gabrielsen's? On top of all this, Gabrielsen once even managed to stock up with a lot of fine foods and other delicacies, cheeses and honey and fruits which the fine folk couldn't resist buying. Quite a businessman was Gabrielsen!

Time passed; winter drew on. Pauline was not very happy. She still dressed up in her white frill and her pearl ring, but there was nobody to show them off to. She now found herself occupied with housework; the store had no customers. Joakim was busy on his own affairs, with his potatoes and his corn, and later with threshing. And when the time came for him to join Karolus's crew and go off to the Lofotens, Pauline was left alone with her irritation. If she didn't sell anything, she wouldn't have any ready cash to stock up again with goods. Her business was shutting itself down.

At this point Edevart sends her a money order from some-where on his journey; not much money, a few daler, a tenner or two, but Pauline plucked up courage again. Ah, that big brother of hers! The first thing he wanted to do was redeem his pledge, his note drawn on the store. Anything left over, Pauline could do what she wished with it. Ah, big brother! Really, he always tried to play down anything he did. That was the way he was! There could be no doubt that he needed the money himself; and Pauline was also sure that Joakim would have become furious and re-fused to accept this money. But Pauline bought goods with it. The word soon spread that the store in Polden once again had things to sell, not a huge quantity of things as at Gabrielsen's, but necessities, things people needed, sacks of flour, groats, coffee, American pork. Pauline wrote back to Edevart thanking him for the money and assuring him that it wouldn't be thrown away. The times are not good, she wrote, and there is a certain amount of talk in the village that a particular businessman has been having difficulty lately in settling his accounts. He was here in Polden recently and talked to me, but I won't say anything about that. You must come home now and run your store yourself. You are away and Joakim is away and I have nobody to advise me. I can only do what this wretched brain of mine tells me . . .

And then—in the middle of February, in the worst of the snow and frost—the people of Outer Polden returned from church with the news that Gabrielsen's store had shut for the second time. Gabrielsen had exploited his wife's family to the utmost; and now the last and worst of the notes had fallen due. It was the end.

It must be said that Gabrielsen had done everything possible to save himself. He had been to see the priest, the doctor, and the sheriff to see if he could use their names in a crisis. He didn't even spare Johnsen, the sexton, who was flattered at being thus approached, but was forced to decline like the others. Finally Gabrielsen had come to Pauline and offered to sell goods to her dirt cheap for cash. What kind of goods? Pauline doubtless wondered. Grindstones and round heating stoves? But she talked sensibly to him about it all and didn't snap at him unkindly. Gabrielsen mentioned a number of large and expensive items which he would reduce to whatever price she named. "I haven't any money for those," said Pauline. He listed various necessities, provisions. "I have just bought a stock of those," said Pauline.

No. They did not do business.

It was still severe winter and a hard time for people, though the days were becoming longer and lighter. Then, in March, Joakim returned for a brief visit from the fishing in Lofoten and brought something with him—he brought money for the whole of Polden. How? From that skipper from Ofoten! The fish-drying money from last summer. Joakim was to share it out among the workers in accordance with what they had each earned. What luck! There was money for both adults and children. Practically every house in Polden had occasion to bless the day. They weren't large amounts; but it brought a complete transformation, a golden age compared with before. The store had all its outstanding accounts paid, and once again had some cash in hand. The skipper even paid back the old loan he had had from Edevart.

So had the skipper turned honest all at once? In fact, he had been an honest man all along, an excellent fellow, but things hadn't gone very smoothly for him. His son Nils, the peddler, had drawn rather too heavily on his resources. Maybe he didn't have all that much left, God knows. But now the old skipper had realized that he wouldn't ever be able to return to Polden to dry his fish without first settling up for the previous year. He was honest out of pure necessity. But so well had he now done by the people of Polden that they almost blessed him for postponing payment until the moment when their need was greatest.

Edevart came home late in the spring when everything was looking nice and green. His boat was loaded to the gunwales with goods and he seemed to have enough cash in hand to manage. Remarkable talent this man had for selling things! He'd been far up in Finmark doing business, selling to Lapps and to settlers in the various regions, selling woolen garments and oilskins to people who had never intended to buy anything.

Pauline was looking forward to acquiring the goods with which the boat was loaded.

"You can't have them," said Edevart. "I'm taking them to the fair."

The idea had been August's, who was always ready for a bit of speculation. He had sent word from Fosenland that he'd bought in stock at Knoff's and already booked a stall at Stokmarknes. Since August was a reluctant letter writer, he had once again communicated his idea to his friend by telegram, and suggested to him that he, too, should load up his boat with as many goods as possible so that their stall might be one of the best stocked at the fair. He himself would come by steamer, bringing with him lots of cases and bales.

Clearly August meant to make a killing.

One day Edevart said to his brother: "We should have settled up, but perhaps I'll be in a better position to afford it after the fair."

Joakim was immediately on the defensive. "What is there for us to settle up?"

"For all those goods you bought for the store last autumn."

"I've had the money for that," said Joakim.

"What do you mean—had it? Just dropped out of the sky, eh?"

"I've had that money. I used it to buy the materials for my barn."

"No, you used your Lofoten money to buy those materials."

"Now listen! Pauline!" cried Joakim through the open door.

"You great ape!" said Edevart.

At this Joakim lost his temper. Things might have gone really wrong if strangers had been listening, and not just their old father sitting there in the room trying to understand what the lads were quarreling about. It seemed as though both were in the right. "What are you two arguing about?" he asked.

Edevart: "It's just Joakim being stupid again."

"I don't know that Joakim's all that stupid," said the father. "You've both got talents you can thank God for."

Pauline arrived. She looked from one to the other, then asked: "What's all this?"

"It's Joakim . . ."

"Is it not the case," Joakim asked, "that I got money from you to buy materials?"

"Yes, it is."

"You're in this together! You two have planned this!" jeered Edevart.

Pauline: "Must we always have this nonsense every time you two settle up between you! If neither of you wants to take the other's money, then give it to me. It won't be wasted. I'll make good use of it."

"The fool! He thinks he owes me for those goods!" muttered Joakim.

"I do!"

Pauline: "But, my dear Edevart, didn't you send money home when you were up north?"

"That was nothing."

"There was what you thought you owed the shop, and a lot more besides."

Edevart tears his hair despairingly. "I can't understand your calculations. I reckon I know how to add two and two together."

"But you don't," said Joakim. "Because you only add up what's right in front of your eyes. But that isn't the right answer."

"Listen to the lad, Pauline!"

"Aren't you the one who built the store up?" Joakim asked. Edevart gaped.

The father looked over from his corner and said: "Yes, he is!"

"And didn't the seine net come from you?" asked Joakim.

When Edevart recovered, he snorted contemptuously: "That net? Ha! I got that net for practically nothing. It was both badly made and it was rotten. Knoff was just going to chuck it in the sea."

"It's held long enough for all my catches."

"Your catches! You've gone out year after year, gone raking around in all the herring bays and eaten up all your provisions and spent all your money. Then you make a catch and pretend that that net has been a huge benefit to you. But it hasn't!"

Joakim, vehemently: "Listen to who's talking about going raking around year after year! Have you no shame! What about you—raking around from one end of the country to the other and never staying put anywhere?"

Edevart realized he would get nowhere this way, so he changed tack. "You can say what you like about me traveling around and doing various jobs. But is it so much better to sit here rotting in Polden the way you and Ezra are doing?"

"Ezra! Are you crazy!" shouted Joakim. "Do you know that

in time Ezra will be the owner of the largest farm in Polden? You may not know that, but I do."

"Yes, when he's worn himself out on that place! When he's incapable of walking or even crawling over his own land!"

"What do you mean? Shouldn't he work?"

"And when he's worn out Hosea and made her a slave to her cows and her fields," Edevart continued. "It's painful to see her."

"You fool!" muttered Joakim. "Can't you see how happy and contented they are, those people?"

Something stirred in Edevart's memory. He said: "That's only because they don't know any better."

"What is there better? They have their struggles, but they're happy and don't wish for anything different."

"And after all their struggling, all they can do is live from hand to mouth. That's all."

"No! In the first place, that's not all. They began empty-handed, and now they have a house and home, they have land, they have three cows, and soon they'll have a horse."

"Jabber! jabber!" jeered Edevart.

"Besides that, they have peace of mind. That's more than you have. They go to bed at night and they sleep."

"I dare say they do," said Edevart.

"Yes, but you don't! You who go wandering all around the country and think that's so much grander. I've heard you some nights! You twist and turn like a worm before you get to sleep, and when you're finally snoring, you start shouting all about your waterfall and about August and Florida in America and your farm. That's the kind of rest you get in the night. I wouldn't want to change places with you."

Long silence. The old father said: "Edevart has so many things to think about. You mustn't bother him. He's got so much on his mind!"

"However that might be," said Edevart at length, "I still owe you for these goods."

"I've no patience with you any more!"

Edevart: "What I want is for you to take over the whole store and run it as you want. That's only right."

"Me? The store?" said Joakim. "Oh, no, thank you! Leave me out of it! I'm no businessman. Pauline's the one who runs the business. I've got quite enough pressing things to do already. The first thing I'm going to do is build a barn."

The old father is still convinced that both his lads are to some extent right. Now he joins in and says: "Yes, it's marvelous what Joakim manages to get out of that land. He must build a bigger barn. If only your mother was alive to see it!"

Edevart was getting nowhere. He took out his wallet, placed twenty-five daler on the table, and said: "Look here! Take this for the store for the time being. There'll be more after the fair!"

"No!" said Pauline, startled. "Stop it!"

"He's crazy!" said Joakim, joining in.

Edevart bit his lip and nodded. Suddenly it occurred to him to say: "The only sense I can make of it is that you two want to get rid of me for good and take over the store."

Now Joakim was the one to gape. Pauline threw up her hands, then let them fall. She was speechless. Joakim did not wish to say anything more. He stumped over to the door, tore at the latch, and pushed several times. He wanted to get out, get out quickly; he barged against it—forgetting that the door opened inward. That door which he must have walked through a thousand times!

When he had gone, Pauline said: "You don't mean that!"

Edevart realized he had gone too far. He answered in a low voice: "No, no, not if you say so. I hardly know what to think."

"You must leave Edevart in peace," the father shouted. "He's got so much on his mind."

That's all it required. These fatherly words appealed straight to the heart. Edevart wavered. His obstinacy weakened, and he turned his face away to conceal it.

407

Before he left Pauline said: "You must take your money back, Edevart. You can't go to the fair with nothing in your pocket."

AND OF COURSE things were soon all right again. No harm had been intended on either side. But Joakim had behaved very sensibly—it was a sheer stroke of genius on Joakim's part to have got out before throwing a chair or some other appropriate object at his brother's head . . .

Edevart needed to have a man to accompany him in the boat to the fair. Last winter he had sailed many a difficult sea up off north Norway, but he hadn't been so heavily laden then. Besides, Vestfjord—which he was now to cross—remained Vestfjord, and he knew from experience what that could mean. He spoke to Karolus and tried to get him to come, but Karolus didn't intend going to the fair. Not because, as district chairman, he was all that greatly occupied at the moment with village business, but because he'd had a hint from the priest that his wife, Ane Maria, might perhaps be released before very long.

"I have a piece of good news to communicate to you, Karolus!" the priest had said to him last Sunday. "There is nothing definite or certain about it yet, but people are busy trying to arrange for your wife to come back home to you again!"

That was a piece of good news which almost took Karolus's breath away. He began speculating about all sorts of strange things, and couldn't face any food when he returned from church. And thereafter he continued to eat sparingly, such was the sheer profundity of his thoughts; and when Edevart wanted him to go along with him to the fair, he shook his head decisively and refused. He was in no mood for amusement, he said. That sort of thing was only for you unmarried people.

"You should take Ezra or Teodor with you!"

Edevart objected that they were also married; but Karolus said: Well, yes, they were certainly married, but they didn't have a cross to bear! Edevart didn't understand a word!

And of course he didn't get Ezra to go with him, either. He didn't even mention it to him. Ezra was too occupied in his spare time with his bog. There was a small new stretch which needed draining before he got his horse and could plow it. That "bottomless" bog continued to present him with an endless series of tasks.

Teodor was the last man Edevart would want to take with him on the trip, but there was no avoiding it. He came himself and asked if there was room for him in the boat. He was very anxious to go to the fair and buy a few things. Teodor dragged himself around the village and never did anything. Gray and neglected, if he lost a button he'd stick a little twig in instead. But he was rather grand about the legs: high boots with red edgings. And still he boasted even today about last year's herring catch and how he and the others had saved Polden. He kept up appearances, with pockets empty but a gold ring on his finger. Good potential there, but as a man inferior stuff.

Ah, that married couple, Teodor and Ragna! Both of them born in Polden, both of them of poor family, both of them lazy, dishonest, and poor, but by no means dull-witted. Few brains and slow minds? No, in their own way they were quick and clever, and Ragna had been top of her class at school. They could steal with light-fingered speed, and they covered their tracks with skill. Indeed, to such things as these they devoted considerable mental effort. Their cottage was a mess when you walked in, and there was a child every second year. But things didn't seem to get any worse for them, so that they could in truth laugh and joke as well as the next. And Ragna, with that special curve of her lips, in fact had a sweeter laugh than them all. They weren't well off, but then they knew no better. And thus they passed their days and lived their lives pretty well, with no futile longings. Things were not too bad.

When it was decided that Teodor was to accompany Edevart to the fair, Ragna wanted to go, too.

"What'll you do for clothes?" asked Teodor. "Will you just go in what you stand up in?"

"No," she said, and had to give in.

409

Ah, but they were both equally frivolous, both equally pleasure-seeking. But the boat couldn't take her as well as all the other cargo. And anyway, who would look after her children?

"But you shall have a length of dress material from the fair," Edevart promised.

"That would be very good of you!" she said. "Then I'd be able to go to church along with the others."

Poor Ragna! She bore her poverty pretty well. She might have worn Sunday best every day of the week if she had been born into affluence. And instead of everybody looking down on her for her bad reputation as now, some priest might have felt honored to have her deigning to sit in church listening to him.

Edevart never forgot that in his childhood he had once helped her to look for a shining button in the snow. It had had a crown on it, a lovely shiny button, one of her treasured possessions. He still felt moved when he looked at her; he was not disposed to be bolder; he felt sorry for her. She had remarkably beautiful hands, because she was lazy and never used them much. What could she do to improve things? Poverty had closed in over her; and she had become shiftless in consequence.

Teodor might say to his wife: "When you were down in Karolus's cellar getting potatoes, you might as well have taken enough to see us the week out."

And Ragna might answer her husband: "Yes, perhaps all of us could do better than we do!"

9 YEAR AFTER YEAR THEY GATHER HERE FOR THE FAIR! Miss the fun? Not likely! Here you find young girls in shawls and brightly colored head scarves; and those who consider themselves daughters of better families begin rather timorously to wear hats. That rather wild young man Henrik Sten arrives, having sailed his boat single-handed, ties up, brushes his shoes, and comes ashore. Eide Nikolaisen, the blacksmith, trained in Tromsø, strolls up and down the quayside; for a watch chain he has a hair lanyard with a gold locket; he is a notorious brawler and womanizer, dark-skinned like all black-smiths, and well known for the strength with which he lifts his partners in the dance. There are also more elderly and sedate people; women who have painfully assembled a lot of dairy products for sale; and men who want to buy themselves a boat.

It is still quiet. Few people have arrived. No sounds of barrel organ. No noisy fun.

August has arrived in good time and has taken over his stall. He has set out his wares neatly on shelves and tidied up. But because nobody has turned up yet, his restless soul has become bored. He has locked up the stall and gone out on the loose. The sailor lad has taken shore leave!

He kept an eye open for Edevart and came to meet him when he arrived. Edevart felt somewhat ill at ease when he saw him; he feared that possibly things hadn't gone too well for his friend; for if August had had a full wallet, he would hardly have awarded himself shore leave.

They unloaded the boat, carrying the goods up to the stall. "These are my goods," said August, pointing to the shelves. "Not quite as much as I had thought!" No, it wasn't much: a few dress materials, sewing things, buttons and hooks, thread, woolen scarves, kerchiefs. It was just as well that Edevart had arrived with a boatload of things, for August had hardly anything. No, hardly anything.

They laid things out on the shelves, filling in some of the gaps with empty boxes so that their stall wouldn't look too bare.

August said encouragingly: "I'd be very happy if I owned your stall now as it stands!"

"You own your part of it," replied Edevart.

August, evasively: "Well, we can always talk about that. What's happened to Teodor—has he gone? Well, that's good! I'd rather he wasn't in on things. What I was going to say was: Mattea is here."

"Who? . . . Oh, Mattea!"

"They've opened up a little place. Shall we go there? A booth selling food. She and her husband."

"Have you met her?" Edevart inquired.

"Yes. But I'm not angry with her. I never quarrel with women, not even when they run off with my ring and my watch. You haven't any money on you, have you?"

"I'm not broke."

"Let me have a couple of daler. Changing the subject: Knoff wants to build a mill on your waterfall."

"What? Will anything come of it?"

"They were over having a look at your place, the old boy and Romeo. I rowed them over. Yes, something will come of it. 'What do you think, August?' they said to me, for they knew I'd put up mills in various parts of the world. So I explained it all to them: a turbine, power gratis, and rye from Russia. 'Yes,' they nodded. 'And,' I said, 'Edevart Andreassen can be the miller and run the whole place.' Again they nodded. Here's Mattea's place."

It was a large booth with several tables, each with a number of stools—the same one which Mattea had worked in as a girl when she was engaged to Nils. After trying many things, the couple had now taken on this eating place, and had presumably given up working on that farm in Ofoten.

August was immediately at home and demanded his bottle. "This is my friend," he said. "You recognize him, I imagine?"

Yes, Mattea recognized him.

"So we meet again here," said Edevart.

"Looks like it," she answered curtly.

412

Edevart said with a smile: "I recognize the mark on the ceiling where somebody once threw a chair."

"Ha, ha, ha!" August laughed good-humoredly.

Mattea did not laugh. She looked venomously at Edevart and immediately reminded him that he had once sent her husband a stern demand notice. "It was a scandalous letter!" she said.

Edevart, cravenly and mollifyingly: "It was scandalous, was it? I didn't read it."

"You didn't read it?"

"Somebody else wrote it for me—a big merchant in Fosenland."

Mattea, in a milder tone: "I'd have given that merchant an earful, if I'd had the chance!"

"Yes," said Edevart, laughing. "But he would merely have put his arms around you and kissed you. He's a very good-looking young man."

"I see you are the same as you always were!" she murmured. "But did you receive the money all right? Why didn't you write and say so?"

"You must forgive me. I'm not much of a writer."

They were friends again. None of them was inclined to bear a grudge for life.

"How's your throat?" Edevart asked jestingly.

"My throat? Oh, you remember that. Yes, it got better again!" And at this Mattea actually winked at him and gave him a roguish look.

Nils came in from the kitchen—Nils the peddler, same as ever, unaffected by anything. He had left his father to his troubles. One wonders whether he knew that his old father hadn't managed to buy a full cargo of fish in the Lofotens this year and was now moored at Polden drying only three-quarters of a load? Apparently Nils busied himself in the kitchen and it was probably he who prepared the various hot and cold dishes while his wife served them to the customers. That's what it looked like: he was

413

wearing a kind of apron. He hadn't forgotten the story of the scandalous demand note, either, and he announced that he didn't want any customers like Edevart in the place. But Mattea peremptorily stopped him with a brief explanation. Finally Nils muttered: "Anybody might have thought I couldn't find that kind of money!"

The friends ordered food, and drank beer with it. August also had several drams. He shouted to Nils to come and join him in a glass, but Mattea interposed herself: Nils had other things to do, Nils was to go back in the kitchen.

"I've cooked the pressed meat," he said.

"Then you can chop some wood," she answered. It was no use; Mattea was still the determined one she had always been. Still young and good-looking, both of them; a handsome couple; but Nils had to do what he was told and go.

"Come and sit here, Mattea!" said August.

She came, but sat next to Edevart. August went on drinking drams. "Haven't you any children?" Edevart asked her.

Mattea: "Haven't I any children! Did you ever hear such a question! I have two children. They're at home with their grandparents. The old folk won't let them go . . . Well, they're rich enough to keep them. Children? I should just think I have!"

August: "Well, they're not mine."

"What d'you mean, yours!" cried Mattea, laughing loudly.

"What are you laughing at? Isn't it just a wee bit strange to think of you sitting here, having once been my sweetheart, and now married to somebody else and all that kind of thing?"

"I'm not thinking about that," said Mattea.

"No, you're not thinking about that, oh, no!" And August nodded darkly. "But what if I'm thinking of it! Here you see me, nothing very particular, with neither gold nor jewels! No, nothing very much to look at . . ."

Edevart: "Shut up, August! You've got all sorts of different things in our stall."

"However that may be," said August, "you, Mattea, were once my girl. And I kissed you."

"Did you now! I don't remember!" But now Mattea doubtless became frightened of provoking her old friend too much. He was in his cups and could get worked up. She said: "If we must talk about it, then I am of course married to Nils. He is my husband, that you can't deny. But after him, there's nobody I'm fonder of than you, August, believe you me."

August looked triumphantly at Edevart, as though to say: "Did you hear that!" The credulous sailor lad was content; he downed another dram and asked for coffee. "Well, then! There's no more to be said," he said. "Whatever else, I've got my sweetheart there where I want her. Don't be in any doubt about that. She's a lady so high up that I won't mention her name here. But you should see her when she puts on her hat and fine clothes to take a walk with me! You know her, Edevart."

Edevart nodded.

Did Mattea become jealous? "You asked for coffee," she said, getting up. And then something unexpected happened: Mattea returned from the kitchen wearing a hat. You see! Mattea had also begun to wear a hat like other girls of better situation. Was her husband not the son of a skipper? She had to show these two young men that she was not a nobody, either. She put down the coffee tray and remained standing.

"Are you going out?" Edevart inquired.

She quickly thought to say: "Yes, let's go out and see if people have come."

The two friends drank their coffee, paid their bill, and went out with her. They did a tour of the whole place. A few new boats had arrived with visitors, but there was no real life yet. They went to the merry-go-round, which was being erected, then to the big tent, where the circus was to be, then to a small tent where two knife throwers and acrobats were busy practicing.

"Let's go and see our stall!" August suggested.

Mattea was greatly respectful of their stall and its range of goods. This the two friends were in no way averse to; and August began to boast quite brazenly: "If you hear of anybody wanting to buy and looking for good value, just send them to us, Mattea. Because we have all kinds of things, and there isn't a merchant in the whole of Trondheim who could undercut us."

Mattea promised to stand by them. She would also want to do considerable business with them before she left for home.

They went back to Mattea's booth. A number of people had called in for coffee and sandwiches. Nils, relieved of the task of waiting on tables, once again disappeared into the kitchen. August drank and became more and more loquacious. He had found an audience, and his imagination began to burgeon. To be sure, he pretended he was talking only to Edevart; but he kept glancing to right and left, and spoke in such a loud voice that people couldn't help listening to him. He was in his element.

"That scarf of mine, you remember?" he said. "I was offered big money for it when I left the south there recently."

"You didn't sell?" Edevart asked.

"No! Not on your life! For if somebody offers you four hundred, it must be worth eight—any child can work that out. Anyway, I didn't feel like doing business with them. I had other things to take care of during those days I was there. And I had to watch out when Magnus was on duty on the quayside at night seeing off the boats. That's right! You don't know what I'm talking about, but I finally dispatched that Magnus right enough."

"You dispatched him?"

"Don't you believe me?"

"What did you do to him?"

"What do you expect me to do to a little creep like that? I bumped him off."

"Rubbish! You're not saying you shot him?"

"Yes, I am!" said August.

Edevart: "No! For in that case you wouldn't be sitting here."

"So I wouldn't be sitting here, would I? But was I to let that baboon go spreading it around the whole district that I was frightened at sea? I've been all around the world. I have possessions in many lands. All right, then! Here I am—come and arrest me! But they daren't! Have you a clear recollection of what that Magnus was like? I can't believe you have, because he was nothing but a nothing. A shop lad, and weak in the head. You remember how frightened he was of mice? Fine one he was to talk of being frightened at sea. But *she* on the other hand—she's something quite different. I will not name her name, but I will think of her in my hour of death. It's not as though she didn't keep on saying, 'No, no, no!' But every time she knew what it was I wanted, she laughed and never said a word about it to that baboon of hers. The first night—'No, don't speak about it!' She just laughed; but she still didn't say anything about it to that baboon. You'll see, she'll want to do it eventually, I thought, and I went along the next night. But she wasn't there. She'd gone and hidden herself in a different place. I searched around—but no! The next day I saw her again, but never a sharp word from her . . ."

Edevart asked: "You say you dispatched him. But you didn't shoot to kill, did you?"

August: "He would have deserved it. Anyway, I didn't actually shoot at him. I beat him up with a stone."

August rambled on more and more incoherently, and Edevart wanted to leave, but in vain he tried to get his friend to come away. August sat submerged in memories. They must have been happy memories, for he laughed and shook his head. Perhaps he simply sat there inventing things and letting his imagination run wild. When he spoke again, it was about a Sunday outing at Knoff's at which he had played his accordion. All the store people had been there: the housekeeper, Romeo and Juliet, all the children. Then a little fieldmouse jumped out of the grass. Magnus turned pale and leaped up. 'Let August see to it!' shouted Romeo. This August did; he saw to it, saw to the mouse, and . . . 'Ha! ha! ha!' laughed August at this point and slapped his knees. Then later it was time to eat. They had brought food with them, and the various tins and cans needed to be heated up. Nobody could manage this, so August again had to step forward. He lined a little trench, lit a fire, heated up the tins, and opened them. He organized things so that the baboon was last to be served from a tin of grouse. There were only a few scraps left in the bottom, and into it he placed the mouse.

"Oh!" groaned his audience in the booth, for some of them were sitting there eating.

"Yes!" shouted August, carried away by his own story. "And I stirred the mouse well into the gravy . . . 'Help yourself, Magnus!' Well, Magnus began eating, taking the smaller pieces first. 'What's this?' he said then. 'That?' I said. 'That's just a piece of fillet, or whatever it's called. You'll be all right eating that.' Well, Magnus took a bite of it, but he spat it out immediately, just as though he could tell from the taste that it was a mouse."

"But couldn't he see what it was?" asked the listeners.

"It wasn't easy to see, because I'd cut its legs off and it was covered in gravy."

Silence. Nobody laughed. Finally somebody asked: "But what made you play such a disgusting trick?"

"H'm! What made me do it?" August answered slyly: "I wanted to cure him of his fear of mice. Wasn't that kind of me? That's the same as we do aboard ship for curing seasickness: we make him swallow it again . . . swallow it again . . ."

"Shut up, won't you!" shouted Mattea. "Can't you see people are sitting here eating!"

There were divided opinions about August's actions. One person asked: "But how did it all end up? Didn't he go for you?"

"Yes. And was it not then that I had to hit him with that stone!" August replied. "He didn't understand it was meant for his own good."

But the coolness of those present took the steam out of August's ardor. He couldn't stand disapproval. Perhaps the whole thing was made up, anyway. In any case, he was now too drunk and confused.

EDEVART STOOD at his stall, selling. Things went badly to begin with; but those who had bought from him once came back again and brought others with them. He had, in fact, decided to sell for what he could get and dispose of his boatload at any price.

He didn't get much value out of August, who popped in now and again, game for anything and all ready to go. His schemes were as wild as ever, and he outlined many a strange plan to Edevart. One of these was to sell the boat and use the money to buy a barrel organ.

Edevart shook his head.

August: "If I can get a barrel organ to travel around with, and buy a bear cub down at the circus tent, I'll earn far more than ever you will here at the stall."

Edevart asked him why he wouldn't rather play his accordion.

"No," said August. "I've promised Mattea to play the accordion one day for her to get people to come to her booth. There's going to be a dance. People will come rolling up, I promise you!"

August also had other ideas. "What about inventing a powder for arthritis and selling it here at the fair? Actually, I'm working on something even better than that, but I wouldn't tell you what it is even if you beat me black and blue."

Edevart knew from experience that August could dream up all kinds of schemes, so he did not laugh at these notions. But he wanted to restrain him, and said: "I'm a bit worried about you, August! Don't go and do anything that might get you into trouble!"

August snorted. "Don't you worry about me! And now let me tell you exactly what it is I have in mind. It's pills for women to take to prevent them from having children. I mentioned it to you once before, but you didn't want to hear about it."

"I don't want to hear about it now, either."

"Oh, kiss my you-know-what!" said August, and continued. "It will be very strange if I don't bring it off. And knowing as many languages as I do, including both English and Russian, I ought to be able to think of something to call them. I traveled once with a ship's officer who had a little bottle of snow-white pills. There was quicksilver in them, and he used them on his wife when he was home, he said. But he didn't dare leave them at home. Oh, no! For then his wife could run around all she wanted while he was away, just using these pills. He showed me the bottle. It said *Secale cornutum* on the label. I've always remembered that."

"You might consider serving at the stall and relieving me occasionally," said Edevart.

August paid no attention. "God, how I could sell pills like that to all the lads here—and to the girls, too, for that matter!"

Edevart: "I wouldn't mind going out and getting a bite to eat."

"All right! Fair enough! I'll come back and take over," said August, and he walked off.

But he didn't come back. Edevart shut up the stall in the evening and took a walk up through the streets of the town. He had bought himself some rolls at the baker's, and ate them as he walked.

The fair was now in full swing on that quiet summer evening. There was noisy fun of every kind: whistling and singing and rattling of tin cans. People took the opportunity of enjoying themselves, and with every justification. Some of the lads had got hold of brandy, and they started squaring up to each other, holding up huge, invincible fists.

Edevart recognized a couple of short dark men with a barrel organ—oh, it was the Hungarian and the Armenian again. They kept up their miserable, threadbare performance, whereby one of them turned the handle and the other set about him and beat him up, smearing fruit juice on his face. Once they had learned this trick, they kept on with it. Poor charlatans, they had become too well known; they were a novelty only to small children. And they also did badly: a few pence now and then, and after the assault perhaps a little more.

Papst had arrived, the eternal watch-selling Jew, older, his beard whiter, but as fat as ever as he lumbered along in his trailing overcoat with all those watch chains across his belly. Ah, but he was not so composed as he had been before; he was careworn, and his face was lined and wrinkled. He didn't recognize Edevart at first; but after staring at him for a while, he found the name in his memory without any prompting. It was a miracle after all these years and with all those acquaintances of his all over the country. This was something he had taught himself: to recognize people again. He had trained himself in this skill and had become a master of it.

They fell into friendly conversation. Edevart showed him his watch—that he still had it, and it had never cost him anything in repairs. Papst opened it and said: "Yes, but now it needs cleaning. Let me have it for a couple of days and I'll let you have it back all cleaned."

"Can't it just go on till it stops?" Edevart asked.

"It would be a shame for such a fine movement," said Papst. "Look, you can have this one in the meantime, it goes quite well. And now, what about your perhaps selling a few watches for me, Edevart?"

"I can't. I've got my own stall here at the fair which I must look after."

"So you've got your own stall. You've become a big man since we last met, I'm glad to see. But what about evenings?"

"No, you'll have to excuse me," said Edevart. "I'm serving all day long at the stall, and I have to give myself a little bit of time off in the evenings."

"I have a number of watches I particularly wanted to sell

here. Good watches, cheap watches. I'm selling out. There's no knowing if I'll ever be this way again."

"Are you going away somewhere?"

"I'll maybe die. I am an old man. If you can sell ten watches, you can have the eleventh one free. I want to dispose of them."

Edevart: "No, no, I daren't even think about it. But I have a friend who might do it. He's something extra special when it comes to selling."

"Where is he?"

"I'll send him to you tomorrow . . ."

It was beginning to grow dark. Edevart took a walk down to the quayside to see if the boat was still there, and of course it was. August wouldn't be so stupid as to sell it. He came past Mattea's place and saw there were lots of people outside. It was black with people. The door was open and the inside was also full of people. There was music, accordion music. August was playing. Ah, August! He was doubtless making nothing out of the concert, but that didn't worry him.

Edevart squeezed his way in through the doorway. Both Nils and Mattea were very busy selling food and drinks to a full house. In the heightened atmosphere of that crowded place, the young men and girls sat on each other's lap in the semidarkness. After a rousing march, August beckoned to Mattea and asked: "So what do I get for this?"

Mattea, who was never very scrupulous when it came to making promises, answered: "Whatever you say!"

August nodded, ran his fingers lightly over that tremendous accordion, and surveyed the assembly. What he then did captured everybody's attention and every table fell silent. He sang as he played, sang to his profoundly melancholy accompaniment an English sea shanty, all about love and knives and a girl in Barcelona. Oh, August knew a thing or two!

He finished and sat silent. Nobody had understood his song, but everybody felt that it had been lovely beyond compare. Some wanted to give him money, but Mattea stopped them, whispering to left and to right: "He doesn't need it, this man. He's got a big stall here at the fair absolutely stuffed with goods. You haven't been there? You must go tomorrow! Look, there's his partner!" And she pointed to Edevart. "They're in business together in a big way . . ."

Teodor appeared. He'd been off on his own all this time; but now he turned up and wanted to make his mark. "Yes, we're all three in it together, with our boat. These are my friends! Know them? I'll say I do!"

August settled himself in his chair and, pointing, gave orders for all tables and chairs to be moved back to the wall. For now there was to be dancing! Yes, indeed! They moved everything to clear a space. And there followed a dance which rocked the entire booth. Henrik Sten was there and made one conquest after another, such a ladies' man was he. But there was nobody to compare in strength with Eide Nikolaisen, the blacksmith, when it came to swinging his partner in the dance. Oh, what an evening that was! And even though Nils and Mattea had to serve their customers all lining the walls, they, too, found time to dance a waltz now and again. God knows, Nils had probably had a bit to drink. And, in the small hours, his wife withdrew with Edevart into the darkest corner and threw herself, wild and uninhibited, into his embrace. What a night that was!

As more and more prepared to leave, August stopped playing. Nils and Mattea had had a splendid session, selling hot and cold dishes and beer and illicit brandy. They had every reason to be satisfied. But when the time came for August to have his reward for his music, Mattea had disappeared. Only Nils was around, tidying up in the half dark. August hung around for a while, looked into the kitchen, searching. No, Mattea was nowhere to be seen.

"What do you want with her?" Nils asked.

"To say good night," August replied.

"She's probably gone to bed somewhere," said Nils.

A sad and miserable end to the party. Edevart kept entreating: "Come away, August! There's something I want to talk to you about!"

When August finally left, he muttered savagely: "Fine bunch of flowers she is!"

AUGUST BEGAN WORKING for Papst. It wasn't so bad, damned if it wasn't. August bragged about it. He worked on the job for a day, selling watches on the fairground. People recognized him again as the musician from the night before, the one who played and sang so marvelously in that eating place. The young people were keen to buy from him. And August said nothing about selling for Papst, indeed no. He had no objection to people thinking him capable of running a watch business in addition to the general stall. It made him look more important; even to his own eyes it was something quite dazzling, comparable with selling jewelry and diamonds at Levanger Fair.

In the early evening August came to Edevart and announced that he was finished.

"Finished, why?"

Well, he'd sold ten watches and got the eleventh for himself, so he'd finished.

Edevart shook his head.

"It's no use," said August. "I won't do it. Why should I go fattening up that bloated old piggy bank? Even though he might burst! Have you seen his wallet? If he went around with a wallet like that in any other country, he'd be a dead man before he knew what was happening. And then all those watches! He's got watches all over his body, and more in a huge iron chest in his room. You never saw anything like it! Why should I go around adding to his pile? Be smart for once and get some sense into your head: if all those young lads buy watches, they'll have no money for anything else and they won't come and buy at this stall. I thought it all out—nobody fools me! All the same, I've got a watch for one day's work and that's not bad!" August brushed one sleeve with the other and laughed softly and seemed pleased with himself.

"You know," he said, "we could go straightaway to Mattea's and get something to eat. I haven't had a bite all day."

"I don't want to shut just yet. But you go to Mattea's first," Edevart replied. "And then you can come back and relieve me?"

"Yes. You don't happen to have a couple of daler? Good, because I'm broke."

Edevart realized that his friend was anxious to be away and show off his new pocket watch, so he didn't detain him.

"I'll be straight back," said August in the doorway, nodding.

He didn't come. Edevart stood there till closing time and served lots of people. He had to bear with August, for the truth was that the dance the previous evening, with August's playing and Mattea's publicity, had brought customers to the stall. Edevart had done business as never before and had disposed of expensive cloth and woolen goods which otherwise he would have had to take back home with him. It had been an unexpectedly good day; and before he closed, Edevart put on one side a really fine length of dress material for Ragna back in Polden.

He did as he usually did and ate his supper of rolls as he strolled around. He ran into Teodor and one of the men at the dance last night, Henrik Sten. They stood and talked.

"Tomorrow I start selling watches for Papst," said Teodor.

"Do you now!" said Edevart.

"Yes, he asked me if I would."

Edevart strolled on. He walked down to where the tents and the merry-go-round were. Behind the circus tent stood August embracing a short-haired lady who was with the troupe of animal trainers. She used to appear in riding boots with a bear on one side and a wolf on the other. She was August's latest acquaintance; and when he caught sight of Edevart, he shouted defensively: "I'm just coming!" Edevart turned and walked in a different direction . . .

The following morning old Papst came to his stall and gave him his watch back. "Now it's been cleaned and it's in perfect order," he said.

Edevart looked at it, listened to it, and said: "I think you've been cleaning the outside of it, too. It looks newer, somehow."

Yes, Papst had cleaned the outside a little, too. He began to talk about August. That man had no staying power. A clever salesman, yes; but a bit the worse for drink, and too talkative. "I recognized him again when he came to see me," said Papst. "He was your skipper that time in Kristiansund. Had gold teeth. No, he didn't want to sell watches for another day. But now I have your brother. Perhaps he'll prove more dependable."

"My brother? I haven't any brother here."

"What? He said he was your brother . . . Teodor . . ."

"No, he's not my brother. Did he say that?"

"He came to see me last evening and said he was your brother and he wanted to sell watches for me. Don't you know him?"

"Yes, I do. But he's not my brother. We're not even remotely related. Far from it!"

"I gave him eleven watches this morning," said Papst, making for the door. He had become uneasy, and shook his bearded head. "Look, Edevart," he continued. "I became a little suspicious myself. He was different . . . how shall I say? . . . not your sort. That's why I wanted a word with you. Do you think he might run away?"

"No. He came with me in my boat, so he can't leave until I do."

Silence. Papst thought a while, then said: "I'll let him try. Don't you think I should?"

"Yes. He'll surely never be so crazy as to steal eleven watches . . ."

Again August was away all day. Edevart worked at the stall. He laid out his goods and materials all the way up to the open door and wrote prices on them. This was a clever move; people stopped, read the prices, felt the goods, then came in and bought them. His wallet filled up with notes; and there was still the following day to come, the final day.

In the evening he meets Teodor and says: "What were you doing pretending to be my brother?"

"Who, me?" says Teodor, not letting himself be trapped.

"You told Papst you were my brother."

"Damned liar, that old fat belly! Ah, now I understand!" shouts Teodor, as though relieved. "I didn't say you were my brother. I said we came from the same place and were just like brothers, since we knew each other so well."

Edevart ponders this. It was a good explanation, a very plausible explanation. The old Jew was a foreigner; he might have misunderstood Teodor's words.

"Have you sold any watches?" Edevart asks.

"I've sold eight and I'm on my way to settle up with him. I have two watches left, plus of course my own. I've been wondering a long time about getting a watch . . ."

A few hours later, late in the evening, when it was quite dark, Edevart set off back to the stall to go to bed, when he had a strange experience. It began with him suddenly seeing a man walking some distance ahead of him in the street. He must have come out of one of the houses. There was nothing unusual in that and Edevart paid little attention; but he was a little surprised when the man started to run. He immediately thought of August, and that he might have landed himself in some sort of trouble; so he set off in pursuit. Why was the man running? The night was quiet, and Edevart saw nobody giving chase. Once he called out August's name, but received no reply. The man did not stop, but disappeared around a bend in the road. Edevart ran. He saw the door of a house was half open and was swinging gently. It might have been the wind that made it move; it might also be that somebody had just gone through. Edevart sprang into the house, and the door again swung behind him. He was in a dark passage. "August!" he called out. No answer. Edevart held out his hands

427

in front of him and felt his way along the passage. He came up against a wall and could go no farther. Groping along the wall, he came to a staircase. Just as he began to climb the stairs to an attic, the front door was again torn open and the man dashed out. Edevart after him. He now saw that it wasn't August; but he nevertheless knew the man and wanted to catch up with him and give an explanation. It was one of the men who had been at last night's dance: the blacksmith.

"What on earth are you running for?" Edevart laughed, stopping him.

"What are you running for yourself?" was the reply. "Have I done anything to you?"

Edevart felt he had to explain: he'd thought it was his friend August who had got into some trouble, in which case he wanted to lend a hand. It was all a mistake . . .

"In that case, off you go and leave me!" the man muttered, and started to run off again. He looked all around and was extremely tense and uneasy.

"Where are you going?" Edevart asked.

"That's none of your business. So just get out of my way!"

But that was not what the man should have answered. Edevart wasn't going to give way to that tone of voice. On the contrary, he lunged forward.

"What the devil . . . !" snorted the blacksmith, and lashed out.

In the ensuing tussle, neither man gained the upper hand. But Edevart knew from experience how to keep his end up in a fight, and he held his own. The worst thing was that the blacksmith swung at him with a bunch of keys; he was also strong as a bear, and Edevart couldn't bring him down with his formidable wrestler's throw.

"You little warehouse rat!" he heard the blacksmith hiss.

"Use a bunch of keys, would you!" Edevart yelled back. "Well, I hope Old Nick gets you!" With that he aimed a kick at the blacksmith's body—let it land where it might! It didn't do all money away, he'll snatch the wallet and run. Such evil, such wickedness directed against poor old Papst! There I lie and he can attack and strangle me. I become frightened. I dare not cry out. It is terrible. 'The money!' he will say. 'The wallet!' I rap on the bed as a sign that I submit, that I am afraid. I hear somebody out in the passage—this man!"

"Me?" cries Teodor again. "You saw me?"

"Shut up! He insists he wants to buy a watch. I am quite beside myself and I say: 'If it's my money you are after, it's in the chest.' 'No, under his pillow!' this man shouts from the passage.

"I'd been to settle up with you . . ." began Teodor.

"Yes, and you saw me put the wallet under my pillow afterward. Shut up!"

"No, I came long before the blacksmith came and I left after we had settled up. Did I not settle up properly with you?"

"All he wants is to buy a watch. I am afraid for my life and I beg him and I slap the bed. 'In the chest!' I say. 'That chest on the floor!' He is about to say, 'Hand over the key!' but I risk it and say: 'Look in the chest!' 'Under the pillow!' comes the voice from the passage again. Horrible moment! It means death, two murderers. Then he must have heard something. He listens and becomes frightened. 'Hurry up!' comes the voice from the passage. And sure enough, he rushes out the door. And you, my good friend, you were there, too! Oh, yes!"

Teodor: "That's the biggest lie ever! Did you see me? I ask you. I came and settled up over the eight watches I had sold, and didn't I settle up honestly? What I want to know is: have you any complaint about the way we settled up?"

"Settle . . . settle . . . !" said Papst. "You were with him."

"How could I be with him when the blacksmith came along I'd gone?"

Edevart: "How do you know that the blacksmith came along you'd gone?"

"ha! Yes!" said Papst. "How do you know that?"

that much damage; and the next time he let loose a kick, the blacksmith grabbed his foot like a flash and threw him.

By the time he had got to his feet, the blacksmith had taken to his heels and was already a long way away. Edevart did not immediately set off in pursuit. He was held back by a window being raised and a man's voice asking: "Are you badly hurt?"

"No."

"You have blood on your face."

"He hit me with a bunch of keys."

"Yes, it was the blacksmith. He uses keys when he fights."

"Why was he running away?"

"I don't know."

The blacksmith was now almost out of sight and Edevart gave up the chase. Of what concern to him was that man, anyway? Why shouldn't he run through the streets? Edevart went back the way he had come, stiff and weary. Near the spot where it had all started, he ran once again into Teodor. He was standing there with old Papst, and Papst was gripping his arm. He was greatly agitated.

"Ah, a decent man!" the Jew exclaimed. "Edevart, c〔ome〕 here. They attacked me and wanted to rob me and murde〔r me.〕 This is one of them!"

Edevart looked from one to the other; then he as〔ked Teo〕dor: "Did you attack Papst?"

"Who, me?" shouted Teodor innocently. "N〔o,〕 you attacked him."

"Yes, he *was* one of them," Papst insiste〔d. "There〕 was another man, but he ran away. I had go〔ne . . . here〕 comes a man. I know him. He is black a〔ll over, black〕 beard, black skin, horrible. Papst knows 〔him, the〕 blacksmith. What does he want? Wants 〔me when〕 I'm in bed, tomorrow! No, now, tonigh〔t! And I〕 become frightened because I unde〔rstand. . . .〕 There is somebody out in the passa〔ge. They are in〕 this together. He wants to buy 〔. . .〕

"How do I know . . . ?" An idea seems to come like a flash to the quick-thinking Teodor. He says: "Because I met the blacksmith a long way down the road after I had been here to settle up. Perhaps he then came along here to Papst's. I don't know."

"Why were you standing around here just now? Had you been up to see Papst again?"

"No, I was just strolling about."

"I got dressed and went down. He was standing here," said Papst. "Oh, he was in on it! He'd come back to see how things were. Help me, Edevart!"

What could Edevart do! Nothing of any lasting significance had occurred. Papst had not lost any money; he'd simply had a nasty scare. But the story certainly seemed to ring true: the blacksmith had run away and Edevart had himself overtaken him and fought with him. When things became serious, the blacksmith had himself become frightened and had wanted to get away from the scene. He wasn't a practiced thief, and this was perhaps his first job. There were no big thieves at Stokmarknes Fair, only little innocents, novices who quickly became afraid and fled. August could tell you about real thieves and robbers. How he would laugh at the flight of the blacksmith tonight when he heard about it!

But the existence of the man in the passage made the thing more serious; those hushed calls indicated an accomplice. The police might perhaps have caught the man, but who were the police? Every man was his own policeman here in this peaceful place; it had always been thus at these fairs, and it had worked well. Had it been Teodor standing in the passage? Teodor was no practiced thief, either, merely a petty pilferer. He could easily have been the one who kept under cover while somebody else did the job. Edevart did not trust him. On the other hand, could he really have imagined such a pathetic robbery? Nothing had happened—no robbery, no murder, just an almighty scare for Papst.

While Edevart is thinking about this, Teodor says ingratiatingly: "Look at you—have you hurt yourself?"

Edevart: "You were standing talking to a man just now?"

"Yes," Teodor replied. "A man called Henrik Sten."

"Might it not have been him standing in the passage?"

Teodor cries: "There you have it, you see! Yes, there you have it: it was Henrik Sten, don't you see! For the blacksmith and he are pretty friendly with each other! Well, what do you think now?" he asked Papst triumphantly.

Papst answers shortly: "Out of the question! I'll give my oath . . ."

Whereupon Teodor seemed prepared to brazen it out. He clenched his fist, held it at the Jew's beard, shook it several times, and announced his readiness to take Papst to court for what he had said.

"You *were* there!" Papst maintained stubbornly.

"I have no time for you!" Teodor declared, and left.

The two of them were left alone. Edevart wished to comfort the old man and said: "It was scandalous of them to treat you like that and disturb your night's rest."

Papst nodded his head. "Yes, yes, it was the blacksmith. He would have strangled me. It was a terrible moment . . ."

"I felt pretty certain there was something wrong. I've just been in a fight with the blacksmith."

"What? Out here? With this very same robber? There you are, you see! Black in the face, a murderer. Did you beat him up good and proper?"

"No, he waylaid me."

"We'll report him."

"Good thing you had your wallet in the chest," said Edevart.

"Well, yes . . . sure . . . !"

"Because he couldn't have run off with that heavy iron chest."

"No! Of course not! But you see, Edevart," Papst whispered, "the wallet wasn't in the chest."

"Not in the chest?"

"No. Under the pillow, the man in the passage said. But there I fooled him. It was at the foot of the bed, underneath the bedclothes. Yes, that's what I did. When he came to settle up and

I made a few daler, I put my wallet under the pillow so he could see it. But he didn't seem like an honest man about the eyes, so as soon as he was out the door I put the wallet at the foot of the bed. I fooled him. Papst sees through people. All the same, it was a terrible moment—two murderers."

Papst began to regain his composure; and Edevart started to go.

"It was a pity he waylaid you," said Papst. "You got hurt?"

"Yes, but I drew blood, too."

Papst showed a childlike interest. "Really? You drew blood?"

"He hit me with those keys. But I found a stone," Edevart lied.

"Splendid! You're a great fighter, Edevart!"

It was a pleasure to gladden the old man with so little. And Edevart lied further: "I gave it to him good and proper, believe you me! I kicked out and caught him on the arm and broke it."

"One of his arms fractured!" Papst cried in delight. "One of those frightful arms of his! Did he yell?"

"By God, I ask you, did he yell!"

"Oh, that's wonderful! I'll remember you for this, Edevart! I bless you for it! How did he yell? Did he groan?"

"No, it must have been hellishly painful. He bellowed."

"Bellowed! Oh, thank you, thank you! You paid him for me. Nobody has ever wanted to save my life but you, Edevart. What do any of the others care about Papst's life? Nothing! Look here, Edevart!" says Papst, rummaging in one of his pockets, "I have something for you. Here's your watch. You shall have it back again."

Edevart gapes, speechless.

"I'd switched it and given you the wrong watch. I didn't notice until later. You must excuse an old man. But here it is now. I'm an honest soul and I'll exchange it. Hand over the other one . . ."

Edevart turned for home. He didn't believe Teodor, indeed not. But he didn't believe any longer in Papst, either.

He found the door of the booth open, the lock broken. What

in the world? He stepped in and saw something in the corner where he himself used to sleep at night. Something curled up, hunched, like the beginnings of a human being—it was August. Dead drunk! thought Edevart.

August's voice is like that of a dying man.

"I've been stabbed. They carried me here. We had to break down the door."

"Stabbed, you say? How did that happen?"

"With a knife. They've gone for the doctor."

August was unable to talk much. He was bleeding, he said. But he managed to explain very briefly that he'd been stabbed at the circus by one of the attendants, a madman. August was now feeling very low; any wildness had left him. He was about to die. He knew he was lying in a pool of blood.

"Where's the wound?" Edevart asked. "In your chest? Well, let me bandage it."

"No, no! The others bandaged it up and I'm lying here holding it on. But it's no use. I can feel it draining away. I'm sure to die, Edevart. Now I'm being paid back for what we did. We were crazy. And she died, too."

"Who are you talking about?"

"The Negro girl. We killed her. Four of us set about her, and she couldn't take it. The last one to have her said she'd died—he'd held his hand over her mouth too long."

"You could be such a bloody swine?"

"Yes," said August.

Silence. August gasped for breath and said: "If only I could have hands laid on me!"

Edevart: "Hands?"

"Yes, to bless me. A priest."

"Is that what you wish?"

"I don't know. When I was confirmed and went up to the altar, the priest laid his hand on my head and blessed me, or whatever you call it."

Silence. Edevart asked: "Did you say they'd gone for the doctor?"

"Yes. But it won't help. I can feel I'm bleeding the whole time. You don't know where you could find a priest?"

"No."

"Couldn't you at least make an attempt to find one?"

Edevart remained silent. He was doubtless thinking it was right.

August said wheedlingly: "You wouldn't be doing it for nothing, Edevart. When I'm dead, I want you to go ahead and knock my teeth out."

"What are you saying!" Edevart cries.

"Yes. I want you to. Take some pliers and break them off. They're worth money."

"That I'll never do!"

"You mean I'd return to haunt you? No, don't you worry! I wouldn't be wanting them any longer. It's just like Skaaro's ring —can't he lie there equally blessed without his gold ring? I tell you, Edevart, you are to take my teeth out. I haven't anything else to give you. And that's not very much, either—certainly not what you ought to have if you manage to find a priest. Perhaps the gold in them is poor stuff, junk . . ."

Some people came in through the door. Two men and the doctor. They ask: "Where is he? Isn't there a lamp here? Take him and carry him to the door!"

August clutches his wound in mortal dread, so that the doctor has to force his hand away. All right, some blood on the shirt and on the chest, but there is little or no bleeding now, nothing serious. The doctor asks if the knife went in very deep. "Yes, deep!" August replies. "How deep?" August doesn't know. "Breathe in!" says the doctor. August breathes. The doctor inserts a probe to ascertain the depth of the wound. August grits his teeth during this torment.

"It isn't deep," says the doctor. But August smiles bitterly at this and says: "It hurts right through to my back."

435

"Yes," the doctor answers. "You've been lying in a draft there in the corner."

The wound is bathed with cotton dipped in alcohol, and August winces at the pain. Then he is bandaged, carried back to his corner, and tucked up with various pieces of material taken off the shelves. As Edevart pays the doctor, he inquires: "Is it dangerous?"

"No," comes the answer. "Not a bit! Just give the wound a chance to heal!"

When August hears what the doctor said, he again smiles bitterly. For the whole of the first few days August never smiled anything other than a bitter smile; but later, when his wound began to itch and he realized it was beginning to mend, August sat up and reported how the misfortune had occurred. In this he spared no scorn for the man who had made such a poor job of the stabbing. "Now, if it had been in some other country!" he said.

Of course there was a woman in the case: that selfsame animal trainer with whom August had become friendly. These last few days August had regularly spent all his time down at the circus; and when he'd given evidence of his mastery of the accordion, he signed up to do one number every hour. Whereupon the lady had shown herself especially friendly, and had allowed herself to be kissed. August was to play his most rousing march for her entry, and then stop in the middle of a bar, leaving a deathly silence for her to step forward with her two dangerous wild animals—this was a device August introduced from the wider world. The whole thing had been arranged. The director had promised August two daler every afternoon, and he had designed and printed huge posters announcing August's appearance and hung them up at the entrance to the circus tent.

Fine! August played. And his fame from the dance drew crowds for each hourly performance. The way he had of suddenly stopping playing as though he were himself mortally scared made the spectators gasp. The director rubbed his hands; and the lady was delighted.

Yes, everything went splendidly. There was only one rather tiresome thing. The third time around, a young man, one of the animal trainers, came along and asked him to keep away from the lady. "Oh, yes?" August had replied, laughing with those gold teeth of his. "Yes!" said the trainer, because that lady was his girl.

"I don't believe it," August replied. "You're a bloody liar!"

This made the animal trainer furious, and he threatened with terrible oaths that it would be the worst for August. "On my honor!" he said.

"On your what?" August asked in return.

"Yes, on my honor!"

Whereupon August had laughed and shown all his gold teeth and advised the animal trainer against talking so grand and getting above himself. "Get out!"

And the animal trainer got out.

Then August played for the final occasion and played as though his life depended on it. He wanted to outdo anything he had done before. He thundered out the "Marche Napoleon," which nobody had heard before, made his break in the middle, and that was that. But when the lady had finished her act with the bear and the wolf, there came an extra: August finished the march as she made her exit. This was something additional and extraordinary. The audience shouted and clapped, the lady reappeared several times to take her bow, while August continued to play. Finally he packed up his instrument and left. Now he was to have his reward.

He came backstage; the lady stood waiting for him. She threw her arms passionately around his neck with every sign of sweet surrender. At that moment the animal trainer rushed out at him, delivered his murderous knife thrust, and ran off.

Then there must have followed great commotion. August collapsed. He had enough worries of his own, but he heard cries and shouts all around him. The director appeared; then another man with gold braid on his cap—the policeman. But he posed no threat; somebody threw horse dung in his eyes and he had to run for his life.

"Who threw it?" Edevart asked. "The other animal trainers?"

"No, there was only one of them," said August. "Do you know what I think, so help me God? I think it was that woman herself who threw the dung in order to save her trainer man. Blast her!"

"What happened then?"

"I don't know," answered August. "Some of the people who had been watching the circus came and helped me and carried me here. They also went for the doctor. Nice people. I didn't know them . . . Well, well, well, I might have fallen dead on the spot. Now, Edevart, what you must do is go to the circus and collect my two daler. I haven't a bean."

"Just as long as the circus didn't leave yesterday along with all the others who left," Edevart answered. "I'll see!"

August shouted after him: "Then you must find that woman and get my watch back. I let her borrow it."

Edevart ran off, but returned at once. Of course the circus had left. He shook his head at his friend and said: "So you've lost your watch again! That brand-new watch!"

Well, August himself thought it was a hell of a business. But what could be done about it! She was so helpless, never knowing the time or anything. Could he have been so mean and nasty to her as to say no? "I don't give a damn about that watch, anyway!" said August. "It didn't go properly. It kept stopping."

Teodor joined in. "Yes, those watches we were selling must have come from Old Nick himself. Mine also stops. It only goes when I shake it. And I put in two days' hard work to get it."

MERCHANTS AND general public gone; the fairground cleared; the place silent. Edevart and Teodor stayed on to give

438

August a chance to recover. But then they fixed on a day for the return journey.

August now began to sit up and was really quite well again. But he was extremely embarrassed at having so betrayed himself to Edevart that first evening; in consequence, he never wearied of pouring scorn on his assailant with the knife. That was a rotten job of work he'd done! It made you weep! His fingers must have been paralyzed! August was really indignant. He was used to a situation where a knife thrust meant death, he said. Here all that happened was that people were fooled into thinking they had been killed. If only he'd been able to lay hands on that animal trainer . . .

10 JOAKIM WAS IN THE PROCESS OF EXTENDING HIS BARN. There were to be two additional stalls, not more. Not three stalls, and no stabling for a horse. August immediately tried putting in his oar by suggesting separate space for two calves; but this was turned down. It didn't upset him to be turned down—August was used to that—but Joakim had been specially withering in the way he had done it, asking him if he wanted to make room in the barn for a few canaries as well. August then immediately wanted to lend a hand with laying the foundation; he had got it into his head that he would soon be better, even though he was a bit careless about his wound. But again he was turned down, and this time he did feel hurt, especially when Joakim took on an outside carpenter to help.

But August was not the man to sit around doing nothing; so he set to work one day making a letter box. He painted it blood red and got Joakim to paint *Mail* on it in Gothic lettering. After which he hung it up on the outside wall of the store and surveyed it with pride. People wondered what he was doing making a mailbox without there being any post office. But August asked why, if there were mailboxes outside every store in Australia, it shouldn't be the same here. The people in Polden could now come and put their Lofoten letters and their letters to their dear ones in this box and be sure that they would go regularly once a week via the people who went to church. Anyway, said August, they ought to start demanding a post office now in Polden—it was a big place!

Well, he was pretty wild! He'd been like that all his days. Not even a mortal stab in the breast with a knife had been able to tame him. But August was after all Polden's one and only August, the only man who had sailed all around the world. There was nothing wrong in having him around. Yet why had the girls of the district given a certain amount of attention to him many years ago when he first returned home—and then nothing? Perhaps he wasn't in the best position to promise them support, but who in the area could do that, anyway? As things were now, the girls could openly make fun of him, say that they loved him and would die on his grave; and August sat there defenseless, cringing and smiling.

All the same, it wasn't a bad thing to have this man around. He stirred things up; he left his mark. His star was now in the ascendancy and now in decline. If he had managed to rescue his possessions from a particular shipwreck which struck the barque *Soleglad,* he might have been the greatest businessman in Polden and the entire district. But things were not destined to reach such fantastic heights. The years that followed had not been good ones. But laziness was alien to his nature; and even in his years of impotence he was always active. Look, for example, at this red mailbox: how it hung there like a brilliant flame. It did not disfigure the wall of the store; on the contrary, it made it rather more of a feature. Later that summer, posters were to be pinned up around that mailbox: important announcements from the sheriff or the priest, and perhaps even proclamations concerning matters of inheritance, complete with the official lion seal of Norway. That mailbox helped to make Polden's store a more public affair.

Little Pauline was now in sole command behind the counter. Everything passed through her hands and through her head: purchases and sales, prices and credit. Her business made steady progress. When Edevart returned from the fair, he handed over to her the few goods he hadn't sold, together with all the takings from their trip. It then transpired that Joakim could be repaid and more for what he had expended, and that Edevart was once again sole owner of the store.

"You can keep the store!" said Edevart. "I wouldn't have it if you threw it at me!"

"So what are you going to do now?" his sister inquired.

Indeed, what was Edevart going to do now? He had steadily declined; he allowed the days to go by, lazily, monotonously; he left his hair uncut; he went to bed in the evening but did not fall asleep until near morning. Yet look at August! When he had finished doing the mailbox, he set up a hoist to bring water up from the well. It was a great help to Pauline, who had to provide water for several cows during the winter. When August had completed this, he immediately turned his attention to the building of the new barn and rendered superfluous the services of the hired carpenter. August took charge of the new extension and on his own initiative enlarged the foundations. Joakim himself had now come round to thinking that he needed a place for calves, but he wouldn't admit it. He asked August with an assumed acerbity: "What the devil do you think you're doing?"

"I'm making room for two calves," August replied.

"That huge space!" cried Joakim. "It's enough for six calves!"

August merely murmured something. He pushed on with it, though Joakim threatened him with all manner of vengeance once the barn was finished.

But such was August: busy every day, lively, mad, crazy, yet effective.

And what about Edevart? God alone knew: perhaps he might have to impose on the charity of Hosea and Ezra for bed and board until his dying day. He lived from day to day, ready for whatever he might turn his hand to; but he turned his hand to nothing. What he needed, what might have helped him was not something that could be achieved by a single day's work. The crab needed patiently to retrace its long journey back to where it might find its head again.

He received a letter from Romeo Knoff. A very cordial letter, but with a serious import: whether Romeo shouldn't sell Doppen for him, since Edevart didn't live there, anyway, and couldn't work the land properly? His neighbor Karel had two big lads now and might consider buying Doppen for the older one. Romeo offered to take back the beds and bedding Edevart had been left with and which were virtually unused; and he declared himself generally ready to do what he could to make sure that Edevart's debt to the store was more or less met. The boat could be included in the sale, since it would be indispensable for the new owner. The question of the waterfall, however, they needn't discuss for the present. Edevart could continue to own the waterfall. If later he wished to dispose of it and Romeo should buy it, they might discuss setting up a mill there, in which case Romeo would be delighted to consider putting Edevart in charge of the plant, following the suggestion of his friend August . . .

A nice long letter which ended by sending friendly greetings from his father and from Romeo himself. It was strange, but Edevart had become so rootless that this letter from a strange man in a strange place had something homely about it which moved him. He forgot the lost days and years there, and for a moment longed to be back there again. He got Joakim to reply that he had no objection to selling Doppen and that he thanked Romeo for his kindness.

So now then he was without his place down south. So now he had a store here which he didn't wish to own. So now he was homeless in every way! August was taken into his confidence. He nodded and said: "You must come with me! We must both get away!"

AND THE DAYS PASSED. The extension to the barn got its roof and was to be fitted out with stalls. One fine evening Joakim was persuaded by Pauline to row out and catch some haddock for the table. It was very much needed, she said, for without some fish she wouldn't be able to feed her menfolk properly. It all sounded very innocent, but it was doubtless all a plot. For that night August and Edevart worked till the sweat ran off them, fitting up the barn on their own initiative. Pauline came out and watched them for a while; but as the time approached when Joakim was expected back, she got up and said she was going inside to be out of the way.

When, toward morning, Joakim arrived, the two friends were finished work in the area where the calves were to be. They had partitioned off space sufficient for two calves; but the remainder they had made into a stable—a stable for a horse! And that wasn't all! The horse had to have its own entrance. They had made a new doorway in the wall of the barn.

Joakim stopped and gaped. Ah, but one wonders whether he hadn't had just the slightest suspicion of what was going to happen. God alone knows! He acted as though his legs were almost giving way beneath him; but he did manage to speak. "Have you gone stark raving mad, you two?"

The offenders remained silent.

"I'm asking you! What are you thinking about!"

"Thinking about?" August repeated mildly.

"Is anything wrong?" Edevart asked. And he excused himself, saying that he didn't know any better and that he'd only done as he was told.

August then spoke up. He judged it wise to speak sweetly and ingratiatingly. "You see, Joakim, I came to think in the end that you were right and not me. That place for the calves really

443

was too big. So we sectioned off part for the two beasts. Don't you think it's big enough? I'd like to know what you think . . ."

Joakim gave him a crucifying look. "If I wasn't standing here holding these fish, I'd show you all right what I think!"

Edevart, mild and helpful: "Couldn't you put your string of fish down for a moment?"

August hastened to continue. "Then of course we did have some space left over, there's no getting away from that. But it's still there. We didn't run off with it."

Now Joakim gave every appearance of struggling to control himself, as though not wanting to create a disturbance in the middle of the night. He fumbled about trying to get one haddock off the string. It was doubtless because he was perplexed. At the same time he asked: "Is this a stable you've made here?"

"That's right. A stable for a horse. That's what we thought."

"What horse?"

Now Edevart spoke again. "Oh, is that the way it is! I thought you two had agreed what was to be done. If I'd known there wasn't to be a stable here, I wouldn't have raised a finger to help."

At that moment Joakim managed to free the haddock from the string and he gave Edevart a great clout across the mouth with the raw fish. When August saw what was happening, he stepped slightly to one side to give himself a clear run if necessary. Edevart stood spitting and wiping his face.

Joakim addressed himself to August, slowly edging up on him. "Tomorrow I'm going to pull down that stable of yours. I'm not going to be made a fool of by having a stable and no horse!"

"No, a horse you must have," August admitted.

"What horse? I asked you."

Joakim had now come so close that August moved away a little before he answered. "Edevart didn't think you could run a place with five head of cattle and no horse."

"Who, me?" shouted Edevart, thunderstruck.

"So, Edevart thought that, did he? He's a fine one to think

444

like that!" Joakim answered furiously. "Anyway, I haven't got five cattle! I've got three!"

"Yes, and one cow in Hosea's barn."

"How do you know that?"

"That'll be four," said August.

"Yes, that'll be four," Joakim mimicked furiously. "But however you look at it, that doesn't make five!"

"And then a new cow next year, which makes five," said Edevart, moving well away.

"What the devil are you saying—a new cow next year?"

Edevart, evasively: "That's what Pauline herself told me. Anyway, you yourself have made five stalls, haven't you?"

Joakim was silent for a while. "Pauline?" he said. "What does she know about it? Ah, that Pauline's in league with you two on this. Good I found out! Did you ever hear the likes of it! All right then, Pauline can ask for these fish till she's blue in the face, I tell you flat! I'm going straight off to find some decent people to give them to."

With this, Joakim strode out, managing as he did so to get close enough in all innocence to August to give him a hit over the head with the haddock.

At this all three had to laugh, though Joakim still laughed somewhat bitterly. He stalked over to Martinus's cottage and hung the string of fish on the door latch . . .

Naturally, the stable did not get pulled down. Joakim had to put up with it standing there ready until such time as he got a horse. He had to put up with a good deal more yet from August, that source of all kinds of wild ideas. Thus it was impossible for him to prevent August one night from boarding off a nice little place for the chickens, with perches on the side of the stable, but with a free run for the chickens to all the other animals. Pauline secretly thanked him warmly for this good deed, and promised him something in return. But when Joakim demanded an explanation, August answered shortly: "Well, is Gabrielsen the only one who can keep hens!"

August kept on the go right up to his last days in Polden. He went to Karolus, the district chairman, and demanded a post office to go with his mailbox. August wasn't prepared to tolerate the situation any longer. The box had been hanging on the wall of the store for several weeks now, and not a single letter had been put in it yet. The cause was simply that it lacked a post office. How did Joakim feel about it? Joakim took a newspaper, but he could only get it by going to church every Sunday and collecting it. What the devil was the use of that! The matter was now to go to the county council. Joakim was the one who drafted the petition, and he promised to set it out in his best style: how Polden was a large village, and all the surrounding districts made use of it; how the priest, the sheriff, and others who wrote many letters would come out in full-throated support of a post office, first and foremost Karolus, their chairman, who frequently wrote to the officials and to the government on Polden's business; and how finally there was the store, the firm of Edevart Andreassen and Pauline, who sent letters and large money orders off to their supply merchants all the year round.

"There are no two ways about it," said August. "We must have a post office in Polden!"

Yes, Karolus didn't deny that. It was all very reasonable. Yes, he said; certainly. It would be taken up and discussed at the next council meeting. "And our thanks are due to you, August, for having the idea," said Karolus. "I may have important letters pretty well every day, and I walk about with them in my pocket until they are crumpled and dirty before I can get them sent off. Yes, we'll work on the matter. I regard it as urgent . . ."

Poor Karolus, he would certainly have liked to do something, and he was kind and good-natured. But he had never been particularly quick-witted, and just now he was deeply immersed in his own concerns. He had more than enough to do already. He had his farm to see to; it would very soon be mowing time and there was no help to be got other than Teodor, who had a rupture and was very little use. Moreover, Ane Maria was coming home

446

now. Karolus had had confirmation of this; and he was worried and confused about the details of how he would manage when she came. But all the same, certainly, there would have to be a post office.

"Let me see that you've got it by the time I come back!" said August.

"Are you leaving?"

"Yes, I'm leaving."

"Oh? Where are you going?"

"First I have a mind to pop over to India and South America. I have one or two interests there I ought to see to."

"India and South America!" Karolus repeated. "So you'll not be back in Polden for a long time?"

"No. But when I write a letter or send an iron-bound chest or anything like that, I'll put POLDEN P.O. Then you'll have to have it ready."

AUGUST CUTS LOOSE and leaves. He hasn't persuaded Edevart to join him; but that doesn't mean that Edevart has it in mind to settle down peacefully in Polden. He is quite ready to be off, this wayfarer; and Polden means little to him any more. But he is unwilling to go and ask Pauline for money for his passage, especially since she has only just helped August on his way.

August is on his way to Bergen to sign on some ocean-going vessel. Pauline has kitted him out generously with clothes; Ezra and Hosea both turn up to see him off; the old father takes his hand and invokes God's blessing on his journey; and Joakim and Edevart row him out to the steamer landing stage.

Edevart speaks—that friend, that big brother, who seems detached from everything. "Now, let me see that you sign on and don't waste your time on something else!"

To this August makes no reply; but he does say: "I regret we didn't build on space for a pig while we were at it."

To this Joakim makes no reply.

447

When they got there, the steamer was already in sight out on the fjord. August hastily took Edevart on one side and said: "That story I told you as I lay there that night at the fair—that there were four of us onto her and that we killed her—that was absolute nonsense."

"Sure it was."

"Because what would you think of a thing like that? Four men . . . I never heard anything so stupid. We were only human, after all. You mustn't say a word about it!"

"I won't say a word about it."

"And the fact that you didn't go running for the priest, that's something I'm also grateful for. And you won't pass that on, either!"

"No."

"Because it's just like I told you once before: you'd simply be blackballed. I know somebody it once happened to and he was simply blackballed: every boat and every port. Nobody would sail with him."

"You don't have to warn me," said Edevart.

"All aboard!" called the agent.

The brothers rowed home. They talked about the man they had just seen aboard, and Joakim said: "There's something strange about him—do you think he might be a man with a mission?"

"How do you mean?"

No, Joakim couldn't exactly say, but like a man with a mission. And however it might be, Polden's last twelve years, its life and its way of living, had been fertilized by August. Good times and ill, prosperous times, dissipated times, uncertain times —everything could be traced back to him. Ever since the day that August, that worldwide traveler, had emerged from the depths and from the darkness, he had infected every soul in the village and in the district. He was the source. "He did a lot of good," said Edevart. And Joakim, who was an enterprising young man who took newspapers and everything, agreed to this. But perhaps he'd been in some way an instrument . . . ?

They rowed steadily and powerfully, these two. They were bringing certain goods from the landing stage back to the store, so the boat was heavily loaded; but the weather was fair. As they rowed, Edevart was sitting on the afterthwart, so Joakim saw only his back. So he spoke more freely than if his brother had been facing him. Edevart wondered a little at this volubility; there was also something a little unusual in Joakim's tone of voice, something rather more brotherly—or perhaps not so much brotherly as gentle.

"He was constituted in such a way that he changed us," said Joakim obscurely. "For he raised us up, and also dragged us down. I don't know whether you think the same."

"Yes, you could well be right," Edevart replied.

"Take me now. I could well have managed without a horse."

"No," Edevart replied. "You couldn't."

"That's what you say!"

They rowed and thought, rowed and thought.

"He certainly rallied round to help them with the new buildings," Edevart said.

"Yes, didn't he!" Joakim exclaimed. "But there was something odd about it. It didn't bring us peace and quiet. He was a stranger to us, and he brought alien things into our lives. Now the people in the north of the district have started going in for calves. They fatten them up over a period and then sell them to the village people for slaughter. They make money out of it."

"So what's wrong with that?"

"Nothing, possibly!" said Joakim.

"And is it August's fault?"

"All in all, it might well be, taking one thing with another. Things were peaceful before here. Father was poor, but that didn't mean anything. He bore it quietly and didn't complain. The same with Mother. Do you remember, when we gave her something, she couldn't afford to use it. And can you remember that when we drew some water for her, she said we were making her lazy. And that was when Mother was in poor health."

449

Edevart remembered that.

"There's something evil, something swinish indeed, about those calves," Joakim says. "First you raise them, then you get to know them, and then you dispose of them to the fine folk in the village for food! How were things before? Well, we bred our beasts and grew fond of them. And we never sold a cow without knowing how well it would be looked after in the new place. It was like letting one of our children go. But that's not how things are now. We've changed."

Edevart doesn't quite understand what has come over his young brother, Joakim. But he replies: "Yes, we've changed."

After a long pause, Joakim says: "He was fatherless and motherless, and he had no home of his own. When he came back to us, he was a stranger."

It begins to dawn on Edevart that his young brother is trying to make a particular point with this talk of his. This becomes altogether clear when Joakim suddenly asks: "What do you think would have happened, Edevart, if you and I had had no parents and no home? Then we'd have been no better off than August!" With more and more reference to Edevart, he continues: "I don't think anybody benefits by being homeless and wandering around. We should stay where we belong."

Edevart does not laugh. He takes it seriously, thinks it over, and says: "The thing is whether we shouldn't try ourselves out to see where we belong best."

Joakim: "Don't you think we belong where we were put? Otherwise we wouldn't have been put there. Like August, for instance: as a child he was, as you know, first at one place, and then they didn't have enough coming in to be able to keep him any longer, so he was sent to another place, where he got more food and better clothes. But after three weeks he ran away—back to the first place. You've heard him tell that himself. And you remember he said he'd never been so desperately sad in his life as he was when he had to leave that first poor place again?"

Edevart remembered.

Joakim: "Try to see where we belong best—well, he had the chance to try! Do we belong where we get more food, better clothes, and more money? If so, our father and mother ought not to have lived all their days contentedly and gratefully in Polden. Nor would they then have lived a far happier life than either August or . . . well, other people who rove around and belong nowhere. What do you think?"

"I don't think anything," Edevart mumbled.

"There are various people now in the north of our district who don't want to stay at home any longer. They've begun saving up for the price of a ticket. That's why they treat their calves like that. Occasionally they'll sell a cow. They've been listening to August's foolish chatter. They want to go to America."

"Many have thought of going there," said Edevart.

Joakim: "You haven't been thinking of it, have you?"

"Thought . . . thought . . . but it won't happen now in any case."

"Just as well! 'Wheat fields and loads of money,' said August. But he wasn't from this place. He'd only lived here occasionally. The Lord left him free to rove. We don't become any happier in ourselves by being better off."

Edevart turned around on the thwart, looked his brother in the face, and said: "Then I don't understand why you want five cattle when Father and Mother were content with two."

"Oh, yes, you do," replied Joakim. "You understand all right! In the first place, with Father and Mother there were just the two of them; but now there are four of us, so we need more than two. Then there's the point that we ought to cultivate our own soil, Norway's soil; then we wouldn't have to buy so much of our food from abroad and suffer for it later in taxes and duties. But that's not all. The most important thing is that we then avoid poor August's fate: being torn up by the roots from our own poor soil and set down in a richer one—and nevertheless yearning to be back in the poorer. I've read that it's not always the richness that counts. Indeed, that it's *never* the richness that counts."

"Yes, you read and you read," said Edevart. "Is *that* what counts?"

"It counts for something. I use seaweed as fertilizer. That's something I read about. Richness? I don't know if you've seen those five little aspens growing down by the ford. No, you've stopped walking over the land. Four of them are growing vigorously with masses of leaves, but the fifth was smaller and had fewer leaves. I felt sorry for it and I wanted to help it on. So one Sunday I took a pail of cow manure down with me and I carefully lifted the turf and spread the manure around the roots. Then I watered it and replaced the turf. That was in the autumn of last year. Now this summer—if you please, the little aspen is diseased, it's got a snow-white grainy rash all up the trunk, and its leaves are even more miserable than before. You see, it found itself in an alien situation and it didn't thrive."

"But it wasn't thriving before, either."

"Yes, it was! It was thriving in its own particular way. It was simply smaller in its growth. Not all things can be equally big."

LATER IN THE YEAR, when the mowing began, Edevart worked alternately with Joakim and with Ezra, as they both needed help. He did not spare himself and he was a good worker. It began to look as though he might put down his roots in Polden for good. He was no longer anything fine and grand, no longer a skipper or a storeowner. He was like all the others, and he seemed content to be nothing very much. He did not so much as set foot in the store; but he liked walking in the country round about. He must have taken his kid brother's words to heart, for he also went down to the ford and looked at the five aspen.

So life went on in Polden, an ordinary, uneventful daily life in every way. And thus, too, life went on throughout the whole parish. No great figure dominated; the greatest, perhaps, was still Karolus, who lived quite alone and had acquired a fat belly, and who moreover owned his own farm and owed no man. If there had been a doctor, he would have been the greatest, for a doctor studies for seven years before he is qualified in his magic ways, and neither the postmaster nor the organist does that. No, they didn't have their own doctor here; they shared a doctor with the neighboring parish, and he lived permanently there. But things went along all right that way. All life goes on. The people of the inner village bought calves from the people in the northern outskirts. Johnsen the sexton smoked his pipe every Sunday on the way to church. And the priest was applying for posts in the south . . . in the south. Why shouldn't all life go on!

By August the fish in Polden had been dried, and the Ofoten skipper paid his workers off and set a few coins in circulation again. Poor old man, he'd only been able to afford a three-quarter load this year in order to have money in hand for the drying. And that was a sad thing.

When it came to carefree irresponsibility, however, there were always Teodor and Ragna. Teodor went mowing for Karolus and did what work he could. He wasn't too bad, and if Karolus hadn't wanted to take him on, plenty of others would. Teodor wasn't worried. Besides, he was clever at cutting hair and was in demand by the whole village on Sundays after church. He acquired many a cup of coffee and a bite to eat this way. When he came strutting along, his figure pale and undernourished, wearing high boots and a pocket watch that never went, he presented absolutely the right careless combination of poverty and elegance.

Ragna, little Ragna, his wife, might find him deficient in one way or another; she might indeed. But that did not cause her to rant and rage. Ragna was reasonably content. Had she not had that new dress material from Edevart; and had she not made it up into a dress herself so that she could go to church? That was indeed something. Otherwise, she had a child every other year, got up again, and was the same old Ragna. When her husband told her of his escapade at the fair, Ragna wasn't above spitting and saying: "You should be ashamed of yourself! There you had that fat wallet already as good as in your hands, yet you come home without a thing to show!" Whereupon Teodor could answer: "Ah, well, we could all do better than we do!"

Then a number of unexpected things happened.

Joakim is sitting one Sunday afternoon reading his paper, which he collected after church. "Papst is dead!" he says.

"Papst dead?" Edevart cries. "Read it!"

There was a longish piece about his death, an obituary tinged with sadness. The old watch dealer was a well-known figure all along the coast, and it is doubtful if he left behind a single enemy. He cheated, yes, of course he did. Many amusing stories went the rounds about how old Papst had twisted those young whippersnappers who came up calling him Moses and pretending to know all about watches. He also scattered around a fair number of rotten watches, which would go for a day or two and then stop. But Papst was not always as obvious as he seemed; at times he could be a quite different person from the usual swindler. In Karmsund, for example, he gave away a very expensive silver watch for nothing to a lad he'd scarcely seen before; and when this occasioned great surprise, Papst explained that the lad came of good people and that he had a good heart. Also, up in the north, people had many a tale to tell of similar traits in Papst. How did that come about? There had been many and sometimes cruel swindles; and then, totally unexpectedly, the exact opposite. He could be straightaway touched by the mere sight of a fair face and completely disregard his own profit. Young people in particular appealed to him. He knew the value a lad at that age attached to having a watch chain across his waistcoat; and many were the times when Papst gave credit to a lad who was in need of a watch. Now the venerable old patriarch would no longer be seen at the coastal fairs. He had died in Trondheim in the middle of the month. He was believed to have been a man of substantial means; and it was known that a prominent lawyer had been called to the old man's bedside some time before his death . . .

The next thing that happened was that Pauline came into the house one evening and said: "There was a letter in the mailbox. I just happened to look in and there it was. It's for you." And she handed the letter to Joakim.

Dear God, it was a little crumpled letter from a girl. It must have been dropped into the box one night. Joakim turned crimson as he took it, and immediately went out. In the morning he was gone.

"He must have gone to the north part of the village," said Pauline. "There's a person there who'd been thinking of going to America, but now it seems she might have given up the idea. There are lots of people up there who are thinking about America. They're saving up for the tickets. The question now is whether Joakim can get her to change her mind!"

Yes, there was no problem. When Joakim returned, he was singing and he seemed to have got what he wanted . . .

But one day, as time went by, the most unexpected thing of all happened: Edevart received a large money order through the post. It was from a lawyer in Trondheim: four hundred *kroner*, as he put it, because money was counted in *kroner* and *øre* now. That was one hundred *daler* in good old money—suddenly, crazily, from Papst. From Papst!

Well, a little while ago Edevart would have thanked God for this money and taken himself off to America, since he had a particularly good reason for going. Now he took things more calmly; for the moment he had no particular use for the money. No, he intended to settle down in Polden, to live and die in Polden. What else?

"What good deed did you do for Papst?" Joakim asked.

Edevart shook his head as he replied: "Search me!"

They read over the lawyer's letter. It was short and to the point. Two lines:

Enclosed find four hundred kroner *as a gift from watch dealer Papst, sent in accordance with his death-bed will. Receipt requested.*

Joakim acknowledged the letter.

Ezra came one Sunday inquiring for Edevart. He was not around. He was probably out walking, which he tended to do when he wanted to be off on his own. Ezra had been to church and had brought Joakim's newspaper. He also had a letter for Edevart. A letter from America. They examined it: a yellow, leathery envelope, thin hasty handwriting, lots of stamps.

Pauline was summoned and she looked at the letter.

"Shall we burn it?" Joakim asked.

The other two looked at him and Pauline became alarmed. "No, you can't do that!" she whispered.

"What do you think, Ezra?" Joakim asked.

"I don't know," Ezra replied.

"Then we'll burn it!"

Pauline repeated: "No, we can't do that!"

He took the letter and was walking away when Pauline ran after him and stopped him. "What would you have said if I'd burned your letter that was lying in the mailbox?"

Joakim thought, then quickly handed the letter back to her. "Well, do as you wish!" he said.

Pauline would have given a lot to have seen Edevart's face when he read the letter, but he vanished into his room and stayed there a long time. When about noon he came in for coffee, he looked much as usual, said little, and seemed absentminded. Then he again went off walking.

No further thought was given to Edevart and his letter just then, for Karolus arrived and was more than usually disturbed. He had also been to church and had had final news about Ane Maria: she was now on her way and arriving on the next boat.

456

Karolus was much exercised in his mind. This was a serious matter; and he wanted to have Joakim, his right-hand man, with him to collect his wife at the landing stage.

Yes, Joakim wouldn't say no to this. "That will be the day after tomorrow," he said. "We'll take Edevart's four-oar boat."

"But what about the fact that I've a boat of my own?" said Karolus. "Wouldn't it be better if we took my eight-oar out of the boathouse and used that?"

"Why should we do that?"

"Oh, I don't know. She might have a fair amount of luggage."

Joakim didn't understand and said nothing.

"She could sit more comfortably in an eight-oar," said Karolus. Oh, he was out of his mind. He'd brooded so long over this homecoming that he'd become quite helpless and confused.

"We'll take the four-oar," said Joakim . . .

They rowed off on Tuesday morning and Karolus continued to be uneasy. But in any case the four-oar turned out to be quite large enough. It was a Polden woman who stepped aboard it: Ane Maria, looking pretty good, unmoved, a bundle of clothes under her arm. She shook hands with the two men and greeted them. Karolus, all blushing and bashful, smiled and asked her to sit at the stern of the boat. Then they rowed home.

Quite a woman was Ane Maria! Little changed in all these years, perhaps even wearing the same dress as the one she left in, good-looking and grave. As Karolus was silent and couldn't bring himself to say anything, Joakim asked: "What has the weather been like coming north?"

"Good weather," she said. "Why, it's you, Edevart!"

"No," responded Karolus. "It's his brother, Joakim."

"Joakim?" she said. "And already grown up? Yes, time flies."

Quite a woman! She neither laughed nor cried, but was just as she was before she went away. She must have had not too bad a time of it. "You've grown stouter," she said to her husband.

"Oh, I'll soon be looking just like a pig!" He exaggerated and pretended to be downcast, though otherwise he didn't mind having a paunch, for this made him look important.

She asked for news of Polden. It was a little difficult for the men to report anything, because in each case they had to reckon out how long she had been away. Well, they dry fish here every year now, they said.

"I know that," she interrupted.

And then there were the various marriages and deaths— some of them had occurred before she left, though Martinus had died since, and Teodor and Ragna had got married.

"Then there's Gabrielsen, who went bankrupt. But we have a store in Polden now."

Ane Maria is interested. "It isn't you who has the store, Karolus, is it?"

No, it wasn't he. It was Edevart . . . Pauline. Imagine, tiny little Pauline! Yes, time had flown!

"Yes," said Karolus, getting a grip on himself. "And now we're going to have a post office in Polden. I'm going to raise the matter in the county council. Why shouldn't we have a post office just as much as the inner district?"

Ane Maria wasn't concerned.

"And recently August left."

"What August? Oh, him . . . !"

She was given an account of lots of things and brought up to date about Polden's affairs. What a woman! How composed she was! How little concerned that she was coming out of prison. There had always been an air of superiority, of hauteur about Ane Maria. She would surely make a place for herself again. In any case, Karolus was pleased she wasn't coming back home with tears in her eyes and embraces and a great fuss. The one thing was that, if only because of the wagging tongues, she might perhaps have had more luggage, seeing that she'd been so long away.

* * *

458

Edevart became more and more reserved. People were afraid that one day he might simply be off, and on his way. He had been up to see Hosea at their new place and had held her baby girl in his arms and given her a ten kroner note for her mother to buy her something with. Hosea clapped her hands; but Edevart said that although it was ten of the new-style money, it was worth only two and a half in daler. "Ah, you've always been so good to us all!" said Hosea. And these words must have touched Edevart and left him feeling foolish, for he turned away abruptly and went without saying goodbye.

Joakim and Pauline confer. They speak in whispers, but even so are afraid of being overheard.

"We should have burned that letter," says Joakim.

"Yes," Pauline agrees.

"For it didn't do him any good."

"No."

"If only we could keep him here a while to let him get over it!"

"I've been thinking," says Pauline, that clever, quick-witted Pauline, "whether I might not be able to borrow that money of his for a while."

"Well, if only you could!"

"I might need it for buying stock between now and Christmas."

"Yes! Exactly! That's the solution! For Edevart would never say no to a thing like that. He didn't ever use to say no . . ." And Joakim was so relieved he began to laugh. That was the best thing they could think of, a way out. Whereupon he then said he had to nip up to the north district of the village that night, some necessary business, urgent, something about a fishing crew or something. But he would be back again early the next morning . . .

But in the morning Edevart was gone. He must have heard that Pauline wanted to borrow his money, or else he smelled it in the wind. When Joakim came home and found no brother, he at once ran down to the boathouses. He stared. The four-oar boat was gone.

Well, that was the way he usually went—without any leave-taking.

A gloomy day. They got hold of Ezra and they told the old father. They were as mournful as though there had been a death. Hosea wept loudly. But might it not be that he had merely rowed off somewhere on some errand and would be coming back?

He did not come back—for a long time.